THE HORUS HERESY®
SIEGE OF TERRA

THE HORUS HERESY®

For the full range of Horus Heresy products visit blacklibrary.com

THE HORUS HERESY®

Ben Counter

GALAXY IN FLAMES

The heresy revealed

BLACK LIBRARY

A BLACK LIBRARY PUBLICATION

First published in 2006.
This edition published in Great Britain in 2022 by
Black Library, Games Workshop Ltd., Willow Road,
Nottingham, NG7 2WS, UK.

Represented by: Games Workshop Limited – Irish branch,
Unit 3, Lower Liffey Street, Dublin 1,
D01 K199, Ireland.

18

Produced by Games Workshop in Nottingham.
Cover illustration by Neil Roberts.

ISBN 13: 978-1-84970-753-4

See Black Library on the internet at

blacklibrary.com

Find out more about Games Workshop
and the worlds of Warhammer at

games-workshop.com

Printed and bound by CPI Group (UK) Ltd, Croydon, CR0 4YY

*With extra-special thanks to Graham McNeill,
for making Galaxy in Flames the book it is.*

THE HORUS HERESY®

It is a time of legend.

Mighty heroes battle for the right to rule the galaxy.

The vast armies of the Emperor of Earth have conquered the galaxy in a Great Crusade – the myriad alien races have been smashed by the Emperor's elite warriors and wiped from the face of history.

The dawn of a new age of supremacy for humanity beckons.

Gleaming citadels of marble and gold celebrate the many victories of the Emperor. Triumphs are raised on a million worlds to record the epic deeds of his most powerful and deadly warriors.

First and foremost amongst these are the primarchs, superheroic beings who have led the Emperor's armies of Space Marines in victory after victory. They are unstoppable and magnificent, the pinnacle of the Emperor's genetic experimentation. The Space Marines are the mightiest human warriors the galaxy has ever known, each capable of besting a hundred normal men or more in combat.

Organised into vast armies of tens of thousands called Legions, the Space Marines and their primarch leaders conquer the galaxy in the name of the Emperor.

Chief amongst the primarchs is Horus, called the Glorious, the Brightest Star, favourite of the Emperor, and like a son unto him. He is the Warmaster, the commander-in-chief of the Emperor's military might, subjugator of a thousand thousand worlds and conqueror of the galaxy. He is a warrior without peer, a diplomat supreme, and his ambition knows no bounds.

The stage has been set.

~ DRAMATIS PERSONAE ~

The Primarchs

THE WARMASTER HORUS

    Commander of the Sons of Horus Legion

ANGRON — Primarch of the World Eaters

FULGRIM — Primarch of the Emperor's Children

MORTARION — Primarch of the Death Guard

The Sons of Horus

EZEKYLE ABADDON — First Captain of the Sons of Horus

TARIK TORGADDON — Captain, 2nd Company, Sons of Horus

IACTON QRUZE, 'THE HALF-HEARD'

    Captain, 3rd Company, Sons of Horus

HORUS AXIMAND, 'LITTLE HORUS'

    Captain, 5th Company, Sons of Horus

SERGHAR TARGOST — Captain, 7th Company, Sons of Horus, lodge master

GARVIEL LOKEN — Captain, 10th Company, Sons of Horus

LUC SEDIRAE — Captain, 13th Company, Sons of Horus

TYBALT MARR, 'THE EITHER'

    Captain, 18th Company, Sons of Horus

KALUS EKADDON, CAPTAIN

Catulan Reaver Squad, Sons of Horus

FALKUS KIBRE, 'WIDOWMAKER'

Captain, Justaerin Terminator Squad, Sons of Horus

NERO VIPUS

Sergeant, Locasta Tactical Squad, Sons of Horus

MALOGHURST 'THE TWISTED'

Equerry to the Warmaster

Other Space Marines

EREBUS	First Chaplain of the Word Bearers
KHÂRN	Captain, 8th Assault Company of the World Eaters
NATHANIAL GARRO	Captain of the Death Guard
LUCIUS	Emperor's Children swordsman
SAUL TARVITZ	First Captain of the Emperor's Children
EIDOLON	Lord Commander of the Emperor's Children
FABIUS BILE	Emperor's Children Apothecary

The Legio Mortis

PRINCEPS ESAU TURNET
> Commander of the *Dies Irae*, an Imperator-class Titan

MODERATI PRIMUS CASSAR
> One of the senior crew of the *Dies Irae*

MODERATI PRIMUS ARUKEN
> Another of the *Dies Irae*'s crew

Non-Astartes Imperials

MECHANICUM ADEPT REGULUS
> Mechanicum representative to Horus, he commands the Legion's robots and maintains its fighting machines

ING MAE SING — Mistress of Astropaths

KYRIL SINDERMANN — Primary iterator

MERSADIE OLITON — Official remembrancer, documentarist

EUPHRATI KEELER — Official remembrancer, imagist

PEETER EGON MOMUS — Architect Designate

MAGGARD — Maloghurst's civilian enforcer

PART ONE
LONG KNIVES

ONE

The Emperor protects
Long night
The music of the spheres

'I WAS THERE,' said Titus Cassar, his wavering voice barely reaching the back of the chamber. 'I was there the day that Horus turned his face from the Emperor.'

His words brought a collective sigh from the Lectitio Divinitatus congregation and as one they lowered their heads at such a terrible thought. From the back of the chamber, an abandoned munitions hold deep in the under-decks of the Warmaster's flagship, the *Vengeful Spirit*, Kyril Sindermann watched and winced at Cassar's awkward delivery. The man was no iterator, that was for sure, but his words carried the sure and certain faith of someone who truly believed in the things he was saying.

Sindermann envied him that certainty.

It had been many months since he had felt anything approaching certainty.

As the Primary Iterator of the 63rd Expedition, it
was Kyril Sindermann's job to promulgate the
Imperial Truth of the Great Crusade, illuminating
those worlds brought into compliance of the rule of
the Emperor and the glory of the Imperium. Bringing the light of reason and secular truth to the
furthest flung reaches of the ever-expanding human
empire had been a noble undertaking.

But somewhere along the way, things had gone
wrong.

Sindermann wasn't sure when it had happened.
On Xenobia? On Davin? On Aureus? Or on any one
of a dozen other worlds brought into compliance?

Once he had been known as the arch prophet of
secular truth, but times had changed and he found
himself remembering his Sahlonum, the Sumatu-
ran philosopher who had wondered why the light
of new science seemed not to illuminate as far as
the old sorceries had.

Titus Cassar continued his droning sermon, and
Sindermann returned his attention to the man. Tall
and angular, Cassar wore the uniform of a moderati
primus, one of the senior commanders of the *Dies
Irae*, an Imperator-class Battle Titan. Sindermann
suspected it was this rank, combined with his earlier friendship with Euphrati Keeler, that had
granted his status within the Lectitio Divinitatus;
status that he was clearly out of his depth in han-
dling.

Euphrati Keeler: imagist, evangelist…

…Saint.

He remembered meeting Euphrati, a feisty, supremely self-confident woman, on the embarkation deck before they had left for the surface of Sixty-Three Nineteen, unaware of the horror they would witness in the depths of the Whisperhead Mountains.

Together with Captain Loken, they had seen the warp-spawned monstrosity Xayver Jubal had been wrought into. Sindermann had struggled to rationalise what he had seen by burying himself in his books and learning to better understand what had occurred. Euphrati had no such sanctuary and had turned to the growing Lectitio Divinitatus cult for solace.

Venerating the Emperor as a divine being, the cult had grown from humble beginnings to a movement that was spreading throughout the Expedition fleets of the galaxy – much to the fury of the Warmaster. Where before the cult had lacked a focus, in Euphrati Keeler, it had found its first martyr and saint.

Sindermann remembered the day when he had witnessed Euphrati Keeler stand before a nightmare horror from beyond the gates of the Empyrean and hurl it back from whence it had come. He had seen her bathed in killing fire and walk away unscathed, a blinding light streaming from the outstretched hand in which she had held a silver Imperial eagle. Others had seen it too, Ing Mae Sing, Mistress of the Fleet's astropaths and a dozen of the ship's arms men. Word had spread fast and Euphrati had become, overnight, a saint in the eyes of the faithful and an icon to cling to on the frontier of space.

He was unsure why he had even come to this meeting – not a meeting, he corrected himself, but a service, a religious sermon – for there was a very real danger of recognition. Membership of the Lectitio Divinitatus was forbidden and if he were discovered, it would be the end of his career as an iterator.

'Now we shall contemplate the word of the Emperor,' continued Cassar, reading from a small leather chapbook. Sindermann was reminded of the Bondsman Number 7 books in which the late Ignace Karkasy had written his scandalous poetry. Poetry that had, if Mersadie Oliton's suspicions were correct, caused his murder.

Sinderman thought that the writings of the Lectitio Divinitatus were scarcely less dangerous.

'We have some new faithful among us,' said Cassar, and Sindermann felt every eye in the chamber turn upon him. Used to facing entire continents' worth of audience, Sindermann was suddenly acutely embarrassed by their scrutiny.

'When people are first drawn to adoration of the Emperor, it is only natural that they should have questions,' said Cassar. 'They know the Emperor must be a god, for he has god-like powers over all human species, but aside from this, they are in the dark.'

This, at least, Sindermann agreed with.

'Most importantly, they ask, "If the Emperor truly is a god, then what does he do with his divine power?" We do not see His hand reaching down from the sky, and precious few of us are blessed with visions granted by Him. So does he not care for the majority of His subjects?"

'They do not see the falsehood of such a belief. His hand lies upon all of us, and every one of us owes him our devotion. In the depths of the warp, the Emperor's mighty soul does battle with the dark things that would break through and consume us all. On Terra, he creates wonders that will bring peace, enlightenment and the fruition of all our dreams to the galaxy. The Emperor guides us, teaches us, and exhorts us to become more than we are, but most of all, the Emperor protects.'

'The Emperor protects,' said the congregation in unison.

'The faith of the Lectitio Divinitatus, the Divine Word of the Emperor, is not an easy path to follow. Where the Imperial Truth is comforting in its rigorous rejection of the unseen and the unknown, the Divine Word requires the strength to believe in that which we cannot see. The longer we look upon this dark galaxy and live through the fires of its conquest, the more we realise that the Emperor's divinity is the only truth that *can* exist. We do not seek out the Divine Word; instead, we hear it, and are compelled to follow it. Faith is not a flag of allegiance or a theory for debate; it is something deep within us, complete and inevitable. The Lectitio Divinitatus is the expression of that faith, and only by acknowledging the Divine Word can we understand the path the Emperor has laid before mankind.'

Fine words, thought Sindermann: fine words, poorly delivered, but heartfelt. He could see that they had touched something deep inside those who heard it. An orator of skill could sway entire worlds with such words and force of belief.

Before Cassar could continue, Sindermann heard sudden shouts coming from the maze of corridors that led into the chamber. He turned as a panicked woman hurled the door behind him open with a dull clang of metal. In her wake, Sindermann could hear the hard bangs of bolter rounds.

The congregation started in confusion, looking to Cassar for an explanation, but the man was as non-plussed as they were.

'They've found you,' yelled Sindermann, realising what was happening.

'Everyone, get out,' shouted Cassar. 'Scatter!'

Sindermann pushed his way through the panick-ing crowd to the front of the chamber and towards Cassar. Some members of the congregation were producing guns, and from their martial bearing, Sin-dermann guessed they were Imperial Army troopers. Some were clearly ship's crewmen, and Sindermann knew enough of religion to know that they would defend their faith with violence if they had to.

'Come on, iterator. It's time we got out of here,' said Cassar, dragging the venerable iterator towards one of the many access corridors that radiated from the chamber.

Seeing the worry on his face, Cassar said, 'Don't worry, Kyril, the Emperor protects.'

'I certainly hope so,' replied Sindermann breathlessly.

Shots echoed from the ceiling and bright muzzle flashes strobed from the walls. Sindermann threw a glance over his shoulder and saw the bulky, armoured form of Astartes entering the chamber. His heart skipped a beat at the thought of being the enemy of such warriors.

Sindermann hurriedly followed Cassar into the access corridor and through a set of blast doors, their path twisting through the depths of the ship. The *Vengeful Spirit* was an immense vessel and he had no idea of the layout of this area, its walls grim and industrial compared to the magnificence of the upper decks.

'Do you know where you are going?' wheezed Sindermann, his breath coming in hot, agonised spikes and his ancient limbs already tiring from exertion he was scarcely used to.

'Engineering,' said Cassar. 'It's like a maze down there and we have friends in the engine crew. Damn, why can't they just let us be?'

'Because they are scared of you,' said Sindermann, 'just like I was.'

'AND YOU ARE certain of this?' asked Horus, Primarch of the Sons of Horus Legion and Warmaster of the Imperium, his voice echoing around the cavernous strategium of the *Vengeful Spirit*.

'As certain as I can be,' said Ing Mae Sing, the 63rd Expedition's Mistress of Astropaths. Her face was lined and drawn and her blind eyes were sunken within ravaged eye sockets. The demands of sending hundreds of telepathic communications across the galaxy weighed heavily on her skeletal frame. Astropathic acolytes gathered about her, robed in the same ghostly white as she and wordlessly whispering muttered doggerel of the ghastly images in their heads.

'How long do we have?' asked Horus.

'As with all things connected with the warp, it is difficult to be precise,' replied Ing Mae Sing.

'Mistress Sing,' said Horus coldly, 'precision is exactly what I need from you, now more than ever. The direction of the Crusade will change dramatically at this news, and if you are wrong it will change for the worse.'

'My lord, I cannot give you an exact answer, but I believe that within days the gathering warp storms will obscure the Astronomican from us,' replied Ing Mae Sing, ignoring the Warmaster's implicit threat. Though she could not see them, she could feel the hostile presence of the Justaerin warriors, the Sons of Horus First Company Terminators, lurking in the shadows of the strategium. 'Within days we shall hardly see it. Our minds can barely reach across the void and the Navigators claim that they will soon be unable to guide us true. The galaxy will be a place of night and darkness.'

Horus pounded a hand into his fist. 'Do you understand what you say? Nothing more dangerous could happen to the Crusade.'

'I merely state what I see, Warmaster.'

'If you are wrong...'

The threat was not idle – no threat the Warmaster uttered ever was. There had been a time when the Warmaster's anger would never have led to such an overt threat, but the violence in Horus's tone suggested that such a time had long passed.

'If we are wrong, we suffer. It has never been any different.'

'And my brother primarchs? What news from them?' asked Horus.

'We have been unable to confirm contact with the blessed Sanguinius,' replied Ing Mae Sing, 'and Leman Russ has sent no word of his campaign against the Thousand Sons.'

Horus laughed, a harsh Cthonic bark, and said, 'That doesn't surprise me. The Wolf has his head and he'll not easily be distracted from teaching Magnus a lesson. And the others?'

'Vulkan and Dorn are returning to Terra. The other primarchs are pursuing their current campaigns.'

'That is good at least,' said Horus, brow furrowing in thought, 'and what of the Fabricator General?'

'Forgive me, Warmaster, but we have received nothing from Mars. We shall endeavour to make contact by mechanical means, but this will take many months.'

'You have failed in this, Sing. Co-ordination with Mars is essential.'

Ing Mae Sing had telepathically broadcast a multitude of encoded messages between the *Vengeful Spirit* and Fabricator General Kelbor-Hal of the Mechanicum in the last few weeks. Although their substance was unknown to her, the emotions contained in them were all too clear. Whatever the Warmaster was planning, the Mechanicum was a key part of it.

Horus spoke again, distracting her from her thoughts. 'The other primarchs, have they received their orders?'

'They have, my lord,' said Ing Mae Sing, unable to keep the unease from her voice.

'The reply from Lord Guilliman of the Ultramarines was clean and strong. They are approaching the muster at Calth and report all forces are ready to depart.'

'And Lorgar?' asked Horus.

Ing Mae Sing paused, as if unsure how to phrase her next words.

'His message had residual symbols of… pride and obedience; very strong, almost fanatical. He acknowledges your attack order and is making good speed to Calth.'

Ing Mae Sing prided herself on her immense self-control, as befitted one whose emotions had to be kept in check lest they be changed by the influence of the warp, but even she could not keep some emotion from surfacing.

'Something bothers you Mistress Sing?' asked Horus, as though reading her mind.

'My lord?'

'You seem troubled by my orders.'

'It is not my place to be troubled or otherwise, my lord,' said Ing Mae Sing neutrally.

'Correct,' agreed Horus. 'It is not, yet you doubt the wisdom of my course.'

'No!' cried Ing Mae Sing. 'It is just that it is hard not to feel the nature of your communication, the weight of blood and death that each message is wreathed in. It is like breathing fiery smoke with every message we send.'

'You must trust me, Mistress Sing,' said Horus. 'Trust that everything I do is for the good of the Imperium. Do you understand?'

'It is not my place to understand,' whispered the astropath. 'My role in the Crusade is to do the will of my Warmaster.'

'That is true, but before I dismiss you, Mistress Sing, tell me something.'

'Yes, my lord?'

'Tell me of Euphrati Keeler,' said Horus. 'Tell me of the one they are calling the saint.'

LOKEN STILL TOOK Mersadie Oliton's breath away. The Astartes were astonishing enough when arrayed for war in their burnished plate, but that sight had been nothing compared to what a Space Marine – specifically, Loken – looked like without his armour.

Stripped to the waist and wearing only pale fatigues and combat boots, Loken glistened with sweat as he ducked and wove between the combat appendages of a training servitor. Although few of the remembrancers had been privileged enough to witness an Astartes fight in battle, it was said that they could kill with their bare hands as effectively as they could with a bolter and chainsword. Watching Loken demolishing the servitor limb by limb, Mersadie could well believe it. She saw such power in his broad, over-muscled torso and such intense focus in his sharp grey eyes that she wondered that she was not repelled by Loken. He was a killing machine, created and trained to deal death, but she couldn't stop watching and blink-clicking images of his heroic physique.

Kyril Sindermann sat next to her and leaned over, saying, 'Don't you have plenty of picts of Garviel already?'

Loken tore the head from the training servitor and turned to face them both, and Mersadie felt a thrill of anticipation. It had been too long since the conclusion of the war against the Technocracy and she had spent too few hours with the captain of the Tenth Company. As his documentarist, she knew that she had a paucity of material following that campaign, but Loken had kept himself to himself in the past few months.

'Kyril, Mersadie,' said Loken, marching past them towards his arming chamber. 'It is good to see you both.'

'I am glad to be here, Garviel,' said Sindermann. The primary iterator was an old man, and Mersadie was sure he had aged a great deal in the year since the fire that had nearly killed him in the Archive Halls of the *Vengeful Spirit*. 'Very glad. Mersadie was kind enough to bring me. I have had a spell of exertion recently, and I am not as fit as once I was. Time's winged chariot draws near.'

'A quote?' asked Loken.

'A fragment,' replied Sindermann.

'I haven't seen much of either of you recently,' observed Loken, smiling down at her. 'Have I been replaced by a more interesting subject?'

'Not at all,' she replied, 'but it is becoming more and more difficult for us to move around the ship. The edict from Maloghurst, you must have heard of it.'

'I have,' agreed Loken, lifting a piece of armour and opening a tin of his ubiquitous lapping powder, 'though I haven't studied the particulars.'

The smell of the powder reminded Mersadie of happier times in this room, recording the tales of great triumphs and wondrous sights, but she cast off such thoughts of nostalgia.

'We are restricted to our own quarters and the Retreat. We need permission to be anywhere else.'

'Permission from whom?' asked Loken.

She shrugged. 'I'm not sure. The edict speaks of submitting requests to the Office of the Lupercal's Court, but no one's been able to get any kind of response from whatever that is.'

'That must be frustrating,' observed Loken and Mersadie felt her anger rise at such an obvious statement.

'Well of course it is! We can't record the Great Crusade if we can't interact with its warriors. We can barely even see them, let alone talk to them.'

'You made it here,' Loken pointed out.

'Well, yes. Following you around has taught me how to keep a low profile, Captain Loken. It helps that you train on your own now.'

Mersadie caught the hurt look in Loken's eye and instantly regretted her words. In previous times, Loken could often be found sparring with fellow officers, the smirking Sedirae, whose flinty dead eyes reminded Mersadie of an ocean predator, Nero Vipus or his Mournival brother, Tarik Torgaddon, but Loken fought alone now. By choice or by design, she did not know.

'Anyway,' continued Mersadie, 'it's getting bad for us. No one's speaking to us. We don't know what's going on any more.'

'We're on a war footing,' said Loken, putting down his armour and looking her straight in the eye. 'The fleet is heading for a rendezvous. We're joining up with Astartes from the other Legions. It'll be a complex campaign. Perhaps the Warmaster is just taking precautions.'

'No, Garviel,' said Sindermann, 'it's more than just that, and I know you well enough to know that you don't believe that either.'

'Really?' snarled Loken. 'You think you know me that well?'

'Well enough, Garviel,' nodded Sindermann, 'well enough. They're cracking down on us, cracking down hard. Not so everyone can see it, but it's happening. You know it too.'

'Do I?'

'Ignace Karkasy,' said Mersadie.

Loken's face crumpled and he looked away, unable to hide the grief he felt for the dead Karkasy, the irascible poet who had been under his protection. Ignace Karkasy had been nothing but trouble and inconvenience, but he had also been a man who had dared to speak out and tell the unpalatable truths that needed to be told.

'They say he killed himself,' continued Sindermann, unwilling to let Loken's grief dissuade him from his course, 'but I've never known a man more convinced that the galaxy needed to hear what he had to say. He was angry at the massacre on the embarkation deck and he wrote about it. He was angry with a lot of things, and he wasn't afraid to speak of them. Now he is dead, and he's not the only one.'

'Not the only one?' asked Loken. 'Who else?'

'Petronella Vivar, that insufferable documentarist woman. They say she got closer to the Warmaster than anyone, and now she's gone too, and I don't think it was back to Terra.'

'I remember her, but you are on thin ice, Kyril. You need to be very clear what you are suggesting.'

Sindermann did not flinch from Loken's gaze and said, 'I believe that those who oppose the will of the Warmaster are being killed.'

The iterator was a frail man, but Mersadie had never been more proud to know him as he stood unbending before a warrior of the Astartes and told him something he didn't want to hear.

Sindermann paused, giving Loken ample time to refute his claims and remind them all that the Emperor had chosen Horus as the Warmaster because he alone could be trusted to uphold the Imperial Truth. Horus was the man to whom every Son of Horus had pledged his life a hundred times over.

But Loken said nothing and Mersadie's heart sank.

'I have read of it more times than I can remember,' continued Sindermann. 'The Uranan Chronicles, for example. The first thing those tyrants did was to murder those who spoke out against their tyranny. The Overlords of the Yndonesic Dark Age did the same thing. Mark my words, the Age of Strife was made possible when the doubting voices fell silent, and now it is happening here.'

'You have always taught temperance, Kyril,' said Loken, 'weighing up arguments and never leaping past them into guesswork. We're at war and we have plenty of enemies already without you seeking to find new ones. It will be very dangerous for you and you may not like what you find. I do not wish to see you come to any harm, either of you.'

'Ha! Now you lecture me, Garviel,' sighed Sindermann. 'So much has changed. You're not just a warrior any more, are you?'

'And you are not just an iterator?'

'No, I suppose not,' nodded Sindermann. 'An iterator promulgates the Imperial Truth, does he not? He does not pick holes in it and spread rumours. But Karkasy is dead, and there are... other things.'

'What things?' asked Loken. 'You mean Keeler?'

'Perhaps,' said Sindermann, shaking his head. 'I don't know, but I feel she is part of it.'

'Part of what?'

'You heard what happened in the Archive Chamber?'

'With Euphrati? Yes, there was a fire and she was badly hurt. She ended up in a coma.'

'I was there,' said Sindermann.

'Kyril,' said Mersadie, a note of warning in her voice.

'Please, Mersadie,' said Sindermann. 'I know what I saw.'

'What did you see?' asked Loken.

'Lies,' replied Sindermann, his voice hushed. 'Lies made real: a creature, something from the warp. Somehow Keeler and I brought it through the gates of the Empyrean with the Book of Lorgar. My own damn fault, too. It was... it was sorcery, the one thing that all these years I've been preaching is a lie, but it was real and standing before me as surely as I stand before you now. It should have killed us, but Euphrati stood against it and lived.'

'How?' asked Loken.

'That's the part where I run out of rational explanations, Garviel,' shrugged Sindermann.

'Well, what do you think happened?'

Sindermann exchanged a glance with Mersadie and she willed him not to say anything more, but the venerable iterator continued. 'When you destroyed poor Jubal, it was with your guns, but Euphrati was unarmed. All she had was her faith: her faith in the Emperor. I... I think it was the light of the Emperor that cast the horror back to the warp.'

Hearing Kyril Sindermann talk of faith and the light of the Emperor was too much for Mersadie.

'But Kyril,' she said, 'there must be another explanation. Even what happened to Jubal wasn't beyond physical possibilities. The Warmaster himself told Loken that the thing that took Jubal was some kind of xeno creature from the warp. I've listened to you teach about how minds have been twisted by magic and superstition and all the things that blind us to reality. That's what the Imperial Truth is. I can't believe that the Iterator Kyril Sindermann doesn't believe the Imperial Truth any more.'

'Believe, my dear?' said Sindermann, smiling bleakly and shaking his head. 'Maybe belief is the biggest lie. In ages past, the earliest philosophers tried to explain the stars in the sky and the world around them. One of them conceived of the notion that the universe was mounted on giant crystal spheres controlled by a giant machine, which explained the movements of the heavens. He was laughed at and told that such a machine would be so huge and noisy that everyone would hear it. He simply replied that we are born with that noise all around us, and that we are so used to hearing it that we cannot hear it at all.'

Mersadie sat beside the old man and wrapped her arms around him, surprised to find that he was shivering and his eyes were wet with tears.

'I'm starting to hear it, Garviel,' said Sindermann, his voice quavering. 'I can hear the music of the spheres.'

Mersadie watched Loken's face as he stared at Sindermann, seeing the quality of intelligence and integrity Sindermann had recognised in him. The Astartes had been taught that superstition was the death of the Empire and only the Imperial Truth was a reality worth fighting for.

Now, before her very eyes, that was unravelling.

'Varvarus was killed,' said Loken at last, 'deliberately, by one of our bolts.'

'*Hektor* Varvarus? The Army commander?' asked Mersadie. 'I thought that was the Auretians?'

'No,' said Loken, 'it was one of ours.'

'Why?' she asked.

'He wanted us… I don't know… hauled before a court martial, brought to task for the… killings on the embarkation deck. Maloghurst wouldn't agree. Varvarus wouldn't back down and now he is dead.'

'Then it's true,' sighed Sindermann. 'The naysayers are being silenced.'

'There are still a few of us left,' said Loken, quiet steel in his voice.

'Then we do something about it, Garviel,' said
Sindermann. 'We must find out what has been
brought into the Legion and stop it. We can fight it,
Loken. We have you, we have the truth and there is
no reason why we cannot–'

The sound that cut off Sindermann's voice was
the door to the practice deck slamming open, followed by heavy metal-on-metal footsteps. Mersadie
knew it was an Astartes even before the impossibly
huge shadow fell over her. She turned to see the
cursive form of Maloghurst behind her, robed in a
cream tunic edged in sea green trim. The Warmaster's equerry, Maloghurst was known as 'the
Twisted', as much for his labyrinthine mind as the
horrible injuries that had broken his body and left
him grotesquely malformed.

His face was thunder and anger seemed to bleed
from him.

'Loken,' he said, 'these are civilians.'

'Kyril Sindermann and Mersadie Oliton are official rememberers of the Great Crusade and I can
vouch for them,' said Loken, standing to face Maloghurst as an equal.

Maloghurst spoke with Horus's authority and
Mersadie marvelled at what it must take to stand up
to such a man.

'Perhaps you are unaware of the Warmaster's
edict, captain,' said Maloghurst, the pleasant neu-
trality of his tone completely at odds with the
tension that crackled between the two Astartes.
'These clerks and notaries have caused enough

trouble; you of all people should understand that. There are to be no distractions, Loken, and no exceptions.'

Loken stood face-to-face with Maloghurst and for one sickening moment, Mersadie thought he was about to strike the equerry.

'We are all doing the work of the Great Crusade, Mal,' said Loken tightly. 'Without these men and women, it cannot be completed.'

'Civilians do not fight, captain, they only question and complain. They can record everything they desire once the war has been won and they can spread the Imperial Truth once we have conquered a population that needs to hear it. Until then, they are not a part of this Crusade.'

'No, Maloghurst,' said Loken. 'You're wrong and you know it. The Emperor did not create the primarchs and the Legions so they could fight on in ignorance. He did not set out to conquer the galaxy just for it to become another dictatorship.'

'The Emperor,' said Maloghurst, gesturing towards the door, 'is a long way from here.'

A dozen soldiers marched into the training halls and Mersadie recognised uniforms of the Imperial Army, but saw that their badges of unit and rank had been removed. With a start, she also recognised one face – the icy, golden-eyed features of Petronella Vivar's bodyguard. She recalled that his name was Maggard, and was amazed at the sheer size of the man, his physique bulky and muscled beyond that of the army soldiers who accompanied

him. The exposed flesh of his muscles bore freshly
healing scars and his face displayed a nascent gigantism similar to Loken's. He stood out amongst the
uniformed Army soldiers, and his presence only
lent credence to Sindermann's wild theory that
Petronella Vivar's disappearance had nothing to do
with her returning to Terra.

'Take the iterator and the remembrancer back to
their quarters,' said Maloghurst. 'Post guards and
ensure that there are no more breaches.'

Maggard nodded and stepped forwards. Mersadie
tried to avoid him, but he was quick and strong,
grabbing her by the scruff of her neck and hauling
her towards the door. Sindermann stood of his own
accord and allowed himself to be led away by the
other soldiers.

Maloghurst stood between Loken and the door. If
Loken wanted to stop Maggard and his men, he
would have to go through Maloghurst.

'Captain Loken,' called Sindermann as he was
marched off the practice deck, 'if you wish to
understand more, read the *Chronicles of Ursh* again.
There you will find illumination.'

Mersadie tried to look back. She could see Loken
beyond Maloghurst's robed form, looking like a
caged animal ready to attack.

The door slammed shut, and Mersadie stopped
struggling as Maggard led her and Sindermann
back towards their quarters.

TWO

Perfection
Iterator
What we do best

PERFECTION. THE DEAD greenskins were a testament to it. Deep Orbital DS191 had been conquered in a matchless display of combat, fields of fire overlapping like dancers' fans, squads charging in to slaughter the orks that the guns could not finish. Squad by squad, room by room, the Emperor's Children had killed their way through the xenos holding the space station with all the handsome perfection of combat that Fulgrim had taught his Legion.

As the warriors of his company despatched any surviving greenskins, Saul Tarvitz removed his helmet and immediately recoiled at the stench. The greenskins had inhabited the orbital for some time and it showed. Fungal growths pulsed on the dark metal struts of the main control centre and crude shrines of weapons, armour and tribal fetishes were piled against the command posts. Above him, the transparent dome of the control centre looked onto the void of space.

The Callinedes system, a collection of Imperial worlds under attack by the greenskins was visible amid the froth of stars. Capturing the orbital back from the orks was the first stage in the Imperial relief of Callinedes, and the Emperor's Children and Iron Hands Legions would soon be storming into the enemy strongholds on Callinedes IV.

'What a stink,' said a voice behind Tarvitz, and he turned to see Captain Lucius, the finest swordsman of the Emperor's Children. His compatriot's armour was spattered black and his elegant sword still crackled with the blood sizzling on its blue-hot blade. 'Damned animals, they don't have the sense to roll over and die when you kill them.'

Lucius's face had once been perfectly flawless, an echo of Fulgrim's Legion itself, but now, after one too many jibes about how he looked more like a pampered boy than a warrior and the influence of Serena d'Angelus, Lucius had started to acquire scars, each one uniform and straight in a perfect grid across his face. No enemy blade had etched them into his face, for Lucius was far too sublime a warrior to allow a mere enemy to mark his features.

'They're tough, I'll give them that,' agreed Tarvitz.

'They may be tough, but there's no elegance to their fighting,' said Lucius. 'There's no sport in killing them.'

'You sound disappointed.'

'Well of course I am. Aren't you?' asked Lucius, jabbing his sword through a dead greenskin and carving a curved pattern on its back. 'How can we achieve ultimate perfection with such poor specimens to better ourselves against?'

'Don't underestimate the greenskins,' said Tarvitz. 'These animals invaded a compliant world and slaughtered all the troops we left to defend it. They have spaceships and weapons we don't understand, and they attack as if war is some kind of religion to them.'

He turned over the closest corpse – a massive brute with skin as tough as gnarled bark, its violent red eyes open and its undershot maw still grimacing with rage. Only the spread of entrails beneath suggested it was dead at all. Tarvitz could almost feel the jarring of his broadsword as he had plunged it through the creature's midriff and its tremendous strength as it had tried to force him onto his knees.

'You talk about them as if we need to understand them before we can kill them. They're just animals,' said Lucius with a sardonic laugh. 'You think about things too much. That's always been your problem, Saul, and it's why you'll never reach the dizzying heights I will achieve. Come on, just revel in the kill.'

Tarvitz opened his mouth to respond, but he kept his thoughts to himself as Lord Commander Eidolon strode into the control centre.

'Fine work, Emperor's Children!' shouted Eidolon.

As one of Fulgrim's chosen, Eidolon had the honour of being within the tight circle of officers who surrounded the primarch and represented the Legion's finest artistry of war. Although it was not bred into him to dislike a fellow Astartes, Tarvitz had little respect for Eidolon. His arrogance did not befit a warrior of the Emperor's Children and the antagonism between them had only grown on the fields of Murder in the war against the megarachnids.

Despite Tarvitz's reservations, Eidolon carried a powerful natural authority about him, accentuated by magnificent armour with such an overabundance of gilding that the purple colours of the Legion were barely visible. 'The vermin didn't know what hit them!'

The Emperor's Children cheered in response. It had been a classic victory for the Legion: hard, fast and perfect.

The greenskins had been doomed from the start.

'Make ready,' shouted Eidolon, 'to receive your primarch.'

THE CARGO DECKS of the deep orbital were rapidly cleared of the greenskin dead by the Legion's menials for a portion of the Callinedes battle force to assemble. Tarvitz felt his pulse race at the thought of setting eyes on his beloved primarch once more. It had been too long since the Legion had fought alongside their leader. Hundreds of

Emperor's Children in perfectly dressed ranks stood to attention, a magnificent army in purple and gold.

As magnificent as they were, they were but a poor imitation of the incredible warrior who was father to them all.

The primarch of the Emperor's Children was awe-inspiring, his face pale and sculpted, framed by a flowing mane of albino-white hair. His very presence was intoxicating and Tarvitz felt a fierce pride fill him at the sight of this incredible, wondrous warrior. Created to echo a facet of war, Fulgrim's art was the pursuit of perfection through battle and he sought it as diligently as an imagist strove for perfection through his picts. One shoulder of his golden armour was worked into a sweeping eagle's wing, the symbol of the Emperor's Children, and the symbolism was a clear statement of Legion pride.

The eagle was the Emperor's personal symbol, and he had granted the Emperor's Children alone the right to bear that same heraldry, symbolically proclaiming Fulgrim's warriors as his most adored Legion. Fulgrim wore a golden-hilted sword at his hip, said to have been a gift from the Warmaster himself, a clear sign of the bond of brotherhood between them.

The officers of the primarch's inner circle flanked him – Lord Commander Eidolon, Apothecary Fabius, Chaplain Charmosian and the massive dreadnought body of Ancient Rylanor. Even these heroes of the Legion were dwarfed by Fulgrim's physical size and his sheer charisma.

A line of heralds, chosen from among the young initiates who were soon to complete their training as Emperor's Children, fanned out in front of Fulgrim, playing a blaring fanfare on their golden trumpets to announce the arrival of the most perfect warrior in the galaxy. A thunderous roar of applause swelled from the assembled Emperor's Children as they welcomed their primarch back to his Legion.

Fulgrim waited graciously for the applause to die down. More than anything, Tarvitz aspired to be that awesome golden figure in front of them, though he knew he had already been designated as a line officer and nothing more. But Fulgrim's very presence filled him with the promise that he could be so much better if he was only given the chance. His pride in his Legion's prowess caught light as Fulgrim looked over the assembled warriors, and the primarch's dark eyes shone as he acknowledged each and every one of them.

'My brothers,' called Fulgrim, his voice lilting and golden, 'this day you have shown the accursed greenskin what it means to stand against the Children of the Emperor!'

More applause rolled around the cargo decks, but Fulgrim spoke over it, his voice easily cutting through the clamour of his warriors.

'Commander Eidolon has wrought you into a weapon against which the greenskin had no defence. Perfection, strength, resolve: these qualities are the cutting edge of this Legion and you have shown them all here today. This orbital is in Imperial hands once more, as are the others the greenskins had occupied in the futile hope of fending off our invasion.

'The time has come to press home this attack against the greenskins and liberate the Callinedes system. My brother primarch, Ferrus Manus of the Iron Hands and I shall see to it that not a single alien stands upon land claimed in the name of the Crusade.'

Expectation was heavy in the air as the Legion waited for the order that would send them into battle with their primarch.

'But most of you, my brothers, will not be there,' said Fulgrim. The crushing disappointment Tarvitz felt was palpable, for the Legion had been sent to the Callinedes system with the assumption that it would lend its full strength to the destruction of the invading xenos.

'The Legion will be divided,' continued Fulgrim, raising his hands to stem the cries of woe and lamentation that his words provoked. 'I will lead a small force to join Ferrus Manus and his Iron Hands at Callinedes IV. The rest of the Legion will rendezvous with the Warmaster's 63rd Expedition at the Isstvan system. These are the orders of the Warmaster and of your primarch. Lord Commander Eidolon will lead you to Isstvan, and he will act in my stead until I can join you once more.'

Tarvitz glanced at Lucius, unable to read the expression on the swordsman's face at the news of their new orders. Conflicting emotions warred within Tarvitz: aching loss to be parted from his primarch once more, and excited anticipation at the thought of fighting alongside his comrades in the Sons of Horus.

'Commander, if you please,' said Fulgrim, gesturing Eidolon to step forwards.

Eidolon nodded and said, 'The Warmaster has called upon us to aid his Legion in battle once more. He recognises our skills and we welcome this chance to prove our superiority. We are to halt a rebellion in the Isstvan system, but we are not to fight alone. As well as his own Legion, the Warmaster has seen fit to deploy the Death Guard and World Eaters.'

A muttered gasp spread around the cargo bay at the mention of such brutal Legions.

Eidolon chuckled. 'I see some of you remember fighting alongside our brother Astartes. We all know what a grim and artless business war becomes in the hands of such men, so I say this is the perfect opportunity to show the Warmaster how the Emperor's chosen fight.'

The Legion cheered once more, and Tarvitz knew that whenever the Emperor's Children had a chance to prove their skill and artistry, especially to the other Legions, they took it. Fulgrim had turned pride into a virtue, and it drove each warrior of his Legion to heights of excellence that no other could match.

Torgaddon had called it arrogance and on the surface of Murder Tarvitz had tried to dissuade him of that notion, but hearing the boastful cries of the Emperor's Children around him, he wasn't sure that his friend had been wrong after all.

'The Warmaster has requested our presence immediately,' shouted Eidolon through the cheering. 'Although Isstvan is not far distant, the conditions in the warp have become more difficult, so we must make all haste. The strike cruiser *Andronius* will leave for Isstvan in four hours. When we arrive, it will be as ambassadors for our Legion, and when the battle is done the Warmaster will have witnessed war at its most magnificent.'

Eidolon saluted and Fulgrim led the applause before turning and taking his leave.

Tarvitz was stunned. To commit such a force of Astartes was rare and he knew that whatever foe they would face on Isstvan must be mighty indeed. Even the thrill of excitement he felt at this opportunity to prove themselves before the Warmaster was tempered by a sudden, nagging sense of unease.

'Four Legions?' asked Lucius, echoing his own thoughts as the squads fell out to make ready for the journey to join the 63rd Expedition. 'For one system? That's absurd!'

'Careful Lucius, you veer close to arrogance,' Tarvitz pointed out. 'Are you questioning the Warmaster's decision?'

'Questioning, no,' said Lucius defensively, 'but come on, even you have to admit it's a sledgehammer to crack a nut.'

'Possibly,' conceded Tarvitz, 'but for the Isstvan system to rebel, it must have been compliant at one stage.'

'What's your point?'

'My point, Lucius, is that the Crusade was supposed to be pushing ever outwards, conquering the galaxy in the name of the Emperor. Instead it is turning back on itself to patch up the cracks. I can only assume that the Warmaster wants to make some kind of grand gesture so show his enemies what rebellion means.'

'Ungrateful bastards,' spat Lucius. 'Once we're done with Isstvan they'll beg us to take them back!'

'With four Legions sent against them,' replied Tarvitz, 'I don't think there'll be many Isstvanians left for us to take back.'

'Come, Saul,' said Lucius walking ahead of him, 'did you lose your taste for battle against the greenskins?'

A taste for battle? Tarvitz had never considered such an idea. He had always fought because he wanted to become more than he was, to strive for perfection in all things. For longer than he could remember he had devoted himself to the task of emulating the warriors of the Legion who were more gifted and more worthy than he. He knew his station within the Legion, but knowing one's station was the first step to bettering it.

Watching Lucius's arrogant swagger, Tarvitz was reminded of how much his fellow captain loved battle. Lucius loved it without shame or apology, seeing it as the best way to express himself, weaving between his enemies and cutting a path of bloody ruin through them with his flashing sword.

'It just concerns me,' said Tarvitz.

'What does?' asked Lucius, turning back to face him. Tarvitz could see the hastily masked exasperation on the swordsman's face. He had seen that expression more and more on Lucius's scarred features recently, and it saddened him to know that the swordsman's ego and rampant ambition to rise within the ranks of the Emperor's Children would be the undoing of their friendship.

'That the Crusade has to repair itself at all. Compliance used to be the end of it. Not now.'

'Don't worry,' smiled Lucius. 'Once a few of these rebel worlds get a decent killing this will all be over and the Crusade will go on.'

Rebel worlds... Whoever thought to hear such a phrase?

Tarvitz said nothing as he considered the sheer numbers of Astartes that would be converging on the Isstvan system. Hundreds of Astartes had fought on Deep Orbital DS191, but more than ten thousand Emperor's Children made up the Legion, most of whom would be journeying to Isstvan III. That in itself was enough for several war zones. The thought of four Legions arrayed in battle sent shivers up Tarvitz's spine.

What would be left of Isstvan when four Legions had marched through the system? Could any depths of rebellion really justify that?

'I just want victory,' said Tarvitz, the words sounding hollow, even to him.

Lucius laughed, but Tarvitz couldn't tell if it was in agreement or mockery.

BEING CONFINED TO his quarters was the most exquisite torture for Kyril Sindermann. Without the library of books he was used to consulting in Archive Chamber Three he felt quite adrift. His own library, though extensive by any normal standards, was a paltry thing next to the arcana that had been destroyed in the fire.

How many priceless, irreplaceable tomes had been lost in the wake of the warp beast he and Euphrati had conjured from the pages of the *Book of Lorgar*?

It did not bear thinking about and he wondered how much the future would condemn them for the knowledge that had been lost there. He had already filled thousands of pages with those fragments he could remember from the books he had consulted. Most of it was fragmentary and disjointed. He knew that the task of recalling everything he had read was doomed to failure, but he could no more conceive of giving up than he could stop his heart from beating.

His gift and the gift of the Crusade to the ages yet to come was the accumulated wisdom of the galaxy's greatest thinkers and warriors. With the broad shoulders of such knowledge to stand upon, who knew what dizzying heights of enlightenment the Imperium might reach?

His pen scratched across the page, recalling the philosophies of the Hellenic writers and their early debates on the nature of divinity. No doubt many would think it pointless to transcribe the writings of those long dead, but Sindermann knew that to ignore the past was to doom the future to repeat it.

The text he wrote spoke of the ineffable inscrutability of false gods, and he knew that such mysteries were closer to the surface than he cared to admit. The things he had seen and read since Sixty-Three Nineteen had stretched his scepticism to the point where he could no longer deny the truth of what was plainly before him and which Euphrati Keeler had been trying to tell them all.

Gods existed and, in the case of the Emperor, moved amongst them...

He paused for a moment as the full weight of that thought wrapped itself around him like a comforting blanket. The warmth and ease such simple acceptance gave him was like a panacea for all the ills that had troubled him this last year, and he smiled as his pen idly scratched across the page before him without his conscious thought.

Sindermann started as he realised that the pen was moving across the page of its own volition. He looked down to see what was being written.

She needs you.

Cold fear gripped him, but even as it rose, it was soothed and a comforting state of love and trust filled him. Images filled his head unbidden: the Warmaster strong and powerful in his newly forged suit of black plate armour, the amber eye glowing like a coal from the furnace. Claws slid from the Warmaster's gauntlets and an evil red glow built from his gorget, illuminating his face with a ghastly daemonic light.

'No...' breathed Sindermann, feeling a great and unspeakable horror fill him at this terrible vision, but no sooner had this image filled his head than it was replaced by one of Euphrati Keeler lying supine on her medicae bed. Terrified thoughts were banished at the sight of her and Sindermann felt his love for this beautiful woman fill him as a pure and wondrous light.

Even as he smiled in rapture, the vision darkened and yellowed talons slid into view, tearing at the image of Euphrati.

Sindermann screamed in sudden premonition.

Once again he looked at the words on the page, marvelling at their desperate simplicity.

She needs you.

Someone was sending him a message.

The saint was in danger.

COORDINATING A LEGION'S assets – its Astartes, its spacecraft, staff and accompanying Imperial Army units – was a truly Herculean task. Managing to coordinate the arrival of four Legions in the same place at the same time was an impossible task: impossible for anyone but the Warmaster.

The *Vengeful Spirit*, its long flat prow like the tip of a spear, slid from the warp in a kaleidoscopic display of pyrotechnics, lightning raking along its sides as the powerful warp-integrity fields took the full force of re-entry. In the interstellar distance, the closest star of the Isstvan system glinted, cold and hard against the blackness. The Eye of Horus glared from the top of the ship's prow, the entire vessel having been refitted following the victory against the Technocracy, the bone-white of the Luna Wolves replaced by the metallic grey-green of the Sons of Horus.

Within moments, another ship broke through, tearing its way into real space with the brutal functionality of its Legion. Where the *Vengeful Spirit* had a deadly grace to it, the newcomer was brutish and ugly, its hull a drab gunmetal-grey, its only decoration, a single brazen skull on its prow. The vessel was the *Endurance*, capital ship of the Death Guard fleet accompanying the Warmaster, and a flotilla of smaller cruisers and escorts flew in its wake. All were the same unembellished gunmetal, for nothing in Mortarion's Legion bore any more adornment than was necessary.

Several hours later the powerful, stabbing form of the *Conqueror* broke through to join the Warmaster. Shimmering with the white and blue colours of the World Eaters, the *Conqueror* was Angron's flagship, and its blunt, muscular form echoed the legendary ferocity of the World Eaters' primarch.

Finally, the *Andronius*, at the head of the Emperor's Children fleet, joined the growing Isstvan strike force. The vessel itself was resplendent in purple and gold, more like a flying palace than a ship of war. Its appearance was deceptive however, for the gun decks bristled with weapons manned by well-drilled menials who lived and died to serve Fulgrim's Legion. The *Andronius*, for all its decorative folly, was a compact, lethal weapon of war.

The Great Crusade had rarely seen a fleet of such power assembled in one place.

Until now, only the Emperor had commanded such a force, but his place was on distant Terra, and these Legions answered only to the Warmaster.

So it was that four Legions gathered and turned their eyes towards the Isstvan system.

THE KLAXONS ANNOUNCING the *Vengeful Spirit's* translation back to real space were the spur to action that Kyril Sindermann had been waiting for. Mopping his brow with an already moist handkerchief, he pushed himself to his feet and made his way to the shutter of his quarters.

He took a deep, calming breath as the shutter rose and he was confronted by the hostile stares of two army soldiers, their starched uniforms insignia free and anonymous.

'Can I help you, sir?' asked a tall man with a cold, unhelpful expression.

'Yes,' said Sindermann, his voice perfectly modulated to convey his non-threatening affability. 'I need to travel to the medicae deck.'

'You don't look sick,' said the second guard.

Sindermann chuckled, reaching out to touch the man's arm like a kindly grandfather. 'No, it's not me, my boy, it's a friend of mine. She's rather ill and I promised that I would look in on her.'

'Sorry,' said the first guard, in a tone that suggested he was anything but. 'We've got orders from the Astartes not to let anyone off this deck.'

'I see, I see,' sighed Sindermann, letting a tear trickle from the corner of his eye. 'I don't want to be an inconvenience, my boys, but my friend, well, she's like a daughter to me, you see. She is very dear to me and you would be doing an old man a very real favour if you could just let me see her.'

'I don't think so, sir,' said the guard, but Sindermann could already detect a softening in his tone and pushed a little harder.

'She has… she has… not long left to her, and I was told by Maloghurst himself that I would be allowed to see her before… before the end.'

Using Maloghurst's name was a gamble, but it was a calculated gamble. These men were unlikely to have any formal channel to contact the Warmaster's equerry, but if they decided to check, he would be unmasked.

Sindermann kept his voice low and soft as he played the grandfatherly role, utilising every trick he had learned as an iterator – the precise timbre of

his voice, the frailty of his posture, keeping eye contact and empathy with his audience.

'Do you have children, my boy?' asked Sindermann, reaching out clasp the guard's arm.

'Yes, sir, I do.'

'Then you understand why I have to see her,'
pressed Sindermann, risking the more direct
approach and hoping that he had judged these men
correctly.

'You're just going to the medicae deck?' asked the
guard.

'No further,' promised Sindermann. 'I just need
some time to say my goodbyes to her. That's all.
Please?'

The guards exchanged glances and Sindermann
fought to keep the smile from his face as he knew
he had them. The first soldier nodded and they
moved aside to let him past.

'Just the medicae deck, old man,' said the guard,
scrawling on a chit that would allow him passage
through the ship to the medicae deck and back. 'If
you're not back in your quarters in a couple of
hours, I'll be dragging you back here myself.'

Sindermann nodded, taking the proffered chit
and shaking both men warmly by the hand.

'You're good soldiers, boys,' he said, his voice
dripping with gratitude. 'Good soldiers. I'll be sure
to tell Maloghurst of your compassion for an old
man.'

He turned quickly so that they didn't see the relief
on his face and hurried away down the corridor

towards the Medicae deck. The companionways echoed with their emptiness as he made his way through the twisting maze of the ship, an idiot smile plastered across his puffing features. Entire worlds had fallen under the spell of his oratory and here he was smiling about duping two simple-minded guards to let him out of his room.

How the mighty had fallen.

'Is THERE ANY more news on Varvarus?' asked Loken as he and Torgaddon walked through the Museum of Conquest on their way to the Lupercal's Court.

Torgaddon shook his head. 'The shells were too fragmented. Apothecary Vaddon wouldn't be able to make a match even if we found the weapon that fired the shot. It was one of ours, but that's all we know.'

The museum was brimming with artefacts won from the Legion's many victories, for the Luna Wolves had brought a score of worlds into compliance. A grand statue dominating one wall recalled the days when the Emperor and Horus had fought side by side in the first campaigns of the Great Crusade. The Emperor, sword in hand, fought off slender, masked aliens while Horus, back to back with his father, blazed away with a boltgun.

Beyond the statue, Loken recognised a display of bladed insectoid limbs, a blend of metallic and biological flesh wrested from the megarachnids on Murder. Only a few of these trophies had been won after Horus's investiture as Warmaster, the majority having been taken before the Luna Wolves had been renamed the Sons of Horus in honour of the Warmaster's accomplishments.

'The remembrancers are next,' said Loken. 'They are asking too many questions. Some of them may already have been murdered.'

'Who?'

'Ignace and Petronella Vivar.'

'Karkasy,' said Torgaddon. 'Damn, I'd heard he killed himself, but I should have known they'd find a way to do it. The warrior lodge was talking about silencing him, Abaddon in particular. They didn't call it murder, although Abaddon seemed to think it was the same as killing an enemy in war. That's when I broke with the lodge.'

'Did they say how it was to be done?'

Torgaddon shook his head. 'No, just that it needed to be done.'

'It won't be long before all this is out in the open,' promised Loken. 'The lodge doesn't move under a veil of secrecy any more and soon there will be a reckoning.'

'Then what do we do?'

Loken looked away from his friend, at the high arch that led from the museum and into the Lupercal's Court.

'I don't know,' he said, waving Torgaddon to silence as he caught sight of a figure moving behind one of the furthest cabinets.

'What's up?' asked Torgaddon.

'I'm not sure,' said Loken, moving between display cabinets of gleaming swords captured from an ancient feudal kingdom and strange alien weapons taken from the many species the Legion had destroyed. The figure he had seen was another Astartes, and Loken recognised the colours of the World Eaters upon his armour.

Loken and Torgaddon rounded the corner of a tall, walnut-framed cabinet, seeing a scarred Astartes warrior peering intently at an immense battle-glaive that had been wrested from the hands of a xenos praetorian by the Warmaster himself.

'Welcome to the *Vengeful Spirit*,' said Loken.

The World Eater looked up from the weapon and turned to face them. His face was deeply bronzed, long and noble, contrasting with the bone white and blue of his Legion's colours.

'Greetings,' he said, bringing his forearm across his armoured chest in a martial salute.

'Khârn, Eighth Assault Company of the World Eaters.'

'Loken of the Tenth,' replied Loken.

'Torgaddon of the Second,' nodded Torgaddon.

'Impressive, this,' said Khârn, looking around him.

'Thank you,' said Loken. 'The Warmaster always believed we should remember our enemies. If we forget them, we shall never learn.'

He pointed at the weapon Khârn had been admiring. 'We have the preserved corpse of the creature that carried this weapon somewhere around here. It's the size of a tank.'

'Angron has his share of trophies too,' said Khârn, 'but only from foes that deserve to be remembered.'

'Should we not remember them all?'

'No,' said Khârn firmly. 'There is nothing to gain from knowing your enemy. The only thing that matters is that they are to be destroyed. Everything else is just a distraction.'

'Spoken like a true World Eater,' said Torgaddon.

Khârn looked up from the weapon with an amused sneer. 'You seek to provoke me, Captain Torgaddon, but I already know what other Legions think of the World Eaters.'

'We were on Aureus,' said Loken. 'You are butchers.'

Khârn smiled. 'Hah! Honesty is rare these days, Captain Loken. Yes, we are and we are proud because we are good at it. My primarch is not ashamed of what he does best, so neither am I.'

'I trust you're here for the conclave?' asked Loken, wishing to change the subject.

'Yes. I serve as my primarch's equerry.'

Torgaddon raised an eyebrow. 'Tough job.'

'Sometimes,' admitted Khârn. 'Angron cares little for diplomacy.'

'The Warmaster believes it is important.'

'So I see, but all Legions do things differently,' laughed Khârn, clapping Loken on his shoulder guard. 'As one honest man to another, your own Legion has as many detractors as admirers. Too damn superior, the lot of you.'

'The Warmaster has high standards,' said Loken.

'So does Angron, I assure you,' said Khârn, and Loken was surprised to hear a note of weariness in Khârn's voice. 'The Emperor knew that sometimes the best course of action is to let the World Eaters do what we do best. The Warmaster knows it too; otherwise we would not be here. It may be distasteful to you, captain, but if it were not for warriors like mine, the Great Crusade would have foundered long ago.'

'There we must agree to disagree,' said Loken. 'I could not do what you do.'

Khârn shook his head. 'You're a warrior of the Astartes, captain. If you had to kill every living thing in a city to ensure victory, you would do it. We must always be prepared to go further than our enemy. All the Legions know it; the World Eaters just preach it openly.'

'Let us hope it never comes to that.'

'Do not pin too much on that hope. I hear tell that Isstvan III will be difficult to break.'

'What do you know of it?' asked Torgaddon.

Khârn shrugged. 'Nothing specific, just rumours really; something religious, they say, witches and warlocks, skies turning red and monsters from the warp, all the usual hyperbole. Not that the Sons of Horus would believe such things.'

'The galaxy is a complicated place,' replied Loken carefully. 'We don't know the half of what goes on in it.'

'I'm beginning to wonder myself,' agreed Khârn.

'It's changing,' continued Loken, 'the galaxy, and the Crusade with it.'

'Yes,' said Khârn with relish. 'It is.'

Loken was about to ask Khârn what he meant when the doors to the Lupercal's Court swung open.

'Evidently the Warmaster's conclave will begin soon,' said Khârn, bowing before them both. 'It is time for me to rejoin my primarch.'

'And we must join the Warmaster,' said Loken. 'Perhaps we will see you on Isstvan III?'

'Perhaps,' nodded Khârn, walking off between the spoils of a hundred wars. 'If there's anything left of Isstvan III when the World Eaters finish with it.'

THREE

Horus enthroned
The saint is in danger
Isstvan III

LUPERCAL'S COURT WAS a new addition to the *Vengeful Spirit*. Previously the Warmaster had held briefings and planning sessions on the strategium, but it had been decided that he needed somewhere grander to hold court. Designed by Peeter Egon Momus, it had been artfully constructed to place the Warmaster in a setting more suited to his position as the leader of the Great Crusade and present him as the first among equals to his fellow commanders.

Vast banners hung from the sides of the room, most belonging to the Legion's battle companies, though there were a few that Loken didn't recognise. He saw one with a throne of skulls set against a tower of brass rising from a blood-red sea and another with an eight-pointed black star shining in a white sky. The meaning of such obscure symbols confounded Loken, but he assumed that they represented the warrior lodge that had become integral to the Legion.

Greater than all the majesty designed by the architect designate, was the Primarch of the Sons of Horus himself, enthroned before them on a great basalt throne. Abaddon and Aximand stood to one side. Both warriors were armoured, Abaddon in the glossy black of the Justaerin, Aximand in his pale green plate.

The two officers glared at Loken and Torgaddon – the enmity that had grown between them during the Auretian campaign too great to hide any more. As he met Abaddon's flinty gaze, Loken felt great sadness as the realised that the glorious ideal of the Mournival was finally and irrevocably dead. None of them spoke as Loken and Torgaddon took their places on the other side of the Warmaster.

Loken had stood with these warriors and sworn an oath by the light of a reflected moon on a planet the inhabitants called Terra, to counsel the Warmaster and preserve the soul of the Legion.

That felt like a very long time ago.

'Loken, Torgaddon,' said Horus, and even after all that had happened, Loken felt honoured to be so addressed. 'Your role here is simply to observe and remind our Legion brothers of the solidity of our cause. Do you understand?'

'Yes, my Warmaster,' said Torgaddon.

'Loken?' asked the Warmaster.

Loken nodded and took his allotted position. 'Yes, Warmaster.'

He felt the Warmaster's penetrating eyes boring into him, but kept his gaze fixed firmly on the arches that led into the Lupercal's Court as the doors beneath one of them slid open. The tramp of feet sounded and a blood-red angel of death emerged from the shadows.

Loken had seen the primarch of the World Eaters before, but was still awed by his monstrous, physical presence. Angron was huge, easily as tall as the Warmaster, but also massively broad, with wide hulking shoulders like some enormous beast of burden. His face was scarred and violent, his eyes buried deep in folds of angry red scar tissue. Ugly cortical implants jutted from his scalp, connected to the collar of his armour by ribbed cables. The primarch's armour was ancient and bronze, like that of a feral world god, with heavy metal plates over mail and twin chainaxes strapped to his back.

Loken had heard that Angron had once been a slave before the Emperor had found him, and that his masters had forced the implants on him to turn him into a psychotic killer for their fighting pits.

Looking at Angron, Loken could well believe it.

Angron's equerry, Khârn, flanked the terrifying primarch, his expression neutral where his master's was thunder.

'Horus!' said Angron, his voice rough and brutal. 'I see the Warmaster welcomes his brother like a king. Am I your subject now?'

'Angron,' replied Horus unperturbed, 'it is good that you could join us.'

'And miss all this prettiness? Not for the world,' said Angron, his voice loaded with the threat of a smouldering volcano.

A second delegation arrived through another of the arches, arrayed in the purple and gold of the Emperor's Children. Led by Eidolon in all his magnificence, a squad of Astartes with glittering swords marched alongside the lord commander, their battle gear as ornate as their leader's.

'Warmaster, the Lord Fulgrim sends his regards,' stated Eidolon formally and with great humility. Loken saw that Eidolon had learned the ways of a practiced diplomat since he had last spoken to the Warmaster. 'He assures you that his task is well under way and that he will join us soon. I speak for him and command the Legion in his stead.'

Loken's eyes darted from Angron to Eidolon, seeing the obvious antipathy between the two Legions. The Emperor's Children and the World Eaters were as different as could be – Angron's Legion fought and won through raw aggression, while the Emperor's Children had perfected the art of picking an enemy force apart and destroying it a piece at a time.

'Lord Angron,' said Eidolon with a bow, 'it is an honour.'

Angron did not deign to reply and Loken saw Eidolon stiffen at this insult, but any immediate confrontation was averted as the final delegation to the Warmaster entered the Lupercal's Court.

Mortarion, Primarch of the Death Guard was backed by a unit of warriors armoured in the dull gleam of unpainted Terminator plate. Mortarion's armour was also bare, with the brass skull of the Death Guard on one shoulder guard. His pallid face and scalp were hairless and pocked, his mouth and throat hidden by a heavy collar that hissed spurts of grey steam as he breathed.

A Death Guard captain marched beside the primarch, and Loken recognised him with a smile. Captain Nathanial Garro had fought alongside the Sons of Horus in the days when they had been known as the Luna Wolves. The Terran-born captain had won many friends within the Warmaster's Legion for his unshakeable code of honour and his straightforward, honest manner.

The Death Guard warrior caught Loken's gaze and gave a perfunctory nod of greeting.

'With our brother Mortarion,' said Horus, 'we are complete.'

The Warmaster stood and descended from the elevated throne to the centre of the court as the lights dimmed and a glowing globe appeared above him, hovering just below the ceiling.

'This,' said Horus, 'is Isstvan III, courtesy of servitor-manned stellar cartography drones. Remember it well, for history will be made here.'

JONAH ARUKEN PAUSED in his labours and slipped a small hip flask from beneath his uniform jacket as he checked for anyone watching. The hangar bay was bustling with activity, as it always seemed to be these days, but no one was paying him any attention. The days when an Imperator Titan being made ready for war would pause even the most jaded war maker in his tracks were long past, for there were few here who had not seen the mighty form of the *Dies Irae* being furnished for battle scores of times already.

He took a hit from the flask and looked up at the old girl.

The Titan's hull was scored and dented with wounds the Mechanicum servitors had not yet had time to patch and Jonah patted the thick plates of her leg armour affectionately.

'Well, old girl,' he said. 'You've certainly seen some action, but I still love you.'

He smiled at the thought of a man being in love with a machine, but he'd love anything that had saved his life as often as the *Dies Irae* had. Through the fires of uncounted battles, they had fought together and as much as Titus Cassar denied it, Jonah knew that there was a mighty heart and soul at the core of this glorious war machine.

Jonah took another drink from his flask as his expression turned sour thinking of Titus and his damned sermons. Titus said he felt the light of the Emperor within him, but Jonah didn't feel much of anything any more.

As much as he wanted to believe in what Titus was preaching, he just couldn't let go of the sceptical core at the centre of his being. To believe in things that weren't there, that couldn't be seen or felt? Titus called it faith, but Jonah was a man who needed to believe in what was real, what could be touched and experienced.

Princeps Turnet would discharge him from the crew of the *Dies Irae* if he knew he had attended prayer meetings back on Davin, and the thought of spending the rest of the Crusade as a menial, denied forever the thrill of commanding the finest war machine ever to come from the forges of Mars sent a cold shiver down his spine.

Every few days, Titus would ask him to come to another prayer meeting and the times he said yes, they would furtively make their way to some forsaken part of the ship to listen to passages read from the Lectitio Divinitatus. Each time he would sweat the journey back for fear of discovery and the court martial that would no doubt follow.

Jonah had been a career Titan crewman since the day he had first set foot aboard his inaugural posting, a Warhound Titan called the *Venator*, and he knew that if it came down to a choice, he would choose the *Dies Irae* over the Lectitio Divinitatus every time.

But still, the thought that Titus might be right continued to nag at him.

He leaned back against the Titan's leg, sliding down until he was sitting on his haunches with his knees drawn up to his chest.

'Faith,' he whispered, 'you can't earn it and you can't buy it. Where then do I find it?'

'Well,' said a voice behind and above him, 'you can start by putting that flask away and coming with me.'

Jonah looked up and saw Titus Cassar, resplendent as always in his parade-ready uniform, standing in the arched entrance to the Titan's leg bastions.

'Titus,' said Jonah, hurriedly stuffing the hip flask back into his jacket. 'What's up?'

'We have to go,' said Titus urgently. 'The saint is in danger.'

MAGGARD STALKED ALONG the shadowed companionways of the *Vengeful Spirit* at a brisk pace, marching at double time with the vigour of a man on his way to a welcome rendezvous. His hulking form had been steadily growing over the last few months, as though he were afflicted with some hideous form of rapid gigantism.

But the procedures the Warmaster's apothecaries were performing on his frame were anything but hideous. His body was changing, growing and transforming beyond anything the crude surgeries of House Carpinus had ever managed. Already he could feel the new organs within him reshaping his flesh and bone into something greater than he could ever have imagined, and this was just the beginning.

His Kirlian blade was unsheathed, shimmering with a strange glow in the dim light of the corridor. He wore fresh white robes, his enlarging physique already too massive for his armour. Legion artificers stood ready to reshape it once his flesh had settled into its new form, and he missed its reassuring solidity enclosing him.

Like him, his armour would be born anew, forged into something worthy of the Warmaster and his chosen warriors. Maggard knew he was not yet ready for such inclusion, but he had already carved himself a niche within the Sons of Horus. He walked where the Astartes could not, acted where they could not be seen to act and spilled blood where they needed to be seen as peacemakers.

It required a special kind of man to do such work, efficiently and conscience-free, and Maggard was perfectly suited to his new role. He had killed hundreds of people at the behest of House Carpinus and many more than that before he had been captured by them, but these had been poor, messy killings compared to the death he now carried.

He remembered the sense of magnificent beginnings when Maloghurst had tasked him with the death of Ignace Karkasy.

Maggard had jammed the barrel of his pistol beneath the poet's quivering jaw and blown his brains out over the roof of his cramped room before letting the generously fleshed body crash to the floor in a flurry of bloody papers.

Why Maloghurst had required Karkasy's death did not concern Maggard. The equerry spoke with the voice of Horus and Maggard had pledged his undying loyalty to the Warmaster on the battlefield of Davin when he had offered him his sword.

Later, whether in reward or as part of his ongoing designs, the Warmaster had killed his former mistress, Petronella Vivar, and for that, Maggard was forever in his debt.

Whatever the Warmaster desired, Maggard would move heaven or hell to see it done.

Now he had been ordered to do something wondrous.

Now he was going to kill a saint.

SINDERMANN BEAT HIS middle finger against his chin in a nervous tattoo as he tried to look as if he belonged in this part of the ship. Deck crew in orange jumpsuits and ordnance officers in yellow jackets threaded past him as he awaited his accomplices in this endeavour. He clutched the chit the guard had given him tightly, as though it were some kind of talisman that would protect him if someone challenged him.

'Come on, come on,' he whispered. 'Where are you?'

It had been a risk contacting Titus Cassar, but he had no one else to turn to. Mersadie did not believe in the Lectitio Divinitatus, and in truth he wasn't sure he did yet, but he knew that whatever or whoever had sent him the vision of Euphrati Keeler had meant him to act upon it. Likewise, Garviel Loken was out of the question, for it was certain that his movements would not escape notice.

'Iterator,' hissed a voice from beside him and Sindermann almost cried aloud in surprise. Titus Cassar stood beside him, an earnest expression creasing his slender face. Another man stood behind him, similarly uniformed in the dark blue of a Titan crewman.

'Titus,' breathed Sindermann in relief. 'I wasn't sure you'd be able to come.'

'We won't have long before Princeps Turnet notices we are not at our posts, but your communication said the saint was in danger.'

'She is,' confirmed Sindermann, 'grave danger.'

'How do you know?' asked the second man.

Cassar's brow twisted in annoyance. 'I'm sorry, Kyril, this is Jonah Aruken, my fellow Moderati on the *Dies Irae*. He is one of us.'

'I just know,' said Sindermann. 'I saw… I don't know… a vision of her lying on her bed and I just knew that someone intended her harm.'

'A vision,' breathed Cassar. 'Truly you are one of the chosen of the Emperor.'

'No, no,' hissed Sindermann. 'I'm really not. Now come on, we don't have time for this, we have to go now.'

'Where?' asked Jonah Aruken.

'The medicae deck,' said Sindermann, holding up his chit. 'We have to get to the medicae deck.'

THE SURFACE OF the shimmering globe above Horus resolved into continents and oceans, overlaid with the traceries of geophysical features: plains, forests, seas, mountain ranges and cities.

Horus held up his arms, as if supporting the globe from below like some titan from the ancient myths of old Earth.

'This is Isstvan III,' he repeated, 'a world brought into compliance thirteen years ago by the 27th expeditionary force of our brother Corax.'

'And he wasn't up to the job?' snorted Angron.

Horus shot Angron a dangerous look. 'There was some resistance, yes, but the last elements of the aggressive faction were destroyed by the Raven Guard at the Redarth Valley.'

The battle site flared red on the globe, nestled among a mountain range on one of Isstvan III's northern continents. 'The remembrancer order was not yet foisted upon us by the Council of Terra, but a substantial civilian contingent was left behind to begin integration with the Imperial Truth.'

'Are we to assume that the Truth didn't take?' asked Eidolon.

'Mortarion?' prompted Horus, gesturing to his brother primarch.

'Four months ago the Death Guard received a distress signal from Isstvan III,' said Mortarion. 'It was weak and old. We only received it because one of our supply ships joining the fleet at Arcturan dropped out of the warp for repairs. Given the age of the signal and the time it took for it to be relayed to my command, it is likely that it was sent at least two years ago.'

'What did it say?' asked Angron.

In reply, the holographic image of the globe unfolded into a large flat pane, like a pict-screen hovering in the air, black, with just a hint of shadowy movement. A shape moved on the screen and Loken realised it was a face – a woman's face, orange-lit by a candle flame that provided the only light. She appeared to be in a small, stone walled chamber. Even over the poor quality of the signal, Loken could tell that the woman was terrified, her eyes wide and her breathing rapid and shallow. She gleamed with sweat.

'The insignia on her collar,' said Torgaddon, 'is from the 27th Expedition.'

The woman adjusted the device she was using to record the image and sound flooded into the Lupercal's Court: crackling flames, distant yelling and gunfire.

'It's revolution,' said the woman, her voice warped by static. 'Open revolt. These people, they have… rejected… they've rejected it all. We tried to integrate them, we thought the Warsingers were just some primitive… superstition, but it was much more, it was real. Praal has gone mad and the Warsingers are with him.'

The woman suddenly looked around at something off-screen.

'No!' she screamed desperately and opened fire with a weapon previously held out of view. Violent muzzle flashes lit her and something indescribable flailed against the far wall as she emptied her weapon into it. 'They're closer. They know we're here and… I think I'm the last one.'

The woman turned back to the screen. 'It's madness, complete madness down here. Please, I don't think I'm going to get through this. Send someone, anyone, just... make this stop–'

A hideous, atonal keening sound blared from the pict screen. The woman grabbed her head, her screams drowned by the inhuman sound. The last frames jerked and fragmented, freeze framing through a series of gruesome images: blood in the woman's frenzied eye, a swirling mass of flesh and shattered stone, and a mouth locked open, blood on teeth.

Then blackness.

'There have been no further communications from Isstvan III,' concluded Mortarion, filling the silence that followed. 'The planet's astropaths have either been compromised or they are dead.'

'The name "Praal" refers to Vardus Praal,' said Horus, 'the governor left behind to command Isstvan III in the name of the Imperium, ensure compliance and manage the dismantling of the traditional religious structures that defined the planet's autochthonous society. If he is complicit in the rebellion on Isstvan III, as this recording suggests, then he is one of our objectives.'

Loken felt a shiver travel down his spine at the thought of once again facing a population whose Imperial official had turned traitor. He glanced over at Torgaddon and saw that the similarities with the Davin campaign were not lost on his comrade.

The holo swelled and returned to the image of Isstvan III. 'The cultural and religious capital of Isstvan is here,' said Horus as the image zoomed in on one of the northern cities, which commanded a large hinterland at the foot of a colossal range of mountains.

'The Choral City. This is the source of the distress signal and the seat of Praal's command, a building known as the Precentor's Palace. Multiple speartips will seize a number of strategic objectives, and with the city in our hands, Isstvan will be ours. The first assault will be a combined force made up of Astartes from all Legions with backup from the Titans of the Mechanicum and the Imperial Army. The rest of the planet will then be subjugated by whichever Imperial Army reinforcements can reach us with the warp in its current state.'

'Why not just bombard them?' asked Eidolon. The sudden silence that followed his question was deafening.

Loken waited for the Warmaster to reprimand Eidolon for daring to question one of his decisions, but Horus only nodded indulgently. 'Because these people are vermin, and when you stamp out vermin from afar, some invariably survive. If we are to cut out the problem, we must get our hands dirty and destroy them in one fell swoop. It may not be as elegant as the Emperor's Children would wish, but elegance is not a priority for me, only swift victory.'

'Of course,' said Eidolon, shaking his head. 'To think that these fools should be so blind to the realities of the galaxy.'

'Have no fear, lord commander,' said Abaddon, descending to stand beside the Warmaster, 'they will be illuminated as to the error of their ways.'

Loken risked a sidelong glance at the first captain, surprised at the respect he heard in his voice. All the previous dealings between the Sons of Horus and Eidolon had led him to believe that Abaddon held the arrogant lord commander in contempt.

What had changed?

'Mortarion,' continued Horus. 'Your objective will be to engage the main force of the Choral City's army. If they are anything like they were when the Raven Guard fought them, they will be professional soldiers and will not break easily, even when confronted with Astartes.'

The holo zoomed in to show a map of the Choral City, a handsome conurbation with many and varied buildings that ranged from exquisite mansions and basilica to massive sprawls of housing and tangles of industrial complexes. Artfully formed boulevards and thoroughfares threaded a multi-levelled city of millions, most of whom appeared to be housed in sprawling residential districts, workshops and factories.

The western edge of the city was highlighted, focusing on the scar-like web of defensive trenches and bunkers along the city's outskirts. The opposite side of the Choral City butted up against the sheer cliffs of a mountain range – the natural defences efficiently shielding the city from a conventional land attack.

Unfortunately for the Choral City, the Warmaster clearly wasn't planning a conventional land attack.

'It appears that a sizeable armed force is manning these defences,' said Horus. 'It looks as if they have excellent fortifications and artillery. Many of these defences were added after compliance to protect the seat of Imperial governance on Isstvan, which means they're ours, and they will be strong. It will be ugly work engaging and destroying this force, and there is still much about the Choral City's military we do not know.'

'I welcome this challenge, Warmaster,' said Mortarion. 'This is my Legion's natural battlefield.'

Another location lurched into focus, a spectacular conglomeration of arches and spires, with dozens of labyrinth-like wings and additions surrounding a magnificent central dome faced in polished stone. The city's crowning glory, the structure looked like a jewelled brooch set into the twisted mass of the Choral City.

'The Precentor's Palace,' said Eidolon appreciatively.

'And your Legion will take it,' said Horus, 'along with the World Eaters.'

Again, Loken caught Eidolon's glance at Angron, the lord commander unable to conceal the distaste he felt at the thought of fighting alongside such a barbaric Legion. If Angron was aware of Eidolon's scornful glance he gave no sign of it.

'The palace is one of Praal's most likely locations,' said Horus. 'Therefore, the palace is one of our most important objectives. The palace must be taken, the Choral City's leadership destroyed, and Praal killed. He is a traitor, so I do not expect or wish him to be taken alive.'

Finally, the holo zoomed in on a curious mass of stonework some way east of the Precentor's Palace. To Loken's untutored eye, it looked like a collection of church spires or temples, sacred buildings heaped one on top of one another over the centuries.

'This is the Sirenhold and my Sons of Horus will lead the attack on it,' said Horus. 'Choral City's revolt appears to be religious in nature and the Sirenhold was the spiritual heart of the city. According to Corax's reports, this was the seat of the old pagan religion that was supposed to have been dismantled. It is presumed that it still exists and that the leadership of that religion will be found here. This is another likely location for Vardus Praal, so again I do not require prisoners, only destruction.'

For the first time, Loken saw the battlefield he would soon be fighting on. The Sirenhold looked like difficult ground to take: massive, complicated structures creating a confusing multi-levelled warren with plenty of places to hide. Dangerous ground.

That was why the Warmaster had sent his own Legion to take it. He knew they could do it.

The holo zoomed out again to a view of the planet itself.

'Preliminary operations will involve the destruction of the monitoring stations on the seventh planet of Isstvan Extremis,' said Horus. 'When the rebels are blind the invasion of Isstvan III will commence. The units chosen to lead the first wave will deploy by drop-pod and gunship, with a second wave ready in reserve. I trust you all understand what is required of your Legions.'

'I only have one question, Warmaster,' said Angron.

'Speak,' said Horus.

'Why do we plan this attack with such precision when a single, massive strike will do the job just as well?'

'You object to my plans, Angron?' Horus asked carefully.

'Of course I object,' spat Angron. 'We have four Legions, Titans and starships at our disposal, and this is just one city. We should hit it with everything we have and slaughter them in the streets. Then we will see how many on this planet have the stomach to rebel. But no, you would have us kill them one by one and pick off their leaders as if we are here to preserve this world. Rebellion is in the people, Horus. Kill the people and the rebellion ends.'

'Lord Angron,' said Eidolon reasonably, 'you speak out of turn–'

'Hold your tongue in the presence of your betters,' snarled Angron. 'I know what you Emperor's Children think of us, but you mistake our directness for stupidity. Speak to me again without my consent and I will kill you.'

'Angron!'

Horus's voice cut through the building tension and the primarch of the World Eaters turned his murderous attention away from Eidolon.

'You place little value on the lives of your World Eaters,' said Horus, 'and you believe in the way of war you have made your own, but that does not place you beyond my authority. I am the Warmaster, the commander of everyone and everything that falls under the aegis of the Great Crusade. Your Legion will deploy according to the orders I have given you. Is that clear?'

Angron nodded curtly as Horus turned to Eidolon. 'Lord Commander Eidolon, you are not among equals here, and your presence in this war council is dependent upon my good graces, which will be rapidly worn thin should you conduct yourself as if Fulgrim was here to nursemaid you.'

Eidolon rapidly recovered his composure. 'Of course, my Warmaster, I meant no disrespect. I shall ensure that my Legion is prepared for the assault on Isstvan Extremis and the capture of the Precentor's Palace.'

Horus switched his gaze to Angron, who grunted in assent.

'The World Eaters will be ready, Warmaster,' said Khârn.

'Then this conclave is at an end,' said Horus. 'Return to your Legions and make ready for war.'

The delegations filed out, Khârn speaking quietly with Angron and Eidolon adopting a swagger as if to compensate for his dressing down. Loken thought he saw a gleam of amusement in Mortarion's eyes as he left with Garro and his Terminators in tow.

Horus turned to Abaddon and said, 'Have a stormbird prepared to convey me to the *Conqueror*. Angron must be illuminated as to the proper conduct of this endeavour.'

Horus turned and made his way from the Lupercal's court with Abaddon and Aximand following behind him without so much as a backwards glance at Loken and Torgaddon.

'That was educational,' said Torgaddon when they were alone.

Loken smiled wearily. 'I could feel you willing Angron to strike Eidolon.'

Torgaddon laughed, remembering when he and Eidolon had almost come to blows when they had first met on the surface of Murder.

'If only we could join the Warmaster on the *Conqueror*,' said Torgaddon. 'Now that would be something worth seeing. Horus illuminating Angron. What would they talk about?'

'What indeed?' agreed Loken.

There was so much Loken didn't know, but as he pondered his unhappy ignorance, he remembered the last thing Kyril Sindermann had shouted to him as he was led away by Maloghurst's soldiers.

'Tarik, we have a battle to prepare for, so I want you to get everyone ready. It's going to be a hard fight on Isstvan III.'

'I know,' said Torgaddon. 'The Sirenhold. What a bloody shambles. This is what happens when you give people a god to believe in.'

'Get Vipus up to speed as well. If we're attacking the Sirenhold, I want Locasta with us.'

'Of course,' nodded Torgaddon. 'Sometimes I think you and Nero are the only people I can trust any more. What are you going to be doing?'

'I have some reading to catch up on,' said Loken.

FOUR

Sacrifice
A single moment
Keep her safe

WHEREVER EREBUS WALKED, shadows followed in his wake. Flickering whisperers were his constant companions, invisible creatures that lurked just beyond sight and ghosted in his shadow. The whisperers flitted from Erebus and gathered in the shadowed corners of the chamber, a stone-walled lodge built in the image of the temple room of the Delphos where Akshub had cut his throat.

Deep in the heart of the *Vengeful Spirit*, the lodge temple was low, close and hot, lit by a crackling fire that burned in a pit in the middle of the room. Flames threw leaping shapes across the walls.

'My Warmaster,' said Erebus. 'We are prepared.'

'Good,' replied the Warmaster. 'It has cost us a great deal to reach this point, Erebus. For all our sakes it had better be worth it, but mostly for yours.'

'It will be, Warmaster,' assured Erebus, paying no heed to the threat. 'Our allies are keen to finally speak to you directly.'

Erebus stooped to stare into the fire, the flames reflecting from his shaven, tattooed head and in his armour, recently painted in the deep scarlet colours now adopted by the Word Bearers Legion. As confident as he sounded, he allowed himself a moment of pause. Dealing with creatures from the warp was never straightforward, and should he fail to meet the Warmaster's expectations then his life would be forfeit.

The Warmaster's presence filled the lodge, armoured as he was in a magnificent suit of obsidian Terminator armour gifted to him by the Fabricator General himself. Sent from Mars to cement the alliance between Horus and the Mechanicum of Mars, the armour echoed the colours of the elite Justaerin, but it far surpassed them in ornamentation and power. The amber eye upon the breastplate stared from the armour's torso and shoulder plates, and on one hand Horus sported a monstrous gauntlet with deadly blades for fingers.

Erebus lifted a book from beside the fire and rose to his feet, reverently turning the ancient pages until he came to a complex illustration of interlocking symbols.

'We are ready. I can begin once the sacrifice is made.'

Horus nodded and said, 'Adept, join us.'

Moments later, the bent and robed form of Adept Regulus entered the warrior lodge. The representative of the Mechanicum was almost completely mechanised, as was common among the higher echelons of his order. Beneath his robes his body was fashioned from gleaming bronze, steel and cables. Only his face showed, if it could be called a face, with large augmetic eyepieces and a vocabulator unit that allowed the adept to communicate.

Regulus led the ghostly figure of Ing Mae Sing, her steps fearful and her hands flitting, as if swatting at a swarm of flies.

'This is unorthodox,' said Regulus, his voice like steel wire on the nerves.

'Adept,' said the Warmaster. 'You are here as the representative of the Mechanicum. The priests of Mars are essential to the Crusade and they must be a part of the new order. You have already pledged your strength to me and now it is time you witnessed the price of that bargain.'

'Warmaster,' began Regulus, 'I am yours to command.'

Horus nodded and said, 'Erebus, continue.'

Erebus stepped past the Warmaster and directed his gaze towards Ing Mae Sing. Though the astropath was blind, she recoiled as she felt his eyes roaming across her flesh. She backed against one wall, trying to shrink away from him, but he grasped her arm in a crushing grip and dragged her towards the fire.

'She is powerful,' said Erebus. 'I can taste her.'

'She is my best,' said Horus.

'That is why it has to be her,' said Erebus. 'The symbolism is as important as the power. A sacrifice is not a sacrifice if it is not valued by the giver.'

'No, please,' cried Ing Mae Sing, twisting in his grip as she realised the import of the Word Bearer's statement.

Horus stepped forwards and tenderly took hold of the astropath's chin, halting her struggles and tilting her head upwards so that she would have looked upon his face had she but eyes to see.

'You betrayed me, Mistress Sing,' said Horus.

Ing Mae Sing whimpered, nonsensical protests spilling from her terrified lips. She tried to shake her head, but Horus held her firm and said, 'There is no point in denying it. I already know everything. After you told me of Euphrati Keeler, you sent a warning to someone, didn't you? Tell me who it was and I will let you live. Try to resist and your death will be more agonising than you can possibly imagine.'

'No,' whispered Ing Mae Sing. 'I am already dead. I know this, so kill me and have done with it.'

'You will not tell me what I wish to know?'

'There is no point,' gasped Ing Mae Sing. 'You will kill me whether I tell you or not. You may have the power to conceal your lies, but your serpent does not.'

Erebus watched as Horus nodded slowly to himself, as if reluctantly reaching a decision.

'Then we have no more to say to one another,' said Horus sadly, drawing back his arm.

He rammed his clawed gauntlet through her chest, the blades tearing through her heart and lungs and ripping from her back in a spray of red.

Erebus nodded towards the fire and the Warmaster held the corpse above the pit, letting Ing Mae Sing's blood drizzle into the flames.

The emotions of her death flooded the lodge as the blood hissed in the fire, hot, raw and powerful: fear, pain and the horror of betrayal.

Erebus knelt and scratched designs on the floor, copying them exactly from the diagrams in the book: a star with eight points that was orbited by three circles, a stylised skull and the cuneiform runes of Colchis.

'You have done this before,' said Horus.

'Many times,' said Erebus, nodding towards the fire. 'I speak here with my primarch's voice, and it is a voice our allies respect.'

'They are not allies yet,' said Horus, lowering his arm and letting the body of Ing Mae Sing slide from the claws of his gauntlet.

Erebus shrugged and began chanting words from the *Book of Lorgar*, his voice dark and guttural as he called upon the gods of the warp to send their emissary.

Despite the brightness of the fire, the lodge darkened and Erebus felt the temperature fall, a chill wind gusting from somewhere unseen and unknown. It carried the dust of ages past and the ruin of empires in its every breath, and ageless eternity was borne upon the unnatural zephyr.

'Is this supposed to happen?' asked Regulus.

Erebus smiled and nodded without answering as the air grew icy, the whisperers gibbering in unreasoning fear as they felt the arrival of something ancient and terrible. Shadows gathered in the corners of the room, although no light shone to cast them and a racing whip of malicious laughter spiralled around the chamber.

Regulus spun on hissing bearings as he sought to identify the source of the sounds, his ocular implants whirring as they struggled to find focus in the darkness. Frost gathered on the struts and pipes high above them.

Horus stood unmoving as the shadows of the chamber hissed and spat, a chorus of voices that came from everywhere and nowhere.

'You are the one your kind calls Warmaster?'

Erebus nodded as Horus looked over at him.

'I am,' said Horus. 'Warmaster of the Great Crusade. To whom do I speak?'

'I am Sarr'kell,' said the voice. *'Lord of the Shadows!'*

THE THREE OF them made their way swiftly through the decks of the *Vengeful Spirit*, heading down towards the tiled environment of the medicae deck. Sindermann kept the pace as brisk as he could, his breath sharp and painful as they hurried to save the saint from whatever dark fate awaited her.

'What do you expect to find when we reach the saint, iterator?' asked Jonah Aruken, his nervous hands fingering the catch on his pistol holster.

Sindermann thought of the small medicae cell where he and Mersadie Oliton had stood vigil over Euphrati and wondered that same thought.

'I don't know exactly,' he said. 'I just know we have to help.'

'I just hope a frail old man and our pistols are up to the job.'

'What do you mean?' asked Sindermann, as they descended a wide screw stair that led deeper into the ship.

'Well, I just wonder how you plan to fight the kind of danger that could threaten a saint. I mean, whatever it is must be pretty damn dangerous, yes?'

Sindermann paused in his descent, as much to catch his breath as to answer Aruken.

'Whoever sent me that warning obviously thinks that I can help,' he said.

'And that's enough for you?' asked Aruken.

'Jonah, leave him alone,' cautioned Titus Cassar.

'No, damn it, I won't,' said Aruken. 'This is serious and we could get in real trouble. I mean, this Keeler woman, she's supposed to be all saintly, yes? Then why doesn't the power of the Emperor save her? Why does he need us?'

'The Emperor works through His faithful servants, Jonah,' explained Titus. 'It is not enough to simply believe and await divine intervention to sweep down from the heavens and set the world to rights. The Emperor has shown us the path and it is up to us to seize this chance to do His will.'

Sindermann watched the exchange between the two crewmen, his anxiety growing with every second that passed.

'I don't know if I can do this, Titus,' said Aruken, 'not without some proof that we're doing the right thing.'

'We are, Jonah,' pressed Titus. 'You must trust that the Emperor has a plan for you.'

'The Emperor may or may not have a plan for me, but I sure as hell do,' snapped Aruken. 'I want command of a Titan, and that's not going to happen if we get caught doing something stupid.'

'Please!' cut in Sindermann, his chest hurting with worry for the saint. 'We have to go! Something terrible is coming to harm her and we have to stop it. I can think of no more compelling an argument than that. I'm sorry, but you'll just have to trust me.'

'Why should I?' asked Aruken. 'You've given me no reason to. I don't even know why I'm here.'

'Listen to me, Mister Aruken,' said Sindermann earnestly. 'When you live as long and complex a life as I have, you learn that it always comes down to a *single moment* – a moment in which a man finds out, once and for all, who he really is. This is that moment, Mister Aruken. Will this be a moment you are proud to look back on or will it be one you will regret for the rest of your life?'

The two Titan crewmen shared a glance and eventually Aruken sighed and said, 'I need my head looked at for this, but all right, let's go save the day.'

A palpable sense of relief flooded through Sindermann and the pain in his chest eased.

'I am proud of you, Mr Aruken,' he said, 'and I thank you, your aid is most welcome.'

'Thank me when we save this saint of yours,' said Aruken, setting off down the stairs.

They followed the stairs down, passing several decks until the symbol of intertwined serpents around a winged staff indicated they had arrived at the medicae deck. It had been some weeks since the last casualties had been brought aboard the *Vengeful Spirit* and the sterile, gleaming wilderness of tiled walls and brushed steel cabinets felt empty, a warren of soulless glass rooms and laboratories.

'This way,' said Sindermann, setting off into the confusing maze of corridors, the way familiar to him after all the times he had visited the comatose imagist. Cassar and Aruken followed him, keeping a watchful eye out for anyone who might challenge their presence. At last they reached a nondescript white door and Sindermann said, 'This is it.'

Aruken said, 'Better let us go first, old man.'

Sindermann nodded and backed away from the door, pressing his hands over his ears as the two Titan crewmen unholstered their pistols. Aruken crouched low beside the door and nodded to Cassar, who pressed the release panel.

The door slid aside and Aruken spun through it with his pistol extended.

Cassar was a second behind him, his pistol tracking left and right for targets, and Sinderman awaited the deafening flurry of pistol shots.

When none came he dared to open his eyes and uncover his ears. He didn't know whether to be glad or deathly afraid that they were too late.

He turned and looked through the door, seeing the familiar clean and well maintained medicae cell he had visited many times. Euphrati lay like a mannequin on the bed, her skin like alabaster and her face pinched and sunken. A pair of drips fed her fluids and a small, bleeping machine drew spiking lines on a green display unit beside her.

Aside from her immobility she looked just as she had the last time he had laid eyes on her.

'Just as well we rushed,' snapped Aruken. 'Looks like we were just in time.'

'I think you might be right,' said Sindermann, as he saw the golden-eyed figure of Maggard come into view at the far end of the corridor with his sword unsheathed.

'YOU ARE KNOWN *to us, Warmaster*,' said Sarr'Kell, his voice leaping around the room like a capricious whisper. *'It is said that you are the one who can deliver us. Is that true?'*

'Perhaps,' replied Horus, apparently unperturbed by the strangeness of his unseen interlocutor. 'My brother Lorgar assures me that your masters can give me the power to achieve victory.'

'*Victory,*' whispered Sarr'kell. '*An almost meaning-less word in the scale of the cosmos, but yes, we have much power to offer you. No army will stand before you, no power of mortal man will lay you low and no ambition will be denied you if you swear yourself to us.*'

'Just words,' said Horus. 'Show me something tangible.'

'*Power,*' hissed Sarr'Kell, the sound rippling around Horus like a slithering snake. '*The warp brings power. There is nothing beyond the reach of the gods of the warp.*'

'Gods?' replied Horus. 'You waste your time throwing such words around, they do not impress me. I already know that your "gods" need my help, so speak plainly or we are done here.'

'*Your Emperor,*' replied Sarr'Kell, and for a fleeting moment, Erebus detected a trace of unease in the creature's voice. Such entities were unused to the defiance of a mortal, even one as mighty as a primarch. '*He meddles in matters he does not understand. On the world you call Terra, his grand designs cause a storm in the warp that tears it asunder from within. We care nothing for your realm, you know this. It is anathema to us. We offer power that can help you take his place, Warmaster. Our aid will see you destroy your foes and take you to the very gates of the Emperor's palace. We can deliver the galaxy to you. All we care for is that his works cease and that you take his place.*'

The unseen voice spoke in sibilant tones, slick and persuasive, but Erebus could see that Horus was unmoved. 'And what of this power? Do you understand the magnitude of this task? The galaxy will be divided, brother will fight brother. The Emperor will have his Legions and the Imperial Army, the Custodian Guard, the Sisters of Silence. Can you be the equal of such a foe?'

'The gods of the warp are masters of the primal forces of all reality. As your Emperor creates, the warp decays and destroys. As he brings us to battle, we shall melt away, and as he gathers his strength, we shall strike from the shadows. The victory of the gods is as inevitable as the passing of time and the mortality of flesh. Do the gods not rule an entire universe hidden from your eyes, Warmaster? Have they not made the warp dark at their command?'

'Your gods did this? Why? You have blinded my Legions!'

'Necessity, Warmaster. The darkness blinds the Emperor too, blinds him to our plans and yours. The Emperor thinks himself the master of the warp and he would seek to know his enemies by it, but see how swiftly we can confound him? You will have passage through the warp as you need it, Warmaster, for as we bring darkness, so we can bring light.'

'The Emperor remains ignorant of all that has transpired?'

'Completely,' sighed Sarr'Kell, 'and so, Warmaster, you see the power we can give you. All that remains is for your word, and the pact will be made.'

Horus said nothing, as if weighing up the choices before him, and Erebus could sense the growing impatience of the warp creature.

At last the Warmaster spoke again. 'Soon I shall unleash my Legions against the worlds of the Isstvan system. There I shall set my Legions upon the path of the new Crusade. There are matters that must be dealt with at Isstvan, and I will deal with them in my own way.'

Horus looked over at Erebus and said, 'When I am done with Isstvan, I will pledge my forces with those of your masters, but not until then. My Legions will go through the fire of Isstvan alone, for only then will they be tempered into my shining blade aimed at the Emperor's heart.'

The sibilant, roiling chill of Sarr'Kell's voice hissed as if he took mighty breaths.

'*My masters accept,*' he said at last. '*You have chosen well, Warmaster.*'

The chill wind that had carried the words of the warp entity blew again, stronger this time, its ageless malevolence like the murder of innocence.

Its icy touch slid through Erebus and he drew a cold breath before the sensation faded and the unnatural darkness began to recede, the light of the fire once more illuminating the lodge temple.

The creature was gone and the void of its presence was an ache felt deep in the soul.

'Was it worth it, Warmaster?' asked Erebus, releasing the pent up breath he had been holding.

'Yes,' said Horus, glancing down at Ing Mae Sing's body. 'It was worth it.'

The Warmaster turned to Regulus and said, 'Adept, I wish the Fabricator General to be made aware of this. I cannot contact him directly, so you will take a fast ship and make for Mars. If what this creature says is true, you will make good time. Kelbor-Hal is to purge his order and make ready for its part in my new Crusade. Tell him that I shall contact him when the time comes and that I expect the Mechanicum to be united.'

'Of course, Warmaster. Your will be done.'

'Waste no time, adept. Go.'

Regulus turned to leave and Erebus said, 'We have waited a long time for this day, Lorgar will be exultant.'

'Lorgar has his own battles to fight, Erebus,' replied Horus sharply. 'Should he fail at Calth, all this will be for nothing if Guilliman's Legion is allowed to intervene. Save your celebrations for when I sit upon the throne of Terra.'

SINDERMANN FELT HIS heart lurch in his chest at the sight of Petronella's bodyguard coming towards them. The man's every step was like death approaching and Sindermann cursed himself for having taken so long to get here. His tardiness had killed the saint and would probably see them all dead as well.

Jonah Aruken's eyes widened as he saw the massive form of the saint's killer approaching. He turned quickly and said, 'Titus, grab her. Now!'

'What?' asked Cassar. 'She's hooked up to all these machines, we can't just–'

'Don't argue with me,' hissed Aruken. 'Just do it, we've got company, bad company.'

Aruken turned back to Sindermann and hissed, 'Well, iterator? Is this that single moment you were talking about, where we find out who we really are? If it is, then I'm already regretting helping you.'

Sindermann couldn't reply. He saw Maggard notice them outside Euphrati's room and felt a cold, creeping horror as a slow smile spread across the man's features.

I am going to kill you, the smile said, *slowly*.

'Don't hurt her,' he whispered, the words sounding pathetic in his ears. 'Please…'

He wanted to run, to get far away from the evil smile that promised a silent, agonising death, but his legs were lead weights, rooted to the spot by some immense power that prevented him from moving so much as a muscle.

Jonah Aruken slid from the medicae cell, with Titus Cassar behind him, the recumbent form of Euphrati in his arms. Dripping tubes dangled from her arms and Sindermann found his gaze unaccountably drawn to the droplets as they swelled at the ends of the plastic tubes before breaking free and plummeting to the deck to splash in crowns of saline.

Aruken held his pistol out before him, aimed at Maggard's head.

'Don't come any closer,' he warned.

Maggard did not even slow down and that same deathly smile shone at Jonah Aruken.

With Euphrati still in his arms, Titus Cassar backed away from the relentlessly approaching killer.

'Come on, damn it,' he hissed. 'Let's go!'

Aruken shoved Sindermann after Cassar and suddenly the spell of immobility that had held him
rooted to the spot was broken. Maggard was less
than ten paces from them and Sindermann knew
that they could not hope to escape without bloodshed.

'Shoot him,' shouted Cassar.

'What?' asked Aruken, throwing his fellow crewman a desperate glance.

'Shoot him,' repeated Cassar. 'Kill him, before he
kills us.'

Jonah Aruken tore his gaze back to the approaching Maggard and nodded, pulling the trigger twice
in quick succession. The noise was deafening and
the corridor was filled with blinding light and
careening echoes. Tiles shattered and exploded as
Aruken's bullets cratered the wall behind where
Maggard had been standing.

Sindermann cried out at the noise, backing away
after Titus Cassar as Maggard spun out from the
sunken doorway in which he had taken cover the
instant before Aruken had fired. Maggard's pistol
leapt to his hand and the barrel blazed with light as
he fired three times.

Sindermann cried out, throwing up his arms and
awaiting the awful pain of bullets tearing into his
flesh, ripping through his internal organs and
blowing bloody-rimmed craters in his back.

Nothing happened and Sindermann heard a cry
of astonishment from Jonah Aruken, who had

likewise flinched at the thunderous noise of Maggard's gun. He lowered his arms and his mouth fell open in amazement at the sight before him.

Maggard still stood there, his muscled arm still holding his wide barrelled pistol aimed squarely at them.

A frozen bloom of light expanded at an infinitesimally slow pace from the muzzle and Sindermann could see a pair of bullets held immobile in the air before them, only the glint of light on metal as they spiralled giving any sign that they were moving at all.

As he watched, the pointed nub of a brass bullet began to emerge from the barrel of Maggard's gun and Sindermann turned in bewilderment to Jonah Aruken.

The Titan crewman was as shocked as he was, his arms hanging limply at his side.

'What the hell is going on?' breathed Aruken.

'I d-don't know,' stammered Sindermann, unable to tear his gaze from the frozen tableau standing in front of them. 'Maybe we're already dead.'

'No, iterator,' said Cassar from behind them, 'it's a miracle.'

Sindermann turned, feeling as if his entire body was numb, only his heart hammering fit to break his chest. Titus Cassar stood at the end of the corridor, the saint held tightly to his chest. Where before Euphrati had lain supine, her eyes were now wide in terror, her right hand extended and the silver eagle that had been burned into her flesh glowing with a soft, inner light.

'Euphrati!' cried Sindermann, but no sooner had he given voice to her name than her eyes rolled back in their sockets and her hand dropped to her side. He risked a glance back at Maggard, but the assassin was still frozen by whatever power had saved their lives.

Sindermann took a deep breath and made his way on unsteady legs to the end of the corridor. Euphrati lay with her head against Cassar's chest, as unmoving as she had been for the last year and he wanted to weep to see her so reduced.

He reached up and ran a hand through Euphrati's hair, her skin hot to the touch.

'She saved us,' said Cassar, his voice awed and humbled by what he had seen.

'I think you might be right, my dear boy,' said Sindermann. 'I think you might be right.'

Jonah Aruken joined him, alternating between casting fearful looks at Maggard and Euphrati. He kept his pistol trained on Maggard and said, 'What do we do about him?'

Sindermann looked back at the monstrous assassin and said, 'Leave him. I will not have his death on the saint's hands. What kind of beginning would it be for the Lectitio Divinitatus if the saint's first act is to kill. If we are to found a new church in the name of the Emperor it will be one of forgiveness, not bloodshed.'

'Are you sure?' asked Aruken. 'He will come after her again.'

'Then we will keep her safe from him,' said Cassar. 'The Lectitio Divinitatus has friends aboard the

Vengeful Spirit and we can hide her until she recovers. Iterator, do you agree?'

'Yes, that's what to do,' nodded Sindermann, 'hide her. Keep her safe.'

FIVE

Dark Millennium
Warsinger

LOKEN HAD NOT set foot on the strategium for some time, the construction of the Lupercal's Court rendering it largely without function. In any case, an unspoken order had filtered down from the lodge members that Torgaddon and Loken were no longer to stand alongside the Warmaster and act as the Legion's conscience.

The isolated strategium platform was suspended above the industrious hubbub of the vessel's bridge, and Loken leaned over the rail to watch the senior crew of the *Vengeful Spirit* going about the business of destroying Isstvan Extremis.

Warriors of the Death Guard and Emperor's Children were already in the theatre of war and the enemies of the Warmaster would even now be dying. The thought of not being there to share the danger galled Loken and he wished he could be on that barren rock with his battle-brothers, especially since Torgaddon had told him that Saul Tarvitz was down there.

The last time the Sons of Horus and the Emperor's Children had met was during the war against the Technocracy and bonds of brotherhood had been re-established between the Legions, formally by the primarchs, and informally by their warriors.

He missed the times he had stood in the presence of his fellow warriors when the talk had been of campaigns past and yet to come. The shared cama-raderie of brotherhood was a comfort that was only realised once it was stripped away.

He smiled wryly to himself, whispering, 'I even miss your tales of "better days", Iacton.'

Loken turned away from the bridge below and unfolded the piece of paper he had discovered inside the dust jacket of the *Chronicles of Ursh*.

Once again he read the words hurriedly written in Kyril Sindermann's distinctive spidery scrawl on the ragged page of a notebook.

Even the Warmaster may not deserve your trust. Look for the temple. It will be somewhere that was once the essence of the Crusade.

Remembering Sindermann's words as he had been forced from the training halls by Maloghurst, Loken had sought out the book from the burnt out stacks of Archive Chamber Three. Much of the archive was still in ruins from the fire that had gutted the chamber and put Euphrati Keeler in a coma. Servitors and menials had attempted to save as many books as they could, and even though Loken was no reader, he was saddened by the loss of such a valuable repository of knowledge.

He had located *The Chronicles of Ursh* with the barest minimum of effort, as if the book had been specifically placed for him to find. Opening the cover, he realised that it had indeed been left there for him, as Sindermann's note slipped from its pages.

Loken wasn't sure exactly what he was looking for, and the idea of a temple aboard the *Vengeful Spirit* seemed laughable, but Sindermann had been deadly serious when he had implored Loken to seek out the book and his note.

It will be somewhere that was once the essence of the Crusade.

He looked up from the note and cast his eyes around the strategium: the raised platform where the Warmaster had delivered his briefings, the niches around the edge where Sons of Horus stood as an honour guard and the vaulted dome of dark steel. Banners hung along the curved wall, indistinct in the gloom, company banners of the Sons of Horus. He hammered his fist against his breastplate as he faced the banner of the Tenth.

If anywhere was once the essence of the Crusade it was the strategium.

The strategium was empty, and it was an emptiness that spoke more of its neglect and its obsolescence than simply the absence of people. It had been abandoned and the ideals once hammered out here had been abandoned too, replaced with something else, something dark.

Loken stood in the centre of the strategium and felt an ache in his chest that was nothing to do with any physical sensation. It took him a moment to realise that there was something out of place here, something present that shouldn't be: a smell that he didn't recognise, faint but definitely hanging in the air.

At last he recognised the smell as incense, cloying, and carrying the familiar scent of hot, dry winds that brought sour fragrances of bitter blossoms. His genhanced senses could pick out the subtle aromas mixed into the incense, its scent stronger as he made his way through the strategium hoping to pinpoint its source. Where had he smelt this before?

He followed the bitter smell to the standard of the Seventh, Targhost's company. Had the lodge master flown the banner in some ritual ceremony of the warrior lodge?

No, the scent was too strong for it to be simply clinging to fabric. This was the aroma of burning incense. Loken pulled the banner of the Seventh away from the wall, and he was not surprised to find that, instead of the brushed steel of the strategium wall, there was the darkness of an opening cut into one of the many access passages that threaded the *Vengeful Spirit*.

Had this been here when the Mournival had gathered? He didn't think so.

Look for the temple, Sindermann had said, so Loken ducked beneath the banner and through the doorway, letting the banner fall into place behind him. The smell of incense was definitely here, and it had been burned recently, or was still burning.

Loken suddenly realised where he had smelled this aroma before and he gripped the hilt of his combat knife as he remembered the air of Davin, the scents that filled the yurts and seemed to linger in the air, even through rebreathers.

The passageway beyond was dark, but Loken's augmented eyesight cut through the gloom to reveal a short passageway, recently constructed, that led to an arched doorway with curved sigils etched into the ironwork surrounding it. Although it was simply a door, Loken felt an unutterable dread of what lay beyond it and for a moment he almost considered turning back.

He shook off such a cowardly notion and made his way forwards, feeling his unease grow with every step he took. The door was closed, a stylised skull mounted at eyelevel and Loken felt uncomfortable even acknowledging that it was there let alone looking at it. Something of its brutal form whispered to the killer in him, telling him of the joy of spilling blood and the relish to be taken in slaughter.

Loken tore his eyes from the leering skull and drew his knife, fighting the urge to plunge it into the flesh of anyone waiting behind the door.

He pushed it open and stepped inside.

The space within was large, a maintenance chamber that had been had been cleared and refitted so as to resemble some underground stone chamber. Twin rows of stone benches faced the far wall, where meaningless symbols and words had been painted. Blank-eyed skulls hung from the ceiling, staring and grinning with bared teeth. They swayed gently as Loken passed them, thin tendrils of smoke rising from their eye sockets.

A low wooden table stood against the far wall. A shallow bowl carved into its surface contained flaky dark detritus that he could smell was dried blood. A thick book lay beside the depression.

Was this a temple? He remembered the bottles and glass flasks that had been scattered around the water fane beneath the Whisperheads.

This place and the fane on Sixty-Three Nineteen looked different, but they *felt* the same.

He heard a sudden rustle on the air, like whispers in his ear, and he spun around, his knife whipping out in front of him.

He was alone, yet the sense of someone whispering in his ear had been so real that he would have sworn on his life that another person had been standing right beside him. Loken took a breath and did a slow circuit of the room, his knife extended, on the defensive in case the mysterious whisperer revealed himself.

Bundles of torn material lay by the benches, and he made his way towards the table – the altar, he realised – upon which lay the book he had noticed earlier.

Its cover was leather, the surface cracked, old and blackened by fire.

Loken bent down to examine the book, flipping open the cover with the tip of his knife. The words written there were composed of an angular script, the letters written vertically on the page.

'Erebus,' he said as he recognised the script as identical to that tattooed upon the skull of the Word Bearer. Could this be the *Book of Lorgar* that Kyril Sindermann had been raving about following the fire in the archive chamber? The iterator had claimed that the book had unleashed some horror of the warp and that had been what caused the fire, but Loken saw only words.

How could words be dangerous?

Even as he formed the thought, he blinked, the words blurring on the page in front of him. The symbols twisted from the unknown language of the Word Bearers to the harsh numerical language of Cthonia, before spiralling into the elegant script of Imperial Gothic and a thousand other languages he had never seen before.

He blinked to ward off a sudden, impossible, sense of dizziness.

'What are you doing here, Loken?' a familiar voice asked in his ear.

Loken spun to face the voice, but once again he was alone. The temple was empty.

'How dare you break the trust of the Warmaster?' the voice asked, this time with a sense of weight behind it.

And this time he recognised the voice.

He turned slowly and saw Torgaddon standing before the altar.

'DOWN!' YELLED TARVITZ as gunfire streaked above him, stitching monochrome explosions along the barren rock of Isstvan Extremis. 'Squad Fulgerion, with me. All squads to position and wait for the go!'

Tarvitz ran, knowing that Sergeant Fulgerion's squad would be on his heels as he made for the cover of the closest crater. A web of criss-crossing tracer fire streaked the air before the monitoring station the Isstvanians had set up on Isstvan Extremis, a tall, organ-like structure of towers, domes and antennae. Anchored on the barren rock surface by massive docking claws, the station was dusted in a powdery residue of ice crystals and particulate matter.

The Isstvan system's sun was little more than a cold disc peeking above the horizon, lining everything in a harsh blue light. Automatic gun ports spat fire at the advancing Emperor's Children, more than two hundred Astartes converging in a classic assault pattern to storm the massive blast doors of the station's eastern entrance.

Isstvan Extremis had little atmosphere to speak of and was lethally cold; only the sealed armour of the Space Marines made a ground assault possible.

Tarvitz slid into the crater, turret fire ripping up chunks of grey rock around him. Sergeant Fulgerion and his warriors, shields held high to shelter them from the fire, hit the ground to either side of him. Veterans only truly at home in the thick of the hardest fighting, Fulgerion and his squad had fought together for years and Tarvitz knew that he had some of the Legion's best warriors with him.

'They were ready for us, then?' asked Fulgerion.

'They must have known that we would return to restore compliance,' said Tarvitz. 'Who knows how long they have been waiting for us to come back.'

Tarvitz glanced over the lip of the crater, spotting purple armoured forms fanning out in front of the gates to take up their allotted positions. That was how the Emperor's Children fought, manoeuvring into position to execute perfectly co-ordinated strikes, squads moving across a battle zone like pieces on a chess board.

'Captain Garro of the Death Guard reports that he is in position,' said Eidolon's voice over the vox-net. 'Show them what war really is!'

The Death Guard had been assigned the task of taking the western approach to the station, and Tarvitz smiled as he imagined his old friend Garro marching his men grimly towards the guns, winning through relentless determination rather than any finesse of tactics. Each to their own, he thought as he drew his broadsword.

Such blunt tactics were not the way of the Emperor's Children, for war was not simply about killing, it was art.

'Tarvitz and Fulgerion in position,' he reported. 'All units ready.'

'Execute!' came the order.

'You heard Lord Eidolon,' he shouted. 'Children of the Emperor!'

The warriors around him cheered as he and Fulgerion clambered over the crater lip and gunfire streaked overhead from the support squads. A perfect ballet began with every one of his units acting in complete concert, heavy weapons pounding the enemy guns as assault units moved in to attack and tactical units took up covering positions.

Splintering explosions burst in the sub-zero air, chunks of debris blasted from the surface of the entrance dome as turret guns detonated and threw chains of bursting ammunition into the air.

A missile streaked past Tarvitz and burst against the blast doors, leaving a flaming, blackened crater in the metal. Another missile followed the first, and then another, and the doors crumpled inwards. Tarvitz saw the golden armour of Eidolon flashing in the planet's hard light, the lord commander hefting a mighty hammer with blue arcs of energy crackling around its head.

The hammer slammed into the remains of the doors, blue-white light bursting like a lightning strike as they vanished in a thunderous explosion. Eidolon charged inside the facility, the honour his by virtue of his noble rank.

Tarvitz followed Eidolon in, ducking through the wrecked blast doors.

Inside, the station was in darkness, lit only by the muzzle flashes of bolter fire and sparking cables torn from their mountings by the furious combat. Tarvitz's enhanced vision dispelled the darkness, warm air billowing from the station through the ruptured doors and white vapour surged around him as he saw the enemy for the first time.

They wore black armour with bulky power packs and thick cables that attached to heavy rifles. The plates of their armour were traced with silver scroll-work, perhaps just for decoration, perhaps a pattern of circuitry.

Their faces were hooded, each with a single red lens over one eye. A hundred of them packed the dome, sheltering behind slabs of broken machinery and furniture. The armoured soldiers formed a solid defensive line, and no sooner had Eidolon and the Emperor's Children emerged from the entrance tunnel than they opened fire.

Rapid firing bolts of ruby laser fire spat out from the Isstvanian troops, filling the dome with horizontal red rain. Tarvitz took a trio of shots, one to his chest, one to his greaves and another cracking against his helmet, filling his senses with a burst of static.

Fulgerion was ahead of him, wading through the las-fire that battered his shield. Eidolon surged forwards in the centre of the line and his hammer bludgeoned Isstvanians to death with each lethal swing. A body flew through the air, its torso a crushed ruin and its limbs shattered by the shock of the hammer's impact. The weight of enemy fire faltered and the Emperor's Children charged forwards, overlapping fields of bolter fire shredding the Isstvanians' cover as close combat specialists crashed through the gaps to kill with gory sweeps of chainswords.

Tarvitz's bolt pistol snapped shots at the darting black figures catching one in the throat and spinning him around. Squad Fulgerion took up position at the remains of the barricade, their bolters filling the dome with covering gunfire for Eidolon and his chosen warriors.

Tarvitz killed the enemy with brutally efficient shots and sweeps of his broadsword, fighting like a warrior of Fulgrim should. His every strike was a faultless killing blow, and his every step was measured and perfect. Gunfire ricocheted from his gilded armour and the light of battle reflected from his helmet as if from a hero of ancient legend.

'We have the entrance dome,' shouted Eidolon as the last of the Isstvanians were efficiently despatched by the Astartes around him. 'Death Guard units report heavy resistance inside. Blow the inner doors and we'll finish this for them.'

Warriors with breaching charges rushed to destroy the inner doors, and even over the flames and shots, Tarvitz could hear muffled explosions from the other side. He lowered his sword and took a moment to survey his surroundings now that there was a lull in the fighting.

A dead body lay at his feet, the plates of the man's black armour ruptured and a ragged tear ripped in the hood covering his face. Frozen blood lay scattered around him like precious stones and Tarvitz knelt to pull aside the torn cowl.

The man's skin was covered in an elaborate swirling black tattoo, echoing the silver designs on his armour. A frozen eye looked up at him, hollow and darkened, and Tarvitz wondered what manner of being had the power to force this man to renounce his oaths of loyalty to the Imperium.

Tarvitz was spared thinking of an answer by the dull thump of the interior doors blowing open. He put the dead man from his mind and set off after Eidolon as he held his hammer high and charged into the central dome. He ran alongside his fellow warriors, knowing that whatever the Isstvanians could throw at him, he was an Astartes and no weapon they had could match the will of the Emperor's Children.

Tarvitz and his men moved through the dust and smoke of the door's explosion, the autosenses of his armour momentarily useless.

Then they were through and into the heart of the Isstvan Extremis facility.

He pulled up short as he suddenly realised that the intelligence they had been given on this facility was utterly wrong.

This was not a comms station, it was a temple.

TORGADDON'S FACE WAS ashen and leathery, puckered and scarred around a burning yellow eye. Sharpened metallic teeth glinted in a lipless mouth and twin gashes were torn in the centre of his face.

A star with eight points was gouged in his temple, mirroring its golden twin etched upon his ornate, black armour.

'No,' said Loken, backing away from this terrible apparition.

'You have trespassed, Loken,' hissed Torgaddon. 'You have betrayed.'

A dry, deathly wind carried Torgaddon's words, gusting over him with the smell of burning bodies. As he breathed the noxious wind, a vision of broken steppes spread out before Loken, expanses of desolation and plains of rusted machinery like skeletons of extinct monsters. A hive city on the distant horizon split open like a flower, and from its broken, burning petals rose a mighty tower of brass that punctured the pollution-heavy clouds.

The sky above was burning and the laughter of Dark Gods boomed from the heavens. Loken wanted to scream, this vision of devastation worse than anything he had seen before.

This wasn't real. It couldn't be. He did not believe in ghosts and illusions.

The thought gave him strength. He wrenched his mind away from the dying world, and suddenly he was soaring through the galaxy, tumbling between the stars. He saw them destroyed, bleeding glowing plumes of stellar matter into the void. A baleful mass of red stars glowered above him, staring like a great and terrible eye of flame. An endless tide of titanic monsters and vast space fleets vomited from that eye, drowning the universe in a tide of blood.

A sea of burning flames spat and leapt from the blood, consuming all in its path, leaving black, barren wasteland in its wake.

Was this a vision of some lunatic's hell, a dimension of destruction and chaos where sinners went when they died? Loken forced himself to remember the lurid descriptions from the *Chronicles of Ursh*, the outlandish scenes described by inventions of dark faith.

No, said the voice of Torgaddon, *this is no madman's delusion. It is the future.*

'You're not Torgaddon!' shouted Loken, shaking the whispering voice from his head.

You are seeing the galaxy die.

Loken saw the Sons of Horus in the tide of fiery madness that poured from the red eye, armoured in black and surrounded by leaping, deformed creatures. Abaddon was there, and Horus himself, an immense obsidian giant who crushed worlds in his gauntlets.

This could not be the future. This was a diseased distorted vision of the future.

A galaxy in which mankind was led by the Emperor could never become such a terrible maelstrom of chaos and death.

You are wrong.

The galaxy in flames receded and Loken scrabbled for some solidity, something to reassure him that this terrifying vision could never come to pass. He was tumbling again, his vision blurring until he opened his eyes and found himself in Archive Chamber Three, a place he had felt safe, surrounded by books that rendered the universe down to pure logic and kept the madness locked up in crude pagan epics where it belonged.

But something was wrong, the books were burning around him, this purest of knowledge being systematically destroyed to keep the masses ignorant of their truths. The shelves held nothing but flames and ash, the heat battering against Loken as he tried to save the dying books. His hands blistered and blackened as he fought to save the wisdom of ancient times, the flesh peeling back from his bones.

The music of the spheres. The mechanisms of reality, invisible and all around…

Loken could see it where the flames burned through, the endless churning mass of the warp at the heart of everything and the eyes of dark forces seething with malevolence. Grotesque creatures cavorted obscenely among heaps of corpses, horned heads and braying, goat-like faces twisted by the mindless artifice of the warp. Bloated monsters, their bodies heaving with maggots and filth, devoured dead stars as a brass-clad giant bellowed an endless war cry from its throne of skulls and soulless magicians sacrificed billions in a silver city built of lies.

Loken fought to tear his sight from this madness. Remembering the words he had thrown in Horus Aximand's face at the Delphos Gate, he screamed them aloud once more:

'I will not bow to any fane or acknowledge any spirit. I own only the empirical clarity of Imperial Truth!'

In an instant, the walls of the dark temple slammed back into place around him, the air thick with incense, and he gasped for breath. Loken's heart pumped wildly and his head spun, sick with the effort of casting out what he had seen.

This was not fear. This was anger.

Those who came to this fane were selling out the entire human race to dark forces that lurked unseen in the depths of the warp. Were these the same forces that had infected Xayver Jubal? The same forces that had nearly killed Sindermann in the ship's archive?

Loken felt sick as he realised that everything he knew about the warp was wrong.

He had been told that there were no such things as gods.

He had been told that there was nothing in the warp but insensate, elemental power.

He had been told that the galaxy was too sterile for melodrama.

Everything he had been told was a lie.

Feeding on the strength his anger gave him, Loken lurched towards the altar and slammed the ancient book closed, snapping the brass hasp over the lock. Even shut, he could feel the terrible purpose locked within its pages. The idea that a book could have some sort of power would have sounded ludicrous to Loken only a few months ago, but he could not doubt the evidence of his own senses, despite the incredible, terrifying, unimaginable things he had seen and heard. He gathered up the book and clutching it under one arm, turned and made his way from the fane.

He closed the door and eased past the banner of the Seventh, emerging once more into the secluded darkness of the strategium.

Sindermann had been right. Loken was hearing the music of the spheres, and it was a terrible sound that spoke of corruption, blood and the death of the universe.

Loken knew with utter certainty that it was up to him to silence it.

THE INTERIOR OF the Isstvan Extremis facility was dominated by a wide, stepped pyramid, its huge stone blocks fashioned from a material that clearly had no place on such a world. Each block came from some other building, many of them still bearing architectural carvings, sections of friezes, gargoyles or even statues jutting crazily from the structure.

Isstvanian soldiers swarmed around the base of the pyramid, fighting in desperate close quarters battle with the steel-armoured figures of the Death Guard. The battle had no shape, the art of war having given way to the grinding brutality of simple killing.

Tarvitz's gaze was drawn from the slaughter to the very top of the pyramid, where a bright light spun and twisted around a half-glimpsed figure surrounded by keening harmonics.

'Attack!' bellowed Eidolon, charging forwards as the tip of the spear, assault units the killing edges

around him. Tarvitz forgot about the strange figure
and followed the lord commander, driving Eidolon
forwards by covering him and holding off enemies
who tried to surround him.

More Emperor's Children stormed into the dome
and the battle at the base of the pyramid. Tarvitz
saw Lucius beside Eidolon, the swordsman's blade
shining like a harnessed star.

It was typical that Lucius would be at the front,
demonstrating that he would rise swiftly through
the ranks and take his place alongside Eidolon as
the Legion's best. Tarvitz slashed his weapon left
and right, needing no skill to kill these foes, simply
a strong sword arm and the will to win. He clambered onto the first level of the pyramid, fighting
his way up its side through rank after rank of black
armoured foes.

He stole a glance towards the top of the pyramid,
seeing the burnished Death Guard warriors climbing ahead of him to reach the figure at the summit.

Leading the Death Guard was the familiar, brutal
form of Nathanial Garro, his old friend forging
upwards with powerful strides and his familiar
grim determination. Even amid the furious battle,
Tarvitz was glad to be fighting alongside his sworn
honour brother once again. Garro forced his way
towards the top of the pyramid, aiming his charge
towards the glowing figure that commanded the
battlefield.

Long hair whipped around it, and as sheets of
lightning arced upwards, Tarvitz saw that it was a

woman, her sweeping silk robes lashing like the tendrils of some undersea creature.

Even above the chaos of battle, he could hear her voice and it was singing.

The force of the music lifted her from the pyramid, suspending her above the pinnacle on a song of pure force. Hundreds of harmonies wound impossibly over one another, screeching notes smashing together as they ripped from her unnatural throat. Stones flew from the pyramid's summit, spiralling towards the dome's ceiling as her song broke apart the warp and weft of reality.

As Tarvitz watched, a single discordant note rose to the surface in a tremendous crescendo, and an explosion blew out a huge chunk of the pyramid, massive blocks of stone tumbling in the currents of light. The pyramid shuddered and stones crashed down amongst the Emperor's Children, crushing some and knocking many more from its side.

Tarvitz fought to keep his balance as portions of the pyramid collapsed in a rumbling landslide of splintered stone and rubble. The armoured body of a Death Guard slithered down the slope towards a sheer drop into the falling masonry and Tarvitz saw that it was the bloodied form of Garro.

He scrambled across the disintegrating pyramid and leapt towards the drop, catching hold of the warrior's armour and dragging him towards firmer ground.

Tarvitz pulled Garro away from the fighting, seeing that his friend was badly wounded. One leg was severed at mid thigh and portions of his chest and upper arm were crushed. Frozen, coagulated blood swelled like blown glass around his injuries and shards of stone jutted from his abdomen.

'Tarvitz!' growled Garro, his anger greater than his pain. 'It's a Warsinger. Don't listen.'

'Hold on, brother,' said Tarvitz. 'I'll be back for you.'

'Just kill it,' spat Garro.

Tarvitz looked up, seeing the Warsinger closer as she drifted towards the Emperor's Children. Her face was serene and her arms were open as if to welcome them, her eyes closed as she drew the terrible song from her.

Yet more blocks of stone were lifting from the pyramid around the Emperor's Children. Tarvitz saw one warrior – Captain Odovocar, the Bearer of the Legion banner – dragged from his feet and into the air by the Warsinger's chorus. His armour jerked as if torn at by invisible fingers, sparking sheets of ceramite peeling back as the Warsinger's power took it apart.

Odovocar came apart with it, his helmet ripping free and trailing glittering streamers of blood and bone as it took his head off.

As Odovocar died, Tarvitz was struck by the savage beauty of the song, a song he felt she was singing just for him. Beauty and death were captured in its discordant notes, the wonderful peace that would come if he just gave himself up to it and let the music of oblivion take him. War would end and violence wouldn't even be a memory.

Don't listen to it.

Tarvitz snarled and his bolt pistol kicked in his hand as he fired at the Warsinger, the sound of the shots drowned by the cacophony. Shells impacted against a sheath of shimmering force around the Warsinger, blooms of white light exploding around her as they detonated prematurely. More and more of the Astartes, Emperor's Children and Death Guard both, were being pulled up into the air and sonically dismembered, and Tarvitz knew they didn't have much time before their cause was lost.

The surviving Isstvanian soldiers were regrouping, storming up the pyramid after the Astartes. Tarvitz saw Lucius among them, sword slashing black-armoured limbs from bodies as they fought to surround him.

Lucius could look after himself and Tarvitz forced himself onwards, struggling to keep his footing amid the chaos of the Warsinger's wanton destruction. Gold gleamed ahead of him and he saw Eidolon's armour shining like a beacon in the Warsinger's light. The lord commander bellowed in defiance and pulled himself up the last few levels of the pyramid as Tarvitz climbed to join him.

The Warsinger drew a shining caul of light around her and Eidolon plunged into it, the glare becoming opaque like a shining white shell. Tarvitz's pistol was empty, so he dropped it, taking a two handed grip on his sword and following his lord commander into the light.

The deafening shrieks of the Warsinger filled his head with deathly unmusic, rising to a crescendo as he penetrated the veil of light.

Eidolon was on his knees, his hammer lost and the Warsinger hovering over him. Her hands stretched out in front of her as she battered Eidolon with waves of force strong enough to distort the air.

Eidolon's armour warped around him, his helmet ripped from his head in a wash of blood, but he was still alive and fighting.

Tarvitz charged, screaming, 'For the Emperor!'

The Warsinger saw him and smashed him to the floor with a dismissive flick of her wrist. His helmet cracked with the force of the impact and for a moment his world was filled with the awful beauty of the Warsinger's song. His vision returned in time for him to see Eidolon lunging forwards. His charge had bought Eidolon a momentary distraction, the harmonics of her song redirected for the briefest moment.

The briefest moment was all a warrior of the Emperor's Children needed.

Eidolon's eyes were ablaze, his hatred and revulsion at this foe clear as his mouth opened in a cry of rage. His mouth opened still wider and he let loose his own screeching howl. Tarvitz rolled onto his back, dropping his sword and clutching his hands to his ears at the dreadful sound. Where the Warsinger's song had layered its death in beguiling beauty, there was no such grace in the sonic assault launched by Eidolon, it was simply agonising, deafening volume.

The crippling noise smashed into the Warsinger and suddenly her grace was torn away. She opened her mouth to sing a fresh song of death, but Eidolon's scream turned her cries into a grim dirge.

Sounds of mourning and pain layered over one another into a heavy funereal drone as the Warsinger dropped to her knees. Eidolon bent and picked up Tarvitz's fallen broadsword, his own terrible scream now silenced. The Warsinger writhed in pain, arcing coils of light whipping from her as she lost control of her song.

Eidolon waded through the light and noise. The broadsword licked out and Eidolon cut the Warsinger's head from her shoulders with a single sweep of silver.

Finally the Warsinger was silent.

Tarvitz clung to the crumbling summit of the pyramid and watched as Eidolon raised the sword in victory, still trying to understand what he had seen.

The Warsinger's monstrous harmonies still rang in his head, but he shook them off as he stared in disbelief at the lord commander.

Eidolon turned to Tarvitz, and dropped the broadsword beside him.

'A good blade,' he said. 'My thanks for your intervention.'

'How…?' was all Tarvitz could muster, his senses still overcome with the deafening shriek Eidolon had unleashed.

'Strength of will, Tarvitz,' said Eidolon. 'That's what it was, strength of will. The bitch's damn magic was no match for a pair of warriors like us, eh?'

'I suppose not,' said Tarvitz, accepting a hand up from Eidolon. The dome was suddenly, eerily silent. The Isstvanians who still lived were slumped where they had fallen at the Warsinger's death, weeping and rocking back and forth like children at the loss of a parent.

'I don't understand–' he began as warriors of the Death Guard started securing the dome.

'You don't need to understand, Tarvitz,' said Eidolon. 'We won, that's what matters.'

'But what you did–'

'What I did was kill our enemies,' snapped Eidolon. 'Understood?'

'Understood,' nodded Tarvitz, although he no more understood Eidolon's newfound ability than he did the celestial mechanics of travelling through the warp.

Eidolon said, 'Kill any remaining enemy troops. Then destroy this place,' before turning and making his way down the shattered pyramid to the cheers of his warriors.

Tarvitz retrieved his fallen weapons and watched the aftermath of victory unfolding below him. The Astartes were regrouping and he made his way back down to where he had left the wounded Garro.

The captain of the Death Guard was sitting propped up against the side of the pyramid, his chest heaving with the effort of breathing and Tarvitz could see it had taken a supreme effort of will not to let the pain balms of his armour render him unconscious.

'Tarvitz, you're alive,' said Garro as he climbed down the last step.

'Just about,' he said. 'More than can be said for you.'

'This?' sneered Garro. 'I've had worse than this. You mark my words, lad, I'll be up and teaching you a few new tricks in the training cages again before you know it.'

Despite the strangeness of the battle and the lives that had been lost, Tarvitz smiled.

'It is good to see you again, Nathaniel,' said Tarvitz, leaning down and taking Garro's proffered hand. 'It has been too long since we fought together.'

'It has that, my honour brother,' nodded Garro, 'but I have a feeling we will have plenty of opportunities to fight as one before this campaign is over.'

'Not if you keep letting yourself get injured like this. You need an apothecary.'

'Nonsense, boy, there's plenty worse than me that need a sawbones first.'

'You never did learn to accept that you'd been hurt did you?' smiled Tarvitz.

'No,' agreed Garro. 'It's not the Death Guard way, is it?'

'I wouldn't know,' said Tarvitz, waving over an Emperor's Children apothecary despite Garro's protests. 'You're too barbarous a Legion for me to ever understand.'

'And you're a bunch of pretty boys, more concerned with looking good than getting the job done,' said Garro, rounding off the traditional insults that passed for greetings between them. Both warriors had been through too much in their long friendship and saved each other's lives too many times to allow formality and petty differences between their Legions to matter.

Garro jerked his thumb in the direction of the summit. 'You killed her?'

'No,' said Tarvitz. 'Lord Commander Eidolon did.'

'Eidolon, eh?' mused Garro. 'Never did have much time for him. Still, if he managed to bring her down, he's obviously learned a thing or two since I last met him.'

'I think you might be right,' said Tarvitz.

SIX

The soul of the Legion
Everything will be different
Abomination

LOKEN FOUND ABADDON in the observation dome
that blistered from the hull of the upper decks of
the *Vengeful Spirit*, the transparent glass looking out
onto the barren wasteland of Isstvan Extremis. The
dome was quiet and dark, a perfect place for reflec-
tion and calm, and Abaddon looked out of place,
his power and energy like that of a caged beast
poised to attack.

'Loken,' said Abaddon as he walked into the
chamber. '*You* summoned *me* here?'

'I did.'

'Why?' demanded Abaddon.

'Loyalty,' said Loken simply.

Abaddon snorted. 'You don't know the meaning
of the word. You have never had it tested.'

'Like you did on Davin?'

'Ah,' sighed Abaddon, 'so that is what this is about. Don't think to lecture me, Loken. You couldn't have taken the steps we did to save the Warmaster.'

'Maybe I'm the only one who took a stand.'

'Against what? You would have allowed the Warmaster to die rather than accept that there might be something in this universe you don't understand?'

'I am not here to debate what happened on Davin,' said Loken, already feeling that he had lost control of the conversation.

'Then why are you here? I have warriors to make ready, and I won't waste time with you on idle words.'

'I called you here because I need answers. About this,' said Loken, casting the book he had taken from the fane behind the strategium onto the mosaic floor of the observation dome.

Abaddon stooped to retrieve the book. In the hands of the first captain, it looked tiny, like one of Ignace Karkasy's pamphlets.

'So you're a thief now,' said Abaddon.

'Do not dare speak to me of such things, Ezekyle, not until you have given me answers. I know that Erebus conspired against us. He stole the anathame from the interex and brought it to Davin. I know it and you know it.'

'You know nothing, Loken,' sneered Abaddon. 'What happens in this Crusade happens for the good of the Imperium. The Warmaster has a plan.'

'A plan?' said Loken. 'And this plan requires the murder of innocent people? Hektor Varvarus? Ignace Karkasy? Petronella Vivar?'

'The remembrancers?' laughed Abaddon. 'You really care about those people? They are lesser people, Loken, beneath us. The Council of Terra wants to drown us in these petty bureaucrats to stifle us and strangle our ambitions to conquer the galaxy.'

'Erebus,' said Loken, trying to keep his anger in check, 'why was he on the *Vengeful Spirit*?'

Abaddon crossed the width of the observation dome in a second. 'None of your damn business.'

'This is my Legion!' shouted Loken. 'That makes it my damn business.'

'Not any more.'

Loken felt his choler rise and clenched his hands into murderous fists.

Abaddon saw the tension in him and said, 'Thinking of settling this like a warrior?'

'No, Ezekyle,' said Loken through clenched teeth. 'Despite all that has happened, you are still my Mournival brother and I will not fight you.'

'The Mournival,' nodded Abaddon. 'A noble idea while it lasted, but I regret ever bringing you in. In any case, if it came down to bloodshed do you really think you could beat me?'

Loken ignored the taunt and said, 'Is Erebus still here?'

'Erebus is a guest on the Warmaster's flagship,' said Abaddon. 'You would do well to remember that. If you had joined us when you had the chance instead of turning your back on us, you would have all your answers, but that's the choice you made, Loken. Live with it.'

'The lodge has brought something evil into our Legion, Ezekyle, maybe the other Legions too, something from the warp. It's what killed Jubal and it's what took Temba on Davin. Erebus is lying to all of us!'

'And we're being used, is that right? Erebus is manipulating us all towards a fate worse than death?' spat Abaddon. 'You know so little. If you understood the scale of the Warmaster's designs then you would beg us to take you back.'

'Then tell me, Ezekyle, and maybe I'll beg. We were brothers once and we can be again.'

'Do you really believe that, Loken? You've made it plain enough that you're against us. Torgaddon said as much.'

'For my Legion, for my Warmaster, there is always a way back,' replied Loken, 'as long as you feel the same.'

'But you'll never surrender, eh?'

'Never! Not when the soul of my Legion is at stake.'

Abaddon shook his head. 'We tie ourselves in such knots because men like you are too proud to make compromises.'

'Compromise will be the death of us, Ezekyle.'

'Forget this until after Isstvan, Loken,' ordered Abaddon. 'After Isstvan, this will end.'

'I will not forget it, Ezekyle. I will have my answers,' snarled Loken, turning and walking away from his brother.

'If you fight us, you'll lose,' promised Abaddon.

'Maybe,' replied Loken, 'but others will stand against you.'

'Then they will die too.'

'THANK YOU ALL for coming,' said Sindermann, overwhelmed and a little afraid at the number of people gathered before him. 'I appreciate that you have all taken a great risk to be here, but this is too much.'

Crammed into a dark maintenance space, filthy with grease and hemmed in by low hissing pipe work, the faithful had come from all over the ship to hear the saint's words, mistakenly believing that she was awake. Amongst the crowd, Sindermann saw the uniforms of Titan crewmen, fleet maintenance workers, medical staff, security personnel, and even a few Imperial Army troopers. Men with guns guarded the entrances to the maintenance space and their presence served as a stark reminder of the danger they were in just by being here.

Such a large gathering was dangerous, too easily noticed, and Sindermann knew that he had to disperse them quickly before they were discovered, and do it in such a way as not to incite a riot.

'You have escaped notice thus far thanks to the size of your gatherings, but so many cannot avoid notice for long,' continued Sindermann. 'You will no doubt have heard many strange and wonderful things recently, and I hope you will forgive me for putting you in harm's way.'

The news of Keeler's rescue had spread quickly through the ship. It had been whispered among the grime-covered ratings, it had been communicated through the remembrancer order with the rapidity of an epidemic and it had reached the ears of even the lowliest member of the expedition. Embellishments and wild rumour followed in the wake of the news and tales abounded of the saint and her miraculous powers, incredible stories of bullets turned aside and of visions of the Emperor speaking directly to her in order to show His people the way.

'What of the saint?' asked a voice from the crowd. 'We want to see her!'

Sindermann held up a hand and said, 'The saint is fortunate to be alive. She is well, but she still sleeps. Some of you have heard that she is awake, and that she has spoken, but regrettably this is not the case.'

A disappointed buzz spread throughout the crowd, angry at Sindermann's denial of what many of them desperately wanted to believe. Sindermann was reminded of the speeches he had given on newly-compliant worlds, where he had used his iterator's wiles to extol the virtues of the Imperial Truth.

Now he had to use those same skills to give these people hope.

'The saint still sleeps, it's true, but for one brief, shining moment she arose from her slumbers to save my life. I saw her eyes open and I know that when we need her, she will come back to us. Until then we must walk warily, for there are those in the fleet who would destroy us for our beliefs. The very fact that we must meet in secret and rely on armed guards to keep us safe is a reminder that Maloghurst himself regularly sends troops to break up the meetings of the Lectitio Divinitatus. People have been killed and their blood is on the hands of the Astartes. Ignace Karkasy, Emperor rest his soul, knew the dangers of an unchecked Astartes before any of us realised their hands were around our throats.

'Once, I could not believe in such things as saints. I had trained myself to accept only logic and science, and to cast aside religion as superstition. Magic and miracles were impossible, simply the invention of ignorant people struggling to understand their world. It took the sacrifice of the saint to show me how arrogant I was. I saw how the Emperor protects, but she has shown me that there is so much more than that, for, if the Emperor protects His faithful, who protects the Emperor?'

Sindermann let the question hang.

'We must,' said Titus Cassar, pushing his way towards the front of the crowd and turning to address them. Sindermann had placed Cassar in the crowd with specific instructions on when to speak – a basic ploy of the iterators to reinforce their message.

'We must protect the Emperor, for there is no one else,' said Cassar. The moderati looked back at Sindermann. 'But we must stay alive in order to do so. Is that not right, iterator?'

'Yes,' said Sindermann. 'The faith that this congregation has displayed has caused such fear in the higher echelons of the fleet that they are trying to destroy us. The Emperor has an enemy here; of that I am sure. We must survive and we must stand against that enemy when it finally reveals itself.'

Worried and angry murmurings spread through the crowd as the deadly nature of the threat sank in.

'Faithful friends,' said Sindermann, 'the dangers we face are great, but the saint is with us and she needs shelter. Shelter we can best achieve alone, but watch for the signs and be safe. Spread the word of her safety.'

Cassar moved through the congregation, instructing them to return to their posts. Reassured by Sindermann's words, they gradually began to disperse. As he watched them go, Sindermann wondered how many of them would live through the coming days.

THE GALLERY OF Swords ran the length of the *Andronius* like the ship's gilded spine. Its roof was transparent and the space beneath was lit by the fire of distant stars. Hundreds of statues lined the gallery, heroes of the Emperor's Children with gemstone eyes and stern expressions of judgement. The worth of a hero was said to be measured by how long he could meet their gaze while walking the length of the Gallery of Swords beneath their unforgiving eyes.

Tarvitz held his head high as he entered the gallery, though he knew he was no hero, simply a warrior who did his best. Chapter Masters and commanders from long ago glared at him, their names and noble countenances known and revered by every warrior of the Emperor's Children. Entire wings of the *Andronius* were given over to the fallen battle-brothers of the Legion, but it was here that every warrior hoped to be remembered.

Tarvitz had no expectation of his visage ending up here, but he would strive to end his days in a manner that might be considered worthy of such an honour. Even if such a lofty goal was impossible, it was something to aspire to.

Eidolon stood before the graven image of Lord Commander Teliosa, the hero of the Madrivane Campaign, and even before Tarvitz drew near he turned to face him.

'Captain Tarvitz,' said Eidolon. 'I have rarely seen you here.'

'It is not my natural habitat, commander,' replied Tarvitz. 'I leave the heroes of our Legion to their rest.'

'Then what brings you here now?'

'I would speak with you if you would permit me.'

'Surely your time is better spent attending to your warriors, Tarvitz. That is where your talents lie.'

'You honour me by saying so, commander, but there is something I need to ask you.'

'About?'

'The death of the Warsinger.'

'Ah.' Eidolon looked up at the statue towering over them, the hollow eyes regarding them with a cold, unflinching gaze. 'She was quite an adversary; absolutely corrupt, but that corruption gave her strength.'

'I need to know how you killed her.'

'Captain? You speak as if to an equal.'

'I saw what you did, commander,' Tarvitz pressed. 'That scream, it was some... I don't know... some power I've never heard of before.'

Eidolon held up a hand. 'I can understand why you have questions, and I can answer them, but perhaps it would be better for me to show you. Follow me.'

Tarvitz followed the lord commander as they walked further down the Gallery of Swords, turning into a side passage with sheets of parchment pinned along the length of its walls. Accounts of glorious actions from the Legion's past were meticulously recorded on them and novices of the Legion were required to memorise the many different battles before their elevation to full Astartes.

The Emperor's Children did more than just remember their triumphs; they proclaimed them, because the perfection of the Legion's way of war deserved celebrating.

'Do you know why I fought the Warsinger?' asked Eidolon.

'Why?'

'Yes, captain, why.'

'Because that is how the Emperor's Children fight.'

'Explain.'

'Our heroes lead from the front. The rest of the Legion is inspired to follow their example. They can do this because the Legion fights with such artistry that they are not rendered vulnerable by fighting at the fore.'

Eidolon smiled. 'Very good, captain. I should have you instruct the novices. And you yourself, would you lead from the front?'

Sudden hope flared in Tarvitz's breast. 'Of course! Given the chance, I would. I had not thought you considered me worthy of such a role.'

'You are not, Tarvitz. You are a file officer and nothing more,' said Eidolon, crushing his faint hope that he had been about to be offered a way of proving his mettle as a leader and a hero.

'I say this not as an insult,' Eidolon continued, apparently oblivious to the insult it clearly was. 'Men like you fulfil an important role in our Legion, but I am one of Fulgrim's chosen. The primarch chose me and elevated me to the position I now hold. He looked upon me and saw in me the qualities needed to lead the Emperor's Children. He looked upon you, and did not. Because of this, I understand the responsibilities that come with being Fulgrim's chosen in a way that you cannot, Captain Tarvitz.'

Eidolon led him to a grand staircase that curved downwards into a large hall tiled with white marble. Tarvitz recognised it as one of the entrances to the ship's apothecarion, where the injured from Isstvan Extremis had been brought only a few hours before.

'I think you underestimate me, lord commander,' said Tarvitz, 'but understand that for the sake of my men I must know–'

'For the sake of our men we all make sacrifices,' snapped Eidolon. 'For the chosen, those sacrifices are great. Foremost among these is that fact that *everything* is secondary to victory.'

'Commander, I don't understand.'

'You will,' said Eidolon, leading him through a gilded archway and into the central apothecarion.

'THE BOOK?' ASKED Torgaddon.

'The book,' repeated Loken. 'It's the key. Erebus is on the ship, I know it.'

The ashen darkness of Archive Chamber Three was one of the few places left on the *Vengeful Spirit* where Loken felt at home, remembering many a lively debate with Kyril Sindermann in simpler times. Loken had not seen the iterator for weeks and he fervently hoped that the old man was safe, that he had not fallen foul of Maloghurst or his faceless soldiers.

'Abaddon and the others must be keeping him safe,' said Torgaddon.

Loken sighed. 'How did it come to this? I would have given my life for Abaddon, Aximand, too, and I know they would have done the same for me.'

'We can't give up on this, Garviel. There will be a way out of this. We can bring the Mournival back together, or at least make sure the Warmaster sees what Erebus is doing.'

'Whatever that is.'

'Yes, whatever that is. Guest of the lodge or not, he's not welcome on my ship. He's the key. If we find him, we can expose what's going on to the Warmaster and end this.'

'You really believe that?'

'I don't know, but that won't stop me trying.'

Torgaddon looked around him, stirring the ashes of the charred books on the shelves with a finger and said, 'Why did you have to meet me here? It smells like a funeral pyre.'

'Because no one ever comes here,' said Loken.

'I can't imagine why, seeing as how pleasant it is.'

'Don't be flippant, Tarik, not now. The Great Crusade was once about bringing illumination to the far corners of the galaxy, but now it is afraid of knowledge. The more we learn, the more we question and the more we question the more we see through the lies perpetrated upon us. To those who want to control us, books are dangerous.'

'Iterator Loken,' laughed Torgaddon, 'you've enlightened me.'

'I had a good teacher,' said Loken, again thinking of Kyril Sindermann, and the fact that everything he had been taught to believe was being shaken to its core. 'And there's more at stake here than a split between Astartes. It's… It's philosophy, ideology, religion even… everything. Kyril taught me that this kind of blind obedience is what led to the Age of Strife. We've crossed the galaxy to bring peace and illumination, but the cause of our downfall could be right here amongst us.'

Torgaddon leaned over and put a hand on his friend's shoulder. 'Listen, we're about to go into battle on Isstvan III and the word from the Death Guard is that the enemy is led by some kind of psychic monsters that can kill with a scream. They're not the enemy because they read the wrong books or anything like that; they're the enemy because the Warmaster tells us they are. Forget about all this for a while. Go and fight. That'll put some perspective on things.'

'Do you even know if we'll be headed down there?'

'The Warmaster's picked the squads for the speartip. We're in it, and it looks as if we'll be in charge, too.'

'Really? After all that's happened?

'I know, but I won't look a gift horse in the mouth.'

'At least I'll have the Tenth with me.'

Torgaddon shook his head. 'Not quite. The Warmaster hasn't chosen the speartip by company. It's squad by squad.'

'Why?'

'Because he thinks that confused look on your face is funny.'

'Please. Be serious, Tarik.'

Torgaddon shrugged. 'The Warmaster knows what he's doing. It won't be an easy battle. We'll be dropping right on top of the city.'

'What about Locasta?'

'You'll have them. I don't think you could have held Vipus back anyway. You know what he's like, he'd have stowed away on a drop-pod if he'd been left out. He's like you, he needs to clear his head with a good dose of fighting. After Isstvan things will get back to normal.'

'Good. I'll feel a lot better with Locasta backing us up.'

'Well, it's true that you need the help,' smiled Torgaddon.

Loken chuckled, not because Torgaddon was actually funny, but because even after everything he was still the same, a person that he could trust and a friend he could rely on.

'You're right, Tarik,' said Loken. 'After Isstvan everything will be different.'

THE CENTRAL APOTHECARION gleamed with glass and steel, dozens of medical cells branching off from the circular hub of the main laboratory. Tarvitz felt a chill travel the length of his spine as he saw Captain Odovocar's ruined body suspended in a stasis tank, waiting for its gene-seed to be harvested.

Eidolon marched through the hub and down a
tiled corridor that led into a gilded vestibule dominated by a huge mosaic depicting Fulgrim's victory
at Tarsus, where the primarch had vanquished the
deceitful eldar despite his many grievous wounds.
Eidolon reached up and pressed one of the enam-
elled chips that formed Fulgrim's belt, standing
back as the mosaic arced upwards, revealing a glowing passageway and winding spiral staircase
beyond. Eidolon strode down the passageway, indicating that Tarvitz should follow him.

The lack of ornamentation was a contrast to the
rest of the *Andronius* and Tarvitz saw a cold blue
glow emanating from whatever lay below as he
made his way down the stairs. As they reached the
end of their descent, Eidolon turned to him and
said, 'This, Captain Tarvitz, is your answer.'

The blue light shone from a dozen ceiling-high
translucent cylinders that stood against the sides of
the room. Each was filled with liquid with indistinct shapes suspended in them – some roughly
humanoid, some more like collections of organs or
body parts. The rest of the room was taken up by
gleaming laboratory benches covered in equipment, some with purposes he couldn't even begin
to guess at.

He moved from tank to tank, repulsed as he saw
that some were full of monstrously bloated flesh
that was barely contained by the glass.

'What is this?' asked Tarvitz in horror at such
grotesque sights.

'I fear my explanations would be insufficient,' said Eidolon, walking towards an archway leading into the next room. Tarvitz followed him, peering more closely at the cylinders as he passed. One contained an Astartes-sized body, but not a corpse, more like something that had never been born, its features sunken and half-formed.

Another cylinder contained only a head, but one which had large, multi-faceted eyes like an insect. As he looked closer, Tarvitz realised with sick horror that the eyes had not been grafted on, for he saw no scars and the skull had reshaped itself to accommodate them.

They had been grown there.

He moved on to the last cylinder, seeing a mass of brains linked by fleshy cables held in liquid suspension, each one with extra lobes bulging like tumours.

Tarvitz felt a profound chill coming from the next room, its walls lined with refrigerated metal cabinets. He briefly wondered what was in them, but decided he didn't want to know as his imagination conjured all manner of deformities and mutations. A single operating slab filled the centre of the room, easily large enough for an Astartes warrior to be restrained upon, with a chirurgeon device mounted on the ceiling above.

Neatly cut sections of muscle fibre were spread across the slab. Apothecary Fabius bent over them, the hissing probes and needles of his narthecium embedded in a dark mass of glistening meat.

'Apothecary,' said Eidolon, 'the captain wishes to know of our enterprise.'

Fabius looked up in surprise, his long intelligent face framed by a mane of fine blond hair. Only his eyes were out of place, small and dark, set into his skull like black pearls. He wore a floor-length medicae gown, blood streaking its pristine whiteness with runnels of crimson.

'Really?' said Fabius. 'I had not been made aware that Captain Tarvitz was among our esteemed company.'

'He is not,' said Eidolon. 'Not yet anyway.'

'Then why is he here?'

'My own alterations have come to light.'

'Ah, I see,' nodded Fabius.

'What is going on here?' asked Tarvitz sharply. 'What is this place?'

Fabius cocked an eyebrow. 'So you have seen the results of the commander's augmentations, have you?'

'Is he a psyker?' demanded Tarvitz.

'No, no, no!' laughed Fabius. 'He is not. The lord commander's abilities are the result of a tracheal implant combined with alteration in the gene-seed rhythms. He is something of a success. His powers are metabolic and chemical, not psychic.'

'You have altered the geneseed?' breathed Tarvitz in shock. 'The gene-seed is the blood of our primarch… When he discovers what you are doing here…'

'Don't be naïve, captain,' said Fabius. 'Who do you think ordered us to proceed?'

'No,' said Tarvitz. 'He wouldn't—'

'That is why I had to show you this, captain,' said Eidolon. 'You remember the Cleansing of Laeran?'

'Of course,' answered Tarvitz.

'Our primarch saw what the Laer had achieved by chemical and genetic manipulation of their biological structure in their drive for physical perfection. The Lord Fulgrim has great plans for our Legion, Tarvitz, the Emperor's Children cannot be content to sit on their laurels while our fellow Astartes win the same dull victories. We must continue to strive towards perfection, but we are fast reaching the point where even an Astartes cannot match the standards Lord Fulgrim and the Warmaster demand. To meet those standards, we must change. We must evolve.'

Tarvitz backed away from the operating slab. 'The Emperor created Lord Fulgrim to be the perfect warrior and the Legion's warriors were moulded in his image. That image is what we strive towards. Holding a xenos race up as an example of perfection is an abomination!'

'An abomination?' said Eidolon. 'Tarvitz, you are brave and disciplined, and your warriors respect you, but you do not have the imagination to see where this work can lead us. You must realise that the Legion's supremacy is of greater importance than any mortal squeamishness.'

Such a bold statement, its arrogance and conceit beyond anything he had heard Eidolon say before, stunned Tarvitz to silence.

'But for your unlikely presence at the death of the Warsinger, you would never have been granted this chance, Tarvitz,' said Eidolon. 'Understand it for the opportunity it represents.'

Tarvitz looked up at the lord commander sharply. 'What do you mean?'

'Now you know what we are attempting, perhaps you are ready to become a part of this Legion's future instead of simply one of its line officers.'

'It is not without risk,' Fabius pointed out, 'but I could work such wonders upon your flesh. I can make you more than you are, I can bring you closer to perfection.'

'Think of the alternative,' said Eidolon. 'You will fight and die knowing that you could have been so much more.'

Tarvitz looked at the two warriors before him, both Fulgrim's chosen and both exemplars of the Legion's relentless drive towards perfection.

He saw then that he was very, very far from perfection as they understood it, but for once welcomed such a failing, if failing it was.

'No,' he said, backing away. 'This is… wrong. Can you not feel it?'

'Very well,' said Eidolon. 'You have made your choice and it does not surprise me. So be it. You must leave now, but you are ordered not to speak of what you have seen here. Return to your men, Tarvitz. Isstvan III will be a tough fight.'

'Yes, commander,' said Tarvitz, relieved beyond measure to be leaving this chamber of horrors.

Tarvitz saluted and all but fled the laboratory, feeling as though the specimens suspended in the tanks were watching him as he went.

As he emerged into the brightness of the apothecarion, he could not shake the feeling that he had just been tested.

Whether he had passed or failed was another matter entirely.

SEVEN

The God Machine
A favour
Subterfuge

THE COLD SENSATION snaking through Cassar's mind
was like an old friend, the touch of something reassuring. The metallic caress of the *Dies Irae* as its
cortical interfaces meshed with his consciousness
would have been terrifying to most people, but it
was one of the few constants Moderati Titus Cassar
had left in the galaxy.

That and the Lectitio Divinitatus.

The Titan's bridge was dim, lit by ghostly readouts and telltales that lined the ornate bridge in
hard greens and blues. The Mechanicum had been
busy, sending cloaked adepts into the Titan, and
the bridge was packed with equipment he didn't yet
know the purpose of. The deck crew manning the
plasma reactor at the war machine's heart had been
readying the Titan for battle since the *Vengeful Spirit*

arrived in the Isstvan system, and every indication
was that the *Dies Irae's* major systems were all func-
tioning better than ever.

Cassar was glad of any advantage the war
machine could get, but somewhere deep down he
resented the thought of anyone else touching the
Titan. The interface filaments coiled deeper into his
scalp, sending an unexpected chill through him.
The Titan's systems lit up behind Cassar's eyes as
though they were a part of his own body. The
plasma reactor was ticking over quietly, its pent-up
energy ready to erupt into full battle order at his
command.

'Motivation systems are a little loose,' he said to
himself, tightening the pressure on the massive
hydraulic rams in the Titan's torso and legs.

'Weapons hot, ammunition loaded,' he said,
knowing that it would take no more than a thought
to unleash them.

He had come to regard the power and magnificence of the *Dies Irae* as the Emperor personified.
Cassar had resisted the thought at first, mocking
Jonah Aruken's insistence that the Titan had a soul,
but it had become more and more obvious why he
had been chosen by the saint.

The Lectitio Divinitatus was under threat and the
faithful had to be defended. He almost laughed
aloud as the thought formed, but what he had seen
on the Medicae deck had only deepened the
strength of his conviction that he had chosen the
right path.

The Titan was a symbol of that strength, an avatar of divine wrath, a god-machine that brought the Emperor's judgement to the sinners of Isstvan.

'The Emperor protects,' whispered Cassar, his voice drifting down through the layers of readouts in his mind, 'and he destroys.'

'Does he now?'

Cassar snapped out of his thoughts and the Titan's systems retreated beneath his consciousness. He looked up in sudden panic, but let out a relieved breath as he saw Moderati Aruken standing over him.

Aruken snapped a switch and the bridge lights flickered to life. 'Be careful who hears you, Titus, now more than ever.'

'I was running through pre-battle checks,' said Cassar.

'Of course you were, Titus. If Princeps Turnet hears you saying things like that you'll be for it.'

'My thoughts are my own, Jonah. Not even the princeps can deny me that.'

'You really believe that? Come on, Titus. You know full well this cult stuff isn't welcome. We were lucky on the Medicae deck, but this is bigger than you and me and it's getting too dangerous.'

'We can't back away from it now,' said Cassar, 'not after what we saw.'

'I'm not even sure what I saw,' said Aruken defensively.

'You're joking, surely?'

'No,' insisted Aruken, 'I'm not. Look, I'm telling you this because you're a good man and the *Dies Irae* will suffer if you're not here. She needs a good crew and you're part of it.'

'Don't change the subject,' said Cassar. 'We both know that what we saw on the Medicae deck was a miracle. You have to accept that before the Emperor can enter your heart.'

'Listen, I've been hearing some scuttlebutt on the deck, Titus,' said Aruken, leaning closer. 'Turnet's been asking questions: about us. He's asking about how deep this runs, as though we're part of some hidden conspiracy. It's as if he doesn't trust us any more.'

'Let him come.'

'You don't understand. When we're in battle we're a good team, and if we get… I don't know… thrown in a cell or worse, that team gets broken up and there isn't a better crew for the *Dies Irae* than us. Don't let this saint business break that up. The Crusade will suffer for it.'

'My faith won't allow me to make compromises, Jonah.'

'Well that's all it is,' snapped Aruken. '*Your* faith.'

'No,' said Titus, shaking his head. 'It's your faith too, Jonah, you just don't know it yet.'

Aruken didn't answer and slumped into his own command chair, nodding at the readouts in front of Cassar. 'How's she looking?'

'Good. The reactor is ticking over smoothly and the targeting is reacting faster than I've seen it in a while. The Mechanicum adepts have been tinkering so there are a few more bells and whistles to play with.'

'You say that as if it's a bad thing, Titus. The Mechanicum know what they're doing. Anyway, the latest news is that we've got twelve hours to go before the drop. We're going in with the Death Guard on support duties. Princeps Turnet will brief us in a few hours, but it's basically pounding the ground and scaring the shit out of the enemy. Sound good?'

'It sounds like battle.'

'It's all the same thing for the *Dies Irae* when the bullets are flying,' said Aruken.

'THIS REMINDS ME of why I was so proud,' said Loken, looking at the speartip assembling on the *Vengeful Spirit's* embarkation deck. 'Joining the Mournival, and just to be a part of this.'

'I am still proud,' said Torgaddon. 'This is my Legion. That hasn't changed.'

Loken and Torgaddon, fully armoured and ready for the drop, stood at the head of a host of Astartes. More than a third of the Legion was there, thousands of warriors arrayed for war. Loken saw veterans alongside newly inducted novices, assault warriors with chainswords and bulky jump packs, and devastators hefting heavy bolters and lascannons.

Sergeant Lachost was speaking with his communications squad, making sure they understood the importance of keeping a link with the *Vengeful Spirit* once they were down in the Choral City.

Apothecary Vaddon was checking and re-checking his medical gear, the narthecium gauntlet with its cluster of probes and the reductor that would harvest gene-seeds from the fallen.

Iacton Qruze, who had been a captain for so long that he was as old as an Astartes could be and still count himself a warrior, was lecturing some of the more recent inductees on the past glories of the Legion that they had to live up to.

'I'd be happier with the Tenth,' said Loken, returning his attention to his friend.

'And I with the Second,' replied Torgaddon, 'but we can't always have what we want.'

'Garvi!' called a familiar voice.

Loken turned and saw Nero Vipus approaching them, leaving the veterans of Locasta to continue their preparations for the drop.

'Nero,' said Loken, 'good to have you with us.'

Vipus clapped Loken's shoulder guard with the augmetic hand that had replaced the organic one he'd lost on Sixty-Three Nineteen. 'I wouldn't have missed this,' he said.

'I know what you mean,' replied Loken. It had been a long time since they had lined up on the *Vengeful Spirit* as brothers, ready to fight the Emperor's good fight. Nero Vipus and Loken were the oldest of friends, back from the barely remembered blur of training, and it was reassuring to have another familiar face alongside him.

'Have you heard the reports from Isstvan Extremis?' asked Vipus, his eyes alight.

'Some of them.'

'They say the enemy has got some kind of psychic leadership caste and that their soldiers are fanatics. My choler's up just thinking about it.'

'Don't worry,' said Torgaddon. 'I'm sure you'll kill them all.'

'It's like Davin again,' said Vipus, baring his teeth in a grimace of anticipation.

'It's not like Davin,' said Loken. 'It's nothing at all like Davin.'

'What do you mean?'

'It's not a bloody swamp, for a start,' interjected Torgaddon.

'It would be an honour if you'd go into battle with Locasta, Garvi,' said Vipus expectantly. 'I have a space in the drop-pod.'

'The honour is mine,' replied Loken, taking his friend's hand as a sudden thought occurred to him. 'Count me in.'

He nodded to his friends and made his way through the bustling Astartes towards the solitary figure of Iacton Qruze. The Half-heard watched the preparations for war with undisguised envy and Loken felt a stab of sympathy for the venerable warrior. Qruze was an example of just how little even the Legion's apothecaries knew of an Astartes' physiology. His face was as battered and gnarled as ancient oak, but his body was as wolf-tough, honed by years of fighting and not yet made weary by age.

An Astartes was functionally immortal, meaning that only in death did duty end, and the thought sent a chill down Loken's spine.

'Loken,' acknowledged Qruze as he saw him approach.

'You're not coming down to see the sights of the Sirenhold with us?' asked Loken.

'Alas, no,' said Qruze. 'I am to stay and await orders. I haven't even got a place in the order of battle for the pacification force.'

'If the Warmaster has no plans for you, Iacton, then I have something you could do for me,' said Loken, 'if you would do me the honour?'

Qruze's eyes narrowed. 'What sort of a favour?'

'Nothing too arduous, I promise you.'

'Then ask.'

'There are some remembrancers aboard, you may have heard of them: Mersadie Oliton, Euphrati Keeler and Kyril Sindermann?'

'Yes, I know of them,' confirmed Qruze. 'What of them?'

'They are… friends of mine and I would consider it an honour if you were to seek them out and ask after them. Check on them and make sure that they are well.'

'Why do these mortals matter to you, captain?'

'They keep me honest, Iacton,' smiled Loken, 'and they remind me of everything we ought to be as Astartes.'

'That I can understand, Loken,' replied Qruze. 'The Legion is changing, boy. I know you've heard me bore you with this before, but I feel in my bones that there's something big just over the horizon that we can't see. If these people help keep us honest, then that's good enough for me. Consider it done, Captain Loken.'

'Thank you, Iacton,' said Loken. 'It means a lot to me.'

'Don't mention it boy,' grinned Qruze. 'Now get out of here and kill for the living.'

'I will,' promised Loken, taking Qruze's wrist in the warrior's grip.

'Speartip units to posts,' said the booming voice of the deck officer.

'Good hunting in the Sirenhold,' said Qruze. 'Lupercal!'

'Lupercal!' echoed Loken.

As he jogged towards Locasta's drop-pod, it almost felt as if the events of Davin were forgotten and Loken was just a warrior again, fighting a crusade that had to be won and an enemy that deserved to die.

It took war to make him feel like one of the Sons of Horus again.

'TO VICTORY!' SHOUTED Lucius.

The Emperor's Children were so certain of the perfection of their way of war that it was traditional to salute the victory before it was won. Tarvitz was not surprised that Lucius led the salute; many senior officers attended the pre-battle celebration and Lucius was keen to be noticed. The Astartes seated at the lavish banquet around him joined his salute, their cheers echoing from the alabaster walls of the banqueting hall. Captured banners, honoured weapons once carried by the Chosen of Fulgrim and murals of heroes despatching alien foes hung from the walls, glorious reminders of past victories.

The primarch himself was not present, thus it fell to Eidolon to take his place at the feast, exhorting his fellow Astartes to celebrate the coming victory. Lucius was equally vocal, leading his fellow warriors in toasts from golden chalices of fine wine.

Tarvitz set down his goblet and rose from the table.

'Leaving already, Tarvitz?' sneered Eidolon.

'Yes!' chimed in Lucius. 'We've only just begun to celebrate!'

'I'm sure you will do enough celebrating for both of us, Lucius,' said Tarvitz. 'I have matters to attend to before we make the drop.'

'Nonsense!' said Lucius. 'You need to stay with us and regale us with memories of Murder and how I helped you defeat the scourge of the megarachnids.'

The warriors cheered and called for Tarvitz to tell the story once more, but he held up his hands to quiet their demands.

'Why don't you tell it, Lucius?' asked Tarvitz. 'I don't think I build your part up enough for your liking anyway.'

'That's true,' smiled Lucius. 'Very well, I'll tell the tale.'

'Lord commander,' said Tarvitz, bowing to Eidolon and then turning to make his way through the golden door of the banquet hall. Appealing to Lucius's vanity was the surest way of deflecting his attention. Tarvitz would miss the camaraderie of the celebration, but he had other matters pressing on his thoughts.

He closed the door to the banqueting hall as Lucius began the tale of their ill-fated expedition to Murder, though its horrifying beginnings had somehow become a great triumph, largely thanks to Lucius, if past retellings were anything to go by.

The magnificent processional at the heart of the *Andronius* was quiet, the droning hum of the vessel reassuring in its constancy. The ship, like many in the Emperor's Children fleet, resembled some ancient palace of Terra, reflecting the Legion's desire to infuse everything with regal majesty.

Tarvitz made his way through the ship, passing wondrous spaces that would make the shipwrights of Jupiter weep with awe, until he reached the Hall of Rites, the circular chamber where the Emperor's Children underwent the oaths and ceremonies that tied them to their Legion. Compared to the rest of the ship, the hall was dark, but it was no less magnificent: marble columns supporting a distant domed ceiling, and ritual altars of marble glittering in pools of shadow at its edges.

Fulgrim's Chosen had pledged themselves to the primarch's personal charge here, and he had accepted his appointment as captain before the

Altar of Service. The Hall of Rites replaced opulence with gravity, and seemed designed to intimidate with the promise of knowledge hidden from all but the Legion's most exalted officers.

Tarvitz paused on the threshold, seeing the unmistakable shape of Ancient Rylanor, his dreadnought body standing before the Altar of Devotion.

'Enter,' said Rylanor in his artificial voice.

Tarvitz cautiously approached the Ancient, his blocky outline resolving into a tank-like square sarcophagus supported on powerful piston legs. The dreadnought's wide shoulders mounted an assault cannon on one arm and a huge hydraulic fist on the other. Rylanor's body rotated slowly on its central axis to face Tarvitz, turning from the *Book of Ceremonies* that lay open on the altar.

'Captain Tarvitz, why are you not with your warriors?' asked Rylanor. The vision slit that housed his ocular circuits regarded Tarvitz without emotion.

'They can celebrate well enough without me,' said Tarvitz. 'Besides, I have sat through one too many renditions of Lucius's tales to think I'll miss much.'

'It is not to my taste either,' said Rylanor, a grating bark of electronic noise sounding from the dreadnought's vox-unit. At first Tarvitz thought the Ancient had developed a fault, until he realised that the sound was Rylanor's laughter.

Rylanor was the Legion's Ancient of Rites, and when not on the battlefield he oversaw the ceremonies that marked the gradual ascent of an Astartes from novice to Chosen of Fulgrim.

Decades before, Rylanor had been wounded beyond the skill of the Legion's apothecaries while fighting the duplicitous eldar, and had been interred in a dreadnought war machine that he might continue to serve. Along with Lucius and Tarvitz, Rylanor was one of the senior officers being sent down to take the Choral City's palace complex.

'I wish to speak with you, revered Ancient,' said Tarvitz, 'about the drop.'

'The drop is in a few hours,' replied Rylanor. 'There is little time.'

'Yes, I have left it too late and for that I apologise, but it concerns Captain Odovocar.'

'Captain Odovocar is dead, killed on Isstvan Extremis.'

'And the Legion lost a great warrior that day,' nodded Tarvitz. 'Not only that, but he was to function as Eidolon's senior staff officer aboard the *Andronius*, relaying the commander's orders to the surface. With his death there is no one to fulfil that role.'

'Eidolon is aware of Odovocar's loss. He will have an alternative in place.'

'I request the honour of fulfilling that role,' said Tarvitz solemnly. 'I knew Odovocar well and would consider it a fitting tribute to finish the work he began on this campaign.'

The dreadnought leaned close to Tarvitz, the cold metallic machine unreadable, as the crippled warrior within decided Tarvitz's fate.

'You would renounce the honour of your place in the speartip to take over his duties?'

Tarvitz looked into Rylanor's vision slit, struggling to keep his expression neutral. Rylanor had seen everything the Legion had gone through since the beginning of the Great Crusade and was said to be able to perceive a lie the instant it was told.

His request to remain aboard the *Andronius* was highly unusual and Rylanor would surely be suspicious of his motives for not wanting to go into the fight. But when Tarvitz had learned that Eidolon was not leading the speartip personally, he knew there had to be a reason. The lord commander never passed up the opportunity to flaunt his martial prowess and for him to appoint another in his stead was unheard of.

Not only that, but the deployment orders Eidolon had issued made no sense.

Instead of the normal, rigorously regimented order of battle that was typical of an Emperor's Children assault, the units chosen to make the first attack appeared to have been picked at random. The only thing they had in common was that none were from Chapters led by Eidolon's favoured lord commanders. For Eidolon to sanction a drop without any of the warriors belonging to those lord commanders was unheard of and grossly insulting.

Something felt very wrong about this drop and Tarvitz couldn't shake the feeling that there was some grim purpose behind the selection of these units. He had to know what it was.

Rylanor straightened and said, 'I shall see to it that you are replaced. This is a great sacrifice you make, Captain Tarvitz. You do the memory of Odovocar much honour with it.'

Tarvitz fought to hide his relief, knowing that he had taken an unthinkable risk in lying to Rylanor. He nodded and said, 'My thanks, Ancient.'

'I shall join the troops of the speartip,' said the dreadnought. 'Their feasting will soon be complete and I must ensure that they are ready for battle.'

'Bring perfection to the Choral City,' said Tarvitz.

'Guide us well,' replied Rylanor, his voice loaded with unspoken meaning. Tarvitz was suddenly certain that the dreadnought *wanted* Tarvitz to remain on the ship.

'Do the Emperor's work, Captain Tarvitz,' ordered Rylanor.

Tarvitz saluted and said, 'I will,' as Rylanor set off across the Hall of Rites towards the banquet, his every step heavy and pounding.

Tarvitz watched him go, wondering if he would ever see the Ancient again.

THE DORMITORIES TUCKED into the thick walls running the length of the gantry were dark and hot, and from the doorway Mersadie could see down into the engine compartment where the crew were indistinguishable, sweating figures who worked in the infernal heat and ruddy glow of the plasma reactors. They hurried across gangways that stretched between the titanic reactors and clambered along massive conduits that hung like spider webs in the hellish gloom.

She dabbed sweat from her brow at the heat and close confines of the engine space, unused to the searing air that stole away her breath and left her faint.

'Mersadie,' said Sindermann coming to meet her along the gantry. The iterator had lost weight, his dirty robes hanging from his already spare frame, but his face was alight with the relief and joy of seeing her. The two embraced in a heartfelt hug, both grateful beyond words to see each other. She felt tears pricking her eyes at the sight of the old man, unaware until this moment of how much she had missed him.

'Kyril, it's so good to see you again,' she sobbed. 'You just vanished. I thought they'd got to you. I didn't know what had happened to you.'

'Hush, Mersadie,' said Sindermann, 'it's all right. I'm so sorry I couldn't send word to you at the time. You must understand that had I a choice, I would have done everything I could to keep you out of this, but I don't know what to do any more. We can't keep her down here forever.'

Mersadie looked through the doorway of the dormitory room they stood outside, wishing she had the courage to believe as Kyril did. 'Don't be ridiculous, Kyril. I'm glad you made contact, I thought... I thought Maloghurst or Maggard had killed you.'

'Maggard very nearly did,' said Sindermann, 'but the saint saved us.'

'She saved you?' asked Mersadie. 'How?'

'I don't know exactly, but it was just like in the Archive Chamber. The power of the Emperor was in her. I saw it, Mersadie, just as sure as you're standing here before me. I wish you could have seen it.'

'I wish that too,' she said, surprised to find that she meant it.

She entered the dormitory and stared down at the still form of Euphrati Keeler on the thin cot bed, looking for all the world as if she was simply sleeping. The small room was cramped and dirty, with a thin blanket spread on the deck beside the bed.

Winking starlight streamed in through a small porthole vision block, something greatly prized this deep in the ship, and without asking, she knew that someone had happily volunteered to give up their prized room for the use of the 'saint' and her companion.

Even down here in the dark and the stink, faith flourished.

'I wish I could believe,' said Mersadie, watching the rhythmic rise and fall of Euphrati's chest.

Sindermann said, 'You don't?'

'I don't know,' she said, shaking her head. 'Tell me why I should? What does believing mean to you, Kyril?'

He smiled and took her hand. 'It gives me something to hold on to. There are people on this ship who want to kill her, and somehow… don't ask me how, I just know that I need to keep her safe.'

'Are you're not afraid?' she asked.

'Afraid?' he said. 'I've never been more terrified in
my life, my dear, but I have to hope that the
Emperor is watching over me. That gives me
strength and the will to face that fear.'

'You are a remarkable man, Kyril.'

'I'm not remarkable, Mersadie,' said Sindermann,
shaking his head. 'I was lucky. I *saw* what the saint
did, so faith is easy for me. It's hardest for you, for
you have seen nothing. You have to simply accept
that the Emperor is working through Euphrati, but
you don't believe, do you?'

Mersadie turned from Sindermann and pulled
her hand from his, looking through the porthole at
the void of space beyond. 'No. I can't. Not yet.'

A white streak shot across the porthole like a
shooting star.

Another followed it, and then another.

'What's that?' she asked.

Sindermann leaned over to get a better look
through the porthole.

Even through his exhaustion, she could see the
strength in him that she had previously taken for
granted and she blink-clicked the image, capturing the defiance and bravery she saw in his
features.

'Drop-pods,' he said, pointing at a static gleaming
object stark against the blackness and closer to Isstvan III. Tiny sparks began raining from its
underside towards the planet below.

'I think that's the *Andronius*, Fulgrim's flagship,'
said Sindermann. 'Looks like the attack we've been

hearing about has begun. Imagine how it would be if we could watch it unfolding.'

Euphrati groaned and the attack on Isstvan III was forgotten as they slid across to sit beside her. Mersadie saw Sindermann's love for her clearly as he mopped her brow, her skin so clean that it practically shone.

For the briefest moment, Mersadie saw how people could believe Euphrati was miraculous; her body so pale and fragile, yet untouched by the world around her. Mersadie had known Keeler as a gutsy woman, never afraid to speak her mind or bend the rules to get the magnificent picts for which she was rightly famed, but now she was something else entirely.

'Is she coming round?' asked Mersadie.

'No,' said Sindermann sadly. 'She makes noises, but she never opens her eyes. It's such a waste. Sometimes I swear she's on the brink of waking, but then she sinks back down into whatever hell she's going through in her head.'

Mersadie sighed and looked back out into space.

The pinpoints of light streaked in their hundreds towards Isstvan III.

As the speartip was driven home, she whispered, 'Loken...'

THE CHORAL CITY was magnificent.

Its design was a masterpiece of architecture, light and space so wondrous that Peeter Egon Momus had begged the Warmaster not to assault so brutally. Older by millennia than the Imperium that had come to claim it in the name of the Emperor, its precincts and thoroughfares were soon to become blood-slick battlefields.

While the juggernaut of compliance had made the galaxy a sterile, secular place, the Choral City remained a city of the gods.

The Precentor's Palace, a dizzying creation of gleaming marble blades and arches that shone in the sun, opened like a vast stone orchid to the sky and the polished granite of the city's wealthiest districts clustered around it like worshippers. Momus had described the palace as a hymn to power and glory, a symbol of the divine right by which Isstvan III would be ruled.

Further out from the palace and beyond the architectural perfection of the Choral City, vast multi-layered residential districts sprawled. Connected by countless walkways and bridges of glass and steel, the avenues between them were wide canyons of tree-lined boulevards in which the citizens of the Choral City lived.

The city's industrial heartland rose like climbing skeletons of steel against the eastern mountains, belching smoke as they churned out weapons to arm the planet's armies. War was coming and every Isstvanian had to be ready to fight.

But no sight in the Choral City compared to the Sirenhold.

Not even the magnificence of the palace outshone the Sirenhold, its towering walls defining the

Choral City with their immensity. The brutal battlements diminished everything around them, and
the sacred fortress of the Sirenhold humbled even
the snow-capped peaks of the mountains. Within
its walls, enormous tomb-spires reached for the
skies, their walls encrusted with monumental
sculptures that told the legends of Isstvan's mythi-
cal past.

The legends told that Isstvan himself had sung
the world into being with music that could still be
heard by the blessed Warsingers, and that he had
borne countless children with whom he populated
the first ages of the world. They became night and
day, ocean and mountain, a thousand legends
whose breath could be felt in every moment of
every day in the Choral City.

Darker carvings told of the Lost Children, the
sons and daughters who had forsaken their father
and been banished to the blasted wasteland of the
fifth planet, where they became monsters that
burned with jealousy and raised black fortresses
from which to brood upon their expulsion from
paradise.

War, treachery, revelation and death; all marched
around the Sirenhold in endless cycles of myth, the
weight of their meaning pinning the Choral City to
the soil of Isstvan III and infusing its every inhabi-
tant with their sacred purpose.

The gods of Isstvan III were said to sleep in the
Sirenhold, whispering their murderous plots in the
nightmares of children and ancients.

For a time, the myths and legends had remained as distant as they had always been, but now they walked among the people of the Choral City, and every breath of wind shrieked that the Lost Children had returned.

Without knowing why, the populace of Isstvan III had armed and unquestioningly followed the orders of Vardus Praal to defend their city. An army of well-equipped soldiers awaited the invasion they had long been promised was coming in the western marches of the city, where the Warsingers had sung a formidable web of trenches into being.

Artillery pieces parked in the gleaming canyons of the city pointed their barrels westwards, set to pound any invaders into the ground before they reached the trenches. The warriors of the Choral City would then slaughter any that survived in carefully prepared crossfire.

The defences had been meticulously planned, protecting the city from attack from the west, the only direction in which an invasion could be launched.

Or so the soldiers manning the defences had been told.

The first omen was a fire in the sky that came with the dawn.

A scattering of falling stars streaked through the blood-red dawn, burning through the sky like fiery tears.

The sentries in the trenches saw them falling in bright spears of fire, the first burning object smashing into the trenches amid a plume of mud and flame.

At the speed of thought, the word raced around the Choral City that the Lost Children had returned, that the prophecies of myth were coming true,

They were proven right when the drop-pods burst open and the Astartes of the Death Guard Legion emerged.

And the killing began.

PART TWO

THE CHORAL CITY

EIGHT

Soldiers from hell
Butchery
Betrayal

THIRTY SECONDS!' YELLED Vipus, his voice barely audible over the screaming jets as the drop-pod sliced through Isstvan III's atmosphere. The Astartes of Locasta were bathed in red light and for a moment Loken imagined what they would look like to the people of the Choral City when the assault began – warriors from another world, soldiers from hell.

'What's our landing point looking like?' shouted Loken.

Vipus glanced at the readout on a pict-screen mounted above his head. 'Drifting! We'll hit the target, but off-centre. I hate these things. Give me a stormbird any day!'

Loken didn't bother replying, barely able to hear Nero as the atmosphere thickened beneath the

drop-pod and the jets on its underside kicked in.
The drop-pod shuddered and began heating up as
the enormous forces pushing against it turned to
fire and noise.

He sat through the last few minutes while everything around him was noise, unable to see the
enemy he was about to fight and relinquishing control over his fate until the drop-pod hit.

Nero had been right when he said he had pre-
ferred an assault delivered by stormbird, the
precise, surgical nature of an airborne assault far
preferable to a warrior than this hurtling descent
from above.

But the Warmaster had decided that the speartip
would be deployed by drop-pod, reasoning –
rightly, Loken admitted – that thousands of Astartes
smashing into the defenders' midst without warning would be more psychologically devastating.
Loken ran through the moment the drop-pod
would hit in his mind, preparing himself for when
the hatch charges would blow open.

He gripped his bolter tightly, and checked for the
tenth time that his chainsword was in its scabbard
at his side. Loken was ready.

'Ten seconds, Locasta,' shouted Vipus.

Barely a second later, the drop-pod impacted with
such force that Loken's head snapped back and suddenly the noise was gone and everything went
black.

✠ ✠ ✠

LUCIUS KILLED HIS first foe without even breaking stride.

The dead man's armour was like glass, shimmering and iridescent, and his halberd's blade was fashioned from the same reflective substance. A mask of stained glass covered his face, the mouth represented by leading and filled with teeth of gem-like triangles.

Lucius slid his sword clear, blood smoking from its edge, as the soldier slumped to the floor. A curved arch of marble shone red in the dawn's early light above him and a swirl of dust and debris drifted around the drop-pod he had just leapt from.

The Precentor's Palace stood before him, vast and astonishing, a stone flower with the spire at its centre like a spectacular twist of overlapping granite petals.

More drop-pods hammered into the ground behind him, the plaza around the palace's north entrances the main objective of the Emperor's Children. A nearby drop-pod blew open and Ancient Rylanor stepped from its red-lit interior, his assault cannon already cycling and tracking for targets.

'Nasicae!' yelled Lucius. 'To me!'

Lucius saw a flash of coloured glass from inside the palace, movement beyond the sweeping stone panels of the entrance hall.

More palace guards reacted to the sudden, shocking assault, but contrary to what Lucius had been expecting, they weren't screaming or begging for mercy. They weren't even fleeing, or standing stock still, numb with shock.

With a terrible war cry the palace guard charged and Lucius laughed, glad to be facing a foe with some backbone. He levelled his sword and ran towards them, Squad Nasicae following behind him, weapons at the ready.

A hundred palace guardians ran at them, resplendent in their glass armour. They formed a line before the Astartes, levelled their halberds, and opened fire.

Searing needles of silver filled the air around Lucius, gouging the armour of his shoulder guard and leg. Lucius lifted his sword arm to shield his head and the needles spat from the glowing blade of his sword. Where they hit the stone around the entrance it bubbled and hissed like acid.

One of Nasicae fell beside Lucius, one arm molten and his abdomen bubbling.

'Perfection and death!' cried Lucius, running through the white-hot silver needles. The Emperor's Children and the Palace Guard clashed with a sound like a million windows breaking, the terrible screaming of the halberd-guns giving way to the clash of blade against armour and point-blank bolter fire.

Lucius's first sword blow hacked through a halberd shaft and tore through the throat of the man before him. Sightless glass eyes glared back at him, blood pumping from the guard's ruined throat, and Lucius tore the helm from his foe's head to better savour the sensation of his death.

A plasma pistol spat a tongue of liquid fire that wreathed an enemy soldier from head to foot, but the man kept fighting, sweeping his halberd down to cut deep into one of Lucius's men before another Astartes ripped off his head with a chainsword.

Lucius pivoted on one foot from a halberd strike and hammered the hilt of his sword into his opponent's face, feeling a tight anger that the faceplate held. The guard staggered away from him and Lucius reversed his grip and thrust the blade through the gap between the glass plates at the guard's waist, feeling the blade's energy field burning through abdomen and spine.

These guards were slowing the Emperor's Children down, buying precious moments with their lives for something deeper in the palace. As much as Lucius was revelling in the sensations of the slaughter, the smell of the blood, the searing stink of flesh as the heat of his blade scorched it and the pounding of blood in veins, he knew he could not afford to give the defenders such moments.

Lucius ran onwards, slicing his blade through limbs and throats as he ran. He fought as though following the steps of an elaborate dance, a dance where he played the part of the victor and the enemy were there only to die. The Palace Guard were dying around him and his armour was drenched with their blood. He laughed in sheer joy.

Warriors still fought behind him, but Lucius had to press on before the palace guard was able to stall their advance with more men in front of them.

'Squad Quemondil! Rethaerin! Kill these and then follow me!'

Fire sawed from every direction as the Emperor's Children forced their way towards the junction Lucius had reached. The swordsman darted his head past the corner, seeing a vast indoor seascape. A plume of water cascaded through a hole in the centre of a colossal granite dome, and a shaft of pink light fell alongside the water, sending brilliant rainbows of colour between the arches formed by the petals of the dome's surface.

Islands rose from the indoor sea that took up most of the dome, each topped by picturesque follies of white and gold.

Thousands of palace guards massed in the dome, splashing towards them through the waist-deep sea and taking up positions among the follies. Most wore the glassy armour of the men still dying behind Lucius, but many others were clad in far more elaborate suits of bright silver. Others still were wrapped in long streamers of silk that rippled behind them like smoke as they moved.

Rylanor emerged into the dome behind Lucius, his assault cannon smoking and the chisel-like grips of his power fist thick with blood.

'They're massing,' spat Lucius. 'Where are the damned World Eaters?'

'We shall have to win the palace by ourselves,' replied Rylanor, his voice grating from deep within his sarcophagus.

Lucius nodded, pleased that they would be able to shame the World Eaters. 'Ancient, cover us. Emperor's Children, break and cover fire! Nasicae, keep up this time!'

Ancient Rylanor stepped out from the junction and a spectacular wave of fire sheared through the air around him, a storm of heavy calibre shell casings and oil-soaked fumes streaming from the cannon mounted on his shoulder.

His explosive fire shredded the stone of the foremost island's follies, broken and bloodied bodies tumbling from the shattered wreckage.

'Go!' shouted Lucius, but the Emperor's Children were already charging, their training so thorough that every warrior already knew his place in the complex pattern of overlapping fire and movement that sent the strike force sweeping into the dome.

Savage joy lit up Lucius's face as he charged, the thrill of battle and the sensations of killing stimulating his body with wondrous excess.

In a swirling cacophony of noise, the perfection of death had come to the Choral City.

ON THE SOUTHERN side of the palace, a strange organically formed building clung to the side of the palace like a parasite, its bulging, liquid shape more akin to something that had been grown than something built. Its pale marble was threaded with dark veins and the masses of its battlements hung like ripened fruit. From the expanse of marble monument slabs marking the passing of the city's finest and most powerful citizens, it was clear that this was a sacred place.

Known as the Temple of the Song, it was a memorial to the music that Father Isstvan had sung to bring all things into existence.

It was also the objective of the World Eaters.

The word that the invasion had begun was already out by the time the first World Eaters' drop-pods crashed into the plaza, shattering gravestones and throwing slabs of marble into the air. Strange music keened through the morning air, calling the people of the Choral City from their homes and demanding that they take up arms. The soldiers from the nearby city barracks grabbed their guns as the Warsingers appeared on the battlements of the Temple to sing the song of death for the invaders.

Called by the Warsingers' laments, the people of the city gathered in the streets and streamed towards the battle.

The World Eaters' strike force was led by Captain Ehrlen, and as he emerged from his drop-pod, he was expecting the trained soldiers that Angron had briefed them on, not thousands of screaming citizens swarming onto the plaza. They came in a tide, armed with anything and everything they had in their homes, but it was not the weapons they carried but their sheer numbers and the terrible song that spoke of killing and murder that made them deadly.

'World Eaters, to me!' yelled Ehrlen, hefting his bolter and aiming it into the mass of charging people.

The white-armoured warriors of the World Eaters formed a firing line around him, turning their bolters outwards.

'Fire!' shouted Ehrlen and the first ranks of the Choral City's inhabitants were cut down by the deadly volley, but the oncoming mass rose up like a spring tide as they clambered over the bodies of the dead.

As the gap between the two forces closed, the World Eaters put up their bolters and drew their chainswords.

Ehreln saw the unreasoning hatred in the eyes of his enemies and knew that this battle was soon to turn into a massacre.

If there was one thing at which the World Eaters excelled, it was massacre.

'DAMN IT,' spat Vipus. 'We must have hit something on the way in.'

Loken forced his eyes open. A slice of light where the drop-pod had broken open provided the only illumination, but it was enough for him to check that he was still in once piece.

He was battered, but could feel no evidence of anything more than that.

'Locasta, sound off!' ordered Vipus. The warriors of Locasta shouted their names, and Loken was relieved to hear that none appeared to have been injured in the impact. He undid the buckle of his grav-harness and rolled to his feet, the drop-pod canted at an unnatural angle. He pulled his bolter

from the rack and pushed his way through the nar-
row opening broken in the side of the drop-pod.

As he emerged into the bright sunshine, he saw
that they had struck a projecting pier of stone on
one of the towers, the rubble of its destruction scattered around the ruined drop-pod. He circled the
wreckage, seeing that they were at least two hundred metres above the ground, wedged amongst the
massive battlements of the Sirenhold.

To his left he saw spectacular tomb-spires
encrusted with statues, while to his right was the
Choral City itself, its magnificent structures bathed
in the rosy glow of the sunrise. From this vantage
point Loken could see the whole city, the extraordinary stone flower of the palace and the western
defences like scars across the landscape.

Loken could hear gunfire from the direction of
the palace and realised that the Emperor's Children
and World Eaters were already fighting the enemy.
Gunfire echoed from below, Sons of Horus units
fighting in the tangle of shrines and statuary that
filled the canyons between the tomb-spires.

'We need a way down,' said Loken as Locasta
pulled themselves from the wreckage of the drop-
pod. Vipus jogged over with his gun at the ready.

'Bloody ground surveyors must have missed the
projections,' he grumbled.

'That's what it looks like,' agreed Loken, as he
saw another drop-pod ricochet from the side of a
tomb-spire and careen downwards in a shower of
broken statues.

'Our warriors are dying,' he said bitterly. 'Someone's going to pay for this.'

'We look spread out,' said Vipus, glancing down into the Sirenhold. Between the tomb-spires, smaller shrines and temples butted against one another in a complex jigsaw.

Plumes of black smoke and explosions were already rising from the fighting.

'We need a place to regroup,' said Loken. He flicked to Torgaddon's vox-channel. 'Tarik? Loken here, where are you?'

A burst of static was his only reply.

He looked across the Sirenhold and saw one tomb-spire close to the wall, its many levels supported by columns wrought into the shapes of monsters and its top sheared off by the impact of a drop-pod. 'Damn. If you can hear me, Tarik, make for the spire by the western wall, the one with the smashed top. Regroup there. I'm heading down to you.'

'Anything?' asked Vipus.

'No. The vox is a mess. Something's interrupting it.'

'The spires?'

'It would take more than that,' said Loken. 'Come on. Let's find a way off this damn wall.'

Vipus nodded and turned to his men. 'Locasta, start looking for a way down.'

Loken leaned over the battlements as Locasta fanned out to obey their leader's command. Beneath him he could see the diminutive figures of

Astartes fighting black-armoured warriors in streaming firefight. He turned away, desperate to find a way down.

'Here!' shouted Brother Casto, Locasta's flamer bearer. 'A stairway.'

'Good work,' said Loken, making his way over to see what Casto had found. Sure enough, hidden behind a tall, eroded statue of an ancient warrior was a dark stairway cut into the sand-coloured stone. The passageway looked rough and unfinished, the stone pitted and crumbling with age.

'Move,' said Vipus. 'Casto, lead the way.'

'Yes, captain,' replied Casto, plunging into the gloom of the passageway. Loken and Vipus followed him, the entrance barely wide enough for their armoured bodies. The stairs descended for roughly ten metres before opening into a wide, low-ceilinged gallery.

'The wall must be riddled,' said Vipus.

'Catacombs,' said Loken, pointing to niches cut into the walls that held the mouldering remains of skeletons, some still swaddled in tattered cloth.

Casto led them along the gallery, the bodies becoming more numerous the deeper they went, the skeletal remains piled two or three deep.

Vipus snapped around suddenly, bolter up and finger on the trigger.

'Vipus?'

'I thought I heard something.'

'We're clear behind,' said Loken. 'Keep moving and focus. This could…'

'Movement!' said Casto, sending a blast of orange-yellow fire from his flamer into the darkness ahead of him.

'Casto!' barked Vipus. 'Report! What do you see?'

Casto paused. 'I don't know. Whatever it was, it's gone now.'

The niches ahead guttered with flames, hungrily devouring the bare bones. Loken could see that there was no enemy up ahead, only Isstvanian dead.

'There's nothing there now,' said Vipus. 'Stay focused, Locasta, and no jumping at shadows! You are Sons of Horus!'

The squad picked up the pace, shaking thoughts of hidden enemies from their minds, as they moved rapidly past the burning grave-niches.

The gallery opened into a large chamber, Loken guessing that it must have filled the width of the wall. The only light was from the dancing flame at the end of Casto's flamer, the yellow light picking out the massive stone blocks of a tomb.

Loken saw a sarcophagus of black granite, surrounded by statues of kneeling people with their heads bowed and hands chained before them. Panels set into the walls were covered in carvings where human forms acted out ceremonial scenes of war.

'Casto, move up,' said Vipus. 'Find us a way down.'

Loken approached the sarcophagus, running his hand down its vast length. Its lid was carved to represent a human figure, but he knew that it could not be a literal portrait of the body inside; its face had no features save for a pair of triangular eyes fashioned from chips of coloured glass.

Loken could hear the song from the Sirenhold outside, even through the layers of stone, a single mournful tone that rose and fell, winding its way from the tomb-spires.

'Warsinger,' said Loken bitterly. 'They're fighting back. We need to get down there.'

THE SILVER-ARMOURED palace guards started flying.

Surrounded by burning arcs of white energy, they leapt over the advancing Emperor's Children, gleaming, leaf shaped blades slicing downwards from wrist-mounted weapons.

Lucius rolled to avoid a hail of blades, the silver guard swooping low to behead two of Squad Quemondil, the charged blades cutting through their armour with horrific ease.

He slid into the water, finding that it only reached his waist. Above him, the halberd-guns of the palace guard were spraying silver fire at the Emperor's Children, but the Astartes were moving and firing with their customary discipline. Even the bizarre sight of the palace's defenders did not dissuade them from their patterns of movement and covering fire. A body fell into the water next to him, its head blasted away by bolter fire and blood pouring into the water in a scarlet bloom.

Lucius saw that the silver guards were too quick and turned too nimbly for conventional engagement. He would just have to engage them unconventionally.

One of the silver guards dived towards him and Lucius could see the intricate filigree on the man's armour, the tiny gold threads like veins on the breastplate and greaves and the scrollwork that covered his face.

The guard dived like a seabird, firing a bright blade from his wrist.

Lucius turned the missile aside with his sword and leapt to meet his opponent. The guard twisted in the air, trying to avoid Lucius, but he was too close. Lucius swung his sword and sliced the guard's arm from his body, his crackling sword searing through the armour. Blood sprayed from the smouldering wound and the guard fell, twisting back towards the water.

Lucius fell with the dead man, splashing back into the lake as the Emperor's Children finally reached their enemy. Volleys of bolter fire scoured the islands and his warriors advanced relentlessly on the survivors. The palace guards were backing away, forming a tighter and tighter circle. Glass-armoured guards lay dead in heaps and the artificial lake was ruddy pink and choked with bodies.

Rylanor's assault cannon sent fire tearing through the silk-clad guards, whose preternatural speed couldn't save them as the cannon shells turned the interior of the dome into a killing ground. Another silver guard fell, bolter fire ripping through his armour.

Squad Nasicae joined Lucius and he grinned wolfishly at them, elated at the prospect of fighting more of the silver guards.

'They're running,' said Lucius. 'Keep them on the back foot. Keep pressing on.'

'Squad Kaitheron's reporting from the plaza,' said Brother Scetherin. 'The World Eaters are fighting around the temple on the north side.'

'Still?'

'Sounds like they're holding off half the city.'

'Ha! They can have them. It's what the World Eaters are good at,' laughed Lucius, relishing the certain knowledge of his superiority.

Nothing in the galaxy could match that feeling, but already it was fading and he knew he would have to procure yet more opponents to satisfy his hunger for battle.

'We press on to the throne room,' he said. 'Ancient Rylanor, secure our rear. The rest of you, we're going for Praal. Follow me. If you can't keep up, go and join the Death Guard!'

His warriors cheered as they followed Lucius into the heart of the palace.

Every one of them wanted to kill Praal and hold his head aloft on the palace battlements so the whole of the Choral City could see.

Only Lucius was certain that Praal's head would be his.

THE ANDRONIUS WAS quiet and tense, its palatial rooms dark and its long, echoing corridors empty of all but menials. The ship's engines pulsed dimly in the stern, only the rumble of directional thrusters shuddering through the ship. Every station was manned, every blast door was sealed and Tarvitz knew a battle alert when he saw it.

What confused him was the fact that the Isstvanians had no fleet to fight.

The hull groaned and Tarvitz felt a deep rumbling through the metal deck, sensing the motion of the ship before the artificial gravity compensated. Ever since the first wave of the speartip had launched, the vessel had been moving, and Tarvitz knew that his suspicions of something amiss were well-founded.

According to the mission briefings he had read earlier, Fulgrim's flagship had been assigned the role of launching the second wave once the palace and the Sirenhold had been taken. There was no need to move.

The only reason to move a vessel after a launch was to move into low orbit in preparation for a bombardment. Though he told himself he was being paranoid, Tarvitz knew that he had to see for himself what was going on.

He made his way swiftly through the *Andronius* towards the gun decks, keeping clear of such grand chambers as the Tarselian Amphitheatre and the columned grandeur of the Monument Hall. He kept to the areas of the ship where his presence would go unchallenged, and where those who might recognise him were unlikely to see him.

He had told Rylanor that he wanted to renounce his position of honour in the speartip to replace Captain Odovocar as Eidolon's senior staff officer, relaying the commander's orders to the surface, but it would only be a matter of time before his subterfuge was discovered.

Tarvitz descended into the lower reaches of the ship, far from where the Emperor's Children dwelt in the most magnificent parts of the *Andronius*. The rest of the ship, inhabited by servitors and menials, was more functional and Tarvitz knew he would pass without challenge here.

The darkness closed around Tarvitz and the yawning chasms of the engine structures opened out many hundreds of metres below the gantry on which he stood. Above the engine spaces were the reeking gun decks, where mighty cannons, weapons that could level cities, were housed in massive, armoured revetments.

'Stand by for ordnance,' chimed an automated, metallic voice. Tarvitz felt the ship shift again, and this time he could hear the creak of the hull as the planet's upper atmosphere raised the temperature of the outer hull.

Tarvitz descended an iron staircase at the end of the dark gantry and the vast expanse of the gun deck sprawled before him, a titanic vault that ran the length of the vessel. Huge, hissing cranes fed the guns, lifting tank-sized shells from the magazine decks through blast proof doors. Gunners and loaders sweated with their riggers, each gun serviced by a hundred men who hauled on thick chains and levers in preparation for their firing. Servitors distributed water to the gun crews and Mechanicum adepts maintained vigil on the weapons to ensure they were properly calibrated.

Tarvitz felt his resolve harden and his anger grow at the sight of the guns being made ready. Who were they planning to fire on? With thousands of Astartes on the planet's surface, bombarding the Choral City was absurd, yet here the guns were, loaded and ready to unleash hell.

He doubted that the men crewing these weapons knew which planet they were in orbit over or even who they would be shooting at. Entire communities flourished below the decks of a starship and it was perfectly possible that these men had no idea who they were about to destroy.

He reached the end of the staircase and set foot on the deck, its high ceiling soaring above him like a mighty cathedral to destructive power. Tarvitz heard footsteps approaching and turned to see a robed adept in the livery of the Mechanicum.

'Captain,' inquired the adept, 'is there something amiss?'

'No,' said Tarvitz. 'I am just here to ensure that everything is proceeding normally.'

'I can assure you, lord, that preparations for the bombardment are proceeding exactly as planned. The warheads will be launched prior to the deployment of the second wave.'

'Warheads?' asked Tarvitz.

'Yes, captain,' said the adept. 'All bombardment cannons are loaded with airbursting warheads loaded with virus bombs as specified in our order of battle.'

'Virus bombs,' said Tarvitz, fighting to hold back his revulsion at what the adept was telling him.

'Is everything all right, captain?' asked the adept, noticing the change in his expression.

'I'm fine,' Tarvitz lied, feeling as if his legs would give way any second. 'You can return to your duties.'

The adept nodded and set off towards one of the guns.

Virus bombs…

Weapons so terrible and forbidden that only the Warmaster himself, and the Emperor before him, could ever sanction their use.

Each warhead would unleash the life eater virus, a rampant organism that destroyed life in all its forms and wiped out every shred of organic matter on the surface of a planet within hours. The magnitude of this new knowledge, and its implications, staggered Tarvitz and he felt his breath coming in short, painful gasps as he attempted to reconcile what he knew with what he had just learned.

His Legion was preparing to kill the planet below and he knew with sudden clarity that it could not be alone in this. To saturate a planet with enough virus warheads to destroy all life would take many ships and with a sick jolt of horror, he knew that such an order could only have come from the Warmaster.

For reasons Tarvitz could not even begin to guess at, the Warmaster had chosen to betray fully a third of his warriors, exterminating them in one fell swoop.

'I have to warn them,' he hissed, turning and running for the embarkation deck.

NINE

The power of a god
Regrouping
Honour brothers

THE STRATEGIUM WAS dark, lit only by braziers that burned with a flickering green flame. Where once the banners of the Legion's battle companies had hung from its walls, they were now replaced with those of the warrior lodge. The company banners had been taken down shortly after the speartip had been deployed and the message was clear: the lodge now had primacy within the Sons of Horus. The platform from which the Warmaster had addressed the officers of his fleet now held a lectern upon which rested the *Book of Lorgar*.

The Warmaster sat on the strategium throne, watching reports coming in from Isstvan III on the battery of pict-screens before him.

The emerald light picked out the edges of his armour and reflected from the amber gemstone forming the eye upon his breastplate. Reams of combat statistics streamed past and pict-relays showed the unfolding battles in the Choral City. The World Eaters were in the centre of an epic struggle. Thousands of people were swarming into the plaza before the Precentor's Palace, and the streets flowed with rivers of blood as the Astartes slaughtered wave after wave of Isstvanians that charged into their guns and chainblades.

The palace itself was intact, only a few palls of smoke indicating the battle raging through it as the Emperor's Children fought their way through its guards.

Vardus Praal would be dead soon, though Horus cared nothing for the fate of Isstvan III's rogue governor. His rebellion had simply given Horus the chance to rid himself of those he knew would never follow him on his great march to Terra.

Horus looked up as Erebus approached.

'First chaplain,' said Horus sternly. 'Matters are delicate. Do not disturb me needlessly.'

'There is news from Prospero,' said Erebus, unperturbed. The shadow whisperers clung to him, darting around his feet and the crozius he wore at his waist.

'Magnus?' asked Horus, suddenly interested.

'He lives yet,' said Erebus, 'but not for the lack of effort on the part of the Wolves of Fenris.'

'Magnus lives,' snarled Horus. 'Then he may yet be a danger.'

'No,' assured Erebus. 'The spires of Prospero have fallen and the warp echoes with the powerful sorcery Magnus used to save his warriors and escape.'

'Always sorcery,' said Horus. 'Where did he escape to?'

'I do not know yet,' said Erebus, 'but wherever he goes, the Emperor's dogs will hunt him down.'

'And he will either join us or die alone in the wilderness,' said Horus, thoughtfully. 'To think that so much depends on the personalities of so few. Magnus was nearly my deadliest enemy, perhaps as dangerous as the Emperor himself. Now he has no choice but to follow us until the very end. If Fulgrim brings Ferrus Magnus into the fold then we have as good as won.'

Horus waved dismissively at the viewscreens depicting the battle in the Choral City. 'The Isstvanians believe the gods have come to destroy them and in a way they are right. Life and death are mine to dispense. What is that if not the power of a god?'

'CAPTAIN LOKEN. SERGEANT Vipus. It is good to see you both,' said Sergeant Lachost, hunkered down in the shattered shell of a shrine to one of Isstvan III's ancestors. 'We've been trying to raise all the squads. They're all over the place. The speartip's shattered.'

'Then we'll re-forge it here,' replied Loken.

Sporadic fire rattled through the valley, so he took cover beside Lachost. The sergeant's command squad was arrayed around the shrine ruin, bolters trained and occasionally snapping off shots at the

shapes that darted through the shadows. Vipus and
the survivors of Locasta huddled in the ruins with
them.

The enemy wore the armour of ancient Isstvan,
tarnished bands of silver and black, and carried
strange relic-weapons, rapid-firing crossbows that
hurled bolts of molten silver.

Tales of heroism were emerging from the scores
of individual battles among the tomb-spires as
Sons of Horus units fought off the soldiers of the
Sirenhold.

'We've got good cover, and a position we can
hold,' said Vipus. 'We can gather the squads here
and launch a thrust into the enemy.'

Loken nodded as Torgaddon ducked into cover
beside them, the Sons of Horus he had brought
with him joining Lachost's men at the walls.

He grinned at Loken and said, 'What kept you,
Garvi?'

'We had to come down from the top of the wall,'
said Loken. 'Where are your warriors?'

'They're everywhere,' said Torgaddon. 'They're
making their way to this spire, but a lot of the
squads are cut off. The Sirenhold was garrisoned by
some... elites, I suppose. They had a hell of an
armoury here, ancient things, looks like advanced
tech.'

Loken nodded as Torgaddon continued.

'Well, this spire is clear at least. I've got Vaddon
and Lachost setting up a command post on the
lower level and we can just hold this position for

now. There are three more Legions in the Choral City and the rest of the Sons of Horus in orbit. There's no need–'

'The enemy has the field,' replied Loken sharply. 'They can surround us. There are catacombs beneath our feet they could use to get around us. No, if we stay put they will find a way to get to us. This is their territory. We strike as soon as we can. This is a speartip and it is up to us to drive it home.'

'Where?' asked Torgaddon.

'The tomb-spires,' said Loken. 'We hit them one by one. Storm them, kill whatever we find and move on. We keep going and force them onto the back foot.'

'Most of our speartip is on its way, captain,' said Lachost.

'Good,' replied Loken, looking up at the spires around the shrine.

The shrine was in a valley formed by the spire they had come down and the next spire along, a brutal cylinder of stone with glowering faces carved into its surface. Dozens of arches around its base offered entrance and cover, their darkness occasionally lit by a brief flash of gunfire.

A tangle of shrines littered the ground between the towers, statues of the Choral City's notable dead jutting from piles of ornate architecture or the ruins of temples.

Loken pointed to the tomb-spire across the valley. 'As soon as we have enough warriors for a full thrust, that's what we hit. Lachost, start securing the shrines around us to give us a good jumping-off point, and get some men up on the first levels of this spire to provide covering fire. Heavy weapons if you've got them.'

Gunfire echoed from the east and Loken saw the forms of Astartes moving towards them: Sons of Horus in the livery of Eskhalen Squad. More warriors were converging on their position, each fighting their own running battles among the shrines as they sought to regroup.

'This is more than a burial ground,' said Loken. 'Whatever happened to Isstvan III, it started here. This force is religious and this is their church.'

'No wonder they're crazy,' replied Torgaddon scornfully. 'Madmen love their gods.'

THE CONTROLS OF the Thunderhawk were loose, the ship trying to flip away from Tarvitz and go tumbling through space. He had only the most rudimentary training on these newer additions to the Astartes armoury, and most of that had been in atmosphere, skimming low over battlefields to drop troops or add fire support.

Tarvitz could see Isstvan III through the armoured glass of the viewing bay, a crescent of sunlight creeping across its surface. Somewhere near the edge of the shining crescent was the city where his battle-brothers, and those of three other Legions, were fighting, unaware that they had already been betrayed.

'Thunderhawk, identify yourself,' said a voice through the gunship's vox. He must have entered the engagement envelope of the *Andronius* and the defence turrets had acquired him as a target. If he was lucky, he would have a few moments before the turrets locked on, moments when he could put as much distance between his stolen Thunderhawk and the *Andronius*.

'Thunderhawk, identify yourself,' repeated the voice and he knew that he had to stall in order to give himself time to get clear of the defence turrets.

'Captain Saul Tarvitz, travelling to the *Endurance* on liaison duty.'

'Wait for authorisation.'

He knew he wouldn't get authorisation, but each second took him further from the *Andronius* and closer to the planet's surface.

He pushed the Thunderhawk as hard as he dared, listening to the hiss of static coming from the vox, hoping against hope that somehow they would believe him and allow him to go on his way.

'Stand down, Thunderhawk,' said the voice. 'Return to the *Andronius* immediately.'

'Negative, *Andronius*,' replied Tarvitz. 'Transmission is breaking up.'

It was a cheap ploy, but one that might give him a few seconds more.

'I repeat, stand–'

'Go to hell,' replied Tarvitz.

Tarvitz checked the navigational pict for signs of pursuit, pleased to see that there were none yet, and wrenched the Thunderhawk down towards Isstvan III.

✠ ✠ ✠

'THE PRIDE OF *the Emperor* is in transit,' announced Saeverin, senior deck officer of the *Andronius*. 'Though the vessel's Navigator claims to be encountering difficulties. Lord Fulgrim will not be with us any time soon.'

'Does he send any word of his mission?' asked Eidolon, standing at his shoulder.

'Communications are still very poor,' said Saeverin hesitantly, 'but what we have does not sound encouraging.'

'Then we will have to compensate with the excellence of our conduct and the perfection of our Legion,' said Eidolon. 'The other Legions may be more savage or resilient or stealthy, but none of them approaches the perfection of the Emperor's Children. No matter what lies ahead, we must never let go of that.'

'Of course, commander,' said Saeverin, as his console lit up with a series of warning lights. His hands danced over the console and he turned to face Eidolon.

'Lord commander,' he said. 'We may have a problem.'

'Do not speak to me of problems,' said Eidolon.

'Defence control has just informed me that they have picked up a Thunderhawk heading for the planet's surface.'

'One of ours?'

'It appears so,' confirmed Saeverin, bending over his console. 'Getting confirmation now.'

'Who's piloting it?' demanded Eidolon. 'No one is authorised to travel to the surface.'

'The last communication with the Thunderhawk indicates that it is Captain Saul Tarvitz.'

'Tarvitz?' said Eidolon. 'Damn him, but he is a thorn in my side.'

'It's certainly him,' said Captain Saeverin. 'It looks like he took one of the Thunderhawks from the planetside embarkation deck.'

'Where is he heading?' asked Eidolon, 'exactly.'

'The Choral City,' replied Saeverin.

Eidolon smiled. 'He's trying to warn them. He thinks he can make a difference. I thought we could use him, but he's too damn stubborn and now he's got it into his head that he's a hero. Saeverin, get some fighters out there and shoot him down. We don't need any complications now.'

'Aye, sir,' nodded Saeverin. 'Fighters launching in two minutes.'

MERSADIE WRANG OUT the cloth and draped it over Euphrati's forehead. Euphrati moaned and shook, her arms thrashing as if she was throwing a fit. She looked as pale and thin as a corpse.

'I'm here,' said Mersadie, even though she suspected the comatose imagist couldn't hear her. She didn't understand what Euphrati was going through, and it made her feel so useless.

For reasons she didn't quite understand, she had stayed with Kyril Sindermann and Euphrati as they moved around the ship. The *Vengeful Spirit* was the size of a city and it had plenty of places in which to hide.

Word of their coming went ahead of them and wherever they went, grime-streaked engine crewmen or boiler-suited maintenance workers were there to show them to safety, supply them with food and water and catch a glimpse of the saint. At present, they sheltered inside one of the engine housings, a massive hollow tube that was normally full of burning plasma and great thrusting pistons. Now the engine was decommissioned for maintenance and it made for a good bolt-hole, hidden and secret despite its vast dimensions.

Sindermann slept on a thin blanket beside Euphrati and the old man had never looked more exhausted. His thin limbs were spotted and bony, his cheeks sunken and hollow.

One of the engine crew hurried up to the nook where Keeler lay on a bundle of blankets and clothes. He was stripped to the waist and covered in grease, a huge and muscular man who was moved to kneel meekly a short distance from the bed of his saint.

'Miss Oliton,' he said reverentially. 'Is there anything you or the saint need?'

'Water,' said Mersadie. 'Clean water, and Kyril asked for more paper, too.'

The crewman's eyes lit up. 'He's writing something?'

Mersadie wished she hadn't mentioned it.

'He's collecting his thoughts for a speech,' she said. 'He's still an iterator, after all. If you can find some medical supplies as well, that would be useful, she's dehydrated.'

'The Emperor will preserve her,' said the crewman, worry in his voice.

'I'm sure he will, but we have to give him all the help we can,' replied Mersadie, trying not to sound as condescending as she felt.

The effect the comatose Euphrati had on the crew was extraordinary, a miracle in itself. Her very presence seemed to focus the doubts and wishes of so many people into an iron-strong faith in a distant Emperor.

'We'll get what we can,' said the crewman. 'We have people in the commissary and medical suites.'

He reached forward to touch Euphrati's blanket and murmured a quiet prayer to his Emperor. As the crewman left she whispered her own perfunctory prayer. After all, the Emperor was more real than any of the so-called gods the Crusade had come across.

'Deliver us, Emperor,' she said quietly, 'from all of this.'

She looked down sadly and caught her breath as Euphrati stirred and opened her eyes, like someone awakening from a deep sleep. Mersadie reached down slowly, afraid that if she moved too quickly she might shatter this brittle miracle, and took the imagists hand in hers.

'Euphrati,' she whispered softly. 'Can you hear me?'

Euphrati Keeler's mouth fell open and she screamed in terror.

'ARE YOU SURE?' asked Captain Garro of the Death Guard, limping on his newly replaced augmetic leg.

The gyros had not yet meshed with his nervous system and, much to his fury, he had been denied a place in the Death Guard speartip. The bridge of the *Eisenstein* was open to the workings of the ship, as was typical with the Death Guard fleet, since Mortarion despised ornamentation of any kind.

The bridge was a skeletal framework suspended among the ship's guts with massive coolant pipes looming overhead like knots of metallic entrails. The bridge crew bent over a platform inset with cogitator banks, their faces illuminated in harsh greens and blues.

'Very sure, captain,' replied the communications officer, reading from the data-slate in his hand. 'An Emperor's Children Thunderhawk is passing through our engagement zone.'

Garro took the data-slate from the officer and sure enough, there was a Thunderhawk gunship passing close to the *Eisenstein*, a pack of fighters at its heels.

'Smells like trouble,' said Garro. 'Put us on an intercept course.'

'Yes, captain,' said the deck officer, turning smartly and heading for the helm.

Within moments the engines flared into life, vast pistons pumping through the oily shadows that surrounded the bridge. The *Eisenstein* tilted as it began a ponderous turn towards the approaching Thunderhawk.

* * *

THE SCREAM HURLED Kyril Sindermann from sleep with the force of a thunderbolt and he felt his heart thudding against his ribs in fright.

'What?' he managed before seeing Euphrati sitting bolt upright in bed and screaming fit to burst her lungs. He scrambled to his feet as Mersadie tried to put her arms around the screaming imagist. Keeler thrashed like a madwoman and Sindermann rushed over to help, putting his arms out as if to embrace them both.

The moment his fingers touched Euphrati he felt the heat radiating from her, wanting to recoil in pain, but feeling as though his hands were locked to her flesh. His eyes met Mersadie's and he knew from the terror he saw there that she felt the same thing.

He whimpered as his vision blurred and darkened, as though he were having a heart attack. Images tumbled through his brain, dark and monstrous, and he fought to hold onto his sanity as visions of pure evil assailed him.

Death, like a black seething mantle, hung over everything. Sinderman saw Mersadie's delicate, coal dark face overcome with it, her features sinking in corruption.

Tendrils of darkness wound through the air, destroying whatever they touched. He screamed as he saw the flesh sloughing from Mersadie's bones, looking down at his hands to see them rotting away before his eyes. His skin peeled back, the bones maggot-white.

Then it was gone, the black, rotting death lifted from him and Sindermann could see their hiding place once again, unchanged since he had laid down to catch a few fitful hours of sleep. He stumbled away from Euphrati and with one look saw that Mersadie had experienced the same thing – horrendous, concentrated decay.

Sindermann put a hand to his chest, feeling his old heart working overtime.

'Oh, no...' Mersadie was moaning. 'Please... what is...?'

'This is betrayal,' said Keeler, her voice suddenly strong as she turned towards Sindermann, 'and it is happening now. You need to tell them. Tell them all, Kyril!'

Keeler's eyes closed and she slumped against Mersadie, who held her as she sobbed.

TARVITZ WRESTLED WITH the Thunderhawk controls. Streaks of bright crimson sheared past the cockpit – the fighter craft were on his tail, spraying ruby-red lances of gunfire at him.

Isstvan III wheeled in front of him as the gunship spun in the viewscreen.

Impacts thudded into the back of the Thunderhawk and he felt the controls lurch in his hands. He answered by ripping his craft upwards, hearing the engines shriek in complaint beneath him as they flipped the gunship's mass out of the enemy lines of fire. Loud juddering noises from behind him spoke of something giving way in one of the engines. Red warning lights and crisis telltales lit up the cockpit.

The angry blips of the fighters loomed large in the tactical display.

The vox-unit sparked again and he reached to turn it off, not wanting to hear gloating taunts as he was destroyed and any hope of warning was lost. His hand paused as he heard a familiar voice say, 'Thunderhawk on a closing course with the *Eisenstein*, identify yourself.'

Tarvitz wanted to cry in relief as he recognised the voice of his honour brother.

'Nathaniel?' he cried. 'It's Saul. It's good to hear your voice, my brother!'

'Saul?' asked Garro. 'What in the name of the Emperor is going on? Are those fighters trying to shoot you down?'

'Yes!' shouted Tarvitz, tearing the Thunderhawk around again, Isstvan III spinning below him. The Death Guard fleet was a speckling of glittering streaks against the blackness, crisscrossed by red laser blasts.

Tarvitz gunned the stormbird's remaining engine as Garro said, 'Why? And be quick, Saul. They almost have you!'

'This is treachery?' shouted Tarvitz. 'All of this! We are betrayed. The fleet is going to bombard the planet's surface with virus bombs.'

'What?' spluttered Garro, disbelief plain in his voice, 'That's insane.'

'Trust me,' said Tarvitz, 'I know how it sounds, but as my honour brother I ask you to trust me like you have never trusted me before. On my life I swear I do not lie to you, Nathaniel.'

'I don't know, Saul,' said Garro.

'Nathaniel!' screamed Tarvitz in frustration. 'Ship to surface vox has been shut off, so unless I can get a warning down there, every Astartes on Isstvan III is going to die!'

CAPTAIN NATHANIEL GARRO could not tear his eyes from the hissing vox-unit, as if seeking to discern the truth of what Saul Tarvitz was saying just by staring hard enough. Beside him, the tactical plot displayed the weaving blips that represented Tarvitz's Thunderhawk and the pursuing fighters. His experienced eye told him that he had seconds at best to make a decision and his every instinct screamed that what he was hearing could not possibly be true.

Yet Saul Tarvitz was his sworn honour brother, an oath sworn on the bloody fields of the Preaixor Campaign, when they had shed blood and stood shoulder to shoulder through the entirety of a bloody, ill-fated war that had seen many of their most beloved brothers killed.

Such a friendship and bond of honour forged in the hell of combat was a powerful thing and Garro knew Saul Tarvitz well enough to know that he never exaggerated and never, ever lied. To imagine that his honour brother was lying to him now was beyond imagining, but to hear that the fleet was set to bombard their battle-brothers was equally unthinkable..

His thoughts tumbled like a whirlwind in his head and he cursed his indecision. He looked down at the eagle Tarvitz had carved into his vambrace so long ago and knew what he had to do.

TARVITZ PULLED THE Thunderhawk into a shallow dive, preparing to chop back the throttle and deploy his air brakes, hoping that he had descended far enough to allow the atmosphere of the planet below to slow him down sufficiently for what he planned…

He glanced down at the tactical display, seeing the fighters moving to either side of him, preparing to bracket him as his speed bled off. Judging the moment was crucial.

Tarvitz hauled back the throttle and hit the air brakes.

The grav seat harness pulled tight on his chest as he was hurled forwards and the cockpit was suddenly lit by brilliant flashes and a terrific juddering seized the gunship. He heard impacts on the hull and felt the Thunderhawk tumble away from his control.

He yelled in anger as he realised that those who sought to betray the Astartes had won, that his defiance of their treachery had been in vain. Blooms of fire surged past the cockpit and Tarvitz waited for the inevitable explosion of his death.

But it never came.

Amazed, he took hold of the gunship's controls and wrestled with them as he fought to level out his flight. The tactical display was a mess of interference, electromagnetic hash and radioactive debris clogging it with an impenetrable fog of a massive detonation. He couldn't see the fighters, but with such interference they could still be out there, even now drawing a bead on him.

What had just happened?

'Saul,' said a voice, heavy with sadness and Tarvitz knew that his honour brother had not let him down. 'Ease down, the fighters are gone.'

'Gone? How?'

'The *Eisenstein* shot them down on my orders,' said Garro. 'Tell me, Saul, was I right to do so, for if you speak falsely, then I have condemned myself alongside you.'

Tarvitz wanted to laugh and wished his old friend was standing next to him so he could throw his arms around him and thank him for his trust, knowing that Nathaniel Garro had made the most monumental decision in his life on nothing but what had passed between them moments ago. The depth of trust and the honour Garro had done him was immeasurable.

'Yes,' he said. 'You were right to trust me, my friend.'

'Tell me why?' asked Garro.

Tarvitz tried to think of something reassuring to tell his old friend, but knew that nothing he could say would soften the blow of this treachery. Instead, he said, 'Do you remember what you once told me of Terra?'

'Yes, my friend,' sighed Garro. 'I told you it was old, even back in the day.'

'You told me of what the Emperor built there,' said Tarvitz. 'A whole world, where before there had been nothing, just barbarians and death. You spoke of the scars of the Age of Strife, whole glaciers burned away and mountains levelled.'

'Yes,' agreed Garro. 'I remember. The Emperor took that blasted planet and he founded the Imperium there. That's what I fight for, to stand against the darkness and build an empire for the human race to inherit.'

'That's what is being betrayed, my friend,' said Tarvitz.

'I will not allow that to happen, Saul.'

'Nor I, my friend,' swore Tarvitz. 'What will you do now?'

Garro paused, the question of what to do, now that he had chosen a side, uppermost in his mind. 'I'll tell the *Andronius* that I shot you down. The flare of the explosion and the fact that you're in the upper atmosphere should cover you long enough to get to the surface.'

'And after that?'

'The other Legions must be warned of what is going on. Only the Warmaster would have the daring to conceive of such betrayal and he would not have begun an endeavour of this magnitude without swaying some of his brother primarchs to join him. Rogal Dorn or Magnus would never forsake the Emperor and if I can get the *Eisenstein* out of the Isstvan system, I can bring them here: all of them.'

'Can you do it?' asked Tarvitz. 'The Warmaster will soon realise what you attempt.'

'I have some time before they will suspect, but then the whole fleet will be after me. Why is it that men have to die every time any of us tries to do what is right?'

'Because that's the Imperial Truth,' said Tarvitz. 'Can you keep control of the *Eisenstein* once this gets out?

'Yes,' said Garro. 'It will be messy, but enough of the crew are staunch Terrans, and they will side with me. Those who do not will die.'

The port engine juddered and Tarvitz knew that he didn't have much time before the gunship gave out beneath him.

'I have to make for the surface, Nathaniel,' said Tarvitz. 'I don't know how much longer this ship will stay in the air.'

'Then this is where we part,' said Garro, an awful note of finality in his voice.

'The next time we see one another, it'll be on Terra,' said Tarvitz.

'*If* we meet again, my brother.'

'We will, Nathaniel,' promised Tarvitz. 'By the Emperor, I swear it.'

'May the luck of Terra be with you,' said Garro and the vox went dead.

Moments ago, he had been on the brink of death, but now he had hope that he might succeed in preventing the Warmaster's treachery from unfolding.

That was what the Imperial Truth meant, he realised at last.

It meant hope: hope for the galaxy; hope for humanity.

Tarvitz gunned the Thunderhawk's engine, fixed its course towards the Precentor's Palace and arrowed it towards the heart of the Choral City.

TEN

The most precious truth
Praal
Death's tomb

THE SUB-DECK WAS packed with people come to hear the words of the saint's apostle. Apostle: that was what they called him now, thought Sindermann, and it gave him comfort to know that even in these turbulent times, he was still a person that others looked up to. Vanity, he knew, but still… one takes what one can when circumstances change beyond one's control.

Word had spread quickly through the *Vengeful Spirit* that he was to speak and he glanced nervously around the edges of the sub-deck for any sign that word had reached beyond the civilians and remembrancers. Armed guards protected the approaches to the sub-deck, but he knew that if the Astartes or Maggard and his soldiers came in force, then not all of them would escape alive.

They were taking a terrible risk, but Euphrati had made it very clear that he needed to speak to the masses, to spread the word of the Emperor and to tell of the imminent treachery that she had seen.

Thousands of people stared expectantly at him and he cleared his throat, glancing over his shoulder to where Mersadie and Euphrati watched him standing at the lectern raised on a makeshift platform of packing crates. A portable vox-link had been rigged up to carry his words to the very back of the sub-deck, though he knew his iterator trained voice could be heard without any mechanical help. The vox-link was there to carry his words to those who could not attend this gathering, faithful among the technical staff of the ship having spliced the portable unit into the ship's principal vox-caster network.

Sindermann's words would be heard throughout the Expedition fleet.

He smiled at the crowd and took a sip of water from the glass beside him.

A sea of expectant faces stared back at him, desperate to hear his words of wisdom. What would he tell them, he wondered? He looked down at the scribbled notes he had taken over the time he had been sequestered in the bowels of the ship. He looked back over his shoulder at Euphrati and her smile lifted his heart.

He turned back to his notes, the words seeming trite and contrived.

He screwed the paper into a ball and dropped it by his side, feeling Euphrati's approval like a tonic in his veins.

'My friends,' he began. 'We live in strange times and there are events in motion that will shock many of you as they have shocked me. You have come to hear the words of the saint, but she has asked me to speak to you, that I may tell you of what she has seen and what all men and women of faith must do.'

His iterator's voice carried the precise amount of gravitas mixed with a tone that spoke to them of his regret at the terrible words of doom he was about to impart.

'The Warmaster has betrayed the Emperor,' he said, pausing to allow the inevitable howls of denial and outrage to fill the chamber. Shouted voices rose and fell like waves on the sea and Sindermann let them wash over him, knowing the exact moment when he should speak.

'I know, I know,' he said. 'You think that such a thing is unthinkable and only a short time ago, I would have agreed, but it is true. I have seen it with my own eyes. The saint showed me her vision and it chilled my very soul to see it: war-tilled fields of the dead, winds that carry a cruel dust of bone and the sky-turned eyes of men who saw wonders and only dreamed of their children and friendship. I tasted the air and it was heavy with blood, my friends, its stink reeking on the bodies of men we have learned to call the enemy. And for what? That they decided they did not want to be part of our warmongering Imperium? Perhaps they saw more than we? Perhaps it takes the fresh eyes of an outsider to see what we have become blind to.'

The crowd quietened, but he could see that most people still thought him mad. Many here were of the Faithful, but many others were not. While almost all of them could embrace the Emperor as divine, few of them could countenance the Warmaster betraying such a wondrous being.

'When we embarked on this so-called "Great Crusade" it was to bring enlightenment and reason to the galaxy, and for a time that was what we did. But look at us now, my friends, when was the last time we approached a world with anything but murder in our hearts? We bring so many forms of warfare with us, the tension of sieges and the battlefield of trenches soaked in mud and misery while the sky is ripped with gunfire. And the men who lead us are no better! What do we expect from cultures who are met by men named "Warmaster", "Widowmaker" and "the Twisted"? They see the Astartes, clad in their insect carapaces of plate armour, marching to the grim sounds of cocking bolters and roaring chainswords. What culture would *not* try to resist us?'

Sindermann could feel the mood of the crowd shifting and knew he had stoked their interest. Now he had to hook their emotions.

'Look to what we leave behind us! So many memorials to our slaughters! Look to the Lupercal's

Court, where we house the bloody weapons of war in bright halls and wonder at their cruel beauty as they hang waiting for their time to come again. We look at these weapons as curios, but we forget the actuality of the lives these savage instruments took. The dead cannot speak to us, they cannot plead with us to seek peace while the remembrance of them fades and they are forgotten. Despite the ranks of graves, the triumphal arches and eternal flames, we forget them, for we are afraid to look at what they did lest we see it in ourselves.'

Sindermann felt a wondrous energy filling him as he spoke, the words flowing from him in an unstoppable torrent, each word seeming to spring from his lips of its own volition, as though each one came from somewhere else, somewhere more eloquent than his poor, mortal talent could ever reach.

'We have made war in the stars for two centuries, yet there are so many lessons we have never learned. The dead should be our teachers, for they are the true witnesses. Only they know the horror and the ever repeating failure that is war; the sickness we return to generation after generation because we fail to hear the testament of those who were sacrificed to martial pride, greed or twisted ideology.'

Thunderous applause spread from the people directly in front of Sindermann, spreading rapidly through the chamber and he wondered if such scenes were being repeated on any of the other ships of the fleet that could hear his words.

Tears sprang to his eyes as he spoke, his hands gripping the lectern tightly as his voice trembled with emotion. 'Let the battlefield dead take our hands in theirs and illuminate us with the most precious truth we can ever learn, that there must be peace instead of war!'

Lucius skidded to the floor of what appeared to be some kind of throne room. Inlaid with impossibly intricate mosaic designs, the floor was covered in scrollwork so tightly wound that it seemed to ripple with movement. Bolter fire stitched through the room, showering him with broken pieces of mosaic as he rolled into the cover of an enormous harpsichord.

Music from the dawn of creation boomed around him, filling the central spire of the Precentor's Palace. Crystal chandeliers hung from the petals at the centre of the great granite flower, shimmering and vibrating in time with the cacophony of battle far below. Instruments filled the room, each one played by a servitor refitted to play the holy music of the Warsingers. Huge organs with pipes that reached up through the shafts of milky morning light stood next to banks of gilded bells and rank upon rank of bronze cages held shaven-headed choristers who sang with blind adulation.

Harp strings snapped and twanged in time with the gunfire and discordant notes boomed as bolter shots ripped through the side of the organ. Storms of weapons' fire flew, filling the air with hot metal and death, the battle and the music competing to make the loudest din.

Lucius felt his limbs become energised just listening to the crashing volume of the noise, each blaring note and booming shot filling his senses with the desire to do violence.

He glanced round the side of the harpsichord, exhausted and elated to have reached so far, so quickly. They had fought their way through the palace, killing thousands of the black- and silver-armoured guards, before finally reaching the throne room.

From his position of cover, Lucius saw that he was in the second ring of instruments, beyond which lay the Precentor's Dais. A mighty throne with its back to him sat upon the dais, a confection of gold and emerald set in a ring of lecterns that each held a massive volume of musical notations.

Gunfire blew one book apart and a blizzard of sheet music fluttered around the throne.

The palace guard massed on the opposite side of the throne room, surrounding a tall figure in gold armour with a collection of tubes and what looked like loudspeakers fanning out from his back. A storm of silver fire flew and Lucius saw yet more guards charging in from the other entrances, a ferocious struggle erupting as these new arrivals charged the Emperor's Children.

'They have courage, I'll give them that,' he muttered to himself.

Chainblades and bolt pistols rang from armour
and storms of silver fire ripped between the patches
of cover offered by the gilded instruments. Each
volley tore up the hardwood frames and sawed
through servitors as they sat at the ornate key-
boards or plucked at strings with metal fingers.

And still the music played.

Lucius glanced behind him. One of Nasicae fell
as he ran to join Lucius, silver filaments punched
through his skull. The body clattered to the floor
beside Lucius. Only three of Nasicae remained, and
they were cut off from their leader.

'Ancient Rylanor, engage!' yelled Lucius into the
vox. 'Get me cover! Tactical squads, converge on the
throne and draw the palace guard in! Purity and
death!'

'Purity and Death!' echoed the Emperor's Children, and with exemplary co-ordination they
surged forward. A silver-armoured guard was shredded by bolter fire and flopped, broken, to the
ground. Glass-armoured bodies lay shattered and
bloody over bullet-scarred instruments. Servitors
moved jerkily, still trying to play even though their
hands were smoking ruins of bone and wire.

The Emperor's Children moved squad by squad,
volley by volley, advancing through the fire as only
the most perfect of Legions could.

Lucius broke cover and ran into the whirlwind of
fire. Silver shards shattered against him.

Behind him, Rylanor's dreadnought body
smashed through a titanic bank of drums and bells,

the noise of its destruction appalling as Rylanor opened fire on the enemy. Acrobatic guards, clad in armour wound with long streamers of silk, darted and leapt away from chainblades and bolts like dancers, slashing limbs with monofilament wire-blades.

Glass-armoured guards charged forward in solid ranks, stabbing with their halberds, yet none of the foes was a match for the disciplined counter-charges of the Emperor's Children. The slick perfection of their pattern-perfect warfare kept its edge even amid the storm of fire and death that filled the throne room.

Lucius ducked and wove through the fire towards the gold armoured figure, shrapnel flashing against the energised edge of his sword blade.

The man's armour was ancient, yet gloriously ornate, the equal in finery of a lord commander of the Emperor's Children. He carried a long spear, its shaft terminated at both ends by a howling ripple of lethal harmonies. Lucius ducked under a swipe of the weapon, stepping nimbly to the side and bringing his sword up towards his opponent's midriff.

Faster than he would have believed possible, the spear reversed and a tremendous blast of noise battered his sword away before it struck. Lucius danced back as a killing wave of sound blared from the tubes and speakers mounted on the golden warrior's back, a whole section of the mosaic floor ploughed in a torn gouge by the sound.

One of the palace guards fell at Lucius's feet, his chest blown open by Rylanor's fire, and another toppled as one of Nasicae sliced off his leg.

The Emperor's Children surged forwards to help him, but he waved them back – this was to be his kill. He leapt onto the throne pedestal, the golden warrior silhouetted in the light streaming from the distant ceiling.

The screaming spear came down and Lucius ducked to avoid it, pushing himself forwards. He stabbed with his sword, but a pitch perfect note sent his sword plunging towards the floor of the dais instead of its intended target. Lucius hauled his sword clear as the spear stabbed for him again, the musical edge shearing past him and blistering the purple and gilt of his armour. The battle raged ferociously around him, but it was an irrelevance, for Lucius knew that he must surely be fighting the leader of this rebellion.

Only Vardus Praal would surround himself with such fearsome bodyguards.

Lucius pivoted away from another strike, spinning around behind Praal and shearing his sword through the speaker tubes and loudspeakers upon his back. He felt a glorious surge of satisfaction as the glowing edge cut through the metal with ease.

A terrific, booming noise blared from the severed pipes and Lucius was hurled from the dais by the force of the blast.

His armour cracked with the force, and the music leapt in clarity as he felt its power surge around his body in a glorious wash of pure, unadulterated sensation. The music sang in his blood, promising yet more glories, and the unfettered excess of music, light and hedonistic indulgence.

Lucius felt the music in his soul and knew that he wanted it, wanted it more than he had wanted anything in his life.

He looked up as the golden warrior leapt lightly from the throne, seeing the music as swirling lines of power and promise that flowed like water in the air.

'Now you die,' said Lucius as the song of death took hold of him.

IN LATER MOMENTS they would name it Death's Tomb, and Loken had never felt such disgust at the sights he saw within it. Even Davin's moon, where the swamps had vomited up the living dead to attack the Sons of Horus, had not been this bad.

The sound of battle was a hellish music of screaming, rising in terrible crescendos, and the sight was horrendous. Death's Tomb was brimming with corpses, festering in charnel heaps and bubbling with corruption.

The tomb-spire Loken and the Sons of Horus fought within was larger inside than out, the floor sunken into a pit where the dead had been thrown. The tomb was that of Death itself. A mausoleum of bloodstained black iron carved into swirls and scrollwork dominated the pit, topped with a sculpture of Father Isstvan himself, a massive bearded sky-god who took away the souls of the faithful and cast the rest into the sky to languish with his Lost Children.

A Warsinger perched on Father Isstvan's black shoulder, screaming a song of death that jarred at Loken's nerves and sent jangling pain along his limbs. Hundreds of Isstvanian soldiers surrounded the pit, firing from the hip as they ran towards the Astartes, driven forward by the shrieking death song.

'At them!' yelled Loken, and before he could draw breath again the enemy was upon them. The Astartes of the spearhead streamed through the many archways leading into the tomb-spire, guns blazing as soon as they saw the enemy swarming towards them. Loken fired a fusillade of shots before the two sides clashed.

More than two thousand Sons of Horus charged into battle and Death's Tomb became a vast amphitheatre for a great and terrible slaughter, like the arenas of the ancient Romanii.

'Stay close! Back to back, and advance!' cried Loken, but he could only hope that his fellow warriors could hear him over the vox. The screaming was deafening, every Isstvanian soldier's mouth jammed open and howling in the shrieking cadences of the Warsinger's music.

Loken cut a gory crescent through the bodies pressing in on him, Vipus matching him stroke for stroke with his long chainsword. Strategy and weapons meant nothing now. The battle was simply a brutal close quarters fight to the death.

Such a contest could have only one outcome.

Loathing filled Loken. Not at the blood and death around him, he had seen much worse before, but at the sheer waste of this war. The people he was killing… their lives could have meant something. They could have accepted the Imperial Truth and helped forge a galaxy where the human race was united and the wisdom of the Emperor ushered them towards a future filled with wonders. Instead they had been betrayed and turned into fanatical killers by a corrupt leader, destined to die for a cause that was a lie.

Good lives wasted. Nothing could be further from the purpose of the Imperium.

'Torgaddon! Bring the line forwards. Force them back and give the guns some room.'

'Easier said than done, Garvi!' replied Torgaddon, his voice punctuated with the sharp crack of breaking bones.

Loken glanced around, saw one of Lachost's squad dragged down by the mass of enemy warriors and tried to bring his bolter to bear. Bloodied, ruined hands forced his aim down and the battle-brother was lost. He dropped his shoulder and barged forwards, bodies breaking beneath him, but others were on top of him, blades and bullets beating at his armour.

With a roar of anger, Loken ripped his chainsword through an armoured warrior before him, forcing the enemy back for the split second he needed to open up with his bolter. A full-throated volley sent a magazine's worth of shells into the mass, blasting them apart in a red ruin of shattered faces and broken armour.

He rapidly swapped in a new bolter magazine and fired among the warriors trying to swamp his fellow Sons of Horus. The Astartes used the openings to forge onwards or open up spaces to bring their own weapons up. Others lent their gunfire to the battle-brothers fighting behind them.

The tone of the Warsinger's screaming changed and Loken felt as though rusty nails were being torn up his spine. He staggered and the enemy were upon him.

'Torgaddon!' he shouted over the din. 'Get the Warsinger!'

'MY APOLOGIES, WARMASTER,' began Maloghurst, nervous at interrupting the Warmaster's concentration on the battle below. 'There has been a development.'

'In the city?' asked Horus without looking up.

'On the ship,' replied Maloghurst.

Horus looked up in irritation. 'Explain yourself.'

'The Prime Iterator, Kyril Sindermann…'

'Old Kyril?' said Horus. 'What of him.'

'It appears we have misjudged the man's character, my lord.'

'In what way, Mal?' asked Horus. 'He's just an old man.'

'That he is, but he may be a greater threat than anything we have yet faced, my lord,' said

Maloghurst. 'He is a leader now, an apostle they call him. He–'

'A leader?' interrupted Horus, 'of whom?'

'Of the people of the fleet, civilians, ships' crew, and the Lectitio Divinitatus. He has just finished a speech to the fleet calling on them to resist the Legion, saying that we are warmongers and seek to betray the Emperor. We are trying to trace where the signal came from, but it is likely he will be long gone before we find him.'

'I see,' said Horus. 'This problem should have been dealt with before Isstvan.'

'And we have failed you in this,' said Maloghurst. 'The iterator mixed calls for peace with a potent brew of religion and faith.'

'This should not surprise us,' said Horus. 'Sindermann was selected for duty with my fleet precisely because he could convince even the most fractious rabble to do anything. Mix that skill with religious fervour and he is indeed a dangerous man.'

'They believe the Emperor is divine,' said Maloghurst, 'and that we commit blasphemy.'

'It must be an intoxicating faith,' mused Horus, 'and faith can be a very powerful weapon. It appears, Maloghurst, that we have underestimated the potential that even a civilian possesses so long as he has genuine faith in something.'

'What would you have me do, my lord?'

'We did not deal with this threat properly,' said Horus. 'It should have ceased to exist when Varvarus and those troublesome remembrancers were illuminated. Now it takes my attention when our plan is at its most sensitive stage. The bombardment is imminent.'

Maloghurst bowed his head. 'Warmaster, Sindermann and his kind will be destroyed.'

'The next I hear of this will be that they are all dead,' ordered Horus.

'It will be done,' promised Maloghurst.

'FOOL!' SPAT PRAAL, his voice a disgusted rasp. 'Have you not seen this world? The wonders you would destroy? This is a city of the gods!'

Lucius rolled to his feet, still stunned from the sonic shockwave that had hurled him from the throne dais, but knowing that the song of death was being sung for him and him alone. He lunged, but Praal batted aside his attack, bringing his spear up in a neat guard.

'This is the city of my enemies,' laughed Lucius. 'That is all that matters to me.'

'You are deaf to the music of the galaxy. I have heard far more than you,' said Praal. 'Perhaps you are to be pitied, for I have listened to the sound of the gods. I have heard their song and they damn this galaxy in their wisdom!'

Lucius laughed in Praal's face. 'You think I care? All I want to do is kill you.'

'The gods have sung what your Imperial Truth will bring to the galaxy,' shrieked Praal, his musical voice heavy with disdain. 'It is a future of fear and hatred. I was deaf to the music before they opened me to their song of oblivion. It is my duty to end your Crusade!'

'You can try,' said Lucius, 'but even if you kill us all, more will come: a hundred thousand more, a million, until this planet is dust. Your little rebellion is over; you just don't know it yet.'

'No, Astartes,' replied Praal. 'I have fulfilled my duty and brought you here, to this cauldron of fates. My work is done! All that remains is to blood myself in the name of Father Isstvan.'

Lucius danced away as Praal attacked once more with the razor-sharp feints of a master warrior, but the swordsman had faced better opponents than this and prevailed. The song of death rippled behind his eyes and he could see every move Praal made before he made it, the song speaking to him on a level he didn't understand, but instinctively knew was power beyond anything he had touched before.

He launched a flurry of blows at Praal, driving him back with each attack and no matter how skilfully Praal parried his strikes, each one came that little bit closer to wounding him.

The flicker of fear he saw in Praal's eyes filled him with brutal triumph. The shrieking, musical spear blared one last atonal scream before it finally shattered under the energised edge of Lucius's sword.

The swordsman pivoted smoothly on his heel and drove his blade, two-handed, into Praal's golden chest, the sword burning through his armour, ribs and internal organs.

Praal dropped to his knees, still alive, his mouth working dumbly as blood sprayed from the massive wound. Lucius twisted the blade, relishing the cracks as Praal's ribs snapped.

He put a foot on Praal's body and pulled the sword clear, standing triumphant over the body of his fallen enemy.

Around him, the Emperor's Children slew the remaining palace guards, but with Praal dead, the song in his blood diminished and his interest in the fight faded. Lucius turned to the throne itself, already aching for the music to surge through his body once again.

The throne's back was to him and he couldn't see who was seated there. A control panel worked furiously before it, like a monstrously complicated clockwork keyboard.

Lucius stepped around the throne and looked into the glassy eyes of a servitor.

Its head was mounted on a skinny body of metal armatures, the complex innards stripped out and replaced with brass clockwork. Chattering metal tines reached from the chest cavity to read the music printed in the books mounted around the throne and the servitor's hands, elaborate, twenty-fingered constructions of metal and wire, flickered over the control panel.

Without Praal, the music was out of tune and time, its syncopated rhythms falling apart. Lucius knew that this was a poor substitute for what had fuelled his battle with Praal.

Suddenly angry beyond words, Lucius brought his blade down in a glittering arc, shattering the control panel in a shower of orange sparks. The hideous music transformed into a howling death shriek, shaking the stone petals of the palace with its terrible, deafening wail before fading like a forgotten dream.

The music of creation ended and all across Isstvan the voices of the gods were silenced.

A VOLLEY OF gunfire caught Loken's attention as he desperately fought the dozens of guards who stabbed at him with their gleaming halberds. Behind him, Torgaddon brought the speartip up into a firing line, and bolter fire battered against the black iron of Death's mausoleum. The Warsinger was broken like a dying bird against the statue of Father Isstvan.

The Warsinger fell, her final scream tailing off as her shattered form cracked against the ornate carvings of Death's mausoleum.

'She's down!' said Torgaddon's voice over the vox, sounding surprised at the ease with which she had been killed.

'Who have we lost?' asked Loken, as the enemy soldiers fell back at the Warsinger's death, suspecting that there was more to this withdrawal than simply her death. Something fundamental had changed on Isstvan, but he didn't yet know what.

'Most of Squad Chaggrat,' replied Torgaddon, 'and plenty of others. We won't know until we get out of here, but there's something else...'

'What?' asked Loken.'

'Lachost says we've lost contact with orbit,' said Torgaddon. 'There's no signal. It's as if the *Vengeful Spirit* isn't even up there.'

'That's impossible,' said Loken, looking around for the familiar sight of Sergeant Lachost.

He saw him at the edge of the charnel pit and marched over to him. Torgaddon and Vipus followed him and Torgaddon said, 'Impossible or not, it's what he tells me.'

'What about the rest of the strike force?' asked Loken, crouching beside Lachost. 'What about the palace?'

'We're having more luck with them,' replied Lachost. 'I managed to get through to Captain Ehrlen of the World Eaters. It sounds like they're outside the palace. It's an absolute massacre over there –, thousands of civilians dead.'

'In the name of Terra!' said Loken, imagining the World Eaters' predilection for massacre and the rivers of blood that would be flowing through the streets of the Choral City. 'Have they managed to contact anyone in orbit?'

'They've got their hands full, captain,' replied Lachost. 'Even if they've managed to raise the *Conqueror*, they're in no position to relay anything from us. I could barely get anything out of Ehrlen other than that he was killing them with his bare hands.'

'And the palace?'

'Nothing, I can't get through to Captain Lucius of the Emperor's Children. The palace has been playing hell with communications ever since they went in. There was some kind of music, but nothing else.'

'Then try the Death Guard. They've got the *Dies Irae* with them, we can use it to relay for us.'

'I'll try, sir, but it's not looking hopeful.'

'This was supposed to be over by now,' spat Loken. 'The Choral City isn't just going to collapse with their leaders dead. Maybe the World Eaters have the right idea. We're going to have to kill them all. We need the second wave down here now and if we can't even speak to the Warmaster this is going to be a very long campaign.'

'I'll keep trying,' said Lachost.

'We need to link up with the rest of the strike force,' said Loken. 'We're cut off here. We need to make for the palace and find the World Eaters or the Emperor's Children. We're not doing any good sitting here. All we're doing is giving the Isstvanians a chance to surround us.'

'There're a lot of soldiers between us and the rest of the strike force,' Torgaddon pointed out.

'Then we advance in force. We won't take this city by waiting to be attacked.'

'Agreed. I saw the main gates along the western walls. We can get into the city proper there, but it'll be a tough slog.'

'Good,' said Loken.

'IT's A TRAP,' said Mersadie. 'It has to be.'

'You're probably right,' agreed Sindermann.

'Of course I'm right,' said Mersadie. 'Maloghurst tried to have Euphrati killed. His pet monster, Maggard, almost killed you too, remember?'

'I remember very well,' said Sindermann, 'but think of the opportunity. There will be thousands there and they couldn't possibly try anything with that many people around. They probably won't even notice we're there.'

Mersadie looked down her nose at Sindermann, unable to believe that the old iterator was being so dense. Had he not spoken to hundreds of people only hours before of the Warmaster's perfidy? And now he wanted to gather in a room with him?

They had been woken from their slumbers by one of the engineering crew who pressed a rolled leaflet into Sindermann's shaking hand. Sharing a worried glance with Mersadie, Sindermann had read it. It was a decree from the Warmaster authorising all remembrancers to gather in the *Vengeful Spirit's* main audience chamber to bear witness to the final triumph on Isstvan III. It spoke of the gulf that had, much to the Warmaster's great sorrow, opened between the Astartes and the remembrancers. With this one, grand gesture, the Warmaster hoped to allay any fears that such a gulf had been engineered deliberately.

'He must think we are stupid,' said Mersadie. 'Does he really think we would fall for this?'

'Maloghurst is a very cunning man,' said Sindermann, rolling up the leaflet and placing it on the bed. 'You'd hardly take him for a warrior any more.

He's trying to flush the three of us out, hoping that no remembrancer could resist such an offer. If I were a less moral man I might admire him.'

'All the more reason not to fall into his trap!' exclaimed Mersadie.

'Ah, but what if it's genuine, my dear?' asked Sindermann. 'Imagine what we'd see on the surface of Isstvan III!'

'Kyril, this is a big ship and we can hide out for a long time. When Loken comes back he can protect us.'

'Like he protected Ignace?'

'That's not fair, Kyril,' said Mersadie. 'Loken can help us get off the ship once we leave the Isstvan system.'

'No,' said a voice behind Mersadie and they both turned to see Euphrati Keeler. She was awake again, and her voice was stronger than Mersadie had heard it for a long time. She looked healthier than she had been since the terror in the archive. To see her standing, walking and talking after so long was still a novelty for Mersadie and she smiled to see her friend once again.

'We go,' she said.

'Euphrati?' said Mersadie. 'Do you really…'

'Yes, Mersadie,' she said. 'I mean it. And yes, I am sure.'

'It's a trap.'

'I don't need a vision from the Emperor to see that,' laughed Euphrati, and Mersadie thought there was something a little sinister and forced to it.

'But they'll kill us.'

Euphrati smiled. 'Yes they will. If we stay here, they'll hunt us down eventually. We have faithful among the crew, but we have enemies, too. I will not have the Church of the Emperor die like that. This will not end in shadows and murder.'

'Now, Miss Keeler,' said Sindermann with a forced lightness of tone. 'You're starting to sound like me.'

'Maybe they will find us eventually, Euphrati,' said Mersadie, 'but there's no reason to make it easy for them. Why let the Warmaster have his way when we can live a little longer?'

'Because you have to see,' said Euphrati. 'You have to see it. This fate, this treachery, it's too great for any of us to understand without witnessing it. Have faith that I am right about this, my friends.'

'It's not a question of faith now, is it?' said Sindermann. 'It's a—'

'It is time for us to stop thinking like remembrancers,' said Euphrati, and Mersadie saw a light in her eyes that seemed to grow brighter with every word she spoke. 'The Imperial Truth is dying. We have watched it wither ever since Sixty-Three Nineteen. You either die with it or you follow the Emperor. This galaxy is too simple for us to hide in its complexity any more and the Emperor cannot work His will through those who do not know if they even believe at all.'

'I will follow you,' said Sindermann, and Mersadie found herself nodding in agreement.

ELEVEN

Warning
Death of a World
The Last Cthonian

SAUL TARVITZ'S FIRST sight of the Choral City was the magnificent stone orchid of the Precentor's Palace. He stepped from the battered Thunderhawk onto the roof of one of the palace wings, the spectacular dome soaring above him. Smoke coiled in the air from the battles within the palace and the terrible sound of screaming came from the square to the north, along with the powerful stench of freshly-spilled blood.

Tarvitz took it in at a glance, the thought hitting him hard that at any moment it would all be gone. He saw Astartes moving along the roof towards him, Emperor's Children, and his heart leapt to see Nasicae Squad with Lucius at its head, his sword smoking from the battle.

'Tarvitz!' called Lucius, and Tarvitz thought he detected even more of a swagger to the swordsman's stride. 'I thought you'd never make it! Jealous of the kills?'

'Lucius, what's the situation?' asked Tarvitz.

'The palace is ours and Praal is dead, killed by my own hand! No doubt you can smell the World Eaters; they're just not at home unless everything stinks of blood. The rest of the city's cut off. We can't raise anyone.'

Lucius indicated the city's far west, where the towering form of the *Dies Irae* blazed fire upon the hapless Isstvanians out of sight below. 'Though it looks like the Death Guard will soon run out of things to kill.'

'We have to contact the rest of the strike force, now,' said Tarvitz, 'the Sons of Horus and the Death Guard. Get a squad on it. Get someone up to higher ground.'

'Why?' asked Lucius. 'Saul, what's happening?'

'We're going to be hit. Something big. A virus strike.'

'The Isstvanians?'

'No,' said Tarvitz sadly. 'We are betrayed by our own.'

Lucius hesitated. 'The Warmaster? Saul, what are you–'

'We've been sent down here to die, Lucius. Fulgrim chose those who were not part of their grand plan.'

'Saul, that's insane!' cried Lucius. 'Why would our primarch do such a thing?'

'I do not know, but he would not have done this without the Warmaster's command,' said Tarvitz. 'This is but the first stage in some larger plan. I do not know its purpose, but we have to try and stop it.'

Lucius shook his head, his features twisted in petulant bitterness. 'No. The primarch wouldn't send me to die, not after all the battles I fought for him. Look at what I've become. I was one of Fulgrim's chosen! I've never faltered, never questioned! I would have followed Fulgrim into hell!'

'But I wouldn't, Lucius,' said Tarvitz, 'and you are my friend. I'm sorry, but we don't have time for this. We have to get the warning out and then find shelter. I'll take word to the World Eaters, you raise the Sons of Horus and Death Guard. Don't go into the details, just tell them that there is a virus strike inbound and to find whatever shelter they can.'

Tarvitz looked at the reassuring solidity of the Precentor's Palace and said, 'There must be catacombs or deep places beneath the palace. If we can reach them we may survive this. This city is going to die, Lucius, but I'll be damned if I am going to die with it.'

'I'll get a vox-officer up here,' said Lucius, a steel anger in his voice.

'Good. We don't have much time, Lucius, the bombs will be launched any moment.'

'This is rebellion,' said Lucius.

'Yes,' said Tarvitz, 'it is.'

Beneath his ritualistic scars, Lucius was still the perfect soldier he had always been, a talisman whose confidence could infect the men around him, and Tarvitz knew he could rely on him. The swordsman nodded and said, 'Go, find Captain Ehrlen. I'll raise the other Legions and get our warriors into cover. I will speak with you again.'

'Until then,' said Tarvitz.

Lucius turned to Nasicae, barked an order, and ran back towards the palace dome. Tarvitz followed, looking down on the northern plaza and glimpsing the seething battle there, hearing the screams and the sound of chainblades.

He looked up at the late morning sky. Clouds were gathering.

Any moment, falling virus bombs would bore through those clouds.

The bombs would fall all over Isstvan III and billions of people would die.

AMONG THE TRENCHES and bunkers that sprawled to the west of the Choral City, men and Astartes died in storms of mud and fire. The *Dies Irae* shuddered with the weight of fire it laid down. Moderati Cassar felt it all, as though the immense, multi-barrelled Vulcan bolter were in his own hand. The Titan had suffered many wounds, its legs scarred by missile detonations and furrows scored in its mighty torso by bunker-mounted cannons.

Cassar felt them all, but a multitude of wounds could not slow down the *Dies Irae* or turn it from its course. Destruction was its purpose and death was the punishment it brought down on the heads of the Emperor's enemies.

Cassar's heart swelled. He had never felt so close to his Emperor, at one with the God-Machine, a fragment of the Emperor's own strength instilled in the *Dies Irae*.

'Aruken, pull to starboard!' ordered Princeps Turnet from the command chair. 'Avoid those bunkers or they'll foul the port leg.'

The *Dies Irae* swung to the side, its immense foot taking the roofs from a tangle of bunkers and shattering artillery emplacements as it crashed forwards. A scrum of Isstvanian soldiers scrambled from the ruins, setting up heavy weapons to pour fire into the Titan as it towered over them.

The Isstvanians were well-drilled and well-armed, and though the majority of their weapons weren't the equal of a lasgun, trenches were a great leveller and a man with a rifle was a man with a rifle when the gunfire started.

The Death Guard slaughtered thousands of them as they bludgeoned their way through the trenches, but the Isstvanians were more numerous and they hadn't run. Instead they had fallen back trench by trench, rolling away from the relentless advance of the Death Guard.

The Isstvanians, with their drab green-grey helmets and mud-spattered flak-suits, were hard to pick out against the mud and rubble with the naked eye, but the sensors on the *Dies Irae* projected a sharp-edged image onto Cassar's retina that picked them out in wondrously clear detail.

Cassar fired a blast of massive-calibre shells, watching as columns of mud and bodies sprayed into the air like splashes in water. The Isstvanians disappeared, destroyed by the hand of the Emperor.

'Enemy forces massing to the port forward quadrant,' said Moderati Aruken.

To Cassar his voice felt distant, though he was just across the command bridge of the Titan.

'The Death Guard can handle them,' replied Turnet. 'Concentrate on the artillery. That can hurt us.'

Below Cassar, the gunmetal forms of the Death Guard glinted around the bunkers as two squads of them threw grenades through the gun ports and kicked down the doors, spraying the Isstvanians who still lived inside with bolter fire or incinerating them with sheets of fire from their flamers. From the head of the *Dies Irae*, the Death Guard looked like a swarm of beetles, with the carapaces of their power armour scuttling through the trenches.

A few Death Guard lay where they had fallen, cut down by artillery fire or the massed guns of the Isstvanian troops, but they were few compared to the Isstvanian corpses strewn at every intersection of trenches. Metre by metre the defenders were being driven towards the northernmost extent of the trenches, and when they reached the white marble of a tall Basilica with a spire shaped like a trident, they would be trapped and slaughtered.

Cassar shifted the weapon arm of the *Dies Irae* to aim at a booming artillery position some five hundred metres away, as it belched tongues of flame and threw explosive shells towards the Death Guard lines.

'Princeps!' called Cassar. 'Enemy artillery moving up on the eastern quadrant.'

Turnet didn't answer him, too intent on something being said to him on his personal command channel. The princeps nodded at whatever order he had just received and shouted, 'Halt! Aruken, cease the stride pattern. Cassar, shut off the ammunition feed.'

Cassar instinctively switched off the cycling of the weapon that thundered from the Titan's arm and the shock forced his consciousness back to the command bridge. He no longer looked through the eyes of the *Dies Irae*, but was back with his fellow officers.

'Princeps?' asked Cassar, scanning the readouts. 'Is there a malfunction? If there is, I'm not seeing it. The primary systems are reading fine.'

'It's not a malfunction,' replied Turnet sharply. Cassar looked up from information scrolling across his vision in unfocused columns.

'Moderati Cassar,' barked Turnet. 'How's our weapon temperature?'

'Acceptable,' said Cassar. 'I was going to push it on that artillery.'

'Close up the coolant ducts and seal the magazine feeds as soon as possible.'

'Princeps?' said Cassar in confusion. 'That will leave us unarmed.'

'I know that,' replied Turnet, as though to a simpleton. 'Do it. Aruken, I need us sealed.'

'Sealed, sir?' asked Aruken, sounding as confused as Cassar felt.

'Yes, sealed. We have to be airtight from top to bottom,' said Turnet, opening a channel to the rest of the mighty war machine's crew.

'All crew, this is Princeps Turnet. Adopt emergency biohazard posts, right now. The bulkheads are being sealed. Shut off the reactor vents and be prepared for power down.'

'Princeps,' said Aruken urgently. 'Is it a biological weapon? Atomics?'

'The Isstvanians have a weapon we didn't know about,' replied Turnet, but Cassar could tell he was lying. 'They're launching it soon. We have to lock down or we'll be caught in it.'

Cassar looked down at the trenches through the Titan's eyes. The Death Guard were still advancing through the trenches and bunker ruins. 'But princeps, the Astartes–'

'You have your orders, Moderati Cassar,' shouted Turnet, 'and you will follow them. Seal us up, every vent, every hatch or we die.'

Cassar willed the *Dies Irae* to shut its hatches and seal all its entranceways, his reluctance making the procedures sluggish.

On the ground below, he watched the Death Guard continue to grind their way through the

Choral City's defences, apparently unconcerned that the Isstvanians were about to launch Throne knew what at them, *or unaware.*

As the battle raged on, the *Dies Irae* fell silent.

THE MAIN AUDIENCE chamber of the *Vengeful Spirit* was a colossal, columned chamber with walls of marble and pilasters of solid gold. Its magnificence was like nothing Sindermann had ever seen, and the thousands of remembrancers who filled the chamber wore the expressions of awed children who had been shown some new, unheard of wonder. Seeing many familiar faces, Sindermann guessed that the fleet's entire complement of remembrancers was present for the Warmaster's announcement.

The Warmaster and Maloghurst stood on a raised podium at the far end of the hall, too far away for either of them to recognise Sindermann, Mersadie or Euphrati.

Or at least he hoped so. Who knew how sharp an Astartes eyesight was, let alone a primarch's?

Both Astartes were wrapped in cream robes edged in gold and silver and a detail of warriors stood beside them. A number of large pict screens had been hung from the walls.

'It looks like an iterators' rally on a compliant world,' said Mersadie, echoing his own thoughts. So similar was it that he began to wonder what message was to be imparted and how it would be reinforced. He looked around for plants in the

audience who would clap and cheer at precise
points to direct the crowd in the desired manner.
Each of the screens displayed a slice of Isstvan III,
set against a black backdrop scattered with bright
silver specks of the Warmaster's fleet.

'Euphrati,' said Mersadie as they made their way
through the crowds of remembrancers. 'Remember
how I said that this was a bad idea?'

'Yes?' said Euphrati, her face creased in a wide,
innocent smile.

'Well, now I think that this was a *really* bad idea.
I mean, look at the number of Astartes here.'

Sindermann followed Mersadie's gaze, already
starting to sweat at the sight of so many armed warriors surrounding them. If even one of them
recognised their faces, it was all over.

'We have to see,' said Euphrati, turning and grabbing his sleeve. '*You* have to see.'

Sindermann felt the heat of her touch and saw the
fire behind her eyes, like thunder before a storm and
he realised with a start, that he was a little afraid of
Euphrati. The crowd milled in eager impatience and
Sindermann kept his face turned from the Astartes
staring into the middle of the audience chamber.

Euphrati squeezed Mersadie's hand as the pict
screens leapt to life and a gasp went up from the
assembled remembrancers as they saw the bloody
streets of the Choral City. Clearly shot from an air-
craft, the images filled the giant pict screens and
Sindermann felt his gorge rise at the sight of so
much butchery.

He remembered the carnage of the Whisperheads and reminded himself that this was what the Astartes had been created to do, but the sheer visceral nature of that reality was something he knew he would never get used to. Bodies filled the streets and arterial gore covered almost every surface as though the heavens had rained blood.

'You remembrancers say you want to see war,' said Horus, his voice easily carrying to the furthest corners of the hall. 'Well, this is it.'

Sindermann watched as the image shifted on the screen, pulling back and panning up through the sky and into the dark, star-spattered heavens above.

Burning spears of light fell towards the battle below.

'What are those?' asked Mersadie.

'They're bombs,' said Sindermann in horrified disbelief. 'The planet is being bombarded.'

'And so it begins,' said Euphrati.

THE PLAZA WAS a truly horrendous sight, ankle-deep in blood and strewn with thousands upon thousands of bodies. Most were blown open by bolter rounds, but many had been hacked down with chainblades or otherwise torn limb from limb.

Tarvitz hurried towards the makeshift strongpoint at its centre, the battlements formed from carved up bodies heaped between the battered forms of fallen drop-pods.

A World Eater with blood-soaked armour and a scarred face nodded to him as he climbed the gruesome ramp of bodies. The warrior's armour was so drenched in blood that Tarvitz wondered for a moment why he hadn't just painted himself red to begin with.

'Captain Ehrlen,' said Tarvitz. 'Where is he?'

The warrior wasted no breath on words and simply jerked a thumb in the direction of a warrior with dozens of fluttering oath papers hanging from his breastplate. Tarvitz nodded his thanks and set off through the strongpoint. He passed wounded Astartes who were tended by an apothecary who looked as if he had fought as hard as any of his patients. Beside him lay two fallen World Eaters, their bodies unceremoniously dumped out of the way.

Ehrlen looked up as Tarvitz approached. The captain's face had been badly burned in some previous battle and his axe was clotted with so much blood that it better resembled a club.

'Looks like the Emperor's Children have sent us reinforcements!' shouted Ehrlen, to grunts of laughter from his fellow World Eaters. 'One whole warrior! We are blessed, the enemy will run away for sure.'

'Captain,' said Tarvitz, joining Ehrlen at the barricade of Isstvanian dead. 'My name is Captain Saul Tarvitz and I'm here to warn you that you have to get your squads into cover.'

'Into cover? Unacceptable,' said Ehrlen, nodding towards the far side of the plaza. Shapes moved in their windows and between the mansions. 'They're regrouping. If we move now they will overwhelm us.'

'The Isstvanians have a bio-weapon,' said Tarvitz, knowing a lie was the only way to convince the World Eaters. 'They're going to fire it. It'll kill everyone and everything in the Choral City.'

'They're going to destroy their own capital? I thought this place was some kind of church? Holy to them?'

'They've shown how much they value their own,' replied Tarvitz quickly, indicating the heaps of dead in front of them. 'They'll sacrifice this city to kill us. Driving us from their planet is worth more to them than this city.'

'So you would have us abandon this position?' demanded Ehrlen, as if Tarvitz had personally insulted his honour. 'How do you know all this?'

'I just got here from orbit. The weapon has already been unleashed. If you're above ground when the virus strike hits you will die. If you believe nothing else, believe that.'

'Then where do you suggest we move to?'

'Just to the west of this position, captain,' said Tarvitz, stealing a glance at the sky. 'The edge of the trench system is thick with bunkers, blast proof shelters. If you get your men into them, they should be safe.'

'Should be?' snapped Ehrlen. 'That's the best you can offer me?'

Ehrlen stared at Tarvitz for a moment. 'If you are wrong the blood of my warriors will be on your hands and I will kill you for their deaths.'

'I understand that, captain,' urged Tarvitz, 'but we don't have much time.'

'Very well, Captain Tarvitz,' said Ehrlen. 'Sergeant Fleiste, left flank! Sergeant Wronde, right! World Eaters, general advance to the west, blades out!'

The World Eaters drew their chainaxes and swords. The bloodstained assault units hurried to the front and stepped over the makeshift barricades of corpses.

'Are you coming, Tarvitz?' asked Ehrlen.

Tarvitz nodded, drawing his broadsword and following the World Eaters into the plaza.

Although they were fellow Astartes, he knew he was a stranger among them as they ran, spitting battle curses and splashing through the dead towards the potential safety of the bunkers.

Tarvitz glanced up at the gathering clouds and felt his chest tighten.

The first burning streaks were falling towards the city.

'IT'S STARTED,' SAID Loken.

Lachost looked up from the field vox. Fire was streaking through the sky towards the Choral City. Loken tried to judge the angle and speed of the falling darts of fire – some of them would come down between the spires of the Sirenhold, just like the Sons of Horus's own drop-pods had done hours earlier, and they would hit in a matter of minutes.

'Did Lucius say anything else?'

'No,' said Lachost. 'Some bio-weapon. That was all. It sounded like he ran into a fire fight.'

'Tarik,' shouted Loken. 'We need to get into cover, now. Beneath the Sirenhold.'

'Will that be enough?'

'If they dug their catacombs deep enough, then maybe.'

'And if not?'

'From what Lucius said, we'll die.'

'Then we'd better get a move on.'

Loken turned to the Sons of Horus advancing around him. 'Incoming! Get to the Sirenhold and head down! Now!'

The closest spire of the Sirenhold was a towering monstrosity of grotesque writhing figures and leering gargoyle faces, a vision taken from some ancient hell of Isstvan's myths. The Sons of Horus broke their advance formation and ran towards it.

Loken heard the distinctive boom of an airborne detonation high above the city and pushed himself harder as he entered the darkness of the tomb-spire. Inside, it was dark and ugly, the floor paved with tortured, half-human figures who reached up with stone hands, as if through the bars of a cage.

'There's a way down,' said Torgaddon. Loken followed as Astartes ran towards the catacomb entrance, a huge monstrous stone head with a passageway leading down its throat.

As the darkness closed around him, Loken heard a familiar sound drifting from beyond the walls of the Sirenhold.

It was screaming.

It was the song of the Choral City's death.

THE FIRST VIRUS bombs detonated high above the Choral City, the huge explosions spreading the deadly payloads far and wide into the atmosphere. Designed to kill every living thing on the surface of a planet, the viral strains released on Isstvan III were the most efficient killers in the Warmaster's arsenal. The bombs had a high enough yield to murder the planet a hundred times over and were set to burst at numerous differing altitudes and locations across the surface of the planet.

The virus leapt through forests and plains, sweeping along algal blooms and riding air currents across the globe. It crossed mountains, forded rivers, burrowed through glaciers. The Imperium's deadliest weapons, the Emperor himself had been loath to use them.

The bombs fell all across Isstvan III, but most of all, they fell on the Choral City.

THE WORLD EATERS were the furthest from cover and suffered the worst of the initial bombardment. Some had reached the safety of the bunkers, but many more had not. Warriors fell to their knees as the virus penetrated their armoured bodies, deadly corrosive agents laced into the viral structure of the weapons dissolving exposed pipes and armour joints, or finding their way inside through battle damage.

Astartes screamed. The sound was all the more shocking for its very existence rather than for the horror of its tone. The virus broke down cellular bonds at the molecular level and its victims literally dissolved into a soup of rancid meat within minutes of exposure, leaving little but sloshing suits of rotted armour. Even many of those who reached the safety of the sealed bunkers died in agony as they shut the doors only to find they had brought the lethal virus inside with them.

The virus spread through the civilian populace of Isstvan III at the speed of thought, leaping from victim to victim in the time it took to breathe in its foul contagion. People dropped where they stood, the flesh sloughing from their skeletons as their nervous systems collapsed and their bones turned to the consistency of jelly.

Bright explosions fed the viral feast, perpetuating the fatal reactions of corruption. The very lethality of the virus was its own worst enemy, for without a host organism to carry it from victim to victim, the virus quickly consumed itself.

However, the bombardment from orbit was unrelenting, smothering the entire planet in a precisely targeted array of overlapping fire plans that ensured that nothing would escape the virus.

Entire kingdoms and vassal states across the surface were obliterated in minutes. Ancient cultures that had survived Old Night and endured the horror of invasion a dozen times over fell without even knowing why, millions dying in screaming agony as their bodies betrayed them and fell apart, reducing them to rotted, decaying matter.

SINDERMANN WATCHED THE bloom of darkness spread across the slice of the planet visible on the giant pict screens. It spread in a wide black ring, eating its way across the surface of the planet with astonishing speed, leaving grey desolation behind it. Another wave of corruption crept in from another part of the surface, the two dark masses meeting and continuing to spread like the symptom of a horrible disease.

'What… what is it?' whispered Mersadie.

'You have already seen it,' said Euphrati. 'The Emperor showed you, through me. It is death.'

Sindermann's stomach lurched as he remembered the hideous vision of decay, his flesh disintegrating before him and black corruption consuming everything around him.

That was what was happening on Isstvan III.

This was the betrayal.

Sindermann felt as though the blood had drained from him. An entire world was bathed in the immensity of death. He felt an echo of the fear it brought to the people of Isstvan III, and that fear, multiplied across all those billions of people was beyond his comprehension.

'You are remembrancers,' said Keeler, a quiet sadness in her voice. 'Both of you. Remember this and pass it on. Someone must know.'

He nodded dumbly, too numbed by what he was seeing to say anything.

'Come on,' said Euphrati. 'We have to go.'

'Go?' sobbed Mersadie, her eyes still fixed on the death of a world. 'Go where?'

'Away,' smiled Euphrati, taking their hands and leading them through the immobile, horrified throng of remembrancers towards the edge of the chamber.

At first, Sindermann let her lead him, his limbs unable to do more than simply place one foot in front of another, but as he saw she was taking them towards the Astartes at the edge of the chamber, he began to pull back in alarm.

'Euphrati!' he hissed. 'What are you doing? If those Astartes recognise us–'

'Trust me, Kyril,' she said. 'I'm counting on that.'

Euphrati led them towards a hulking warrior who stood apart from the others, and Sindermann knew enough of body language to know that this man was as horrified as they were at what was happening.

The Astartes turned to face them, his face craggy and ancient, worn like old leather.

Euphrati stopped in front of him and said, 'Iacton. I need your help.'

Iacton Qruze. Sindermann had heard Loken speak of him. The 'half-heard'.

He was a warrior of the old days, whose voice carried no weight amongst the higher echelons of command.

A warrior of the old days…

'You need my help?' asked Qruze. 'Who are you?'

'My name is Euphrati Keeler and this is Mersadie Oliton,' said Euphrati, as if her introductions in the midst of such carnage were the most normal thing in the world, 'and this is Kyril Sindermann.'

Sindermann could see the recognition in Qruze's face and he closed his eyes as he awaited the inevitable shout that would see them revealed.

'Loken asked me to look out for you,' said Qruze.

'Loken?' asked Mersadie. 'Have you heard from him?'

Qruze shook his head, but said, 'He asked me to keep you safe while he was gone. I think I know what he meant now. '

'What do you mean?' asked Sindermann, not liking the way Qruze kept casting wary glances at the armed warriors that lined the walls of the chamber.

'Never mind,' said Qruze.

'Iacton,' commanded Euphrati, her voice laden with quiet authority. 'Look at me.'

The craggy-featured Astartes looked down at the slight form of Euphrati, and Sindermann could feel the power and determination that flowed from her.

'You are the half-heard no longer,' said Euphrati. 'Now your voice will be heard louder than any other in your Legion. You cling to the old ways and wish them to return with the fond nostalgia of the venerable. Those days are dying here, Iacton, but with your help we can bring them back again.'

'What are you talking about, woman?' snarled Qruze.

'I want you to remember Cthonia,' said Euphrati, and Sindermann recoiled as he felt an electric surge of energy spark from her, as if her very skin was charged.

'What do you know of the planet of my birth?'

'Only what I see inside you, Iacton,' said Euphrati, a soft glow building behind her eyes and filling her words with promise and seduction. 'The honour and the valour from which the Luna Wolves were forged. You are the only one who remembers, Iacton. You're the only one left that still embodies what it is to be an Astartes.'

'You know nothing of me,' he said, though Sindermann could see her words were reaching him, breaking down the barriers the Astartes erected between themselves and mortals.

'Your brothers called you the Half-heard, but you do not take them to task for it. I know this is because a Cthonian warrior is honourable and cares not for petty insults. I also know that your counsel is not heard because yours is the voice of a past age, when the Great Crusade was a noble thing, done not for gain, but for the good of all humankind.'

Sindermann watched as Qruze's face spoke volumes of the conflict raging within his soul.

Loyalty to his Legion vied with loyalty to the ideals that had forged it.

At last he smiled ruefully and said, '"Nothing too arduous" he said.'

He looked over towards the Warmaster and Maloghurst.

'Come,' he said. 'Follow me.'

'Where to?' asked Sindermann.

'To safety,' replied Qruze. 'Loken asked me to look out for you and that's what I'm going to do. Now be silent and follow me.'

Qruze turned on his heel and marched towards one of the many doors that led out of the audience chamber. Euphrati followed the warrior and Sindermann and Mersadie trotted along after her, unsure as to where they were going or why. Qruze reached the door, a large portal of polished bronze guarded by two warriors, moving them aside with a chopping wave of his hand.

'I'm taking these ones below,' he said.

'Our orders are that no one is to leave,' said one of the guards.

'And I am issuing you new orders,' said Qruze, a steely determination that Sindermann had not noticed earlier underpinning his words. 'Move aside, or are you disobeying the order of a superior officer?'

'No, sir,' said the warriors, bowing and hauling open the bronze door.

Qruze nodded to the guards and gestured that the four of them should pass through.

Sindermann, Euphrati and Mersadie left the audience chamber, the door slamming behind them with an awful finality. With the sounds of the dying planet and the gasps of shock suddenly cut off, the silence that enveloped them was positively unnerving.

'Now what do we do?' asked Mersadie.

'I get us as far away from the *Vengeful Spirit* as possible,' answered Qruze.

'Off the ship?' asked Sindermann.

'Yes,' said Qruze. 'It is not safe for your kind now. Not safe at all.'

TWELVE

Cleansing
Let the galaxy burn
God Machine

THE SCREAMING OF the Choral City's death throes came in tremendous waves, battering against the Precentor's Palace like a tsunami. In the streets below and throughout the palace, the people of the Choral City were decaying where they stood, bodies coming apart in torrents of disintegrating flesh.

The people thronged in the streets to die, keening their hatred and fear up at the sky, imploring their gods to deliver them. Millions of people screamed at once and the result was a terrible black-stained gale of death. A Warsinger soared overhead, trying to ease the agony and terror of their deaths with her songs, but the virus found her too, and instead of singing the praises of Isstvan's gods she coughed out black plumes as the virus tore through her insides. She fell like a shot bird, twirling towards the dying below.

A bulky shape appeared on the roof of the Precentor's Palace. Ancient Rylanor strode to the edge of the roof, overlooking the scenes of horror below, the viral carnage seething between the buildings. Rylanor's dreadnought body was sealed against the world outside, sealed far more effectively than any Astartes armour, and the deathly wind swirled harmlessly around him as he watched the city's death unfold.

Rylanor looked up towards the sky, where far above, the Warmaster's fleet was still emptying the last of its deathly payload onto Isstvan III. The ancient dreadnought stood alone, the only note of peace in the screaming horror of the Choral City's death.

'GOOD JOB WE built these bunkers tough,' said Captain Ehrlen.

The darkness of the sealed bunker was only compounded by the sounds of death from beyond its thick walls. Pitifully few of the World Eaters had made it into the network of bunkers that fringed the edge of the trench network and barricaded themselves inside. They waited in the dark, listening to the virus killing off the city's population more efficiently than even their chainaxes could.

Tarvitz waited amongst them, listening to the deaths of millions of people in mute horror. The

World Eaters appeared to be unmoved, the deaths of civilians meaning nothing to them.

The screaming was dying down, replaced by a dull moaning. Pain and fear mingled in a distant roar of slow death.

'How much longer must we hide like rats in the dark?' demanded Ehrlen.

'The virus will burn itself out quickly,' said Tarvitz. 'That's what it's designed to do: eat away anything living and leave a battlefield for the enemy to take.'

'How do you know?' asked Ehrlen.

Tarvitz looked at him. He could tell Ehrlen the truth, and he knew that he deserved it, but what good would it do? The World Eaters might kill him for even saying it. After all, their own primarch was part of the Warmaster's conspiracy.

'I have seen such weapons employed before,' said Tarvitz.

'You had better be right,' snarled Ehrlen, sounding far from satisfied with Tarvitz's answer. 'I won't cower here for much longer!'

The World Eater looked over his warriors, their bloodstained armoured bodies packed close together in the darkness of the bunker. He raised his axe and called, 'Wrathe! Have you raised the Sons of Horus?'

'Not yet,' replied Wrathe. Tarvitz could see he was a veteran, with numerous cortical implants blistered across his scalp. 'There's chatter, but nothing direct.'

'So they're still alive?'

'Maybe.'

Ehrlen shook his head. 'They got us. We thought we'd taken this city and they got us.'

'None of us could have known,' said Tarvitz.

'No. There are no excuses.' Ehrlen's face hardened. 'The World Eaters must always go further than the enemy. When they attack, we charge right back at them. When they dig in, we dig them out. When they kill our warriors, we kill their cities, but this time, the enemy went further than we did. We attacked their city, and they destroyed it to take us with them.'

'We were all caught out, captain,' said Tarvitz. 'The Emperor's Children, too.'

'No, Tarvitz, this was our fight. The Emperor's Children and the Sons of Horus were to behead the beast, but we were sent to cut its heart out. This was an enemy that could not be scared away or thrown into confusion. The Isstvanians had to be killed. Whether the other Legions acknowledge it or not, the World Eaters were the ones who had to win this city, and we take responsibility for our failures.'

'It's not your responsibility,' said Tarvitz.

'A lesser soldier pretends that his failures are those of his commanders,' said Ehrlen. 'An Astartes realises they are his alone.'

'No, captain,' said Tarvitz. 'You don't understand. I mean–'

'Got something,' said Wrathe from the corner of the bunker.

'The Sons of Horus?' asked Ehrlen.

Wrathe shook his head. 'Death Guard. They took cover in the bunkers further west.'

'What do they say?'

'That the virus is dying down.'

'Then we could be out there again soon,' said Ehrlen with relish. 'If the Isstvanians come to take their city back, they'll find us waiting for them.'

'No,' said Tarvitz. 'There's one more stage of the viral attack still to come.'

'What's that?' demanded Ehrlen.

'The firestorm,' said Tarvitz.

'You SEE NOW,' said Horus to the assembled remembrancers. 'This is war. This is cruelty and death. This is what we do for you and yet you turn your face from it.'

Weeping men and women clung to one another in the wake of such monstrous genocide, unable to comprehend the scale of the slaughter that had just been enacted in the name of the Imperium.

'You have come to my ship to chronicle the Great Crusade and there is much to be said for what you have achieved, but things change and times move on,' continued Horus as the Astartes warriors along the flanks of the chamber closed the doors and stood before them with their bolters held across their chests.

'The Great Crusade is over,' said Horus, his voice booming with power and strength. 'The ideals it once stood for are dead and all we have fought for has been a lie. Until now. Now I will bring the

Crusade back to its rightful path and rescue the galaxy from its abandonment at the hands of the Emperor.'

Astonished gasps and wails spread around the chamber at Horus's words and he relished the freedom he felt in saying them out loud. The need for secrecy and misdirection was no more. Now he could unveil the grandeur of his designs for the galaxy and cast aside his false façade to reveal his true purpose.

'You cry out, but mere mortals cannot hope to comprehend the scale of my plans,' said Horus, savouring the looks of panic that began to spread around the audience chamber.

No iterator could ever have had a crowd so completely in the palm of his hand.

'Unfortunately, this means that there is no place for the likes of you in this new crusade. I am to embark on the greatest war ever unleashed on the galaxy, and I cannot be swayed from my course by those who harbour disloyalty.'

Horus smiled.

The smile of an angelic executioner.

'Kill them,' he said. 'All of them.'

Bolter fire stabbed into the crowd at the Warmaster's order. Flesh burst in wet explosions and a hundred bodies fell in the first fusillade. The screaming began as the crowd surged away from the Astartes who marched into their midst.

But there was no escape.

Guns blazed and roaring chainswords rose and fell.

The slaughter took less than a minute and Horus turned away from the killing to watch the final death throes of Isstvan III. Abaddon emerged from the shadows where he and Maloghurst had watched the slaughter of the remembrancers.

'My lord,' said Abaddon, bowing low.

'What is it, my son?'

'Ship surveyors report that the virus has mostly burned out.'

'And the gaseous levels?'

'Off the scale, my lord,' smiled Abaddon. 'The gunners await your orders.'

Horus watched the swirling, noxious clouds enveloping the planet below.

All it would take was a single spark.

He imagined the planet as the frayed end of a fuse, a fuse that would ignite the galaxy in a searing conflagration and would lead to an inexorable conclusion on Terra.

'Order the guns to fire,' said Horus, his voice cold. 'Let the galaxy burn!'

'EMPEROR PRESERVE US,' whispered Moderati Cassar, unable to hide his horror and not caring who heard him. The miasma of rancid, putrid gasses still hung thickly around the Titan and he could only dimly see the trenches again, along with the Death Guard emerging from the bunkers. Shortly after the order to seal the Titan had been given, the Death Guard had taken cover, clearly in receipt of the same order as the *Dies Irae*.

The Isstvanians had received no such order. The Death Guard's withdrawal had drawn the Isstvanian soldiers forwards and they had borne the full brunt of the bio-weapon.

Masses of mucus-like flesh choked the trenches, half-formed human corpses looming from them, faces melted and rot-bloated bodies split open. Thousands upon thousands of Isstvanians lay in rotting heaps and thick streams of sluggish black corruption ran the length of the trenches.

Beyond the battlefield, death had consumed the forests that lay just outside the Choral City's limits, now resembling endless graveyards of blackened trunks, like scorched skeletal hands. The earth beneath was saturated with biological death and the air was thick with foul gasses released by the oceans of decaying matter.

'Report,' said Princeps Turnet, re-entering the cockpit from the Titan's main dorsal cavity.

'We're sealed,' said Moderati Aruken on the other side of the bridge. 'The crew's fine and I have a zero reading of contaminants.'

'The virus has burned itself out,' said Turnet. 'Cassar, what's out there?'

Cassar took a moment to gather his thoughts, still struggling with the hideous magnitude of death that he couldn't have even imagined had he not seen it through the eyes of the *Dies Irae*.

'The Isstvanians are… gone,' he said. He peered through the swirling clouds of gas at the mass of the city to one side of the Titan. 'All of them.'

'The Death Guard?'

Cassar looked closer, seeing segments of gunmetal armour partially buried in gory chokepoints, marking where Astartes had fallen.

'Some of them were caught out there,' he said. 'A lot of them are dead, but the order must have got to most of them in time.'

'The order?'

'Yes, princeps. The order to take cover.'

Turnet peered through the Titan's eye on Aruken's side of the bridge, seeing Death Guard warriors through the greenish haze securing the trenches around their bunkers and treading through the foul remains of the Isstvanians.

'Damn,' said Turnet.

'We are blessed,' said Cassar. 'They could so easily have been–'

'Watch your mouth, Moderati! That religious filth is a crime by the order of–'

Turnet's voice cut off as movement caught his eyes.

Cassar followed his gaze in time to see the clouds of gas lit up by a brilliant beam of light as a blazing lance strike slashed through the clouds of noxious, highly flammable gasses.

ALL IT TOOK was a single spark.

An entire planet's worth of decaying matter wreathed the atmosphere of Isstvan III in a thick shawl of combustible gasses. The lance strike from the *Vengeful Spirit* burned through the upper atmosphere into the choking miasma and its searing beam ignited the gas with a dull *whoosh* that seemed to suck the oxygen from the air.

In a second, the air itself caught light, ripping across the landscape in a howling maelstrom of fire and noise. Entire continents were laid bare, their landscapes seared to bare rock, their decayed populations vaporised in seconds as winds of fire swept across their surfaces in a deadly gale of blazing destruction.

Cities exploded as gas lines went up, blazing towers of fire whipping madly in the deadly firestorm. Nothing could survive and flesh, stone and metal were vitrified or melted in the unimaginable temperatures.

Entire sprawls of buildings collapsed, the bodies of their former occupants reduced to ashen waste on the wind, palaces of marble and industrial heartlands destroyed in gigantic mushroom clouds as the storm of destruction swept around Isstvan III with relentless, mindless destruction until it seemed as though the entire globe was ablaze.

Those Astartes who had survived the viral attack found themselves consumed in flames as they desperately sought to find cover once more.

But against this firestorm there could be no cover for those who had dared to brave the elements.

By the time the echoes of the recoil had faded on the Warmaster's flagship, billions had died on Isstvan III.

✠ ✠ ✠

MODERATI CASSAR HUNG on for dear life as the tempestuous firestorm raged around the *Dies Irae*. The colossal Titan swayed like a reed in the wind, and he just hoped that the new stabilising gyros the Mechanicum had installed held firm in the face of the onslaught.

Across from him, Aruken gripped the rails surrounding his chair with white knuckled hands, staring in awed terror at the blazing vortices spinning beyond the command bridge.

'Emperor save us. Emperor save us. Emperor save us,' he whispered over and over as the flames billowed and surged for what seemed like an eternity. The heat in the command bridge was intolerable since the coolant units had been shut down when the Titan was sealed off from the outside world.

Like a gigantic pressure cooker, the temperature inside the Titan climbed rapidly until Cassar felt as if he could no longer draw breath without searing the interior of his lungs. He closed his eyes and saw the ghostly green scroll of data flash through his retinas. Sweat poured from him in a torrent and he knew that this was it, this was how he would die: not in battle, not saying the Lectitio Divinitatus, but cooked to death inside his beloved *Dies Irae*.

He had lost track of how long they had been bathed in fire when the professional core of his mind saw that the temperature readings, which had been rising rapidly since the firestorm had hit, were beginning to flatten out. Cassar opened his eyes and saw the madly churning mass of flame through the viewing bays of the Titan's head, but he also saw spots of sky, burned blue as the fire incinerated the last of the combustible gasses released by the dead of Isstvan.

'Temperature dropping,' he said, amazed that they were still alive.

Aruken laughed as he too realised they were going to live.

Princeps Turnet slid back into his command chair and began bringing the Titan's systems back on line. Cassar slid back into his own chair, the leather soaking wet where his sweat had collected. He saw the readouts of the external surveyors come to life as the princeps once again opened their systems to the outside world.

'Systems check,' ordered Turnet.

Aruken nodded, mopping his sweat-streaked brow with his sleeve. 'Weapons fine, though we'll need to watch our rate of fire, since they're already pretty hot.'

'Confirmed,' said Cassar. 'We won't be able to fire the plasma weapons any time soon either. We'll probably blow our arm off if we try.'

'Understood,' said Turnet. 'Initiate emergency coolant procedures. I want those guns ready to fire as soon as possible.'

Cassar nodded, though he was unsure as to the cause of the princeps's urgency. Surely there could be nothing out there that would have survived the firestorm? Certainly nothing that could threaten a Titan.

'Incoming!' called Aruken, and Cassar looked up to see a flock of black specks descending rapidly through the crystal sky, flying low towards the blackened ruins of the burned city.

'Aruken, track them,' snapped Turnet.

'Gunships,' said Aruken. 'They're heading for the centre of the city, what's left of the palace.'

'Whose are they?'

'Can't tell yet.'

Cassar sat back in the cockpit seat and let the filaments of the Titan's command systems come to the fore of his mind once again. He engaged the Titan's targeting systems and his vision plunged into the target reticule, zooming in on the formation of gunships disappearing among the crumbling, fire-blackened ruins of the Choral City. He saw bone-white colours trimmed with blue and the symbol of fanged jaws closing over a planet.

'World Eaters,' he said out loud. 'They're the World Eaters. It must be the second wave.'

'There is no second wave,' said Turnet, as if to himself. 'Aruken, get the vox-mast up and connect me to the *Vengeful Spirit*.'

'Fleet command?' asked Aruken.

'No,' said Turnet, 'the Warmaster.'

IACTON QRUZE LED them through the corridors of the *Vengeful Spirit*, past the Training Halls, past the Lupercal's Court and down through twisting passageways none of them had traversed before, even when they had been hiding from Maggard and Mal-oghurst.

Sindermann's heart beat a rapid tattoo on his ribs, and he felt a curious mix of elation and sorrow fill him as he realised what Qruze had saved them from. There could be little doubt as to what must have happened to those remembrancers in the Audience Chamber and the thought of so many wonderful creative people sacrificed to serve the interests of those with no understanding of art or the creative process galled him and saddened him in equal measure.

He glanced at Euphrati Keeler, who appeared to have become stronger since their escape from death. Her hair was golden and her eyes bright, and though her skin was still pallid, it only served to highlight the power within her.

Mersadie Oliton, by contrast, was visibly weakening.

'They will come after us soon,' said Keeler, 'if they are not already.'

'Can we escape?' Mersadie asked, hoarsely.

Qruze only shrugged. 'We will or we won't.'

'Then this is it?' asked Sindermann.

Keeler shot him an amused glance. 'No, you should know better than that, Kyril. It is never "it", not for a believer. There's always more, something to look forward to when it's all over.'

They passed a number of observation domes that looked out into the cold void of space, the sight only serving to remind Sindermann of just how tiny they were in the context of the galaxy. Even the faintest speck of light that he could see was actually a star, perhaps surrounded by its own worlds, its own people and entire civilisations.

'How is it that we find ourselves at the centre of such momentous events and yet we never saw them coming?' he whispered.

After a while, Sindermann began to recognise his surroundings, seeing familiar signs scraped into bulkheads, and insignia he recognised, telling him that they were approaching the embarkation decks. Qruze led the way unerringly, his stride sure and confident, a far cry from the wretched sycophant he had heard described.

The blast doors to the embarkation deck were closed, the tattered remnants of the votive papers and offerings made to the Warmaster when his sons took him to the Delphos still fixed to the surrounding structure.

'In here,' said Qruze. 'If we're lucky, there will be a gunship we can take.'

'And go where?' demanded Mersadie. 'Where can we go that the Warmaster won't find us?'

Keeler reached out and placed her hand on Mersadie's arm. 'Don't worry. We have more friends than you know, Sadie. The Emperor will show me the way.'

The doors rumbled open and Qruze marched confidently onto the embarkation deck. Sindermann smiled in relief when the warrior said, 'There. Thunderhawk Nine Delta.'

But the smile fell from his face as he saw the gold-
armoured form of Maggard standing before the
machine.

SAUL TARVITZ WATCHED the look of utter disbelief on
Captain Ehrlen's face as he took in the scale of the
destruction wrought by the firestorm. Nothing
remained of the Choral City as they had known it.
Every scrap of living tissue was gone, burned to
atoms by the flames that roared and howled in the
wake of the virus attack.

Every building was black, burned and collapsed
so that Isstvan III resembled a vision of hell, its
tumbled buildings still ablaze as the last combustible materials burned away. Tall plumes of fire
poured skyward in defiance of gravity, fuel lines
and refineries that would continue to burn until
their reserves were exhausted. The stench of
scorched metal and meat was pungent and the vista
before them was unrecognisable as that which they
had fought across only minutes before.

'Why?' was all Ehrlen could ask.

'I don't know,' said Tarvitz, wishing he had more
to tell the World Eater.

'This wasn't the Isstvanians, was it?' asked Ehrlen.

Tarvitz wanted to lie, but he knew that the World
Eater would see through him instantly.

'No,' he said. 'It wasn't.'

'We are betrayed?'

Tarvitz nodded.

'Why?' repeated Ehrlen.

'I have no answers for you, brother, but if they hoped to kill us all in one fell swoop, then they have failed.'

'And the World Eaters will make them pay for that failure,' swore Ehrlen, as a new sound rose over the crackle of burning buildings and tumbling masonry.

Tarvitz heard it too and looked up in time to see a flock of World Eaters' gunships streaking towards their position from the outskirts of the city. Gunfire came down in a burning spray, punching through the ruins around them, boring holes in the black marble of the ground.

'Hold!' shouted Ehrlen.

Heavy fire thudded down among the World Eaters as the gunships roared overhead. Tarvitz crouched at a smashed window opening beside Ehrlen, hearing one of the World Eaters grunt in pain as a shell found its mark.

The gunships passed and soared up into the sky, looping around above the shattered palace before angling down for another run.

'Heavy weapons! Get some fire up there!' yelled Ehrlen.

Gunfire stuttered up from the gaps in partially collapsed roofs, chattering heavy bolters and the occasional ruby flare of a lascannon blast. Tarvitz ducked back from the window as return fire thundered down, stitching lines of explosions through the World Eaters. More of them fell, blown off their feet or blasted apart.

One World Eater slumped down beside Tarvitz, the back of his head a pulsing red mass.

The gunships banked, spraying fire down at their position.

Tarvitz could see the World Eaters zeroing in on them as they flew back towards their position. Return fire lanced upwards and one gunship fell, its engine spewing flames, to smash to pieces against a burning ruin.

Tarvitz could see dozens of gunships, surely the whole of the World Eaters' arsenal.

The lead Thunderhawk dropped through the ruins, hovering a few metres above the ground with its assault ramp down and bolter fire sparking around the opening.

Ehrlen turned towards Tarvitz.

'This isn't your fight,' he yelled over the gunfire. 'Get out of here!'

'Emperor's Children never run!' replied Tarvitz, drawing his sword.

'They do from this!'

No Space Marine could have survived the storm of fire that blazed away at the interior of the gunship, but it was no ordinary Space Marine that was borne within it.

With a roar like a hunting animal, Angron leapt from the gunship and landed with a terrible crash in the midst of the ruined city.

He was a monster of legend, huge and terrible. The primarch's hideous face was twisted in hatred, his huge chainaxes battered and stained with decades of bloodshed. As the mighty primarch landed, World Eaters dropped from the other gunships.

Thousands of World Eaters loyal to the Warmaster followed their primarch into the Choral City, accompanied by the war cries that echoed Angron's own bestial howl as he charged into his former brethren.

HORUS PUT HIS fist through the pict-screen that showed the transmission from the *Dies Irae*. The image of the World Eaters' gunships splintered under the assault as his anger at Angron's defiance boiled over. One of his allies – no, one of his subordinates – had disobeyed his direct order.

Aximand, Abaddon, Erebus and Maloghurst eyed him warily and Horus could imagine their trepidation at the news of Angron's impetuous attack on the survivors of the virus bombing.

That there were survivors at all was galling, but Angron's actions put a whole new spin on the Isstvan campaign.

'And yet,' he said, choking back his rage, 'I am surprised at this.'

'Warmaster,' said Aximand, 'what do you–'

'Angron is a killer!' snapped Horus, rounding on his Mournival son. 'He solves every problem with raw violence. He attacks first and thinks later, if he thinks at all. And yet I never saw this! What else would he do when he saw the survivors of his Legion in the Choral City? Would he sit back and watch the rest of the fleet bombard them from orbit? Never! And yet I did nothing!'

Horus glanced at the smashed remains of the pict-display. 'I will never be caught out like this again. There will be no twists of fate I do not see coming.'

'The questions remains,' said Aximand. 'What shall we do about Angron?'

'Destroy him with the rest of the city,' said Abaddon without a pause. 'If he cannot be trusted to obey his Warmaster then he is a liability.'

'The World Eaters are an exceptionally effective weapon of terror,' retorted Aximand. 'Why destroy them when they can wreak so much havoc among those loyal to the Emperor?'

'There are always more soldiers,' said Abaddon. 'Many will beg to join the Warmaster. There is no room for those who can't follow orders.'

'Angron is a killer, yes, but he is predictable,' put in Erebus, and Horus bristled at the implicit insult in the first chaplain's words. 'He can be kept obedient by letting him off the leash every now and again.'

'The Word Bearers may live by treachery and lies,' snarled Abaddon, 'but in the Sons of Horus you are loyal or you are dead!'

'What do you know of my Legion?' asked Erebus, rising to meet the first captain's ire, his mask of smirking calm slipping. 'I know secrets that would destroy your mind! How dare you speak to me of deceit? This, this reality, all you know, this is the lie!'

'Erebus!' roared Horus, ending the confrontation instantly. 'This is not the place to evangelise your Legion. I have made my decision and these are wasted words.'

'Then Angron will be destroyed in the bombardment?' asked Maloghurst.

'No,' replied Horus. 'He will not.'

'But Warmaster, even if Angron prevails he could be down there for weeks,' said Aximand.

'And he will not fight alone. Do you know, my sons, why the Emperor appointed me Warmaster?'

'Because you were his favoured son,' replied Maloghurst. 'You are the greatest warrior and tactician of the Great Crusade. Whole worlds have fallen at the mention of your name.'

'I did not ask for flattery,' snarled Horus.

'Because you never lose,' said Abaddon levelly.

'I never lose,' nodded Horus, glaring between the four Astartes, 'because I see only victory. I have never seen a situation that cannot be turned into triumph, no disadvantage that cannot be turned to an advantage. *That* is why I was made Warmaster. On Davin I fell, yet came through that ordeal stronger. Against the Auretian Technocracy we faced dissent from within our own fleet, so I used the conflict to rid us of those fomenting rebellion. There is no failing I cannot turn to a component in my victories. Angron has decided to turn Isstvan III into a ground assault – I can consider this a failure and limit its impact by bombing Angron and his World Eaters into dust along with the rest of the planet, or I can forge a triumph from it that will send echoes far into the future.'

Maloghurst broke the silence that followed. 'What would you have us do, Warmaster?'

'Inform the other Legions that they are to prepare for a full assault on the loyalists in the Choral City. Ezekyle, assemble the Legion. Have them ready to launch the attack in two hours.'

'I shall be proud to lead my Legion,' said Abaddon.

'You will not lead them. That honour will go to Sedirae and Targhost.'

Anger flared in Abaddon. 'But I am the first captain. This battle, where resolve and brutality are qualities required for victory, is tailor-made for me!'

'You are a captain of the Mournival, Ezekyle,' said Horus. 'I have another role in mind for you and Little Horus in this fight. One I feel sure you will relish.'

'Yes, Warmaster,' said Abaddon, the frustration disappearing from his face.

'As for you, Erebus…'

'Warmaster?'

'Stay out of our way. To your duties, Sons of Horus.'

THIRTEEN

Maggard
Factions
Luna Wolves

PRINCEPS TURNET LISTENED intently as the orders came through, though Cassar couldn't hear the orders piped into the princeps's ear and he didn't want to – it was all he could do to keep from vomiting. Every time he let his mind wander outside the systems of the *Dies Irae*, he saw nothing but the tangles of charred ruins. His consciousness retreated within the machine, pulling his perception back into the massive form of the Titan.

The *Dies Irae* was coming back to life around him; he could sense the god-machine's limbs flood with power and could feel the weapons reloading. The plasma reactor at its heart was beating in time with his own, a ball of nuclear flame that burned with the Emperor's own righteous strength.

Even here, among all this death and horror, the Emperor was with him. The god-machine was the instrument of His will, standing firm among the destruction. That thought comforted Cassar and helped him focus. If the Emperor was here, then the Emperor would protect.

'Orders in from the *Vengeful Spirit*,' said Turnet briskly. 'Moderati, open fire.'

'Open fire?' said Aruken. 'Sir? The Isstvanians are gone. They're dead.'

To Cassar, Aruken's voice sounded distant, for he was subsumed in the systems of the Titan, but he heard Turnet's voice as clearly as if he had spoken in his own ear.

'Not at the Isstvanians,' replied Turnet, 'at the Death Guard.'

'Princeps?' said Aruken. 'Fire on the Death Guard?'

'I am not in the habit of repeating my orders, moderati,' replied Turnet, 'and they are to fire on the Death Guard. They have defied the Warmaster.'

Cassar froze. As if there wasn't enough death on Isstvan III, now the *Dies Irae* was to fire on the Death Guard, the very force they had been sent to support.

'Sir,' he said. 'This doesn't make any sense.'

'It doesn't need to!' shouted Turnet, his patience finally at an end. 'Just do as I order.'

Looking straight into Turnet's eyes, the truth hit Titus Cassar as though the Emperor had reached out from Terra and filled him with the light of truth.

'The Isstvanians didn't do this, did they?' he asked. 'The Warmaster did.'

Turnet's face creased in a slow smile and Cassar saw his hand reaching towards his holstered sidearm.

Cassar didn't give him the chance to get there first and snatched for his own autopistol.

Both men drew their pistols and fired.

MAGGARD TOOK A step forwards, drawing his golden Kirlian blade and unholstering his pistol. His bulk was even more massive than Sindermann remembered, grossly swollen to proportions beyond human and more reminiscent of an Astartes. Had that been Maggard's reward for his services to the Warmaster?

Without wasting words of preamble, Qruze raised his bolter and fired, but Maggard's armour was the equal of Astartes plate and the shot simply signalled the beginning of a duel.

Sindermann and Mersadie ducked as Maggard's pistol spat fire, the noise appalling as the two warriors ran towards one another with their guns blazing.

Keeler watched calmly as Maggard's gunfire blew chunks from Qruze's armour, but before he could fire any more, Qruze was upon him.

Qruze smashed his fist into Maggard's midriff, but the silent killer rode the punch and swung his sword for the Astartes's head. Qruze ducked back from the great slash of Maggard's sword, the blade

slicing though the armour at the Astartes warrior's
stomach.

Blood sprayed briefly from the wound and Qruze
dropped to his knees in sudden pain before drawing his combat knife, the blade as long as a mortal
warrior's sword.

Maggard leapt towards him and his sword hacked
a deep gouge in Qruze's side. Yet more blood
spilled from the venerable Astartes's body. Another
killing strike slashed towards Qruze, but this time
combat knife and Kirlian blade met in a shower of
fiery sparks. Qruze recovered first and stabbed his
blade through the gap between Maggard's greaves.
The assassin stumbled backwards and Qruze rose
unsteadily to his feet.

The assassin stepped in close and lunged with his
sword. Maggard was almost the equal of Qruze in
physique and had youth on his side, but even Sindermann could see he was slower, as if his new
form was unfamiliar, not yet worn in.

Qruze sidestepped a huge arcing strike of Maggard's sword and swung inside his opponent's
defence, reaching around to lock his head in the
crook of his elbow.

His other arm snapped round to plunge the knife
into Maggard's throat, but a fist seized Qruze's
hand in an iron grip, halting the blade inches from
the man's pulsing jugular.

Qruze fought to force the blade upwards, but
Maggard's newly enhanced strength was the greater
and he began to force the blade to one side. Beads

of sweat popped on Qruze's face, and Sindermann knew that this was a struggle he could not win alone.

He pushed himself to his feet and ran towards Maggard's fallen pistol, its matt black finish cold and lethal-looking. Though designed for a mortal grip, the pistol still felt absurdly huge in his hands.

Sindermann held the heavy pistol outstretched and marched towards the struggling warriors. He couldn't risk a shot from any kind of distance, he was no marksman and was as likely to hit their deliverer as their killer.

He walked up to the fight and placed the muzzle of the pistol directly on the bleeding wound where Qruze had stabbed Maggard. He pulled the trigger and the recoil of the shot almost shattered his wrist, but the effect of his intervention more than made up for the trauma.

Maggard opened his mouth in a silent scream and his entire body flinched in sudden agony. Maggard's grip on the knife weakened and, with a roar of anger, Qruze punched it into the base of his opponent's jaw and through the roof of his mouth.

Maggard buckled and fell to the side with the force of a falling tree. The golden armoured assassin and the Astartes rolled and Qruze was on top of his enemy, still gripping the knife.

Face to face for a moment, Maggard spat a mouthful of blood into Qruze's face. Qruze pushed the knife deeper into Maggard's jaw, plunging it into his opponent's brain.

Maggard spasmed, his huge bulk thrashing briefly, and when he stopped Qruze was looking into a pair of blank, dead eyes.

Qruze pushed himself from Maggard's body.

'Face to face,' said Qruze, breathing heavily with the exertion of killing Maggard. 'Not with treachery, from a thousand miles up. Face to face.'

He looked at Sindermann and nodded his thanks. The warrior was wounded and exhausted, but there was a calm serenity to him.

'I remember how it used to be,' he said. 'We were brothers on Cthonia. Not just among ourselves, but with our enemies, too. That was what the Emperor saw in us when he came to the hives. We were gangs of killers as existed on a thousand other worlds, but we believed in a code that was more precious than life. That was what he wrought into the Luna Wolves. I thought that even if none of the rest of us remembered, the Warmaster would, because he was the one the Emperor chose to lead us.'

'No,' said Keeler, 'you are the last one.'

'And when I realised that I just... told them what they wanted to hear. I tried to be one of them, and I succeeded. I almost forgot everything, until... until now.'

'The music of the spheres,' said Sindermann quietly.

Qruze's eyes focused again on Keeler and his face hardened.

'I did nothing, Half-heard,' said Keeler, answering his unasked question. 'You said so yourself. The ways of Cthonia were the reason the Emperor chose you and your brothers for the Luna Wolves. Perhaps it was the Emperor who reminded you.'

'I saw this coming for so long, but I let it, because I thought that was my code now, but nothing changed, not really. The enemy just moved from out there to amongst us.'

'Look, as profound as this all is, can we get the hell out of here?' asked Mersadie.

Qruze nodded and beckoned them towards the Thunderhawk gunship. 'You're right, Miss Oliton, let's get off this ship. It is dead to me now.'

'We're with you, captain,' said Sindermann as he gingerly picked his way over Maggard's body after Qruze. The years seemed to have dropped from him, as if the energy lost in the fight was returning with interest. Sindermann saw a light in his eyes he hadn't seen before.

Watching the light of understanding rekindled in Iacton Qruze reminded Sindermann that there was still hope.

And there was nothing so dangerous in the galaxy as a little hope.

TURNET'S SHOT WENT high, and Cassar's went wide. Jonah Aruken ducked for cover as the rounds ricocheted on the curved ceiling of the bridge. Turnet rolled down behind the command chair as Cassar pulled himself from his own chair, set deep into the cockpit floor and level with the Titan's eye. Cassar fired again and sparks showered as the autopistol

round hit the electronics arrayed around Turnet's
chair.

Turnet fired back and Cassar dropped into the
cover of the depression formed by his own seat. The
connectors had torn free from his scalp as he
moved and tears of blood streaked his face, metallic monofilament wires clinging wetly to the back
of his neck.

His mind throbbed with the suddenness of being
ripped away from the god-machine.

'Titus!' yelled Aruken. 'What are you doing?'

'Moderati, surrender or you will die here!'
shouted Turnet. 'Throw down your weapon and
surrender.'

'This is treachery!' shouted Cassar. 'Jonah, you
know I am right. The Warmaster did this. He
brought death to this city to kill the believers!'

Turnet fired blindly from behind the elaborate
machinery of the command seat. 'Believe? You
would betray your Warmaster because of this religion? You're diseased, do you know that? Religion
is a sickness, and I should have put you down a
long time ago.'

Cassar thought rapidly. There was only one way
out of the cockpit – the doorway that led into the
Titan's dorsal cavity where the plasma generator
was located along with the detail of engineer crewmen who operated it. He couldn't run, for fear of
Turnet shooting him dead as he broke from cover.

But the same was true of Turnet.

They were both trapped.

'You knew,' said Cassar, 'about the bombard-ment.'

'Of course I knew. How can you be so ignorant? Don't you even know what's happening on this planet?'

'The Emperor is being betrayed,' said Cassar.

'There is no Emperor,' shouted Turnet. 'He abandoned us. He left the Imperium that men died to conquer for him. He doesn't care. But the Warmaster cares. He conquered this galaxy and it is his to rule, but there are fools who don't understand that. They are the ones who have forced the Warmaster into this so that he can do what must be done.'

Cassar's mind reeled. Turnet had betrayed everything the Emperor had built, and the combat within the command bridge struck Cassar as representative of what was happening in the wider conflict.

Turnet rose and fired wildly as he ran for the door, both shots smacking into the bridge wall behind Cassar.

'I won't let you do this!' yelled Cassar, returning fire. His first shot went wide, but now Princeps Turnet was struggling with the wheel lock of the door.

Cassar lined up his shot on Turnet's back.

'Titus! Don't do it!' shouted Aruken, wrenching the Titan's primary motor controls around. The Titan lurched madly, the whole bridge tipping like the deck of a ship in a storm. Cassar was thrown back against the wall, the opportunity to take his shot gone. Turnet hauled the door open, throwing himself from the Titan's bridge and out of Cassar's firing line.

Cassar scrambled to his feet again as the Titan rocked upright. A shape moved in front of him and he almost fired before realising it was Jonah Aruken.

'Titus, come on,' said Aruken. 'Don't do this.'

'I don't have a choice. This is treachery.'

'You don't have to die.'

Cassar jerked his head towards the Titan's eye, through which they could still see the Death Guard moving through the death-slicked trenches. 'Neither do they. You know I am right, Aruken. You know the Warmaster has betrayed the Imperium. If we have the *Dies Irae* then we can do something about it.'

Aruken looked from Cassar's face to the gun in his hand. 'It's over, Cassar. Just... just give this up.'

'With me or against me, Jonah,' said Cassar levelly. 'The Emperor's faithful or His enemy? Your choice.'

IT HAD OFTEN been said that a Space Marine knew no fear.

Such a statement was not literally true, a Space Marine *could* know fear, but he had the training and discipline to deal with it and not let it affect him in battle. Captain Saul Tarvitz was no exception, he had faced storms of gunfire and monstrous aliens and even glimpsed the insane predators of the warp, but when Angron charged, he ran.

The primarch smashed through the ruins like a juggernaut. He bellowed insanely and with one sweep of his chainaxe carved two loyal World Eaters in two, bringing his off-hand axe down to bite through the torso of a third. His traitor World Eaters dived over the rubble, blasting with pistols or stabbing with chainblades.

'Die!' bellowed Captain Ehrlen as the loyalists counter-charged, throwing themselves into the enemy as one. Tarvitz was used to Astartes who fought in feints and counter-charges, overlapping fields of fire, picking the enemy apart or sweeping through his ranks with grace and precision. The World Eaters did not fight with the perfection of the Emperor's Children. They fought with anger and hatred, with brutality and the lust for destruction.

And they fought with more hatred than ever before against their own, against the battle-brothers they had warred alongside for years.

Tarvitz scrambled back from the carnage. World Eaters shouldered past him as they charged at Angron, but the butchered bodies lying around showed what fate awaited them. Tarvitz put his shoulder down and hammered through a ruined wall, sprawling into a courtyard where statues stood scarred and beheaded by the day's earlier battles.

He glanced behind him. Thousands of World Eaters were locked in a terrible hurricane of carnage, scrambling to get at one another. At the centre of the bloody hurricane was Angron, massive and terrible as he laid about him with his axes.

Captain Ehrlen crashed down a short distance from him and the World Eater's eyes flickered over Tarvitz before he rolled onto his back and pulled himself to his feet. Ehrlen's face was torn open, a red mask of blood with his eyes the only recognisable feature. A pack of World Eaters descended on him, piling him to the ground and working at him as though they were carving up a side of meat.

Volleys of bolter shots thudded through the walls and the battle spilled into the courtyard, World Eaters wrestling with one another and forcing bolters up to fire point blank or disembowelling their battle-brothers with chainaxes. Tarvitz kicked himself to his feet and ran as a wall collapsed and a dozen traitors surged forward.

He threw himself behind a pillar, bolt shells blasting chunks of marble from it in concussive impacts. The sound of battle followed him and Tarvitz knew that he had to try and find the Emperor's Children. Only with his fellow warriors alongside him could he impose some form of order on this chaotic fight.

Tarvitz ran, realising that gunfire was directed at him from all angles. He charged through the ruins of a grand dining hall and into a cavernous stone-walled kitchen,

He kept running and smashed his way through the ruins until he found himself in the streets of the Choral City. A burning gunship streaked overhead and crashed into a building in an orange plume of flame as gunfire stuttered throughout the ruins he had just vacated and Angron's roaring cut through the din of battle.

The magnificent dome of the Precentor's Palace rose above the battle unfolding across the blackened remains of the city.

As Tarvitz made his way through the carnage towards his beloved Emperor's Children, he promised that if he was to meet his death on this blasted world, then he would meet it amongst his battle-brothers, and in death defy the hatred the Warmaster had sown amongst them.

LOKEN WATCHED THE Sons of Horus landing on the far side of the Sirenhold. His Space Marines – he couldn't think of them as 'Sons of Horus' any more – were arrayed around the closest tomb-spire in a formidable defensive formation.

His heavy weapons commanded the valley of shrines through which attackers would have to advance and the Tactical Marines held hard points of ruins where they would fight on their own terms.

But the enemy was not the Isstvanian army, they were his brothers.

'I thought they'd bomb us,' said Torgaddon.

'They should have done,' replied Loken. 'Something went wrong.'

'It'll be Abaddon' said Torgaddon. 'He must have been itching for a chance to take us on face-to-face. Horus couldn't have held him back.'

'Or Sedirae,' echoed Loken, distaste in his voice. The afternoon sun hung in veils between the shadows cast by the walls and the tomb-spires.

'I never thought it would end like this, Tarik,' said Loken. 'Maybe storming some alien citadel or defending... defending Terra, like something from the epic poems, something romantic, something the remembrancers could get their teeth into. I never thought it could end defending a hole like this against my own battle-brothers.'

'Yes, but then you always were an idealist.'

The Sons of Horus were coming down on the far side of the tomb-spire across the valley, the optimal point to strike from, and Loken knew that this would be the hardest battle he would ever have to fight.

'We don't have to die here,' said Torgaddon.

Loken looked at him. 'I know, we can win. We can throw everything we have at them. I'll lead them in from the front and then there's a chance that–'

'No,' said Torgaddon. 'I mean we don't have to hold them *here*. We know we can get through the main gates into the city. If we strike for the Precentor's Palace we could link up with the Emperor's Children or the World Eaters. Lucius said the warning came from Saul Tarvitz so they know we are betrayed.'

'Saul Tarvitz is on Isstvan III?' asked Loken, sudden hope flaring in his heart.

'Apparently so,' nodded Torgaddon. 'We could help them. Fortify the palace.'

Loken looked back across at the tangle of shrines and tomb-spires. 'You would retreat?'

'I would when there's no chance of victory and we can fight on better terms elsewhere.'

'We'll never have another chance to face them on our own terms, Tarik. The Choral City is gone, this whole damn planet is dead. It's about punishing them for their betrayal and the brothers we have lost.'

'We all lost brothers here, Garvi, but dying need-lessly won't bring them back. I will have my vengeance, too, but I'm not throwing away the few warriors I have left in a knee jerk act of defiance. Think about this, Loken. Really think, about why you want to fight them here.'

Loken could hear the first bursts of gunfire and knew Torgaddon was right. They were still the best trained, most disciplined of the Legions and he knew that if he wanted to fight those who had betrayed him, he had to fight with his head and not his heart.

'You're right, Tarik,' said Loken. 'We should link up with Tarvitz. We need to get organised to launch a counter-attack.'

'We can really make them suffer, Garvi, we can force them into a battle and delay them. If Tarvitz got the warning out here, who's to say that there aren't others carrying a warning to Terra? Maybe the other Legions already know what's happened. Someone underestimated us, they thought this would be a massacre, but we'll go one better. We'll turn Isstvan III into a war.'

'Do you think we can?'

'We're the Luna Wolves, Garvi. We can do anything.'

Loken took his friend's hand, accepting the truth of his words. He turned to the squads arrayed behind him, scanning the valley through their gunsights.

'Astartes!' he shouted. 'You all know what has happened and I share your pain and outrage, but I need you to focus on what we must now do and not let passion blind you to the cold facts of war. Bonds of brotherhood have been shattered and we are no longer the Sons of Horus, that name has no meaning for us now. We are once again the Luna Wolves, soldiers of the Emperor!'

A deafening cheer greeted his words as Loken continued, 'We are giving the enemy this position and will break through the gates to strike for the palace. Captain Torgaddon and I will take the assault units and lead the speartip.'

Within moments, the newly re-christened Luna Wolves were ready to move out, Torgaddon barking orders to put the assault squads up front. Loken gathered a body of warriors to him, forming a pocket of resistance in the shadow of the tombspire.

'Kill for the living and kill for the dead,' said Torgaddon as they prepared to move out.

'Kill for the living,' replied Loken as the speartip, numbering perhaps two thousand Luna Wolves, moved out across the tombscape of the Sirenhold towards the massive gates.

Loken turned back to the valley, seeing the shapes of Sons of Horus moving towards him. Larger, darker shapes loomed in the distance, grinding the battle-scarred shrines and statues to dust as they went: Rhino APCs, lumbering Land Raiders, and even the barrel-shaped silhouette of a dreadnought.

He felt he should be filled with sadness at the tragedy of fighting his brothers, but there was no sadness.

There was only hatred.

ARUKEN'S EYES WERE hollow and he was sweating. Cassar was shocked to see his normal, cocky arrogance replaced by fear. Despite that fear, Cassar knew that he could not fully trust Jonah Aruken.

'This has to end, Titus,' said Aruken. 'You don't want to be a martyr do you?'

'Martyr? That's a strange choice of words for someone who claims not to believe.'

A small smile appeared on Aruken's face. 'I'm not as stupid as you think, Titus. You're a good man and a damn good crewman. You *believe* in things, which is more than most people can manage. So, I'd rather you didn't die.'

Cassar didn't respond to Aruken's forced levity. '*Please*, I know you're just saying that for the princeps's benefit. I've no doubt he can hear every word.'

'Probably, yes, but he knows that as soon as he opens that door you'll blow his head off. So I guess you and I can just say what we damn well like.'

Cassar's grip on the gun relaxed. 'You're not in his pocket?'

'Hey, we've been through some scary shit recently, haven't we?' said Aruken. 'I know what you're going through.'

Cassar shook his head. 'No you don't, and I know what you're trying to do. I can't back down, I'm making a stand in the name of my Emperor. I won't just surrender.'

'Look, Titus, if you believe then you believe, but you don't have to prove that to anyone.'

'You think I'm doing this for show?' asked Cassar, aiming his gun at Aruken's throat.

Aruken held out his hands and walked carefully around the princeps's command chair to stand across the bridge from him.

'The Emperor isn't just a figurehead to cling to,' said Cassar. 'He is a god. He has a saint and miracles and I have seen them. And so have you! Think of all you have seen and you'll realise you have to help me, Jonah!'

'I saw some odd things, Titus, but–'

'Don't deny them,' interrupted Cassar. 'They happened. As sure as you and I are standing in this war machine. Jonah, there is an Emperor and He is watching over us. He judges us by the choices we make when those choices are hard. The Warmaster has betrayed us and if I stand back and let it happen then I am betraying my Emperor. There are principles that must be defended, Aruken. Don't you even see that much? If none of us take a stand,

After a long pause, the voice returned. 'The̶ ̶ ̶ ̶ see a
̶e welcome on my ship, Iacton Qruze.' ̶ ̶ ̶ o the
'And who are you?' asked Qruze. ̶ ̶ ̶ os-
'I am Captain Nathaniel Garro of the *Eisenstein*.'

then the Warmaster will win and there won't even
be the memory of this betrayal.'

Aruken shook his head in frustration. 'Cassar, if I
could just make you see–'

'You're trying to tell me you haven't seen anything
to believe in?' asked Cassar, turning away in disappointment. He looked through the scorched panes
of the viewing bay at the assembling Death Guard.

'Titus, I haven't believed in anything for a long
time,' said Aruken. 'For that I'm truly sorry, and I'm
sorry for this too.'

Cassar turned to see that Jonah Aruken had
drawn his pistol and had it aimed squarely at his
chest.

'Jonah?' said Cassar. 'You would betray me? After
all we have seen?'

'There's only one thing I want, Titus, and that's
command of my own Titan. One day I want to be
Princeps Aruken and that's not going to happen if I
let you do this.'

Cassar said, 'To know that this whole galaxy is
starved of belief and to think that you might be the
only one who believes… and yet to still believe in
spite of all that. That is faith, Aruken. I wish that
you could understand that.'

'It's too late for that, Titus,' said Aruken. 'I'm
sorry.'

Aruken's gun barked three times, filling the
bridge with bursts of light and noise.

✠ ✠ ✠

TARVITZ COULD SEE the battle from the shadow of an entrance arch leading into the Precentor's Palace. He had escaped the cyclone of carnage that Angron had slaughtered into life, to link up with his own warriors in the palace, but the sight of the World Eater's primarch was still a vivid red horror in his mind.

Tarvitz glanced back into the palace, its vaulted hallways strewn with the bodies of the dead palace guard darkening as late afternoon turned the shadows long and dim. Soon it would be night.

'Lucius,' voxed Tarvitz, static howling. 'Lucius, come in.'

'Saul, what do you see?'

'Gunships and drop-pods too, our colours, landing just north of here.'

'Has the primarch blessed us with his presence?'

'Looks like Eidolon,' said Tarvitz with relish. The vox was heavy with static and he knew that the Warmaster's forces would be attempting to jam their vox-channels without blocking their own.

'Listen, Lucius, Angron is going to break through here. The loyal World Eaters down there won't be able to hold him. He's going to head for the palace.'

'Then there will be a battle,' deadpanned Lucius. 'I hope Angron makes it a good fight. I think I might have found a decent fencing opponent at last.'

'You're welcome to him. We need to make this stand count. Start barricading the central dome.

We'll move to fortifying the main [d...] tions if Angron gives us that long.'

'Since when did you become the [...] asked Lucius petulantly. 'I was the on[...] Vardus Praal.'

Tarvitz felt his anger rise at his frien[d...] ness at such a volatile time, but bit back [...] to say, 'Get in there and help man the b[...] We don't have long before we'll be in the th[...]

THE THUNDERHAWK SPED away from the V[...] *Spirit*, gathering speed as Qruze kicked in the [...] burners. Mersadie felt unutterably light-heade[d...] be off the Warmaster's ship at last, but the cold r[...] isation that they had nowhere to go sobered her[...] she saw glinting specks of the fleet all around ther[...]

'Now what?' asked Qruze. 'We're away, but wher[...] to next?'

'I told you we were not without friends, did I not, [...] Iacton?' said Euphrati, sitting in the co-pilot's chair beside the Astartes warrior.

The warrior gave her a brief sideways look. 'Be that as it may, remembrancer. Friends do us little good if we die out here.'

'But what a death it would be,' said Keeler, with the trace of a ghostly smile.

Sindermann shared a worried glance with her, no doubt wondering if they had overreached themselves in trusting that Euphrati could deliver them to safety out in the dark of space. The old man looked tiny and feeble and she took his hand in hers.

PART THREE

BROTHERS

FOURTEEN

Until it's over
Charmoisan
Betrayal

'I'VE LOST COUNT of the days,' said Loken, crouching by one of the makeshift battlements that looked over the smouldering ruins of the Choral City.

'I don't think Isstvan III has days and nights any more,' replied Saul Tarvitz.

Loken looked into the steel grey sky, a mantle of cloud kicked up by the catastrophic climate change forced on Isstvan III by the sudden extinction of almost all life on its surface. A thin drizzle of ash rained, the remains of the firestorm swept up by dry, dead winds a continent away.

'They're massing for another attack,' said Tarvitz, indicating the tangle of twisted, ash-wreathed rubble that had once been a vast mass of tenement blocks to the east of the palace.

Loken followed his gaze. He could just glimpse a flash of dirty white armour.

'World Eaters.'

'Who else?'

'I don't know if Angron even knows another way to fight.'

Tarvitz shrugged. 'He probably does. He just likes his way better.'

Tarvitz and Loken had first met on Murder, where the Sons of Horus had fought alongside the Emperor's Children against hideous megarachnid aliens. Tarvitz had been a fine warrior, devoid of the grandstanding of his Legion that had so antagonised Torgaddon.

Loken barely remembered the journey back through the Sirenhold, scrambling through shattered tombs and burning ruins. He remembered fighting through men he had once called brother towards the great gates of the Sirenhold, and he had not stopped until he had his first proper sight of the Precentor's Palace and its magnificent rose-granite petals.

'They'll hit within the hour,' said Tarvitz. 'I'll move men over to the defences.'

'It could be a feint,' said Loken, vividly remembering the first days of the battle for the palace. 'Angron hits one side, Eidolon counter-attacks.'

His first sight of Tarvitz's warriors in battle had resembled a great game with the Emperor's Children as pieces masterfully arranged in feints and counter-charges. A lesser man than Saul Tarvitz would have allowed his force to be picked apart by them, but the captain of the Emperor's Children had somehow managed to weather three days of non-stop attacks.

'We'll be ready for it,' said Tarvitz, looking down into the depths of the palace.

Loken and Tarvitz had climbed into the structure of a partially collapsed dome, one of the many sections of the Precentor's Palace that had been ruined during the firestorm and fighting.

Sheared sections of granite petals formed the cover behind which Loken and Tarvitz were sheltering, while in the rubble-choked dome below, hundreds of the survivors were manning the defences. Luna Wolves and Emperor's Children manned barricades made of priceless sculptures and other artworks that had filled the chambers beneath the dome.

Now these monumental sculptures of past rulers lay on their sides with Astartes crouched behind them.

'How much longer do you think we can hold?' asked Loken.

'We'll stay until it's over,' said Tarvitz. 'You said so yourself, every second we survive, the chance grows that the Emperor hears of this and sends the other Legions to bring Horus to justice.'

'If Garro makes it,' said Loken. 'He could be dead already, or lost in the warp.'

'Perhaps, but I have to hope that Nathaniel made it out,' said Tarvitz. 'Our job is to hold them off for as long as we can.'

'That's what worries me. This probably all started when Angron slipped the leash, but the Warmaster could have just pulled his Legions out and bombed this city into dust. He would have lost some of them, but even so… this planet should have been dead a long time ago.'

Tarvitz smiled. 'Four primarchs, Garviel. That's your answer. Four warriors not given to backing down. Who would be the first to leave? Angron? Mortarion? If Eidolon's leading the Emperor's Children then he's got a lot to prove alongside the primarchs, and I have never known Horus show weakness, not when his brother primarchs might see it.'

'No,' agreed Loken. 'The Warmaster does not back down from a battle once he's committed.'

'Then they'll have to kill us all,' said Tarvitz.

'Yes, they will,' said Loken grimly.

The vox-beads in both their helmets chimed and Torgaddon's voice sounded.

'Garvi, Saul!' said Torgaddon. 'I've got reports that the World Eaters are massing. We can hear them chanting, so they'll be coming soon. I've reinforced the eastern barricades, but we need every man down here.'

'I'll pull my men back from the gallery dome,' voxed Tarvitz. 'I'll send Garviel to join you.'

'Where are you going?' asked Loken.

'I'm going to make sure the west and north are still covered and to get some guns on the chapel too,' said Tarvitz, pointing through the ruins of the dome to the strange organic shape of the Warsingers' Chapel adjoining the palace complex.

The survivors had instinctively avoided the chapel and few of them had even seen inside it. Its very walls were redolent of the corruption that had consumed the soul of the Choral City.

'I'll take the chapel and Lucius can take the ground level,' continued Tarvitz, turning back to Loken. 'I swear that sometimes I think Lucius is actually enjoying this.'

'A little too much, if you ask me,' replied Loken. 'You need to keep an eye on him.'

A familiar dull explosion sounded and a tower of rubble and smoke burst from the Choral City's tortured cityscape to the north of the palace.

'Amazing,' said Tarvitz, 'that there are any Death Guard left alive over there.'

'Death Guard are tough to kill,' replied Loken, heading for the makeshift ladder that led down to the remains of the gallery dome.

Despite his words, he knew that it really *was* amazing. Mortarion, never one to do things with finesse, had simply landed one of his fleet's largest orbital landers on the edge of the western trenches and saturated the defences with turret fire while his Death Guard deployed.

That had been the last anyone had heard of the Death Guard in the Choral City.

Though from the haphazardly aimed artillery shells that landed daily in the traitors' camps, it was clear that some loyal Death Guard still resisted Mortarion's efforts to exterminate them.

'I only hope we live as long,' said Tarvitz. 'We're running low on supplies and ammunition. Soon we'll start running low on Astartes.'

'As long as one is alive, captain, we'll fight,' promised Loken. 'Horus picked some unfortunate enemies in you and me. We'll make him regret ever taking us on.'

'Then we'll speak again after Angron's been sent scurrying,' said Tarvitz.

'Until then.'

Loken dropped down into the dome, leaving Tarvitz alone for a moment to look across the blasted city. How long had it been since he had been surrounded by anything other than the nightmarish place the Choral City had become? Two months? Three?

Ashen skies and smouldering ruins surrounded the palace for as far as the eye could see in all directions, the city resembling the kind of hell the Isstvanians themselves might once have believed in.

Tarvitz shook the thought from his mind.

'There are no hells, no gods, no eternal rewards or punishments,' he told himself.

LUCIUS COULD HEAR the killing. He could read the sound of it as though it were written down before him like sheet music. He knew the difference between the war-cries of a World Eater and those of a Son of Horus, and the variance between the tonal quality of a volley of bolter fire launched to support an attack or to defend an obstacle.

The chapel Saul had tasked him with defending was a strange place to be the site of the Great Crusade's last stand. Not so long ago it had been the nerve centre of an enemy regime, but now its makeshift defences were the only thing holding off the far superior traitor forces.

'Sounds like a nasty one,' said Brother Solathen of Squad Nasicae, hunched down by the sill of the chapel window. 'They might break through.'

'Our friend Loken can handle them,' sneered Lucius. 'Angron wants to get some more kills. That's all he wants. Listen? Can you hear that?'

Solathen cocked his head as he listened. Astartes hearing, like most of their senses, was finely honed, but Solathen didn't seem to recognise Lucius's point. 'Hear what, captain?'

'Chainaxes. But they're not cutting into ceramite or other chainblades; they're cutting into stone and steel. The World Eaters can't get to grips with the Sons of Horus over there, so they're trying to hack through the barricades.'

Solathen nodded and said, 'Captain Tarvitz knows what he's doing. The World Eaters only know one way to fight. We can use that to our advantage.'

Lucius frowned at Solathen's praise of Saul Tarvitz, aggrieved that his own contributions to the defences appeared to have been overlooked. Hadn't he killed Vardus Praal? Hadn't he managed to get his men to safety when the virus bombs and the firestorm had hit?

He turned his bitter expression away and stared through the chapel window across the plaza still stained dark with charred ruins. Amazingly, the chapel window was still intact, although its panes had been distorted by the heat of the firestorm, bulging and discoloured with vein-like streaks that reminded Lucius of an enormous insectoid eye.

The chapel itself was more bizarre inside than out, constructed from curved blocks of green stone in looming biological shapes that looked as though a cloud of noxious-looking fumes had suddenly petrified as it billowed upwards. The altar was a great spreading membrane of paler purple stone, like a complex internal organ opened up and pinned for study against the far wall.

'The World Eaters aren't the ones you should be worried about, brother,' continued Lucius idly. 'It's us.'

'Us, captain?'

'The Emperor's Children,' said Lucius. 'You know how our Legion fights. They're the dangerous ones out there.'

Most of the surviving loyalist Emperor's Children were holding the chapel. Tarvitz had taken a force to cover the nearest gate, but several squads were arrayed among the odd organ-like protrusions on the floor below. Squad Nasicae had only four members left, including Lucius himself, and they headed the assault element of the survivors' force along with Squads Quemondil and Raetherin.

Tarvitz had deployed Sergeant Kaitheron on the roof of the chapel with his support squad as well as the majority of the Emperor's Children's remaining heavy weapons. Astartes from the tactical squads were at the chapel windows or in cover further inside. The rest of Lucius's troops were stationed in cover outside the chapel, among the barricades of fallen stone slabs they had set up in the early days of the siege.

Two thousand Space Marines, enough for an entire battle zone of the Great Crusade, were defending a single approach to the palace with the Warsingers' Chapel as the lynchpin of their line.

Movement caught Lucius's eye and he peered through the distorted window into the blackened buildings across from him.

There! A glimpse of gold.

He smiled, knowing full well how the Emperor's Children fought.

'Contact!' he announced to the rest of his force. 'Third block west, second floor.'

'On it,' replied Sergeant Kaitheron, a no-nonsense weapons officer who treated war as a mathematical problem to be solved with angles and weight of fire. Lucius heard the squads moving on the roof, training weapons on the area he had indicated.

'West front, make ready!' ordered Lucius. Several of the tactical squads hurried into firing positions along Lucius's side of the chapel.

The tension was delicious, and Lucius felt a surge of ecstatic sensation crawling along his veins as he heard the song of death building in his blood. A raw, toe-to-toe conflict meant opportunities to exercise perfection in war, but to make it truly memorable it needed these moments of feverish anticipation when the full weight of potential death and glory surged around his body.

'Got them,' called Kaitheron from the chapel roof. 'Emperor's Children. Major force over several floors. Armour too. Land Raiders and Predators. Lascannon, to the fore! Heavy bolters, cover the open ground mid-range and overlap!'

'Eidolon,' said Lucius.

Lucius could see them now, hundreds of Astartes in the purple and gold of the Legion he idolised, gathering in the dead eyes of ruined structures.

'They'll get the support into position first,' said Lucius. 'Then they'll use the Land Raiders to bring the troops in. Mid- to close-range the infantry will move in. Hold your fire until then.'

Tracks rumbled as the Land Raiders, resplendent with gilded eagle's wings and frescoes of war on their armour-plated sides, ground through the shattered ruins of the Choral City. Each was full of Emperor's Children, the galaxy's elite, primed by Eidolon and Fulgrim to treat the men they had once called brothers as foes worthy only of extermination.

To Eidolon, the survivors of the first wave were ignorant and mindless, deserving only death, but they had reckoned without Lucius. He licked his lips at the thought of once again facing the warriors of his Legion; warriors worthy of the name. Enemies he could respect.

Or earn the respect of…

Lucius could practically see the enemy squads deploying with such rapid confidence that they looked more like players in a complex parade-ground move than soldiers at war.

He could taste the moment when the battle would really begin.

He wanted it right there and then, but he also knew how much more delicious the taste of battle was when the timing was perfect.

Windows shattered as fire from the tanks ripped through the chapel, kicking up shards of marble and glass.

'Hold!' ordered Lucius. Despite everything, his Astartes were still Emperor's Children and they would not break ranks like undisciplined World Eaters.

He risked a glance through the splintered glass to see the Land Raiders churning up the marble of the plaza. Predator battle tanks followed them, acting as mobile gun platforms that blew great shuddering chunks from the chapel's battlements. Lascannon fire streaked back and forth, Kaitheron's men attempting to cripple the advancing vehicles and the Land Raiders' sponson-mounted weapons trying to pick off the Astartes on the roof.

A Predator tank slewed to a halt as its track was blown off and another vehicle burst into multi-coloured flames. Purple-armoured bodies tumbled past the window; corpses served as an appetiser to the great feast of death.

Lucius drew his sword, feeling the music build inside him until he felt he could no longer contain it. The familiar hum of his sword's energy field became part of the rhythm and he felt himself slipping into the duellist's dance, the weaving stream of savagery he had perfected over centuries of killing.

How many men were in the assault? Certainly a large chunk of Eidolon's command.

Lucius had fewer men, but this battle was all about winning glory and spectacle.

A tank round shot through a window and burst against the ceiling, showering them in fragments and smoke.

Lucius saw streaks of bolter fire from the palace entrance – Tarvitz was drawing Eidolon in and Eidolon had no choice but to dance to his tune. He heard a musical clang and saw the assault ramps of the Land Raiders slam open and Lucius glimpsed the close-packed armoured bodies within.

'Go!' he yelled and the jump packs of the assault units opened up behind him, catapulting the warriors into battle. Lucius followed in their wake, vaulting through the chapel window. Squad Nasicae came after him and the rest of his warriors followed in turn.

Battle: the dance of war. Lucius knew that against an enemy like Eidolon, there would be no time for anything but the most intense applications of his martial perfection. His consciousness shifted and everything was snapped into wondrous focus, every colour becoming bright and dazzling and every sound blaring and discordant along his nerves.

The duellist's dance took him into the enemy as battle erupted in all its perfectly marshalled chaos around him. Heavy fire streaked down from the roof and Land Raiders twisted on their tracks to bring their guns to bear on the Emperor's Children charging from the chapel.

The Space Marines outside the chapel charged at the same instant, and Eidolon's force was attacked from two sides at once.

Lucius ducked blades and bolts, his sword lashing like a serpent's tongue. Eidolon's force reeled. Squad Quelmondil battled ferociously with the enemy warriors emerging from the nearest Land Raider. He danced past them, savage joy kicking in his heart and he rolled under a spray of bolter fire to come up and stab his blade through the abdomen of an enemy sergeant.

Death was an end in itself, expressing Lucius's superiority through the lives he took, but he had a higher purpose. He knew what he had to do, and his strangely distorted senses sought out the glint of gold or the flutter of a banner, anything indicating the presence of one of Fulgrim's chosen.

Then he saw it; armour trimmed in black instead of gold, a helmet worked into a stern, grimacing skull: Chaplain Charmosian.

The black-armoured warrior stood proud of the top hatch of a Land Raider, directing the battle with sharp chops of his eagle-winged crozius. Lucius grinned manically, setting off through the battle to face Charmosian and slay him in a fight worthy of the Legion's epics.

'Charmosian!' he yelled, his voice sounding like the most vibrant music imaginable. 'Keeper of the Will! I am Lucius, once your brother, now your nemesis!'

Charmosian turned his skull helmet towards Lucius and said, 'I know who you are!'

The chaplain clambered from the hatch and stood on top of the Land Raider, daring Lucius to approach him. Charmosian was a battlefield leader and to fulfil that role he needed the respect of the Legion, respect that could only be earned fighting from the front.

He would be a worthy foe, but that wasn't why Lucius had sought him out.

Lucius leapt onto the Land Raider's track mounting and charged up its glacis until he was face to face with Charmosian. Bolter fire flew in all directions, but it was irrelevant.

This was the only battle in Lucius's mind.

'We taught you too much pride,' said Charmosian, bringing his lethal crozius around in a strike designed to crush Lucius's chest. He brought his blade up to deflect the crozius, and the dance entered a new and urgent phase. Charmosian was good, one of the Legion's best, but Lucius had spent many years training for a fight such as this.

The chaplain's crozius was too heavy to block full-on, so the swordsman let it slide from his blade as Charmosian swung at him time and time again, frustrating him into putting more strength into his blows.

A little longer. A few more moments, and Lucius would have his chance.

He loved the way Charmosian hated him, feeling it as something bright and refreshing.

Lucius could read the pattern of Charmosian's attacks and laughed as he saw the clumsy intent written over every blow. Charmosian wanted to kill Lucius with one almighty stroke, but his crozius rose too far, held too long inert as the chaplain gathered his strength.

Lucius lunged, his sword sweeping out in a high cut that slashed through the chaplain's upraised arms. The crozius tumbled to the ground and Charmosian roared in pain as his arms from the elbows down fell with it.

The battle raged around the scene and Lucius let the noise and spectacle of it fill his over-stimulated senses. The battle was around him, and his victory was all that mattered.

'You know who I am,' said Lucius. 'Your last thought is of defeat.'

Charmosian tried to speak but before the words were out Lucius spun his sword in a wide arc and

Charmosian's head was sliced neatly from his shoulders.

Crimson sprayed across the gold of the Land Raider's hull. Lucius caught the head as it spun through the air and held it high so the whole battlefield could see it.

Around him, thousands of the Emperor's Children fought to the death as Eidolon's force, hit from two sides, reeled against the palace defences and fell back. Tarvitz led the counter-strike and Eidolon's attack was melting away.

He laughed as he saw Eidolon's command tank, a Land Raider festooned with victory banners, rise up over a knot of rubble as it retreated from the fighting.

The loyalists had won this battle, but Lucius found that he didn't care.

He had won his own battle, and pulling Charmosian's head from the skull faced helmet and throwing it aside, he knew he had what he needed to ensure that the song of death kept playing for him.

THE WARSINGERS' CHAPEL was quiet. Hundreds of new bodies lay around it, purple and gold armour scorched and split, runnels of blood gathering between the stained marble tiles. In some places they lay alongside the blackened armour of the World Eaters who had died in the initial assaults on the Choral City.

The palace entrance was heavily barricaded and in the closest dome of the palace, the few apothecaries in the loyalist force were patching up their wounded.

Tarvitz saw Lucius cleaning his sword, alternating between wiping the blade and using its tip to carve new scars on his face. A skull-faced helmet sat beside him.

'Is that really necessary?' asked Tarvitz.

Lucius looked up and said, 'I want to remember killing Charmosian.'

Tarvitz knew he should discipline the swordsman, reprimand him for practices that might be considered barbaric and tribal, but here, amid this betrayal and death, such concerns seemed ridiculously petty.

He squatted on the ground next to Lucius, his limbs aching and his armour scarred and dented from the latest battle at the entrance to the palace.

'Fair enough,' he said, jerking his thumb in the direction of the enemy. 'I saw you kill him. It was a fine strike.'

'Fine?' said Lucius. 'It was better than fine. It was art. You never were much for finesse, Saul, so I'm not surprised you didn't appreciate it.'

Lucius smiled as he spoke, but Tarvitz saw a very real flash of annoyance cross the swordsman's features, a glimpse of hurt pride that he did not like the look of.

'Any more movement?' he asked, changing the subject.

'No,' said Lucius. 'Eidolon won't come back before he's regrouped.'

'Keep watching,' ordered Tarvitz. 'Eidolon could catch us unawares while our guard's down.'

'He won't breach us,' promised Lucius, 'not while I'm here.'

'He doesn't have to,' said Tarvitz, wanting to make sure Lucius understood the reality of their position. 'Every time he attacks, we lose more warriors. If he strikes fast and pulls out, we'll be whittled down until we can't hold everywhere at once. The ambush from the temple cost him more than he'd like, but he still took too many of us down.'

'We saw him off though,' said Lucius.

'Yes,' agreed Tarvitz, 'but it was a close run thing, so I'll send a squad to help keep the watch.'

'So you don't trust me to keep watch now, is that it?'

Tarvitz was surprised at the venom in Lucius's voice and said, 'No, that's not it at all. All I want is to make sure that you have enough warriors here to fend off another attack. Anyway, I need to attend to the western defences.'

'Yes, off you go and lead the big fight, you're the hero,' snapped Lucius.

'We will win this,' said Tarvitz, placing his hand on the swordsman's shoulder.

'Yes,' said Lucius, 'we will. One way or another.'

LUCIUS WATCHED TARVITZ go, feeling his anger at his assumption of command. Lucius had been the one earmarked for promotion and greatness, not Tarvitz. How could his own glorious accomplishments have been overshadowed by the plodding leadership of Saul Tarvitz? All the glories that he had earned in the crucible of combat were forgotten and he felt his bitterness rise up in a choking wave in his gullet.

He had felt a moment's guilt as he had formed his plan, but remembering Tarvitz's patronising condescension, he felt that guilt vanish like snow in the sunshine.

The temple was quiet and Lucius checked to make sure that he was alone, moving to sit on one of the outcroppings of smooth grey-green stone and lifting Charmosian's helmet.

He peered into the bloodstained helmet until he saw the glint of silver, and then reached in and pulled out the small metallic scrap that was Charmosian's helmet communicator.

Once again he checked to see that he was alone before speaking into it.

'Commander Eidolon?' he said, his frustration growing as he received no answer.

'Eidolon, this is Lucius,' he said. 'Charmosian is dead.'

There was a brief crackle of static, and then, 'Lucius.'

He smiled as he recognised Eidolon's voice. As one of the senior officers among the Emperor's Children, Charmosian had been in direct contact with Eidolon, and, as Lucius had hoped, the channel had still been open when the chaplain had died.

'Commander!' said Lucius, his voice full amuse-ment. 'It is good to hear your voice.'

'I have no interest in listening to your taunts, Lucius,' snarled Eidolon. 'You must know we will kill you all eventually.'

'Indeed you will,' agreed Lucius, 'but it will take a very long time. A great many Emperor's Children will die before the palace falls. Sons of Horus and World Eaters, too. And Terra knows how many of Mortarion's Death Guard have died already in the trenches. You will suffer for this, Eidolon. The War-master's whole force will suffer. By the time the other Legions get here he may have lost too many on Isstvan III to win through.'

'Keep telling yourself that, Lucius, if it makes it easier.'

'No, commander,' he said. 'You misunderstand me. I am saying that I wish to make a deal with you.'

'A deal?' asked Eidolon. 'What kind of deal?'

Lucius's scars tightened as he smiled. 'I will give you Tarvitz and the Precentor's Palace.'

FIFTEEN

No shortage of wonders
Old friends
Perfect failure

THE STRATEGIUM WAS dimly lit, the only illumination coming from the flickering pict screens gathered like supplicants around the Warmaster's throne and a handful of torches that burned low with a fragrant aroma of sandalwood. The back wall of the strategium had been removed during the fighting on Isstvan III, revealing a fully fashioned temple adjoining the *Vengeful Spirit*'s bridge.

The Warmaster sat alone. None dared disturb his bitter reveries as he sat brooding on the conflict raging below. What should have been a massacre had turned into a war – a war he could ill afford the time to wage.

Despite his brave words to his brother primarchs, the battle on Isstvan III worried him. Not for any fear that his warriors would lose, but for the fact that they were engaged at all. The virus bombing should have killed every one of those he believed would not support him in his campaign to topple the Emperor from the Golden Throne of Terra.

Instead, the first cracks had appeared in what should have been a faultless plan.

Saul Tarvitz of the Emperor's Children had taken a warning to the surface…

And the *Eisenstein*…

He remembered Maloghurst's fear as he had come to tell him of the debacle with the remembrancers, the fear that the Warmaster's wrath would prove his undoing.

Maloghurst had limped towards the throne with his hooded head cast down.

'What is it Maloghurst?' Horus had demanded.

'They are gone,' said Maloghurst. 'Sindermann, Oliton and Keeler.'

'What do you mean?'

'They are not amongst the dead in the Audience Chamber,' explained Maloghurst. 'I checked every corpse myself.'

'You say they are gone?' asked the Warmaster at last. 'That implies you know where they have gone. Is that the case?'

'I believe so, my lord,' nodded Maloghurst. 'It appears they boarded a Thunderhawk and flew to the *Eisenstein*.'

'They stole a Thunderhawk,' repeated Horus. 'We are going to have to review our security procedures regarding these new craft. First Saul Tarvitz and now these remembrancers; it seems anyone can steal one of our ships with impunity.'

'They did not steal it on their own,' explained Maloghurst. 'They had help.'

'Help? From whom?'

'I believe it was Iacton Qruze. There was a struggle and Maggard was killed.'

'Iacton Qruze?' laughed Horus mirthlessly. 'We have seen no shortage of wonders, but perhaps this is the greatest of them. The Half-heard growing a conscience.'

'I have failed in this, Warmaster.'

'It is not a question of failure, Maloghurst! Mistakes like this should never occur. More and more of my efforts are distracted from this battle. Tell me, where is the *Eisenstein* now?'

'It attempted to break through our blockade to reach the system jump point.'

'You say "attempted",' noted Horus. 'It did not succeed?'

Maloghurst paused before answering. 'Several of our ships intercepted the *Eisenstein* and heavily damaged it.'

'But they did not destroy it?'

'No, my lord, before they could do so, the *Eisenstein's* commander made an emergency jump into the warp, but the ship was so badly damaged that we do not believe it could survive such a translation.'

'If it does, then the whole timetable of my designs will be disrupted.'

'The warp is dark, Warmaster. It is unlikely that–'

'Do not be so sure of yourself, Maloghurst,' warned Horus. 'The Isstvan V phase is critical to our success and if the *Eisenstein* carries word of our plans to Terra, then all may be lost.'

'Perhaps, Warmaster, if we were to withdraw from the Choral City and blockade the planet, we could ensure that the Isstvan V phase proceeds as planned.'

'I am the Warmaster and I do not back down from a battle!' shouted Horus. 'There are goals to be won in the Choral City that you cannot comprehend.'

Horus was shaken from his memories by the chiming of the communications array fitted into the arm of his throne.

'This is the Warmaster.'

A holomat installed beneath the floor projected a large square plane on which swirled an image, high above the Warmaster's temple. The image resolved into the face of Lord Commander Eidolon, evidently inside his command Land Raider. The sound of distant explosions washed through the static.

'Warmaster,' said Eidolon. 'I bring news that I feel you should hear.'

'Tell me,' said Horus, 'and it had better be good news.'

'Oh, it is, my lord,' said Eidolon.

'Well, don't drag this out, Eidolon,' warned Horus. 'Tell me!'

'We have an ally inside the palace.'

'An ally? Who?'

'Lucius.'

THE AFTERMATH OF a battle was the worst part.

An Astartes warrior was used to the tension of waiting for an attack to come, and even the din and pain of battle itself. But Loken never wished for a time without war more than when he saw what was left after the battle had finished. He didn't experience fear or despair in the manner of a mortal man, but he felt sorrow and guilt as they did.

Angron's latest attack had been one of the fiercest yet, the primarch himself leading it, charging through the ruins of the palace dome towards Loken's defences. Thousands of blood covered World Eaters had followed him and many of those warriors still lay where they had fallen.

Once this place had been part of the palace, a handsome garden with summer-houses, ornamental lakes and a roof that opened up to the sun. Now it was a rubble-strewn ruin, its roof collapsed and only an incongruous decorated post or the splintered remains of an ornamental bridge remaining of its finery.

The bodies of the World Eaters were concentrated on the forward barricade, a line of heaped rubble and metal spikes constructed by the Luna Wolves. Angron had attacked it in force and Torgaddon had relinquished it, letting the World Eaters die for it before his Astartes fell back to the defences at the entrance of the palace's central dome. The ruse had worked and the World Eaters had been strung out as they charged at Loken's position. Many had died to the guns Tarvitz had stationed above the barricades, and by the time Loken's sword had left its sheath it was only momentum that kept the World Eaters fighting – victory was beyond them.

Luna Wolves were mixed in with the World Eaters' dead, warriors Loken had known for years. Although the sounds of battle had faded, Loken fancied he could still hear echoes of the fighting, chainblades ripping through armour and volleys of bolter rounds splitting the air.

'It was a close run thing, Garviel,' said a voice from behind Loken, 'but we did it.'

Loken glanced round to see Saul Tarvitz emerging from the central dome. Loken smiled as he saw his friend and battle-brother, a man who had come a long way from the line officer he had been back on Murder to command the survivors of Horus's treachery.

'Angron will be back,' said Loken.

'Their ruse failed, though,' said Tarvitz.

'They don't need to break in, Saul,' said Loken. 'Horus will whittle us down until there's no one left. Then Eidolon and Angron can just roll over us.'

'Not forgetting the Warmaster's Sons of Horus,' said Tarvitz.

Loken shrugged. 'There's no need for them to get involved yet. Eidolon wants the glory and the World Eaters are hungry for blood. The Warmaster will happily let the other Legions wear us down before they strike.'

'That's changed,' said Tarvitz.

'What do you mean?'

'I've just had word from Lucius,' explained Tarvitz. 'He tells me that his communications specialists have broken the Sons of Horus communiqués. Some old friends of yours are coming down from the *Vengeful Spirit* to lead the Legion.'

Loken turned from the battlefield, suddenly interested. 'Who?'

'Ezekyle Abaddon and Horus Aximand,' said Tarvitz. 'Apparently they are to bring the Warmaster's own wrath down upon the city. The Sons of Horus will be playing their hand soon enough, I think.'

Abaddon and Aximand, the arch-traitors, men Loken had admired for so long and the heart of the Mournival. Both warriors stood at Horus's right hand and possibilities flashed through Loken's mind. Deprived of the last of its Mournival, a crucial part of the Legion would die and it would start unravelling without such inspirational figureheads.

'Saul, are you certain?' asked Loken urgently.

'As sure as I can be, but Lucius seemed pretty excited by the news.'

'Did this intercept say where they would be landing?' demanded Loken.

'It did,' smiled Lucius. 'The Mackaran Basilica, just beyond the palace. It's a big temple with a spire in the shape of a trident.'

'I have to find Tarik,'

'He is with Nero Vipus, helping Vaddon with the wounded.'

'Thank you for bringing me this news, Saul,' said Loken with a cruel smile. 'This changes everything.'

LUCIUS PEERED PAST the bullet-riddled pillar, scanning through the darkness of one of the many battlefields scattered throughout the ruins of the palace. Bodies, bolters and chainaxes lay on the shattered tiles where they had been dropped and many of the bodies were still locked in their last, fatal combat.

It had not been difficult for Lucius to slip out of the palace. The biggest danger had been the snipers of the recon squads the Warmaster's forces had deployed among the ruins. Lucius had spied movement in the ruined buildings several times and had taken cover in shell craters or behind heaps of corpses.

Squirming through the filth and darkness like an animal – it had been humiliating, though the sights, sounds and smells of these battlefields still filled his senses in an arousing way. He stepped warily into the courtyard. The bodies that lay everywhere had been butchered, hacked apart with chainblades or battered to death with fists.

It was an ugly spectacle, yet he relished the image of how intense their deaths must have been.

'No artistry,' he said to himself as a gold and purple armoured figure detached from the shadows. A score of warriors followed him and Lucius smiled as he recognised Lord Commander Eidolon.

'Lord commander,' said Lucius, 'it is a pleasure to stand before you once more.'

'Damn your blandishments!' spat Eidolon. 'You are a traitor twice over.'

'That's as maybe,' said Lucius, slouching on a fallen pillar of black marble, 'but I am here to give you what you want.'

'Ha!' scoffed Eidolon. 'What can you give us, traitor?'

'Victory,' said Lucius.

'Victory?' laughed Eidolon. 'You think we need your help to give us that? We have you in a vice! One by one, death by death, victory will be ours!'

'And how many warriors will you lose to achieve it?' retorted Lucius. 'How many of Fulgrim's chosen are you willing to throw into a battle that should never have been fought at all? You can end this right now, right here, and keep all your Astartes alive for the real battle! When the Emperor sends his reply to Horus's treachery you will need every single one of your battle-brothers and you know it.'

'And what would be your price for this invaluable help?' asked Eidolon.

'Simple,' said Lucius. 'I want to rejoin the Legion.'

Eidolon laughed in his face and Lucius felt the song of death surge painfully through his body, but he forced its killing music back down inside him.

'Are you serious, Lucius?' demanded Eidolon. 'What makes you think we *want* you back?'

'You need someone like me, Eidolon. I want to be part of a Legion that respects my skills and ambition. I am not content to stay a captain for the rest of my life like that wretch Tarvitz. I will be at Fulgrim's side where I belong.'

'Tarvitz,' spat Eidolon. 'Does he still live?'

'He lives,' nodded Lucius, 'although I will gladly kill him for you. The glory of this battle should be mine, yet he lords over us all as if he is one of the chosen.'

Lucius felt his bitterness rise and fought to maintain his composure. 'He was once happy to trudge alongside his warriors and leave better men to the glory, but he has chosen this battle to discover his ambition. It's thanks to him that I'm down here at all.'

'You ask for a great deal of trust, Lucius,' said Eidolon.

'I do, but think what I can give you: the palace, Tarvitz.'

'We will have these things anyway.'

'We are a proud Legion, lord commander, but we never send our brothers to their deaths to prove a point.'

'We follow the orders of the Warmaster in all things,' replied Eidolon guardedly.

'Indeed,' noted Lucius, 'but what if I said I can give you a victory so sudden it will be yours and yours alone. The World Eaters and the Sons of Horus will only flounder in your wake.'

Lucius could see he had caught Eidolon's interest and suppressed a smile. Now all he had to was reel him in.

'Speak,' commanded Eidolon.

'I'M COMING WITH you, Garvi,' said Nero Vipus, walking into the only dome of the palace not to be ruined by the siege. It had once been an auditorium with a stage and rows of gilded seats, where the music of creation had once played to the Choral City's elite, but now it was mouldering and dark.

Loken rose from his battle meditation, seeing Vipus standing before him and said, 'I knew you would wish to come, but this is something Tarik and I have to do alone.'

'Alone?' said Vipus. 'That's madness. Ezekyle and Little Horus are the best soldiers the Legion has ever had. You can't go up against them alone.'

Loken placed his hand on his friend's shoulder and said, 'The palace will fall soon enough with or without Tarik and me. Saul Tarvitz has done unimaginable things in keeping us all alive as long as he has, but ultimately the palace will fall.'

'Then what's the point of throwing your life away hunting down Ezekyle and Little Horus?' demanded Vipus.

'We only have one goal on Isstvan III, Nero, and that's to hurt the Warmaster. If we can kill the last of the Mournival then the Warmaster's plans suffer. Nothing else matters.'

'You said we were supposed to be holding the traitors here while the Emperor sent the other Legions to save us. Is that not true any more? Are we on our own?'

Loken shook his head and retrieved his sword from where he had propped it against the wall. 'I don't know, Nero. Maybe the Emperor has sent the Legions to rescue us, maybe he hasn't, but we have to assume that we're on our own. I'm not going to fight with nothing but blind hope to keep me going. I'm going to make a stand.'

'And that's what I want to do,' said Vipus, 'at my friend's side.'

'No, you need to stay here,' said Loken. 'Your stand must be made here. Every minute you keep the traitors here is another minute for the Emperor to bring the Warmaster to justice. This killing is Mournival business, Nero. Do you understand?'

'Frankly, no,' said Nero, 'but I will do as you ask and stay here.'

Loken smiled. 'Don't mourn me yet, Nero. Tarik and I may yet prevail.'

'You'd better,' said Vipus. 'The Luna Wolves need you.'

Loken felt humbled by Nero's words and embraced his oldest friend. He dearly wished he could tell him that there was yet hope and that he expected to return alive from this mission.

'Garviel,' said a familiar voice from the entrance to the dome.

Loken and Nero released each other from their brotherly embrace and saw Saul Tarvitz, framed in the wan light of the auditorium's entrance.

'Saul,' said Loken.

'It's time,' said Tarvitz. 'We're ready to create the diversion you requested.'

Loken nodded and smiled at the two brave warriors, men he had fought through hell for and would do so a hundred times more. The honour they did him just by being his friends made his chest swell with pride.

'Captain Loken,' said Tarvitz formally. 'It may be that this is the last time we will meet.'

'I do not think,' replied Loken, 'there is any "maybe" about it.'

'Then I will wish you all speed, Garviel.'

'All speed, Saul,' said Loken, offering his hand to Tarvitz. 'For the Emperor.'

'For the Emperor,' echoed Tarvitz.

With his farewells said, Loken made his way from the auditorium, leaving Tarvitz and Vipus to organise the defences for the next attack.

Surviving tactical maps indicated that the Mackaran Basilica lay to the north of their position and as he made his way towards the point he had selected as the best place to leave the palace he found Torgaddon waiting for him.

'You saw Vipus?' asked Torgaddon.

'I did,' nodded Loken. 'He wanted to come with us.'

Torgaddon shook his head. 'This is Mournival business.'

'That's what I told him.'

Both warriors took deep breaths as the enormity of what they were about to attempt swept over them once again.

'Ready?' asked Loken.

'No,' said Torgaddon. 'You?'

'No.'

Torgaddon chuckled as he turned to the tunnel that led from the palace.

'Aren't we a pair?' he said and Loken followed him into the darkness.

For good or ill, the final battle for Isstvan III was upon them.

'YOU DARE RETURN to me in failure?' bellowed Horus, and the bridge of the *Vengeful Spirit* shook with the fury of his voice. His face twisted in anger at the wondrous figure standing before him, struggling to comprehend the scale of this latest setback.

'Do you even understand what I am trying to do here?' raged Horus. 'What I have started at Isstvan will consume the whole galaxy, and if it is flawed from the outset then the Emperor will break us!'

Fulgrim appeared uncowed by his anger, his brother's features betraying an insouciance quite out of character for the primarch of the Emperor's Children. Though he had but recently arrived on his flagship, *Pride of the Emperor*, Fulgrim looked as magnificent as ever.

His exquisite armour was a work of art in purple and gold, bearing many new embellishments and finery with a flowing, fur-lined cape swathing his body. More than ever, Horus thought Fulgrim looked less like a warrior and more like a rake or libertine. His brother's long white hair was pulled back in an elaborate pattern of plaits and his pale cheeks were lightly marked with what appeared to be the beginnings of tattoos.

'Ferrus Manus is a dull fool who would not listen to reason,' said Fulgrim. 'Even the mention of the Mechanicum's pledge did not–'

'You swore to me that you could sway him! The Iron Hands were essential to my plans. I planned Isstvan III with your assurance that Ferrus Manus would join us. Now I find that I have yet another enemy to contend with. A great many of our Astartes will die because of this, Fulgrim.'

'What would you have had me do, Warmaster?' smiled Fulgrim, and Horus wondered where this new, sly mocking tone had come from. 'His will was stronger than I anticipated.'

'Or you simply had an inflated opinion of your own abilities.'

'Would you have me kill our brother, Warmaster?' asked Fulgrim.

'Perhaps I will,' replied Horus unmoved. 'It would be better than leaving him to roam free to destroy our plans. As it is he could reach the Emperor or one of the other primarchs and bring them all down on our heads before we are ready.'

'Then if you are quite finished with me, I shall return to my Legion,' said Fulgrim, turning away.

Horus felt his choler rise at Fulgrim's infuriating tone and said, 'No, you will not. I have another task for you. I am sending you to Isstvan V. With all that has happened, the Emperor's response is likely to arrive more quickly than anticipated and we must be prepared for it. Take a detail of Emperor's Children to the alien fortresses there and prepare it for the final phase of the Isstvan operation.'

Fulgrim recoiled in disgust. 'You would consign me to a role little better than a castellan, as some prosaic housekeeper making it ready for your grand entrance? Why not send for Perturabo? This kind of thing is more to his liking.'

'Perturabo has his own role to play,' said Horus. 'Even now he prepares to lay waste to his home world in my name. We shall be hearing more of our bitter brother very soon. Have no fear of that.'

'Then give this task to Mortarion. His grimy foot-sloggers will relish such an opportunity to muddy their hands for you!' spat Fulgrim. 'My Legion was the chosen of the Emperor in the years when he still deserved our service. I am the most glorious of his heroes and the right hand of this new Crusade. This is… this is a betrayal of the very principles for which I chose to join you, Horus!'

'Betrayal?' said Horus, his voice low and dangerous. 'A strong word, Fulgrim. Betrayal is what the Emperor forced upon us when he abandoned the galaxy to pursue his quest for godhood and gave over the conquests of our Crusade to scriveners and bureaucrats. Is that the charge you would level at me now, to my face, here on the bridge of my own ship?'

Fulgrim took a step back, his anger fading, but his eyes alight with the excitement of the confrontation. 'Perhaps I do, Horus. Perhaps someone needs to tell you a few home truths now that your precious Mournival is no more.'

'That sword,' said Horus, indicating the venom-sheened weapon that hung low at Fulgrim's waist. 'I gave you that blade as a symbol of my trust in you, Fulgrim. We alone know the true power that lies within it. That weapon almost killed me and yet I gave it away. Do you think I would give such a weapon to one I do not trust?'

'No, Warmaster,' said Fulgrim.

'Exactly. The Isstvan V phase of my plan is the most critical,' said Horus, stoking the dangerous embers of Fulgrim's ego. 'Even more so than what is happening below us. I can entrust it to no other. You *must* go to Isstvan V, my brother. All depends on its success.'

For a long, frightening moment, violent potential crackled between Horus and the primarch of the Emperor's Children.

Fulgrim laughed and said, 'Now you flatter me, hoping my ego will coerce me into obeying your orders.'

'Is it working?' asked Horus as the tension drained away.

'Yes,' admitted Fulgrim. 'Very well, the Warmaster's will be done. I will go to Isstvan V.'

'Eidolon will stay in command of the Emperor's Children until we join you at Isstvan V,' said Horus and Fulgrim nodded.

'He will relish the chance to prove himself further,' said Fulgrim.

'Now leave me, Fulgrim,' said Horus, 'You have work to do.'

SIXTEEN

Enemy within
The Eightfold Path
Honour must be satisfied

APOTHECARY VADDON FOUGHT to save Casto's life.
The upper half of the warrior's armour had been
removed and his bare torso was disfigured by a gory
wound, flaps of skin and chunks of muscle blown
aside like the petals of a bloody flower by an
exploding bolter round.

'Pressure!' said Vaddon as he flicked over the set-
tings on his narthecium gauntlet. Scalpels and
syringes cycled as Brother Mathridon, an Emperor's
Children Astartes who had lost a hand in the earlier
fighting and served as Vaddon's assistant, kept pressure on the wound. Casto bucked underneath him,
his teeth gritted against pain that would kill anyone
but an Astartes.

Vaddon selected a syringe and pushed it into
Casto's neck. The vial mounted on the gauntlet

emptied, pumping Casto's system with stimulants to keep his heart forcing blood around his ruptured organs. Casto shook, nearly snapping the needle.

'Hold him still,' snapped Vaddon.

'Yes,' said a voice behind them. 'Hold him still. It will make it easier to kill him.'

Vaddon's head snapped up and he saw a warrior clad in the armour of an Emperor's Children lord commander. He carried an enormous hammer, purple arcs of energy playing around its massive head. Behind the warrior, Vaddon could see a score of Emperor's Children in purple and gold finery, their armour sheened with lapping powder and oil.

Instantly, he knew that these were no loyalists and felt a cold hand clutch at his chest as he saw that they were undone.

'Who are you?' demanded Vaddon, though he knew the answer already.

'I am your death, traitor!' said Eidolon, swinging his hammer and crushing Vaddon's skull with one blow.

HUNDREDS OF EMPEROR'S Children streamed into the palace from the east, on a tide of fire and blood. They fell upon the wounded first, Eidolon himself butchering those who lay waiting for Vaddon's ministrations, taking particular relish in killing the loyalist Emperor's Children he found there. The warriors of his Chapter swarmed through the palace around him, the defenders discovering to their horror that their flank had somehow been turned and that more and more of the traitors were pouring into the palace.

Within moments, the last battle had begun. The loyalists turned from their defences and faced the Emperor's Children. Assault Marines' jump packs gunned them across ruined domes to crash into Eidolon's assault units. Heavy weapons troopers and scout snipers amongst the ruined battlements shot down into the enemy, swapping tremendous volleys of fire across the shattered domes.

It was a battle without lines or direction as the fighting spilled into the heart of the Precentor's Palace. Each Astartes became an army of his own as all order broke down and every warrior fought alone against the enemies that surrounded him. Emperor's Children jetbikes screamed insanely through the precincts of the palace and ripped crazed circuits around the domes, spraying fire into the Astartes battling below them.

Dreadnoughts tore up chunks of fallen masonry with their mighty fists and hurled them at the loyalists holding the barricades against which so many of their foes had died only a short while before.

Everything was swirling madness, horror and destruction, with Eidolon at the centre of it, swinging his hammer and killing all who came near him as he led his perfect warriors deeper into the heart of the defences.

LUC SEDIRAE, WITH his blond hair and smirking grin, looked completely out of place among the rusting industrial spires of the Choral City. Beside him, Serghar Targhost, Captain of the Seventh Company, seemed far more at home, his older, darker skin and heavy fur cloak more in keeping with a murdered world.

Sedirae stood on top of a rusting slab of fallen machinery before thousands of Sons of Horus arrayed for war. War paint was fresh on their breastplates and new banners dedicated to the warrior lodges flapped in the wind.

'Sons of Horus!' bellowed Sedirae, his voice brimming with the confidence that came to him so easily. 'For too long we have waited for our brother Legions to open the gate for us so we can put the doubters and the feeble-minded to the sword! At last, the hour has come! Lord Commander Eidolon has broken the siege and the time has come to show the Legions how the Sons of Horus fight!'

The warriors cheered and the lodge banners were raised high, displaying the facets of the beliefs underpinning the lodge philosophies. A brazen claw reached down from the sky to crush a world in its fist, a black star shone eight rays of death upon a horde of enemies and a great winged beast with two heads stood resplendent on a mountain of corpses.

Images from beyond, conjured by the words of Davinite priests who could look into the warp, they displayed the Sons of Horus's allegiance to the powers their Warmaster embraced.

'The enemy is in disarray,' shouted Sedirae over the cheering. 'We will fall upon them and sweep them away. You know your duties, Sons of Horus, and you all know that the paths you have followed have led you towards this day. For here we destroy the last vestiges of the old Crusade, and march towards the future!'

Sedirae's confidence was infectious and he knew they were ready.

Targhost stepped forward and raised his hands. He bore the rank of lodge captain himself, privy to the secrets of the Davinite ways and as much a holy man as a commander. He opened his mouth and unleashed a stream of brutal syllables, guttural and dark, the tongue of Davin wrought into a prayer of victory and blood.

The Sons of Horus answered the prayer, their voices raised in a relentless chant that echoed around the dead spires of the Choral City.

And when the prayers were done, the Sons of Horus marched to war.

FIRE STORMED AROUND Tarvitz. Emperor's Children Terminators raked the central dome with fire and the sounds of brutal hand-to-hand combat came from the shattered gallery. Tarvitz ducked and ran as bolter fire kicked up fragments around him, sliding into cover beside Brother Solathen of Squad Nasicae.

Solathen and about thirty loyalist Emperor's Children were pinned down behind a great fallen column, a few Luna Wolves among them.

'What in the Emperor's name happened?' shouted Tarvitz. 'How did they get in?'

'I don't know, sir,' replied Solathen. 'They came from the east.'

'We should have had some warning,' said Tarvitz. 'That's Lucius's sector. Have you seen him at all?'

'Lucius?' asked Solathen. 'No, he must have fallen.'

Tarvitz shook his head. 'Not likely. I have to find him.'

'We can't hold out here,' said Solathen. 'We have to pull back and we won't be able to wait for you.'

Tarvitz nodded, but knew that he had to try and find Lucius, even if it was just to recover his body. He doubted Lucius could ever really die, but knew that, amid this carnage, anything was possible.

'Very well,' said Tarvitz. 'Go. Fall back in good order to the inner domes and the temple, there are barricades there. Go! And don't wait for me!'

He put his head briefly over the pillar and fired his bolter, kicking a burst of shots towards Eidolon's Emperor's Children swarming all over the far side of the dome. More covering fire sprayed from his warriors' guns as they began falling back by squads.

The dome between him and his goal was littered with bodies, some of them chewed into unrecognisable sprays of torn flesh. He waited until his warriors had put enough distance between them and the enemy and broke from cover.

Bolter shots tore up the ground beside him and he rolled into the cover of a fallen pillar, crawling as fast as he could to reach the passageway that led from the dome and curved around its columned circumference towards the east wing of the Precentor's Palace.

Lucius was somewhere in these ruins and Tarvitz had to find him.

LOKEN DUCKED AND threw himself to the floor, skidding along the fire-blackened tiles of the plaza. The palace loomed above him, whirling as Loken spun on his back and fired up at the closest World Eater. One shot caught the warrior in the leg and he collapsed in a roaring heap. Torgaddon leapt upon him, plunging his sword into the traitor's back.

Loken climbed to his feet as more fire stuttered across the plaza. He tried to get a bearing on the enemy among the heaps of the dead and the jagged slabs of marble sticking up from the edges of shell craters, but it was impossible.

The plaza between the chaos of the palace and the dark mass of the city was infested with World Eaters, charging forwards to exploit the breach made by the Emperor's Children.

'There's a whole squad out here,' said Torgaddon, wrenching his sword from the World Eater. 'We're right in the middle of them.'

'Then we keep going,' said Loken.

Back on his feet, he reloaded his bolter as they hurried through the wreckage and charnel heaps, scanning the darkness for movement. Torgaddon kept close behind him, sweeping his bolter between chunks of tiling or fallen masonry. Fire snapped around them and the sounds of battle coming from the palace became ever more terrible, the war-cries and explosions tearing through the violent night.

'Down!' yelled Torgaddon as a burst of plasma fire lanced from the darkness. Loken threw himself to the ground as the searing bolt flashed past him and bored a hole in a slab of fallen stone behind him. A dark shape came at him and Loken saw the flash of a blade, bringing his bolter up in an instinctive block. He felt chainblade teeth grinding against the metal of his gun and kicked out at his attacker's groin.

The World Eater pivoted away from the blow easily, turning to smash Torgaddon to the ground with the butt of his chainaxe. Torgaddon's attack gave Loken a chance to regain his feet and he threw aside the ruined bolter to draw his own sword.

Torgaddon wrestled with another World Eater on the ground, but his friend would have to fend for himself as Loken saw that his opponent was a captain, and not just any captain, but one of the World Eaters' best.

'Khârn!' said Loken as the warrior attacked.

Khârn paused in his attack and, for the briefest moment, Loken saw the noble warrior he had spoken with in the Museum of Conquest, before something else swamped it again – something that twisted Khârn's face with hatred.

That second was enough for Loken, allowing him to dodge back behind a fan of broken stone jutting from the edge of crater. Bullets still carved through the air and somewhere beyond his sight, Torgaddon was fighting his own battle, but Loken could not worry about that now.

'What happened, Khârn?' cried Loken. 'What did they turn you into?'

Khârn screamed an incoherent bellow of rage and leapt towards him with his axe held high. Loken braced his stance and brought his blade up to catch Khârn's axe as it slashed towards him and the two warriors clashed in a desperate battle of strength

'Khârn...' said Loken through gritted teeth as the World Eater forced the chainaxe's whirling teeth towards his face. 'This is not the man I knew! What have you become?'

As their eyes met, Loken saw Khârn's soul and despaired. He saw the warrior who had sworn oaths of brotherhood and pledged himself to the Crusade as he himself had done, the warrior who had seen the terrors and tragedies of the Crusade as well as its victories. And he saw the dark madness that had swamped that in bloodshed and betrayals yet to be enacted.

'I am the Eightfold Path,' snapped Khârn, his every words punctuated by a froth of blood.

'No!' shouted Loken, pushing the World Eater away. 'It doesn't have to be this way.'

'It does,' said Khârn. 'There is no way off the Path. We must always go further.'

The humanity drained from Khârn's face and Loken knew that the World Eater was truly gone and that only in death would this battle end.

Loken backed away, fending off a flurry of blows from Khârn's axe, until he was forced back against a slab of rubble. His foe's axe buried itself in the stone beside him and Loken slammed the pommel of his sword into Khârn's head. Khârn rode the blow and smashed his forehead into Loken's face, grabbing his sword arm and wrestling him to the ground.

They struggled in the mud like animals, Khârn trying to grind Loken's face into the shattered stone and Loken trying to throw him off. Loken rolled onto his back as he heard the rumble of an engine like an earthquake and the glare of floodlights stabbed out and threw Khârn's outline into silhouette.

Knowing what was coming, Loken hammered his fist into Khârn's face over and over again, pushing him upright with a hand clasped around his neck. The World Eater struggled in Loken's grip as the light grew stronger and the roaring form of a Land Raider crested the ridge of rubble behind them like a monster rising from the deep.

Loken felt the huge impact as the Land Raider's dozer blade slammed into Khârn, the sharpened prongs at its base punching through the World Eater's chest. He released Khârn's body and rolled to the edge of the crater as the Land Raider rose up, carrying the struggling Khârn with it. The mighty tank crashed back down and Loken pressed his body into the mud as it ground over him, the roaring of its engine passing inches above him.

Then it was over, the tank rumbled onwards, carrying the impaled World Eater before it like some gory trophy. Tanks were all around him, the Eye of Horus glaring from their armoured hulls, and Loken recognised the livery they were painted in.

The Sons of Horus.

For a moment, Loken just stared at the force surging towards the palace. Gunfire flared as they drove towards their prize.

A hand reached down and grabbed Loken, dragging him, battered and bloody, into cover from the guns of the tanks. He looked up and saw Torgaddon, similarly mauled by the encounter with the World Eaters.

Torgaddon nodded in the direction of the Land Raider. 'Was that–?'

'Khârn,' nodded Loken. 'He's gone.'

'Dead?'

'Maybe, I don't know.'

Torgaddon looked up at the Sons of Horus speartip driving for the palace. 'I think even Tarvitz might have trouble holding the palace now.'

'Then we'll have to hurry.'

'Yes. Stay low and let's keep out of any more trouble,' said Torgaddon, 'unless Abaddon and Little Horus aren't challenging enough on their own.'

'Saul will make them pay for every piece of rubble they capture,' said Loken, pulling himself painfully to his feet. Khârn had hurt him, but not so much that he couldn't fight. 'For his sake, let's make that count for something.'

The two friends forged through the rubble once again, towards the Mackaran Basilica.

Where lay one last chance of a victory on Isstvan III.

THE SOUNDS OF battle echoed from all around him and Tarvitz hugged the shadows as he made his careful way through the ruins of the east wing of the palace. Squads of Emperor's Children swarmed through the palace grounds, sweeping through the shattered domes and gunfire riddled rooms as they plunged the knife of their attack into the heart of the defences.

Here and there he saw squad markings he recognised and had to fight the ingrained urge to call out to them. But these warriors were the enemy and there would be no brotherly embrace or comradely welcome were they to discover him.

The very obsessiveness of their attack was working in Tarvitz's favour as these warriors possessed the same single mindedness as Eidolon, fixated on the prize of the palace rather than proper battlefield awareness. For once, Eidolon's flaws were working in his favour, thought Tarvitz, as he ghosted through the strobe lit wasteland of the palace.

'You're going to need to tighten up discipline, Eidolon,' he whispered, 'or someone's going to make you pay.'

The eastern sectors he had assigned Lucius and his men to watch over were bombed out ruins, the frescoes burned from the walls by the firestorm, and the mighty statue gardens pulverised by constant shelling and the battles that had raged furiously over the past months. To have held out this long was a miracle in itself and Tarvitz was not blind enough to try and fool himself into thinking that it could last much longer.

He saw dozens of bodies and checked every one for a sign that the swordsman had fallen. Each body was a warrior he knew, a warrior who had followed him into battle at the palace and trusted that he could lead them to victory. Each set of eyes accused him of their death, but he knew that there was nothing more he could have done.

The further eastward he went the less he encountered the invading Emperor's Children, their attack pushing into the centre of the Precentor's Palace rather than spreading out to capture its entirety.

Trust Eidolon to go for the glory rather than standard battlefield practice.

Give me a hundred Space Marines and I would punish your arrogance, thought Tarvitz.

Even as the thought occurred to him, a slow smile spread across his face. He *had* a hundred Space Marines. True, they were engaged in battle, but if any force of warriors could disengage from battle in good order and hand over to a friendly force in the middle of a desperate firefight, it was the Emperor's Children.

He crouched in the shadow of a fallen statue and opened a vox-channel. 'Solathen,' he hissed. 'Can you hear me?'

Static washed from the vox bead in his ear and he cursed at the idea of his plan being undone by something as trivial as a failure of communications.

'I hear you, captain, but we're a little busy right now!' said Solathen's voice.

'Understood,' said Tarvitz, 'but I have new orders for you. Disengage from the fight and hand over to the Luna Wolves. Let them take the brunt of the fighting and gather as many warriors as you can rally to you. Then converge on my position.'

'Sir?'

'Take the eastern passages along the servants' wing. That should bring you to me without too much trouble. We have an opportunity to hurt these bastards, Solathen, so I need you to get here with all possible speed!'

'Understood, sir,' said Solathen, signing off.

Tarvitz froze as he heard a voice say, 'It won't do any good, Saul. The Precentor's Palace is as good as lost. Even you should be able to see that.'

He looked up and saw Lucius standing in the centre of the dome in front of him, his shimmering sword in one hand and a shard of broken glass in the other. He raised the glass to his face and sliced its razor edge along his cheek, drawing a line of blood from his skin that dripped to the dome's floor.

'Lucius,' said Tarvitz, rising to his feet and entering the dome to meet the swordsman. 'I thought you were dead.'

Bright starlight filled the dome and Tarvitz saw it was filled with the corpses of Emperor's Children.

Not traitors, but loyalists and he could see that not one had fallen to a gunshot wound, but had been carved up by a powerful edged weapon. These warriors had been cut apart, and a horrible suspicion began to form in his mind.

'Dead?' laughed Lucius. '*Me*? Remember what Loken said to me when I humbled him in the practice cages?'

Wary now, Tarvitz nodded. 'He said there was someone out there who could beat you.'

'And do you remember what I told him?'

'Yes,' replied Tarvitz, sliding his hand to the hilt of his broadsword. 'You said, "Not in this lifetime," didn't you?'

'You have a good memory,' said Lucius, dropping the bloody shard of glass to the floor.

'Who's that latest scar for?' asked Tarvitz.

Lucius smiled, though there was no warmth to it.

'It's for you, Saul.'

THE GREAT FORUM of the Mackaran Basilica was a desert of ashen bone, for as the virus bombs had dropped, thousands of Isstvanians had gathered there in the hope that the parliament house at one end of the forum would receive them. They had thronged the place and died there, their scorched remains resembling an ancient swamp from which rose the columns that bounded the forum on three sides. On the fourth was the parliament house itself, befouled by black tendrils of ash that reached up from the forum.

The building had been the seat of the Choral City's civilian parliament, a counterpart to the nobles who had ruled from the Precentor's Palace, but the prominent citizens who had taken shelter inside had died as surely as the horde of civilians outside.

Loken pushed through the sea of black bones, his sword ready in his hand as he forged through the thicket of bone. A skull grinned up at him, its burned and empty eye sockets accusing. Behind him, Torgaddon covered the forum beyond them.

'Wait,' said Loken quietly.

Torgaddon halted and looked round. 'Is it them?'

'I don't know, maybe,' said Loken, looking up at the parliament house. Beyond it he could just see the lines of a spacecraft, a stormbird in Sons of Horus colours. 'Someone landed here, that's for sure.'

They continued onwards to the edge of the parliament building, climbing the smooth marble steps. Its great doors had been thick studded oak, but they had been eaten away by the virus and burned to ash by the firestorm.

'Shall we?' asked Torgaddon.

Loken nodded, suddenly wishing that they had not come here, as a terrible feeling of doom settled on him. He looked at Torgaddon and wished he had some fitting words to say to him before they took these last, fateful steps.

Torgaddon seemed to understand what he was thinking and said, 'Yes. I know, but what choice do we have?'

'None,' said Loken, marching through the archway and into the parliament house.

The interior of the building had been protected from the worst of the virus bombing and firestorm, only a few tangled blackened corpses lying sprawled among the dark wood panels and furnishings. The walls of the circular building were adorned with faded frescoes of the Choral City's magnificent past, telling the tales of its growth and conquests.

The benches and voting-tables of the parliament were arranged around a central stage with a lectern from which the debates were led.

On the stage, in front of the lectern, stood Ezekyle Abaddon and Horus Aximand.

'YOU BETRAYED US,' said Tarvitz, the hurt and disappointment almost too much to bear. 'You killed your own men and let Eidolon and his warriors into the palace. Didn't you?'

'I did,' said Lucius, swinging his sword in loops around his body as he loosened his muscles in preparation for the fight Tarvitz knew must come next. 'And I'd do it again in a heartbeat.'

Tarvitz circled the edge of the dome, his steps in time with those of the swordsman. He had no illusions as to the outcome of this fight, Lucius was the pre-eminent blade master of the Legion, perhaps all the Legions. He knew he could not defeat Lucius, but this betrayal demanded retribution.

Honour must be satisfied.

'Why, Lucius?' asked Tarvitz.

'How can you ask me that, Saul?' demanded Lucius, drawing the circle closer and, step by step, the distance between the two warriors shrank. 'I am only here thanks to my misplaced acquaintance with you. I know what the lord commander and Fabius offered you. How could you turn such an opportunity down?'

'It was an abomination, Lucius,' said Tarvitz, knowing he had to keep Lucius talking for as long as he could. 'To tamper with the gene-seed? How can you possibly believe that the Emperor would condone such a thing?'

'The Emperor?' laughed Lucius. 'Are you so sure he would disapprove? Look at what he did to create the primarchs? Aren't *we* the result of genetic manipulation? The experiments Fabius is conducting are the logical next link in that evolutionary chain. We are a superior race and we must establish that superiority over any lesser beings that stand in our way.'

'Even your fellow warriors?' spat Tarvitz, gesturing to the corpses around the dome's circumference with the blade of his sword.

Lucius shrugged. 'Even them. I am going to rejoin my Legion and they tried to stop me. What choice did I have? Just like you are going to try and stop me.'

'You'll kill me too?' asked Tarvitz. 'After all the years we've fought together?'

'Don't try and appeal to my sense of fond reminiscences, Saul,' warned Lucius. 'I am better than you and I am going to achieve great things in the service of my Legion. Neither you or any foolish sense of misplaced loyalty are going to stop me.'

Lucius lifted the blade of his sword and dropped into a fighting crouch as Tarvitz approached him. The dome seemed suddenly silent as the two combatants circled one another, each searching for a weakness in the other's defences. Tarvitz drew his combat knife in his left hand and reversed the blade, knowing he would need as many blades between him and Lucius as humanly possible.

Tarvitz knew there were no more words to be spoken. This could only end in blood.

Without warning, he leapt towards Lucius, thrusting with the smaller blade, but even as he attacked he saw that Lucius had been expecting it.

Lucius swayed aside and swept the hilt of his sword down, smashing the knife from his hand. The swordsman ducked as Tarvitz turned on his heel and slashed high with his sword.

Tarvitz's blade cut only air and Lucius hammered his elbow into his side.

He danced away, expecting Lucius to land a blow, but the swordsman merely smiled and danced around him lightly on the balls of his feet. Lucius was playing with him, and he felt his anger mount in the face of such mockery.

Lucius advanced towards Tarvitz, darting in with the speed of a striking snake to thrust at his stomach. Tarvitz blocked the thrust, rolling his wrists over Lucius's blade and slashing for his neck, but the swordsman had anticipated the move and nimbly dodged the blow.

Tarvitz attacked suddenly, his blade a flashing blur of steel that forced Lucius back step by step. Lucius parried a vicious slash aimed at his groin, spinning with a laugh to launch a lightning riposte at his foe.

Tarvitz saw the blade cut the air towards him, knowing he was powerless to prevent it landing. He hurled himself back, but felt a red-hot line of agony as the energised edge bit deep into his side. He clamped a hand to his side as blood spilled down his armour, gasping in pain before his armour dispensed stimulants that blocked it.

Tarvitz backed away from Lucius and the swordsman followed with a grin of anticipation.

'If that's the best you've got, Saul, then you'd best give up now,' smirked Lucius. 'I promise I'll make it quick.'

'I was just about to say the same thing, Lucius,' gasped Tarvitz, lifting his sword once again.

The two warriors clashed once more, their swords shimmering streaks of silver and blue as coruscating sparks spat from their blades. Tarvitz fought with every ounce of courage, strength and skill he could muster, but he knew it was hopeless. Lucius parried his every attack with ease and casually landed cut after cut on his flesh, enough to draw blood and hurt, but not enough to kill.

Blood gathered in the corner of his mouth as he staggered away from yet another wounding blow.

'A hit,' sniggered Lucius. 'A palpable hit.'

Tarvitz knew he was fighting with the last of his reserves and the fight could not go on much longer. Soon Lucius would tire of his poor sport and finish him, but perhaps he had held him here for long enough.

'Had enough?' coughed Tarvitz. 'You don't have to die here.'

Lucius cocked his head to one side as he advanced towards him and said, 'You're serious, aren't you? You actually think you can beat me.'

Tarvitz nodded and spat blood. 'Come on and have a go if you think you can kill me.'

Lucius leapt forwards to attack and Tarvitz dropped his sword and leapt to meet him. Surprised by such an obviously suicidal move, Lucius was a fraction of a second too late to dodge Tarvitz's attack.

The two warriors clashed in the air and Tarvitz smashed his fist into the swordsman's face. Lucius turned his head to rob the blow of its force, but Tarvitz gave him no chance to right himself as they fell to the floor, and pistoned his fist into his former comrade's face. Lucius's sword skittered away and they fought with fists and elbows, knees and feet.

At such close quarters, skill with a blade was irrelevant and Tarvitz let his hate and anger spill out in every thunderous hammer blow he landed. They rolled and grappled like brawling street thugs, Tarvitz punching Lucius with powerful blows that would have killed a mortal man a dozen times over, the swordsman struggling to push Tarvitz clear.

'I also remember what Loken taught you the first time he brought you down,' gasped Tarvitz as he saw movement at the edge of the dome. 'Understand your foe and do whatever is necessary to bring him down.'

He released his grip on Lucius and rolled clear, pushing himself as far away from the swordsman as he could. Lucius sprang to his feet in an instant, scrambling across the floor to retrieve his weapon.

'Now, Solathen!' shouted Tarvitz. 'Kill him! He betrayed us all!'

He watched as Lucius turned towards the dome's entrance, seeing the warriors Solathen had rallied and brought to him. Solathen obeyed Tarvitz's command instantly, as a good Emperor's Children should, and the dome was suddenly filled with the bark of gunfire. Lucius dived out of the way, but even he wasn't quick enough to avoid a volley of bolter shells.

Lucius jerked and danced in the fusillade, sparks and blood flying from his armour. He rolled across the floor, scrabbling for a hole in the wall blasted by the months of battle as the gunfire of the loyalist Emperor's Children tore into him.

'Kill him!' yelled Tarvitz, but Lucius was faster than he would have believed possible, diving from the dome as shells tore up scorched frescoes around him.

Tarvitz pushed himself to his feet and staggered over towards where Lucius had escaped.

Beyond the dome, the outer precincts of the palace were a nightmarish landscape of craters and blackened ruins. A pall of smoke hung over the battlefield the palace had become and he smashed his fist into the wall in frustration as he saw that the swordsman had vanished.

'Captain Tarvitz?' said Solathen. 'Reporting as ordered.'

Tarvitz turned from his search for Lucius, pushing his frustrations aside and focusing on the more immediate matter of counter-attacking Eidolon's warriors.

'My thanks, Solathen. I owe you my life,' he said.

The warrior nodded as Tarvitz picked up a fallen bolter and checked the magazine to make sure he had a full load.

'Now come on,' he said grimly. 'Let's show these bastards how the real Emperor's Children fight!'

SEVENTEEN

Winning is survival
Dies Irae
The end

'BETRAYER,' SAID LOKEN, stepping into the parliament house.

'There was nothing to betray,' retorted Abaddon.

Even after all that had happened on Isstvan III, the word betrayal had the power to ignite the ever-present anger inside him.

'I envy you this, Loken,' continued Abaddon. 'To you the galaxy must seem so simple. So long as there's someone you can call enemy you'll fight to the death and think you are right.'

'I know I am right, Ezekyle!' shouted Loken. 'How can this be anything but wrong? The death of this city and the murder of your brothers? What has happened to you, Abaddon, to turn you into this?'

Abaddon stepped down off the stage, leaving Aximand to stand alone at the lectern. In his

Terminator armour Abaddon was far taller than
Loken and he knew from witnessing the first captain in battle that he could still fight as skilfully as
any Astartes in power armour.

'Isstvan III was forced upon us by the inability of
small minds to understand reality,' said Abaddon.
'Do you think I have been a part of this, and that I
am here, because I enjoy killing my brothers? I
believe, Loken, as surely as you do. There are powers
in this galaxy that even the Emperor does not
understand. If he leaves humanity to wither on the
vine in his selfish quest for godhood then those
powers will swamp us and every single human
being in this galaxy will die. Can you understand
the enormity of that concept? The whole human
race! The Warmaster does, and that is why he must
take the Emperor's place to deal with these threats.'

'Deal with them?' said Torgaddon, shaking his
head. 'You are a fool, Ezekyle, we saw what Erebus
was doing. He has lied to you all. You have made a
pact with evil powers.'

'Evil?' said Aximand. 'They saved the Warmaster's
life. I have seen their power and it is within the Warmaster's ability to control them. You think we are
fools, that we are blind? The forces of the warp are
the key to this galaxy. That is what the Emperor cannot understand. The Warmaster will be lord of the
warp as well of the Imperium and then we will rule
the stars.'

'No,' replied Loken. 'The Warmaster has become
corrupted. If he takes the throne it will not be

humanity that rules the galaxy, it will be something else. You know that, Little Horus, even if Ezekyle doesn't. He doesn't care about the galaxy; he just wants to be on the winning side.'

Abaddon smiled, slowly approaching Loken as Torgaddon circled towards Horus Aximand. 'Winning is survival, Loken. You die, you lose, and nothing you ever believed ever meant anything. I live, I win, and you might as well have never existed. Victory, Loken. It's the only thing in the galaxy that means anything. You should have spent more time being a soldier, maybe then you would have ended up on the winning side.'

Loken held up his sword, trying to gauge Abaddon's movements. 'There is always time to decide who wins.'

He could see Abaddon tensing up, ready to strike, and knew that the first captain's taunting was just a cover.

'Loken, you have come so far,' said Abaddon, 'and you still don't understand what we're doing here. We're not so far from human that we're not allowed a few mistakes, but to fight us instead of realising what the Warmaster is trying to achieve… that's unforgivable.'

'Then what's your mistake, Ezekyle?'

'Talking too much,' replied Abaddon, launching himself towards Loken with his bladed fist bathed in lethal energies.

✠ ✠ ✠

TORGADDON WATCHED AS Abaddon charged towards Loken, taking that as his cue to attack Little Horus. His former comrade had seen the intent in his eyes and leapt to meet him as Loken and Abaddon smashed apart the pews along the nave.

They met in a clatter of battle plate, fighting with all the strength and hatred that only those who were once brothers, but are now bitter enemies, can muster. They grappled like wrestlers until Aximand flung Torgaddon's arms wide and smashed his elbow into his jaw.

He fell back, blocked the right cross slashing for his face, and closed with Aximand, cracking an armoured knee into his opponent's midriff.

Little Horus stumbled and Torgaddon knew that it would take more than a knee in the guts to halt a warrior such as Aximand. His former brother was powerfully built, his strength, poise and skill the equal of Torgaddon's.

The two warriors faced one another, and Torgaddon could see a look of regret flash across Little Horus's face.

'Why are you doing this?' asked Torgaddon.

'You said you were against us,' replied Aximand.

'And we are.'

Both warriors lowered their guards; they were brothers, members of the Mournival who had seen so many battles together that there was no need for posturing. They both knew how the other fought.

'Tarik,' said Aximand, 'if this could have ended another way, we would have taken it. None of us would have chosen this way.'

'Little Horus, when did you realise how far you had gone? Was it when the Warmaster told you we were going to be bombed, or some time before?'

Aximand glanced over to where Loken and Abaddon fought. 'You can walk away from this, Tarik. The Warmaster wants Loken dead, but he said nothing about you.'

Torgaddon laughed. 'We called you Little Horus because you looked so like him, but we were wrong. Horus never had that doubt in his eyes. You're not sure, Aximand. Maybe you're on the wrong side. Maybe this is the last chance you've got to end your life as a Space Marine and not as a slave.'

Aximand smiled bleakly. 'I've seen it, Tarik, the warp. You can't stand against that.'

'And yet here I am.'

'If you had just taken the chance the lodge gave you, you would have seen it too. They can give us such power. If you only knew, Tarik, you'd join us in a second. The whole future would be laid out before you.'

'You know I can't back down. No more than you can.'

'Then this is it?'

'Yes, it is. As you said, none of us would have chosen this.'

Aximand readied himself. 'Just like the practice cages, Tarik.'

'No,' said Torgaddon, 'nothing like that.'

The energised claw swung at Loken's head, and he ducked, too late seeing it for the feint it was. Abaddon grabbed him by the edge of his shoulder guard and drove his knee into Loken's stomach. Ceramite buckled and Loken felt pain knife into him as bones broke.

Abaddon released him and punched him in the face. He was thrown against the wall of the parliament, scorched plaster and brick falling around him.

'The Warmaster wanted me to bring the Justaerin, but I told him it was an insult.'

Loken saw his sword lying on the floor beside him and slid down the wall to grab it. He pushed off the wall, pivoting past Abaddon's slashing fist, swinging the blade towards the first captain's face.

Abaddon blocked the blow with his forearm, reaching out to pluck Loken from his feet and hurl him towards the parliament building's wall. The world spun away from him and suddenly there was pain.

His vision blurred as he smacked into the ground and shards of stone flew up around him. The pain within him felt strange, as if it belonged to someone else. It felt as if his back was broken and a treacherous voice in his mind whispered that the pain would go away if he just gave up and let it all go away in a fog of oblivion. His grip tightened on his sword and he let his anger fuel his strength to fight against the voice in his head that told him to give up.

A long time ago, Loken had sworn an oath to his Emperor, and that oath was never to give up, even as the moment of death approached. His vision swam back into focus, and he looked up to see the hole in the parliament house's wall his body had smashed.

Loken rolled onto his front as Abaddon's massive armoured form charged towards him, smashing aside the blackened remains of the breach.

He scrambled to his feet and backed away, letting Abaddon's fist swing past him. He darted in, stabbing with his sword, but the thick plates of his enemy's armour turned the blade aside. He scrambled back up the steps of the parliament house, hearing Torgaddon and Little Horus fighting within and knowing that he needed his brother's strength to triumph.

'You can't run forever!' roared Abaddon as he turned to follow him, his steps ponderous and heavy.

SAUL TARVITZ GRINNED like a hunter who had finally run his prey to ground. The warriors he and Solathen led cut a bloody swathe through Eidolon's warriors, killing them without mercy as they themselves had been killed so recently. What had once been an attack that threatened to overwhelm them utterly was now in danger of becoming a rout for the traitors.

Gunfire echoed fiercely through the palace as the loyalists unleashed volley after volley of gunfire at anything that moved. Loyalist Space Marines surrounded Eidolon's assault force and, attacked on two fronts. The lord commander's force was buckling.

Tarvitz could see warriors with missing limbs or massive open wounds struggling in the desperate fight, jostling to get a position where they could kill the traitors who had so nearly overrun them. His own sword reaped a bloody tally as he killed warriors he had once fought with and bled alongside, each sword blow a cruel twist of fate that brought aching sadness as much as it did cathartic satisfaction.

He saw Eidolon in the centre of the battle, smashing warriors to ruin with each swing of his hammer and fought his way through the battle to reach the lord commander. His own body ached from the duel with Lucius, but he knew that there was no point in calling for an apothecary. Whatever wounds he was suffering from would never have a chance to heal. It would end here, Tarvitz knew, but it would be a hell of a fight and he had never felt more proud to lead these brave warriors into battle.

To have such noble fighters almost undone by a supposedly loyal comrade's betrayal was a galling, yet somehow fitting end to their struggle. Lucius had very nearly cost them this battle and Tarvitz swore that if he lived through this hell, he would see the bastard dead once and for all.

The lord commander was almost within his reach, but no sooner had Eidolon seen him than the traitors began falling back in disciplined ranks. Tarvitz wanted to scream in frustration, but knew better than to simply hurl himself after his foe.

'Firing line across the nave!' shouted Tarvitz at the top of his voice and instantly, a contingent of Astartes formed up and began firing disciplined volleys of bolter fire at the retreating enemy.

He lowered his sword and leaned against the broken wall as he realised that, against all odds, they had held once more. Before he had a moment to savour the unlikeliness of their latest victory, the vox-bead chimed in his ear.

'Captain Tarvitz,' said a voice he recognised as one of the Luna Wolves.

'Tarvitz here,' he said.

'This is Vipus, captain. The position on the roof is sound but we've got company.'

'I know,' replied Tarvitz. 'The Sons of Horus.'

'Worse than that,' said Vipus. 'To the west, look up.'

Tarvitz pushed through the remains of the battle and scanned the sky above the crumbling, smoke wreathed ruins. Something moved towards the palace, something distant, but utterly huge.

'Sweet Terra,' he said, 'the *Dies Irae*.'

'I'll make the Titan our priority target,' swore Vipus.

'No, you can't hurt it. Just kill enemy Space Marines.'

'Yes, captain.'

'Enemy units!' a voice yelled from near the temple entrance. 'Armour and support!'

Tarvitz pushed himself from the wall, drawing on his last reserves of energy to once again muster his warriors for the defence of the palace. 'Assault units by the doors! All other Astartes, fire at will!'

Tarvitz could see a huge strike force of enemy forces, boxy Land Raiders and Rhinos massing on the outskirts of the Precentor's Palace. Beyond them, Sons of Horus, World Eaters and Emperor's Children set up fields of fire to surround the temple.

The *Dies Irae* would soon be in range to blast them with its enormous weaponry.

'They'll be coming again soon,' shouted Tarvitz, 'but we'll see them off again, my brothers! No matter what occurs, they will not forget the fight we've given them here!'

Looking at the size of the army arrayed for the final assault, Tarvitz knew that there would be no holding against it.

This was the endgame.

TERMINATOR ARMOUR WAS huge. It made a man into a walking tank, but what it added in protection, it lost in speed. Abaddon was skilful and could fight almost as fast as any other Astartes while clad in its thick plates.

But 'almost' wasn't good enough when life or death was at stake

Chunks of rubble spilled into the parliament house as Abaddon battered his way back inside, the brutal high-shouldered shape of his Terminator armour wreathed in chalky plaster dust. As Abaddon smashed his way back inside, he passed beneath a sagging portico that supported a vast swathe of sculpted marble statuary above. Loken struck out at one of the cracked pillars supporting the portico, the fluted support smashing apart under the power of the blow.

The parliament filled with dust as the huge slabs above came down on Abaddon, the entire weight of the statuary collapsing on top of the first captain. Loken could hear Abaddon roaring in anger as the stonework thundered down in a flurry of rubble and destruction.

He turned away from the avalanche of debris and fought his way through the billowing clouds of dust towards the centre of the parliament building.

He saw Torgaddon and Horus Aximand upon the central stage.

Torgaddon was on his knees, blood raining from his body and his limbs shattered. Aximand held his sword upraised, ready to deliver the deathblow.

He saw what would happen next even as he screamed at his former brother to stay his hand. Even over the crash of rubble being displaced as Abaddon forced himself free of the collapsed statues, he heard Aximand's words with a terrible clarity.

'I'm sorry,' said Aximand.

And the sword slashed down against Torgaddon's neck.

THE PLASMA BOLT was like a finger of the sun, reaching down from the guns of the *Dies Irae* and smashing through the wall of the Warsingers' Temple, the liquid fire boring deep into the ground. With a sound like the city dying, one wall of the temple collapsed as dust and fire filled the air and shards of green stone flew like knives. Warriors melted in the heat blast or died beneath the heaps of stone that collapsed around them.

Tarvitz fell to his knees on the winding stairway that climbed to the upper reaches of the temple. A choking mass of burning ash billowed around him and he fought his way upwards, knowing that hundreds of the last loyalist Space Marines were dead. The sound was appalling, the roar of the collapsing temple stark against the silence of the traitors that surrounded the temple on all sides.

A body fell past him, one of the Luna Wolves, his arm blown off by weapons fire hammering the upper floors.

'To the roof!' ordered Tarvitz, not knowing if anyone could hear him over the cacophony of the Titan's guns. 'Abandon the nave!'

Tarvitz reached the gallery running the length of the temple, finding it crammed with Space Marines, their Legion colours unrecognisable beneath layers of grime and blood. Such distinctions were irrelevant, Tarvitz realised, for they were one band of brothers fighting for the same cause.

Above this level was the roof, and Tarvitz spotted Sergeant Raetherin, a solid line officer and veteran of the Murder campaign.

'Sergeant!' he yelled. 'Report!'

Raetherin looked up from the window through which he was aiming his bolter. He had caught a glancing blow to the side of his head and his face streamed with blood

'Not good, captain!' he replied. 'We've held them this long, but we won't hold another attack. There's too many of them and that Titan is going to blow us away any second.'

Tarvitz nodded and risked a glance through a shattered loophole to the ground far below, feeling his hate for these traitors, warriors for whom notions of honour and loyalty were non-existent, swell as he saw the multitude of bodies sprawled around the palace. He knew these dead warriors, having led them in battle these last few months and more than anything, he knew what they represented.

They were the galaxy's best soldiers, the saviours of the human race and the chosen of the Emperor. Their lives of heroic service and sacrifice had been ended by brute treachery and he had never felt so helpless.

'No,' he said, as resolve filled him. 'No, we will not falter.'

Tarvitz met Raetherin's eyes and said. 'The Titan is going to hit the same corner of the temple again, higher up, and then the traitors are going to storm us. Get the men back and make ready for the assault.'

He knew the traitors were just waiting for the temple to fall so they could storm in and kill the loyalists at their leisure. This was not just a battle; it was the Warmaster demonstrating his superiority.

Massive calibre gunfire thundered from the *Dies Irae*, an awesome storm of fire and death that smashed the plaza outside the temple, blasting apart loyalists in great columns of fire.

Infernal heat battered against the temple, and a hot gale blew through the gallery.

'Is that the best you've got?' he yelled in anger. 'You'll never kill us all!'

His warriors looked at him with savage light in their eyes. The words had sounded hollow in his ears, spoken out of rage rather than bravado, but he saw the effect it had and smiled, remembering that he had a duty to these men.

He had a duty to make their last moments mean something.

Suddenly, the air ripped apart as the Titan's plasma gun fired and white heat filled the gallery, throwing Tarvitz to the floor. Molten fragments of stone sprayed him and warriors fell, broken and burning around him. Blinded and deafened, Tarvitz dragged himself away from the destruction. Hot air boomed back into the vacuum blasted by the plasma and it was like a burning wind of destruction come to scour the loyalists from the face of Isstvan III.

He rolled onto his back, seeing that the bolt had ripped right through the temple roof, leaving a huge glowing-edged hole, like a monstrous bite mark, through one corner of the temple. Fully a third of the temple's mass had collapsed in a great rockslide of liquefied stone, flooding out like a long tongue of jade.

Tarvitz tried to shake the ringing from his ears and forced his eyes to focus.

Through the miasma of heat, he could hear a war-cry arise from the enemy warriors.

A similar clamour rose from the other side of the temple, where the World Eaters and the Emperor's Children were arrayed among the ruins of the palace.

The attack was coming.

LOKEN DROPPED TO his knees in horror at the sight of Torgaddon's head parting from his shoulders. The blood fountained slowly, the silver sheen of the sword wreathed in a spray of red.

He screamed his friend's name, watching as his body crashed to the floor of the stage and smashed the wooden lectern to splinters as it fell. His eyes met those of Horus Aximand and he saw a sorrow that matched his own echoed in this brother's eyes.

His choler surged, hot and urgent, but his anger was not directed at Horus Aximand, but at the warrior who pulled himself from the rubble behind him. He turned and forced himself to his feet, seeing Abaddon pulling himself from under the collapsed portico. The first captain had extricated himself from beneath slabs of marble that would have crushed even an armoured Astartes, but he was still trapped and immobile from the waist down.

Loken gave vent to an animal cry of loss and rage and ran towards Abaddon. He leapt, driving a knee down onto Abaddon's arm and pinning it with all his weight and strength to the rubble. Abaddon's free hand reached up and grabbed Loken's wrist as Loken drove his chainsword towards Abaddon's face.

The two warriors froze, locked face to face in a battle that would determine who lived and who died. Loken gritted his teeth and forced his arm down against Abaddon's grip.

Abaddon looked into Loken's face and saw the hatred and loss there.

'There's hope for you yet, Loken,' he snarled.

Loken forced the roaring point of the sword down with more strength than he thought could ever inhabit one body. The betrayal of the Astartes – their very essence – flashed through Loken's mind and he found the target of his hatred embodied in Abaddon's violent features.

The chainblade's teeth whirred. Abaddon forced the point down and it ripped into his breastplate. Sparks sprayed as Loken pushed the point onwards, through thick layers of ceramite. The sword juddered, but Loken kept it true.

He knew where it would break through, straight through the bone shield that protected Abaddon's chest cavity and then into his heart.

Even as he savoured the idea of Abaddon's death, the first captain smiled and pushed his hand upwards. Astartes battle plate enhanced a warrior's strength, but Terminator armour boosted it to levels beyond belief, and Abaddon called upon that power to dislodge Loken.

Abaddon surged upwards from the rubble with a roar of anger and slammed his energised fist into Loken's chest. His armour cracked open and the bone shield protecting his own chest cavity shattered into fragments. He staggered away from Abaddon, managing to keep his feet for a few seconds before his legs gave out and he collapsed to his knees, blood dribbling from his cracked lips in bloody ropes.

Abaddon towered over him and Loken watched numbly as Horus Aximand joined him. Abaddon's eyes were filled with triumph, Aximand's with regret. Abaddon took the bloody sword from Aximand's hand with a smile. 'This killed Torgaddon and it seems only fitting that I use it to kill you.'

The first captain raised the sword and said, 'You had your chance, Loken. Think about that while you die.'

Loken met Abaddon's unforgiving gaze, seeing the madness that lurked behind his eyes like a mob of angry daemons, and waited for death.

But before the blow landed, the parliament building exploded as something vast and colossal, like a primal god of war bestriding the world smashed through the back wall. Loken had a fleeting glimpse of a monstrous iron foot, easily the width of the building itself crashing through the stonework and demolishing the building as it went.

He looked up in time to see a mighty red god, towering and immense striding through the remains of the Choral City, its battlements bristling with weapons and its mighty head twisted in a snarl of merciless anger.

Rubble and debris cascaded from the roof as the *Dies Irae* smashed the parliament building into a splintered ruin of crushed rock, and Loken smiled as the building collapsed around him.

Tremendous impacts smashed the marble floor and the noise of the building's destruction was like the sweetest music he had ever heard, as he felt the world go black around him.

SAUL TARVITZ LOOKED around him at the hundred Space Marines crammed into the tiny square of cover that was all that remained of the Warsingers' temple. They had sat awaiting the final attack of the traitors for what had seemed like an age, but had been no more than thirty minutes.

'Why don't they attack?' asked Nero Vipus, one of the few Luna Wolves still alive.

'I don't know,' said Tarvitz, but whatever the reason I'm thankful for it.'

Vipus nodded, his face lined with a sadness that had nothing to do with the final battles of the Precentor's Palace.

'Still no word from Garviel or Tarik?' asked Tarvitz, already knowing the answer.

'No,' said Vipus, 'nothing.'

'I'm sorry, my friend.'

Vipus shook his head. 'No, I won't mourn them, not yet. They might have succeeded.'

Tarvitz said nothing, leaving the warrior to his dream and turned his attention once again to the terrifying scale of the Warmaster's army. Ten thousand traitors stood immobile in the ruins of the Choral City. World Eaters chanted alongside Emperor's Children while the Sons of Horus and the Death Guard waited in long firing lines.

The colossal form of the *Dies Irae* had thankfully stopped firing, the monstrous Titan marching to tower over the Sirenhold like a brazen fortress.

'They want to make sure we're beaten,' said Tarvitz, 'to plant a flag on our corpses.'

'Yes,' agreed Vipus, 'but we gave them the fight of their lives did we not?'

'That we did,' said Tarvitz, 'that we did, and even once we're gone, Garro will tell the Legions of what they've done here. The Emperor will send an army bigger than anything the Great Crusade has ever seen.'

Vipus looked out over the Warmaster's army and said, 'He'll have to.'

ABADDON SURVEYED THE ruins of the parliament house, its once magnificent structure a heaped pile of shattered stone. His face bled from a dozen cuts and his skin was an ugly, bruised purple, but he was alive.

Beside him, Horus Aximand slumped against a ruined statue, his breathing laboured and his shoulder twisted at an unnatural angle. Abaddon had pulled them both from the wreckage of the building, but looking at Aximand's downcast face, he knew that they had not escaped without scars of a different kind.

But it was done. Loken and Torgaddon were dead.

He had thought to feel savage joy at the idea, but instead he felt only emptiness, a strange void that yawned in his soul like a vessel that could never be filled.

Abaddon dismissed the thought and spoke into the vox. 'Warmaster,' he said, 'it is over.'

'What have we done, Ezekyle?' whispered Aximand.

'What needed to be done,' said Abaddon. 'The Warmaster ordered it and we obeyed.'

'They were our brothers,' said Aximand and Abaddon was astonished to find tears spilling down his brother's cheeks.

'They were traitors to the Warmaster, let that be an end to it.'

Aximand nodded, but Abaddon could see the seed of doubt take root in his expression.

He lifted Aximand and supported him as they made their way towards the waiting stormbird that would take them from this cursed place and back to the *Vengeful Spirit*.

The traitors within the Mournival were dead, but he had not forgotten the look of regret he had seen on Aximand's face.

Horus Aximand would need watching, Abaddon decided.

THE VIEWSCREEN OF the strategium displayed the blackened, barren rock of Isstvan V.

Where Isstvan III had once been rich and verdant, Isstvan V had always been a mass of tangled igneous rock where no life thrived. Once there had been life, but that had been aeons ago, and its only remnants were scattered basalt cities and fortifications. The people of the Choral City had thought these ruins were home to the evil gods of their religion, who waited there plotting revenge.

Perhaps they were right, mused Horus, thinking of Fulgrim and his complement of Emperor's Children who were preparing the way for the next phase of the plan.

Isstvan III had been the prologue, but Isstvan V would be the most decisive battle the galaxy had ever seen. The thought made Horus smile as he looked up to see Maloghurst limping painfully towards his throne.

'What news, Mal?' asked Horus. 'Have all surface units returned to their posts?'

'I have just heard from the *Conqueror*,' nodded Maloghurst. 'Angron has returned. He is the last.'

Horus turned back to the gnarled globe of Isstvan V and said, 'Good. It is no surprise to me that he should be the last to quit the battlefield. So what is the butcher's bill?'

'We lost a great many in the landings and more than a few in the palace,' replied Maloghurst. 'The Emperor's Children and the Death Guard were similarly mauled. The World Eaters lost the most. They are barely above half strength.'

'You do not think this battle was wise,' said Horus. 'You cannot hide that from me, Mal.'

'The battle was costly,' averred Maloghurst, 'and it could have been shortened. If efforts had been made to withdraw the Legions before the siege developed then lives and time could have been saved. We do not have an infinite number of Astartes and we certainly do not have infinite time. I do not believe there was any great victory to be won here.'

'You see only the physical cost, Mal,' said Horus. 'You do not see the psychological gains we have made. Abaddon was blooded, the real threats among the rebels have been eliminated and the World Eaters have been brought to a point where they cannot turn back. If there was ever any doubt as to whether this Crusade would succeed, it has been banished by what I have achieved on Isstvan III.'

'Then what are your orders?' asked Maloghurst.

Horus turned back to the viewscreen and said, 'We have tarried here too long and it is time to move onwards. You are right that I allowed myself to be drawn into a war that we did not have time to fight, but I will rectify that error.'

'Warmaster?'

'Bomb the city,' said Horus. 'Wipe it off the face of the planet.'

LOKEN COULDN'T MOVE his legs. Every heartbeat was agony in his lungs as the muscles of his chest ground against splinters of bone. He coughed up clots of blood with every breath and he was sure that each one would be his last as the will to live seeped from his body.

Through a crack in the rubble pinning him to the ground, Loken could see the dark grey sky. He saw streaks of fire dropping through the clouds and closed his eyes as he realised that they were the first salvoes of an orbital bombardment.

Death was raining down on the Choral City for the second time, but this time it wouldn't be anything as exotic as a virus. High explosives would bring the city down and put a final, terrible exclamation mark at the end of the Battle of Isstvan III.

Such a display was typical of the Warmaster.

It was a final epitaph that would leave no one in any doubt as to who had won.

The first orange blooms of fire burst over the city. The ground shook. Buildings collapsed in waves of fire and the streets boiled with flame once more.

The ground shuddered as though in the grip of an earthquake and Loken felt his prison of debris shift. Hard spikes of pain buffeted him as flames burst across the remains of the parliament building.

Then darkness fell at last, and Loken felt nothing else.

A HUNDRED OF Tarvitz's loyalists remained. They were the only survivors of their glorious last stand, and he had gathered them in the remains of the Warsingers' Temple – Sons of Horus, Emperor's Children, and even a few lost-looking World Eaters. Tarvitz noticed that there were no Death Guard in their numbers, thinking that perhaps a few had survived Mortarion's scouring of the trenches, but knowing that they might as well have been on the other side of Isstvan III.

This was the end. They all knew it, but none of them gave voice to that fact.

He knew all their names now. Before, they had just been grime-streaked faces among the endless days and nights of battle, but now they were brothers, men he would die with in honour.

Flashes of explosions bloomed in the city's north. Shooting stars punched through the dark clouds overhead, scorching holes through which the glimmering stars could be seen. The stars shone down on the Choral City in time to watch the city die.

'Did we hurt them, captain? asked Solathen. 'Did this mean anything?'

Tarvitz thought for a moment before replying.

'Yes,' he said, 'we hurt them here. They'll remember this.'

A bomb slammed into the Precentor's Palace, finally blasting what little remained of its great stone flower into flame and shards of granite. The loyalists did not throw themselves into cover or run for shelter – there was little point.

The Warmaster was bombarding the city, and he was thorough.

He would not let them slip away a second time.

Towers of flame bloomed all across the palace, closing in on them with fiery inevitability.

The battle for the Choral City was over.

THE TEMPLE WAS nearly complete, its high, arched ceiling like a ribcage of black stone beneath which the officers of the new Crusade were gathered. Angron still fumed at the decision to leave Isstvan III before the destruction of the loyalists was complete, while Mortarion was silent and sullen, his Death Guard like a steel barrier between him and the rest of the gathering.

Lord Commander Eidolon, still smarting from the failures his Legion had committed in the eyes of the Warmaster, had several squads of Emperor's Children accompanying him, but his presence was not welcomed, merely tolerated.

Maloghurst, Abaddon and Aximand represented the Sons of Horus, and beside them stood Erebus. The Warmaster stood before the temple's altar, its four faces representing what Erebus called the four faces of the gods. Above him, a huge holographic image of Isstvan V dominated the temple.

An area known as the Urgall Depression was highlighted, a giant crater overlooked by the fortress that Fulgrim had prepared for the Warmaster's forces. Blue blips indicated likely landing sites, routes of attack and retreat. Horus had spent the last hour explaining the details of the operation to his commanders and he was coming to an end.

'At this very moment seven Legions are coming to destroy us. They will find us at Isstvan V and the battle will be great. But in truth it will not be a battle at all, for we have achieved much since last we gathered. Chaplain Erebus, enlighten us as to matters beyond Isstvan.'

'All goes well at Signum, my lord,' said Erebus stepping forward. New tattoos had been inked on his scalp, echoing the sigils carved into the stones of the temple.

'Sanguinius and the Blood Angels will not trouble us, and Kor-Phaeron sends word that the Ultramarines muster at Calth. They suspect nothing and will not be in a position to lend their strength to the loyalist force. Our allies outnumber our enemies.'

'Then it is done,' said Horus. 'The backs of the Emperor's Legions will be broken at Isstvan V.'

'And what then?' asked Aximand.

A strange melancholy had settled upon Horus Aximand since the battles of the Choral City, and he saw Abaddon cast a wary glance in his brother's direction.

'When our trap is sprung?' demanded Aximand. 'The Emperor will still reign and the Imperium will still answer to him. After Isstvan V, what then?'

'Then, Little Horus?' said the Warmaster. 'Then we strike for Terra.'

ABOUT THE AUTHOR

Ben Counter has two Horus Heresy novels to his
name – *Galaxy in Flames* and *Battle for the Abyss*.
He is the author of the Soul Drinkers series and
The Grey Knights Omnibus. He has written the
novellas *Traitor by Deed* and *Arjac Rockfist*, the
Space Marine Battles novels *The World Engine*
and *Malodrax*, and a number of short stories.
He is a fanatical painter of miniatures, a pursuit
that has won him his most prized possession:
a prestigious Golden Demon award. He lives in
Portsmouth, England.

TIMELINE

Millennia	Age	Notes
1-15	Age of Terra	Humanity dominates Earth. Civilisations come and go. The Solar system is colonised. Mankind lives on Mars and the moons of Jupiter, Saturn and Neptune.
15-18	Age of Technology	Mankind begins to colonise the stars using sub-light spacecraft. At first only nearby systems can be reached and the colonies established on them must survive as independent states since they are separated from Earth by up to ten generations of travel.
18-22	Age of Technology	Invention of the warp-drive accelerates the colonising of the galaxy. Federations and empires are founded. First aliens encountered and first Alien Wars are fought. First human psykers scientifically proved to exist. Psykers begin to appear throughout human worlds.
22-25	Age of Technology	First Navigators are born allowing human spaceships to make even longer, quicker warp-jumps. Mankind enters a golden age of enlightenment as scientific and technological

		progress accelerates. Human worlds unite and non-aggression pacts are secured with dozens of alien races.
25-26	Age of Strife	Terrible warp-storms interrupt interstellar travel. Sporadic at first, the storms eventually prevent any warp-jumps being made. The incidence of human mutation increases rapidly. Mankind enters a dark period of anarchy and despair.
26-30	Age of Strife	Human worlds ripped apart by civil wars, revolts, alien predation and invasion. Human psykers and other mutants dominate some worlds and these rapidly fall prey to warp-creatures. Humanity is on the brink of destruction.
30-present	Age of Imperium	Earth is conquered by the Emperor and enters an alliance with the Mechanicum of Mars. Finally the warp-storms abate and interstellar travel is possible again. The Emperor builds the Astronomican and creates the Space Marine Legions. Human worlds reunited by the Emperor in a Great Crusade that lasts for two hundred years.

YOUR
NEXT READ

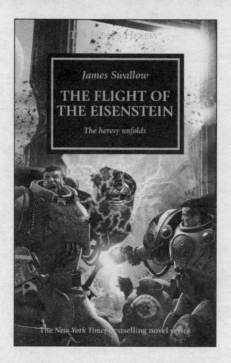

THE FLIGHT OF THE EISENSTEIN
by James Swallow

Having witnessed the terrible massacre on Isstvan III, Death Guard
Captain Garro seizes a ship and sets a course for Terra to warn the
Emperor of Horus's treachery.

YOUR NEXT READ

FULGRIM
by Graham McNeill

As the Great Crusade draws to a close, primarch Fulgrim and the Emperor's Children continue their pursuit of perfection. But pride comes before a fall, and this most proud of Legions is about to fall a very, very long way...

YOUR
NEXT READ

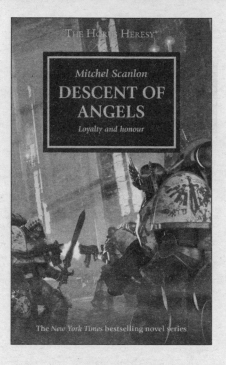

THE HORUS HERESY

Mitchel Scanlon

DESCENT OF ANGELS

Loyalty and honour

The *New York Times* bestselling novel series

DESCENT OF ANGELS
by Mitchel Scanlon

As the mighty Lion El'Jonson strives to unify his feudal home world of Caliban, the coming of the Imperium brings a new destiny – and new division – for his knightly followers.

YOUR NEXT READ

BATTLE FOR THE ABYSS
by Ben Counter

As Horus deploys his forces, a small band of loyal Space Marines from disparate Legions learn that a massive enemy armada is heading to Ultramar, home of the Ultramarines, headed by the most destructive starship ever constructed.